Never Look Back

NEW YORK TIMES BESTSELLING AUTHOR

A.L. JACKSON

A.L. Jackson
www.aljacksonauthor.com
Cover Design by RBA Designs
Editing by SS Stylistic Editing
Proofreading by Julia Griffis, The Romance Bibliophile
Formatting by Champagne Book Design

The characters and events in this book are fictitious. Names, characters, places, and plots are a product of the author's imagination. Any similarity to real persons, living or dead, is coincidental and not intended by the author.

More from

A. L. Jackson

Redemption Hills
Give Me a Reason
Say It's Forever
Never Look Back
Promise Me Always – Coming 2023

The Falling Stars Series
Kiss the Stars
Catch Me When I Fall
Falling into You
Beneath the Stars

Confessions of the Heart
More of You
All of Me
Pieces of Us

Fight for Me
Show Me the Way
Follow Me Back
Lead Me Home
Hold on to Hope

Never Look
Back

Chapter One

Logan

I T WAS JUST AFTER TEN WHEN I PULLED INTO THE CIRCULAR drive of the mansion hidden deep in the forest outside Redemption Hills. Night stretched long and dense across the heavens. It didn't matter. The sun could sit square in the sky, and you would still be able to feel the darkness radiating from within.

A shroud of debauchery.

An oozing of sin.

You didn't get this rich playing by the rules.

That was a *rule* I'd learned at just nineteen.

The moment I came to a stop, the valet opened the door to my Maserati.

"Sir," he said as he stepped back for me to stand. "Welcome."

"It is a beautiful evening, isn't it?" I responded with too bright a smile as I rose from the driver's seat. I inhaled the cold, mountain air and casually readjusted my suit jacket as a bolt of anticipation jumped into my veins. It curled beneath the surface of my skin like a demon that had finally found a place to sink its talons, and a thirst that felt like an old, familiar friend lit in the well of my chest.

Nine cars were parked facing out along the long, curved drive that looped around the front of the house.

Dealt like a hand of dirty cards.

A Bentley.

An Aston Martin.

A G-Wagon, among others.

I was certain I'd be the proud owner of at least one of them tonight.

The valet slipped into the seat of my car so he could park it next to the rest.

Ante up, baby.

I strode toward the expanse of concrete steps that led to the double doors. When I hit the top landing, one side opened, and I was escorted into Haille Manchief's home by a guard named Oz who was dressed in a designer suit. His holster peeked out from under his jacket and a massive scar ran the length of his face.

"Mr. Lawson."

"Oz. It's a pleasure to see you again. Tell me you brought backup." I grinned.

Let's just say the last time I'd visited, there had been a small disagreement when another player had felt *played*.

He roughed a chuckle. "Tell me I'm not going to need any."

I patted his shoulder. "Now what would be the fun in that?"

"You are dangerous, you know?" He smiled when he asked it. "You're lucky the boss likes you."

I ran a hand over my trimmed beard. "I have no idea what you're talking about. Everyone likes me. I mean, come on, man, have you seen me?"

He laughed, his accent thick as he eyed me from the side and said, "I know firsthand that is not true."

"Jealousy. Admiration. *Like.* They're all very closely related. Some people just have a hard time managing the proper way to show them."

Amusement gleamed in his blue eyes. "Like I said, dangerous."

He led me deeper into the bowels of the home decorated in dark woods, plush, oversized rugs, and exposed, raw stone. A giant fireplace roared from beneath a two-story mantle in the main room, accenting the carved staircase that led to the floors above.

Haille Manchief was a rich motherfucker. Bred of old money and wicked schemes.

I'd made him richer.

Legitimate investments that had turned over a multitude of times.

I supposed he'd been returning the favor by inviting me into his underworld. Or maybe he'd only needed one look at me to recognize the vile stain that lived within.

Oz and I edged down a long corridor before we dipped through another set of double doors and headed down the wide, spiral staircase to the basement below.

"Good luck."

"Now you and I both know I won't need it."

Fighting a smile, he dipped his head before heading back up to the main floor.

Downstairs, the air was thinned, dense with the scent of expensive bourbon, cigar smoke, and sweaty expectation.

Gathered around the table were a group of greedy men. Some filthy rich who had plenty to lose and others who would fair far better by packing their shit and leaving before it was too late. Their mistresses lingered around the room, some standing behind them like good luck charms. More likely consolation prizes to soothe them when their egos were stung.

Moving toward an open seat, I glanced around at the men's faces. I knew in a beat, I would win.

Losing cost you everything. Greed was the only way to survive. Pushing ahead. Taking what you needed before someone else stole it from you.

I took my seat, and Haille lifted his chin my direction, the old bastard puffing at his cigar as he rocked back in his chair. He sat three seats to the left, his smile wry, like he knew I would do whatever it required, too, and he took some twisted satisfaction in that fact.

The valet came downstairs and dumped the pile of keys he'd collected onto the middle of the table while the dealer divvied chips for their worth.

The asshole next to me rubbed his hand on the back of his beefy neck as nerves visibly rattled through his body.

A grin pulled at my mouth.

This was going to be fun.

Only the grin slid off my face when I felt the disturbance. This feeling that saturated the air in a clotted dread.

Awareness slipped through my senses.

The kind that promised the faulty foundation I'd been standing on had just been ripped out from under me.

Oz led another player downstairs, and the man slowly rounded down, the clack of his shoes echoing on the wood steps like the tapping of destruction.

The sense only grew as he came more into view, until that awareness turned into shocking recognition.

It pitched the air out of my lungs and sent my defenses to high alert.

Ice slipped down my spine, and any warmth that still remained in my blood went cold.

Jarek Urso crawled to the underbelly of the house like the scum that he was.

A flash of rage singed through my being.

Fierce.

Savage.

A swell of lightheadedness rushed to my brain.

I couldn't fucking breathe.

I had to physically hold onto the arms of the chair to keep from launching myself across the room to snuff him out. To beat a debt out of him that he'd had coming to him for seven years.

He'd taken the one thing from me that had ever mattered. The one thing that could never be replaced.

My hands curled tighter to the chair as my vision clouded over in red when my attention caught on the woman who trailed behind Jarek with her hand twined in his.

It didn't matter that I couldn't see her face.

I'd recognize her from a mile away.

My stomach soured, and hot hatred pounded through my frozen blood, ripping open an old, ugly wound.

Jarek took the last step into the basement, coming up short when he felt the force of my stare, the grudge that burned and the dark ideas that spun too far and too fast.

He angled his head in a clear-cut challenge.

Since her head was downturned, Aster Rose all but collided into his back.

Aster who jerked her attention up to find what had stalled her husband.

Aster whose fire-agate eyes went wide and whose rose-petal lips parted when she found me sitting across the room.

Shock whispered through the air in tendrils of hot static.

Hate and hurt.

Hate and hurt.

I wasn't sure if it was hers or mine.

Jarek's eyes narrowed in possession, and his hand tightened on his wife's.

My jaw clenched, and my heart thrashed.

Haille chuckled as he glanced between us like the snake knew he'd just invited two beasts into the ring, and he was excited by the prospect of us ripping each other to shreds.

A fight to the death.

"Welcome to my home." Haille lifted his arms in a show of pretension. "Please, have a seat. It is time to begin."

Jarek took the last spot directly across from me.

Aster stood behind him like an adornment, long, dark brown hair worn in an intricate, seductive twist, pieces trailing down to kiss the skin of her bare shoulders. A black, silky dress draped over her curves like the sluicing of dark water.

And in a moment, I knew all bets were off.

∽

I wondered if it was possible to drown on hatred as another hand of cards was dealt.

Wondered if my lungs could physically implode with the weight of the loss, with the shape of her presence, if there was a chance we'd be crushed by the carnage strewn between us.

Tension bound the room, and few words had been said, everyone's attention rapt on the duel going down.

It wasn't unusual for a high-stakes game.

But tonight, while I sat there trying to hide the fact I was twitching like a rabid beast, it felt like the purse had shifted.

The goal, the objective, the target—they had blurred and hazed and taken new shape.

Purpose skewed.

Contorting.

Distorting reason and sound mind.

Hours had passed.

Each had whittled away a little more of the exterior—the pretenses and façades—and peeled away my flesh to reveal bare bones.

It seemed I was no longer playing for wealth.

It was pride.

Revenge.

Or maybe it was purely survival because I wasn't sure I was going to make it through this alive.

The only thing I was certain of as I pushed another ten grand into the pot and stared across at the single player who remained was that I was going to destroy him. Take everything he had and ruin what was left.

Jarek tried to keep his expression neutral, the pompous prick with his slicked back black hair and his careless confidence that had been given to him through his name rather than earned.

Like he was confident I would let him reach out and take what was mine.

Not ever again.

Even with the pungent arrogance, I saw the tick of his jaw, the flinch of his eyes, the sheen of sweat that hinted at the edges of his brow and glimmered beneath the dull lights from the chandelier that hung from above.

He glanced at his dwindling chips.

"Your father-in-law would be proud. If only he could see you now." I couldn't help but taunt it as I rocked back in my chair. I did my best to ignore the presence that hovered over him from behind.

A presence that fanned out and teased me like a sinful, decadent dream. A dream that had once been so beautiful it'd coerced me into believing there just might be something better in this life than depravity and greed.

I glanced up in time to catch the worry that riddled those fire-agate eyes. The golden green with flecks of red that were begging for something she didn't deserve to be given.

Mercy.

I tore my attention from the lure of hers and watched as redness clawed at Jarek's throat before he started to push in the chips to meet the bet.

Aster gripped him by the shoulder. "Jarek, don't do this."

I had to wonder exactly what he had riding on the line. Why he was there. Why I could feel the chinks in his armor coming apart.

Flinging off her hand, he cut her a hard glare.

"Don't," he warned.

The word was coated with his humiliation. With desperation.

Ah.

There was the chink.

Weakness wept through the powerful persona.

Reluctantly, Aster withdrew her hand, and her delicate throat trembled as she swallowed. She lifted that stoic chin that I'd caressed more times than I could count.

Okay, fine.

That was a goddamn lie because I remembered every fucking touch. Every glance. Every broken promise she had made.

Jarek met my stare as he pushed nearly the rest of his chips into the pot, raising me by a thousand.

I raised him another ten.

How far are you going to go, asshole? Whatever you have, it's mine.

A soft sound of pain wheezed from Aster's chest. A heave of distressed air.

My gaze followed to where the black dress she wore dipped low between her tits. My heart fisted when I saw what she wore around her neck. It was a star-shaped necklace, dangling down to kiss her cleavage.

I nearly cracked. Lost the control I was holding onto.

It had to be a joke.

A taunt.

A fucking cruel, sick twisted one, the girl coming down here and parading it like a slap to my face.

It made my teeth clench and the fury I was barely constraining flashfire through my veins.

I tore my attention from her when Jarek spat, "Fuck," under his breath.

He still clutched his cards, refusing to give up the fight.

Haille laughed, the sadistic fucker enjoying this far too much. He looked at Jarek. How the hell he knew him, I didn't have a clue, but I didn't believe in a coincidence quite this big. He pulled his cigar from his mouth and jabbed it Jarek's direction. "It seems you're in a small predicament, Mr. Urso. Are you already going to walk? And here I thought you were going to bring something interesting to the table."

Jarek all but growled, and Aster's gaze darted between the three of us. Nerves flew from her soft, caramel flesh. That face carved of perfect lines and smooth skin tightened in dread.

He'd brought something interesting to the table, all right.

"Just cut your losses, Jarek." She begged it quietly, but I heard the strength behind it.

It tugged somewhere deep in my chest. The way she'd come off as shy, maybe even vulnerable, but in truth, she'd just been a listener. Too astute to join in on the superficial. Strong and firm in her own, innocent way.

Too smart to delve into the foolishness of that sordid life.

I guessed I'd been the fool, though, hadn't I?

"Your move." Haille cocked his head as he rocked back in his seat, his attention on Jarek before his eyes slanted to me, curious as they narrowed.

Normally I came off as easygoing. Probably too easygoing. Just another spoiled, rich punk living in excess because I didn't see a point in having it if I didn't use it up.

Money.

Women.

Reckless outside the office. Ruthless inside.

Tonight? Every cell in my body had pulled to a razor-sharp edge.

"What's it going to be?" Haille provoked.

Jarek roughed his hand down his pompous face, and he turned to look at the necklace around Aster's neck as if it could be a solution to his issues.

Aster gasped, and her hand came up to protect it. Tears sprang to her eyes. She took a small step back. "No," she wheezed, like it would physically pain her to remove it.

I wanted to jump to my feet.

Take hold of her and demand answers.

Demand to know *why*.

Why had she done it if she could stand there and look like there was a piece of her that was broken.

Anger and confusion had me in a stranglehold.

Old grief I'd buried deep that was clawing to the surface.

"Give it to me," Jarek grated.

"No." My voice cut through the dense air.

A roll of thunder.

The tolling of a challenge.

Aster froze. Her stare landed on me.

It was pain.

A plea.

Desperation.

It only made the sickness thrum harder.

I looked to Jarek.

"The girl."

The stake came out without thought to repercussions.

Without rationale.

No sense.

Just revenge.

I wanted what never should have been his.

A gasp rocked from her, and she stumbled back farther.

Jarek's eyes sharpened to blades, and there was no question he wanted to reach over the table and choke the life from me.

My fingers itched.

I hoped he tried.

I gave nothing. No smile. No sneer. Just the quiet hatred that emanated from within. The fact I intended to take everything from him. I'd known one day I would. I just hadn't anticipated the opportunity would present itself so soon.

He blinked then jutted his chin at the dealer for the exotic chip.

The one that signified he would hazard my proposition.

It wasn't rare. A bid made for a beach home. A family heirloom. Something that couldn't be replaced. Here, fortunes were won and lost.

"What are you doing? I am not for sale." Aster's voice was aghast. Horrified and filled with disgust.

"He's bluffing, Aster." Jarek tossed in the chip.

It was the first time I let myself fully look at her. To sit back and take her in like she was *mine to take*. Sickened terror ridged her gorgeous face because I was pretty sure she knew this wasn't close to a bluff.

I couldn't do anything but crack a grin. "It seems you are tonight."

Then I laid down my cards.

A straight flush.

Chapter Two

Aster

"YOU BASTARD." THE ACCUSATION FLEW FROM MY MOUTH. Horror that sliced through the pressure-addled air. Through the bitterness that had poisoned the oxygen.

Toxic.

Lethal.

So malignant I thought I would suffocate.

How could he even suggest it? He had no idea what he was doing. How dangerous this was. What was riding on the line.

Logan Lawson merely cocked his head to the side. Vile arrogance lapped from him on waves, the man a stake impaled directly into my mangled heart.

Seeing him had nearly done me in. Dropped me to my knees. But I had to stand strong.

"You can't do this, Logan." My voice was anguished. "I am not an asset. Not a plaything to be bought or sold."

Such a lie. I'd been a possession since the day I was born. Paraded by my father like merchandise.

Logan smirked back like he was enjoying my outrage. Feeding off my pain.

He wanted to hurt me, and it killed me that he did.

What did I expect? Something different than his hatred? It wasn't as if I could wipe the memory of the last time I'd seen him seven years ago. It wasn't like I could forget what had been written in his expression.

I'd crushed him.

Devastated him.

Almost as much as I'd devastated myself.

Now he watched me with this hollowed-out disdain that made my skin crawl.

Like death had come to smother him, but the only thing it'd managed to rob him of was his soul.

Because his body was alive. Bristling with strength. Tall. So tall. The man built of sinewy, bristling muscle. Fierce but trim. A viper who would strike.

Perfect beneath his designer suit. Every chiseled angle of his unforgettable face was ethereal, but there was no mistaking the demon lying underneath.

He wore his beard short and trimmed, his dark, dark hair short but long enough on top that it appeared carelessly mussed.

And his eyes—they were the deepest green set in a thousand, intricate layers. Swirled in blacks and golds and old forgotten dreams that he was supposed to have shared with me.

Now they appeared as stones that would forever haunt me in the night.

Malachite.

I ached just looking at him, like if I stared long enough, maybe I could reach through time and space to the man I'd once believed him to be.

Clearly, that man was long since gone.

In pure arrogance, he stood from his chair as if he thought he'd won, while my spineless husband sat fuming in visions of retaliation, his tongue locked in his ignorant mouth as he fisted and unfisted his hands.

No question, Jarek would make good on the visions. He had a legion of monsters at his beck and call.

And it didn't matter if Logan stood there like he wished death upon me, I wanted to fly around the table, grab him, and tell him not to be a fool.

All while I had the urge to spit in his smug, obscenely handsome face.

I could take his anger, but I wasn't sure how to take the callousness of what he'd become.

"Get your things…a coat would be good." Logan said it so nonchalantly, as if I were just another possession, while he was presented with two sets of keys—his own and another man's who had lost a Mercedes. A man who had laughed and clapped Logan on the back as if it had all been in good fun.

The entire act made me want to throw up. The avarice and gluttony.

"We wouldn't want you to get cold, now, would we?" Logan's head tipped to the side. His chosen words might have indicated he cared, but the arch of his brow was pure condescension.

My heart raced, and I stumbled another step backward. "I'm not going anywhere with you."

Logan's expression darkened as he tucked a stack of cash into the interior pocket of his suit jacket. "That's where you're wrong."

Jarek shoved from his chair, his voice a haggard accusation as he sputtered, "That game was fixed. This was a fucking setup. There is no way he had a straight flush. It's not possible, and everyone here knows it. I'm leaving…with my wife."

Haille Manchief chuckled as he took in the exchange.

Clearly, it was the ulterior games the man was interested in. The carnage and the aftermath.

I'd made it my business to listen, and yesterday, I'd overheard Jarek talking with his bookie that Haille was the one to see if he needed to earn big and quick.

It hadn't gone as he'd planned.

Jarek grabbed me by the elbow. Was it wrong I wanted to punch him in the face? This was his fault. He'd gotten himself into this mess, the details obscured, but I'd heard the rumblings.

Had felt his unease.

A desperation that had underscored his already slimy demeanor.

But these were the types of perilous situations by which he lived.

A rumble of discomfited laughter and quiet speculation floated through the room, and my nerves rushed beneath the surface of my skin as I witnessed the raw amusement in Haille's eyes and the cold caution that ridged the guard who'd led us downstairs.

"We honor our bets when we sit at this table, Mr. Urso," Haille warned in a low voice.

Jarek looked like he was going to snap when he glared at the man.

The rest of the players might have found this entertaining, but from a young age, I'd known that in the end it was always blood on the line.

I wrangled out of Jarek's hold and backed away.

"I'm not going anywhere with either of you." The revulsion and sickness I'd carried for years spewed from my mouth as my attention swung between him and Logan.

I was done. So done. Let the pieces fall where they may, but I was finished being a pawn.

Before anyone could stop me, I turned and ran upstairs, my heels clacking on the wooden steps as I went. I fisted the slippery material of the skirt of my dress to keep myself from tripping over its length.

Hitting the top landing, I flew as fast as five-inch heels would take me, racing across the warmth of the fire-laden room, the flickers of flames that burned from the hearth casting a fake comfort on the house that was nothing but a viper's den.

Footsteps pounded behind me.

Jarek.

He reached me just as I made it to the coat rack in the foyer. He snatched me by the wrist.

Hard enough the sting of it spiked on my skin.

Or maybe it was only the hatred I felt for him.

Whirling around, I tried to yank myself free. "Let me go."

He tightened his hold, nails digging into my flesh, but it was his voice that penetrated like a spear. "Let you go? You're my wife, and you're leaving with me. Right now."

I struggled to get free. "I said to let me go."

When I didn't give in, he shoved me against the wall, his foul being looming over me. "Make me look like a fool and see what happens, Aster. I'm warning you now."

"And if you don't remove your hands from my prize, tomorrow, you no longer exist." The ice in Logan's words froze the air.

Jarek stilled, and my attention whipped around the room. Searching for a way out.

Fight or flight.

I intended both.

Then Jarek laughed. "I think you've forgotten who I am."

Logan smirked, so confident I was afraid he *had* forgotten. I was worried he'd gotten so far from that world he didn't remember what was at stake.

"Nah. I haven't forgotten. I just don't care. Now if you'd let her go." Logan straightened his suit jacket.

Jarek's teeth gnashed, though his hand loosened. I took it as my opportunity to shoot into action, and I wound out from under his hold and rushed for my coat.

I threw it on, and I forced myself not to listen to the words that were exchanged, the vibration of hostility, the blood that would be shed.

All I wanted was to get my things and get out of there.

Get my things.

I almost laughed it was so absurd.

I had nothing. Nothing that was my own.

I tossed open the door and rushed out into the frigid cold.

I could hear the commotion behind me. Shouts and footsteps and a single gunshot.

Oh God.

My chest nearly caved in dread. In a fist of that old, stupid love that should have died long ago. I had to force myself not to turn around and go back to make sure it wasn't Logan at the receiving end of the bullet.

Run to him to ensure he was safe.

That he was whole.

Instead, I let the panic chase me down the stone steps.

Everything burned as I sucked in lungfuls of cold-mountain air.

Above, the stars were strewn on forever, so dense they appeared knitted together, a glittering blanket that went on for an eternity that I refused to continue to live.

A life that had been chosen for me.

My heels clacked against the pavement, my movements inhibited by the ridiculous dress, one that was slit up high on one side, my legs bare underneath.

Another showpiece.

Dressed as a jewel.

I'd worn it to do a man's bidding. A part I refused to continue to play.

Hugging my coat tightly, I ran as quickly as I could down the long driveway.

Ran with the lights of the mansion fading in the distance. Through the gate and out onto the side of the winding road shrouded by thick forest that rose up on all sides and into the cover of snow that blanketed the earth.

I ran until there was only darkness and stars and pavement underneath.

Ran until my breaths puffed in white plumes from my burning lungs, and I heard the loud roar of an engine coming up quick from behind, the spray of headlights illuminating the dense, dark night.

I simply ran.

But I knew, no matter how far I ran, I had nowhere to go.

Chapter Three

Logan

THE ENGINE GROWLED AS I ACCELERATED AND ROUNDED A sharp curve just on the other side of the gate. She couldn't have gotten far, but I still felt like I was in a race against… something.

Dread.

Hate.

Possession.

I didn't know.

I just knew it was straight-up chaos that whipped a tornado of need in my chest.

A toiling that writhed in that cynical pit that festered deep inside me. It seemed no matter how much I had, there was always this thirst for something that was just out of reach.

More, more, more.

I should have known it could never be sated when I'd been fighting for the wrong damned thing.

The bedlam eased a fraction when I saw a flurry of white up ahead, her thick coat glowing in the hazy dome of my headlights, silver heels glinting in the rays as she fumbled down the edge of the road.

Relief pounded through my bloodstream.

Only the sight of her spiked something else, too. A dark pleasure that rattled my bones. A sickening satisfaction that she was there.

I braked hard when I caught up, the car skidding to a stop two feet in front of her. Reaching over the console, I pushed open the passenger door.

"Are you hiding from me?" I couldn't stop it from riding out.

"Screw you, Logan Lawson." She could barely get it out, she was panting so hard.

"Get in." The command gritted from my mouth.

Aster bent over, gasping, the air puffing from her mouth a misty, white vapor.

The temperature on the dash read twenty-eight, and she might have been wearing a white-fur coat, but it only came to her knees, and her feet were bare save for those silver, strappy heels.

I'd gladly lay down another bet there was a frigid draft breezing up beneath that dress.

I had the sudden urge to warm her up.

Fire-agate eyes flashed and flamed as they cut through the night. "I already told you that I'm not going anywhere with you."

She started to move around the door like she found it fit to keep walking down the deserted road. I eased along, keeping pace with her with the door swung open and hot air blasting from the vents.

"You're going to freeze."

Scoffing, she hugged herself tighter. "Like you care, Logan."

"I take good care of my possessions."

She sent me a look meant to slay.

Yeah, I was being a prick. After what she'd done? What she'd caused?

Grief glowered like a dark storm from within.

She deserved it.

And I was the twisted fuck that found some sort of satisfaction in her anger. Like maybe I wanted her to feel even an ounce of what she'd put me through.

The loss she'd caused.

But the thought of her finding actual harm out on this deserted road? It had that chaos rounding double time.

"Get in the car, Aster," I said, keeping my voice as even as possible when I wanted to shout that she was being a fool when she continued to stumble down the road in the freezing cold.

She ignored me.

"If you don't get in, I'll do it for you."

Her head whipped my way. An arrow pierced me in the chest. I hated that she was so goddamn pretty. Hated that I could remember the times when the sight of me had brightened her face with the kind of joy that had felt so real.

Now, she glared at me like I was a monster. It wasn't far from the truth.

"You wouldn't dare."

My brow arched as my car inched down the road. "Wouldn't I?"

Energy crackled in the chilled air. An old spark I resented still had the audacity to thrive. The kind that burned and seared and left nothing but ash.

She lifted her chin, and her voice shifted, went deep the way it used to do, like she wanted to believe I was someone I was not. "I don't think you would."

I rammed on the brake, had the car in park, and was in front of her so fast she nearly tripped. My hands shot out to grip her by the arms to keep her from falling. An avalanche of greed hit me so hard it came close to knocking me from my feet.

Urges slammed me from all sides.

Attraction.

Want.

An old devotion that should have been crushed underfoot.

Clearly, I was the fool.

I gripped her by the chin. "You'd do well not to underestimate me, Aster Rose."

Without giving her a chance to respond, I scooped her up and tossed her frozen ass over my shoulder.

"Are you kidding me?" she shrieked, her legs kicking in a bid to get free. "Put me down."

"Nope. Not going to happen."

She screeched as I tucked her into the front passenger's seat of my car so she wouldn't end up an ice block. I yanked the seatbelt across her body and clicked it into place.

"There." I smiled like I was proud of the great job I'd done.

"Logan." Ferocity and frustration filled every line of her expression.

I just held that smug smile, shut the door, and rounded the front of the car so I could slip into the driver's side.

I didn't dare glance that way as I put the car into drive and gunned it because having her this close promised to do me in.

I ignored the tugging of inevitability. The lure. The draw.

Gravity.

It felt like this moment had been coming for a billion years and there would have been nothing either of us could have done to stop it.

Her breaths were shallow. Short and panted and filling the cabin like an intoxicating dream. Every twitch of her body I felt like a spark.

"What do you want from me, Logan?" Her attention was focused ahead, her fingers clutched together on her lap so tightly her knuckles were white.

"Did you actually think I was going to leave you out there in the snow to fend for yourself?"

I heard the thick swallow that got lodged in her throat. "I can take care of myself."

"You'd get eaten alive out there."

"By you." A ripple of distrust vibrated through her body.

Like I was to blame and not her dumb-as-fuck husband who'd been stupid enough to meet my proposition?

The laughter that ripped from me was low. "There isn't anything within twenty miles, and you aren't going to get service. You really want me to dump you on the side of the road? Fine. Be my guest."

I wouldn't. But fuck. I could barely handle the hatred that emanated from her. The distrust. The disbelief.

How the fuck did we end up here?

Because I remembered...I remembered.

I roughed my fingers through my hair like it could staunch the roil of agony that was threatening to burst.

She inhaled a sharp breath before she released it in surrender, her teeth gritting when she pressed, "Why would you make that bet?"

Because he was a monster.

Because she no longer shined when she was standing at his side.

Because I still didn't fucking understand.

I boiled it down to the barest, most basic thing.

"He took what was mine, so I took it back."

Dejection shook her head. "So that's how it is to you, too? I'm just a possession? A plaything? A commodity to be bought and stolen? Used how you want? What, are you going to force me?"

Her voice was hard, but a single tear slipped down her cheek.

A shock of rage spiraled down my spine at the thought of someone hurting her. It lined my insides in steel. This feeling like I wanted to gather her up. Protect and hold her. Ease whatever horrible shit had been introduced into her life.

But she was the one who'd chosen it, wasn't she?

She didn't fucking wait. Didn't fight. Destroyed the hope we'd been given.

I had to hold every demand back, the *why* that screamed from my brain. My hands cinched tight on the steering wheel to stop myself from doing something stupid like reaching out, touching her, and begging her to stay.

It really fucking sucked loving someone you were supposed to hate.

I forced myself to stare out the windshield when I let the bitterness override. "Who said I wanted to fuck you, Aster?"

The words were daggers.

Lies.

Bred of the years that pledged that neither of us knew the other anymore.

Hurt tangled her fingers together like doing it could keep her from coming apart, the words thin wisps of pain. "Then why are you doing this?"

Nonchalance filtered out with my shrug. "Some people need to be taught a lesson."

Distaste and disbelief filled her scoff. "So that's why you lured Jarek here...for you to teach him that? A lesson? Do you realize how dangerous that is?"

The headlights ate up the pavement, the forest whipping by in a blur as I flew down the winding road.

"I was as surprised to see him as he was to see me," I told her, eyeing her for a clue.

Her expression twisted, more of that confusion. Gut told me she didn't know how Jarek had ended up sitting there any better than I did.

She fidgeted, shifting in hesitation and dread, before the haggard question tremored from her tongue. "Is he dead? I heard a gunshot."

"Do you want him to be?" It was bait.

Aster flinched before she turned to stare out the passenger window at the slur of snow-laden trees. Her voice was quiet with strain. "He's my husband. What do you think?"

"Don't worry, Aster. Your *prince* is just fine." My teeth gritted as I spat it, and I floored the accelerator, flying down the winding road.

As if there was any fucking way to leave that fact behind.

I whipped my car into the rounded drive of the hotel on the outskirts of the small city. Severity bound the cab of my car, that energy thick. Every mile that passed had been painful.

Aster sat up higher in her seat. Uncertainty had her gaze darting to every corner. Her nerves scattered like the wind that gusted through the valleys of the mountain.

"What are we doing here?" she wheezed.

I smirked over at her, though it was bitterness that leaked out with the words. "What, did you think that I was taking you to my place? I'll pass, but thanks."

Hurt blistered through her expression.

My chest squeezed.

Shit.

I had no goddamn clue how to handle this. How to treat her. How to even look at her without coming unglued.

I came to a quick stop in front of the doorway and jumped out before I apologized.

This was the girl who'd fucking wrecked me. Destroyed the good thing I was trying to build. She didn't get my sympathy or worry.

I stormed around to her side and ripped open her door. "Let's go."

She fumbled out, and I could feel her trying to keep up as I strode directly to the lobby clerk. I grabbed a room while Aster wavered behind, unsure of what the hell was going on.

Join the fucking club, baby.

I didn't know what had possessed me to make that proposition. Nothing but how good it'd feel to see the shame written on Jarek's face.

I had his wife, and now I didn't know what the fuck to do with her.

Keep her.

There my head went, deep diving into dangerous things.

"Here you are, Sir." The clerk handed me the key to a room at one of the nicest hotels in Redemption Hills. It was situated on the farthest end of downtown, about a mile from my apartment.

It would be a safe place for her to stay until I figured out a plan because I sure as shit wasn't delivering her back into the hands of that prick. Maybe I should have ended him rather than standing down when Oz had fired the warning shot.

But I knew what putting a man like Jarek Urso into the ground would incite.

A war.

It would endanger my family. My brothers. Their wives. Their kids. I couldn't go there.

No doubt, my actions from tonight already had me neck deep.

"I have a room." I pressed my hand to the small of Aster's back. She shivered.

I rejected the way it wanted to seep into me and take over.

The way her spirit washed and swam, different but familiar.

I had to stop myself from leaning in and inhaling her warmth.

I guided her to the elevator, pushed the button for the third floor, and swiped the card at the door. It opened to the lapping shadows.

We stepped inside the bated silence.

I could feel every violent beat of her heart. Could taste every ragged breath. Could smell her aura coming off her in waves.

Hyacinth and magnolia leaves.

This decadent, exotic scent that sparked the type of memories I couldn't bear.

They drilled a hole through the middle of me.

Resentment.

Hurt.

A new obsession that twisted my guts in a tangle of greed.

It was a volatile, dangerous combination.

I felt the impact of it tremble down her spine as she reluctantly stepped inside. She edged deeper into the living area of the hotel room as I let the door drift shut behind us.

My eyes caressed her shape as a fresh round of those memories surged.

The way she used to be a picture of joy.

The way my heart used to beat out of my chest every time she came into a room.

What a fucking injustice that it still did.

Aster was harder than she'd been then, though. Her once soft, round cheeks were now angled and harsh. Her eyes sharpened and telling. She remained petite, small tits and slim waist and full thighs I could get lost in for days.

She lifted her hands out to the sides. "So, what now, Logan? Have you had your fun? Are you finished playing games?"

Distrust burned from her being. I almost wanted to laugh. Who was she kidding?

"Who said I was playing games?"

A scoff ripped from her lungs, though it shook with agony. "That's all it's ever been, hasn't it? A game to you? To see how fast you can make it to the top? Just how powerful you could be? Obviously, you won, Logan. I think you've proven your point. Where are the stones, anyway?"

The last was a fiery accusation. One that pierced me like a flaming arrow.

I had her spun and pressed against the closest wall before she could process the movement. My hands rested on either side of her head.

Caging her in.

She trembled, her body hot and lush and too goddamn tempting.

Savage seductress.

She gulped, her pulse pounding so hard I could feel it beating through my blood.

"Is that why you're here, Aster? You want to know about the stones?"

Those fucking twin stones that had ruined everything. A treasure that could never compensate for the grief they'd caused.

"It looks like they've afforded you a wonderful life." Bitterness flooded out with her words.

She obviously still didn't have a clue what'd gone down that night since she thought I might possess both.

What bullshit.

"Where are they?" she demanded.

"You think I wanted a bauble? A shiny thing to waste away in a safe? You're right. Because of you, I've been living like a king for all these years. I guess I should thank you."

The lie slipped so easily from my tongue.

"You sold them. You bastard."

A smirk cracked my face. "Bastard? You can do better than that, can't you, Aster?"

After all, she was the slayer of hearts.

"What do you want from me?" Her voice was half-panicked, half a plea, pitched too high from the sultry husk it normally held. "You take me in a bet, force me into your car, and then leave me in a hotel room? What are you going to do, lock me away in here?"

She stared at me in confusion. Like I was the one who'd hurt her.

A breath of condescension left me. "What did you think, Aster? That I was going to sweep you back to my palace and we were going to live happily ever after? You missed that train."

She blinked in pain. "I don't understand what you want or what you're doing."

My fingertips traced her trembling jaw. I was definitely, definitely playing with fire. The way I wanted to sink in. Forget it all and tell her I didn't give a fuck about what'd happened in the past.

That would make me the biggest fool of all.

So I found purpose—one thing I could actually control.

"What do you think? I'm going to destroy your husband." The words slipped out in a vat of subdued darkness.

I'd always intended it. Had thirsted for the moment when I could repay him for what he'd done.

Vengeance the ugliest side of greed.

Agate eyes glowed in the muted light, orbs of molten gold that churned with a concern she shouldn't feel. Her tongue stroked out to wet her lips before she let go of the ragged words. "You can't keep me here. He's going to kill you. If not him, then my father will."

A sound of indifference puffed from my nose. It seemed my life had always been on the line when it came to her.

I started to pull away. She fisted her hands in the lapels of my jacket.

"Logan," she begged. "You need to take me back to my hotel. Where Jarek is. You can't make me stay here."

A rough chuckle scraped free. "Can't I?"

She heaved a frantic breath. A billow of old need punched me in the guts.

Fuck.

This was a bad idea. All of it. And I wanted to go deeper.

"You know they'll come for me. This is a war you don't want to start." Her eyes bored into mine like she could bring me to my senses.

Thing was, I already knew that full well. Just having her here put me in her father's crosshairs.

Aster and I came from dirty families. But hers? Hers was powerful.

The veins of the Costa name were carved throughout the country, stretching out to touch the world.

Brutal.

Ruthless.

It was funny how I'd once believed she was nothing like them.

Throat constricting, I pressed both hands to the wall on either side of her head and leaned down to murmur the question at her ear. "Who is it you belong to, Aster?"

I dared her to say it. To admit this bullshit out loud. That she was one of them. Not one with me.

Her chin quivered, and I thought it was regret that poured out with the words. "Not you."

She gasped when I gripped her by the side and angled back a fraction, words a hiss that I spat at her face. "And your husband is a fool for playing with that truth."

Pained laughter flitted out. "You're a fool for trying to prove that he is. Do you have any idea what you've incited with that stunt? It was reckless, Logan, reckless, and—"

My fingers sank deeper into her side. "He never should have sat at that table if he wasn't willing to see it through."

"And you're an asshole for thinking me a plaything to be divvied and shared." That old ferocity flared in her gaze. The part of her I'd loved most. She'd been sweet and kind and so fucking strong and brave that I'd thought together we could conquer the world.

But it turned out that person hadn't really existed. She'd succumbed. Let them control her the way they always had. Chose that life over the one I'd offered.

I wondered if she had the first clue how deeply it'd destroyed me.

My hand found the soft curve of her neck before it slipped around to the front of her throat. I squeezed just hard enough to force her to meet my gaze, and my voice dropped to the low cut of a threat. "And if you were mine, I would never share you."

Agony lashed through her expression, and her tongue swept out to wet her dry lips before she pushed out the words, "But I'm not, am I? No matter what a bet says."

Her eyes rushed all over my face, taking every intonation in, like I was to blame for that.

I swallowed around the shards of glass that had gathered in my throat. "Is that what you want, Aster? You want me to let you go?"

"Yes." I wondered if she knew it sounded like a lie.

She'd stood up to him and not a half an hour later, she was succumbing again.

"When are you supposed to leave?"

Her lids pressed closed like she didn't want to look at me when she answered. "At nine tomorrow morning."

My chuckle was cruel as I let it spread over her face. That's what living without her had been.

Cruel.

I stepped back, and a tiny sound whimpered from her lips.

I cocked my head. "Fine, Aster. Be ready at seven. I'll pick you up and take you there. Just know Jarek's debt just became greater than he can pay."

Chapter Four

Aster

AT SEVEN A.M., I'D ALREADY BEEN PACING THE LOBBY FLOOR for half an hour.

It wasn't as if I'd gotten any sleep.

I'd tossed in the shadows of the hotel room, the hours ticking by as the howl of winter had raked at the windows and sent shapes crawling over the walls.

I'd been pinned to the bed by shackles of fear and bonds of regret.

Grief and loss so thick I'd drifted on it, three inches below the surface, where reality was a blur of indistinguishable colors and dark waters churned in my soul.

A millennium of demons, and a lifetime of ghosts.

Phantoms that had held on through the years, refusing to let me free of their oppressive weight.

I'd carried them for so long, my spirit drawn toward a destiny that could never be mine, I guessed I shouldn't have been surprised that one day Logan and I would end up here.

Should never have been shocked that our paths would collide.

Least surprising was that seeing him again had hurt almost as badly as the day I had to watch him walk away.

The day I'd told the greatest lie. One that had cracked me apart, cleaved me into a thousand pieces, half of them belonging to the man and the other to what had been forever lost.

I turned and paced the other direction, ignoring the stares I got considering I still wore that slinky black dress, my hair disheveled, my eyes wild.

It made my heart ache that most days the assumptions they were making right then didn't feel that far off.

But I couldn't allow that to cause me concern.

Under Logan's pain and venom last night, beneath the wrath that blazed in his eyes, the menacing recklessness that promised he would do anything to see it through, I'd come to the swift, heartbreaking conclusion that I had to return to Jarek.

My taking off last night had only landed Logan and me in a bed we couldn't sleep in.

A trouble he wouldn't survive, and that was an outcome I wouldn't survive, either.

My only option was getting to the airport so I could climb back onto that private jet we'd arrived on yesterday and pray we could pretend none of this happened. Pray Jarek wouldn't rage and hunger for revenge.

Pray Logan wouldn't be so foolish to set out to do what he'd promised was his intention last night.

To destroy Jarek.

Sorrow spread over me like an oil slick when I thought of the gunshot that I'd heard when I'd been fleeing. How it'd been Logan I'd been concerned for and not Jarek. How I'd had to press that lie from my mouth when Logan had demanded to know how I'd feel if Jarek were gone.

I guessed I'd become the perfector of lies, though I had to remember that sometimes a lie was a gesture of compassion.

The powerful engine of the flashy car that roared into the hotel drive might have turned heads, but I figured I still would have felt the shift in the air even if he hadn't made a sound. The way my chest tightened and my heartbeats flew.

It was the same way I'd felt like I was falling into a fathomless sea of torment when I'd begun to descend those stairs last night.

As if the ground no longer existed below me.

From the moment I'd met Logan Lawson, he'd made it difficult to stand on my own two feet. The ground quaking below, the shockwaves that swept through my body a flood, knocking me from sense and safety.

Steeling myself to the impact of the man, I pasted on that façade as I strode out the door and into the glacial cold of the snowy mountain morning. Vapor streamed from the tailpipes of Logan's car, and I nearly stumbled a step when he pushed to standing from the driver's side.

He was so intimidatingly beautiful he made me fumble.

Heart and soul.

My stomach a fist of old, old want.

Malachite eyes found me through the icy air, unreadable, hardened stones that glinted cold. He wore a fitted suit and a smirk on his face.

"Good morning, darling." It was pure condescension as he rounded the front of his car.

The ground shifted again, cracks that raced out ahead of him.

The man a tornado that had torn up my world.

"I pray you slept well." His gaze raked me like razors. I wondered if he'd still relish in my torment if he'd borne witness to every distressed sob that'd left my throat last night.

"I've had better nights." I attempted to keep my voice even.

"I'm sure you have." His mouth was near my ear when he murmured the innuendo, a carrot dangled to drag me back into the past.

Too bad my heart still remained there.

He set his hand on the small of my back to guide me to his car. Even though I wore the thick coat, I might as well have been bare.

Flesh to flesh.

I tried to suppress the shiver and sank down into the warmth of the heated leather seats. I was slapped in the face by his aura, the cab a dangerous concoction of corruption and clove.

There was no turning away from his shape as he moved back around the front of the car and slipped into the seat next to me.

Everything amplified.

Multiplied.

His scent that mixed with a tinge of something sweet.

Attraction flashed.

Skimmed my flesh.

Something so alive it couldn't be killed no matter how badly it needed to be.

Logan glanced my way. In that bare beat, I swore I saw a million things.

Regret.

Sadness.

Pain.

But it hardened so fast I had to have been imagining it. Searching for something that just wasn't there.

He put the car into drive, and the tires squealed as he hit the street.

Everything was bated, stilled and slowed and coiled as he blew down the road toward the airport on the outskirts of the small city.

I did my best to take it in. To remember this place where Logan had found sanctuary. At least, I hoped he had because the venom that poured from his body as he took sharp turns and gunned the accelerator made me think he'd found no peace.

That maybe he'd spent the entire night tossing, too.

Redemption Hills was quaint, quiet, and beautiful. A million miles away from what I knew.

It was strange how Los Angeles always shouted so loud, how it never slept, how the night cried out and day was a constant crush of people and sounds.

It should be impossible to feel alone in the thick of it, but it's what I'd found.

My reality a lifetime of loneliness.

Of faked smiles and forged pleasantries.

They were my only weapons. Weapons that had kept me alive.

I wondered if I'd ever recognized it as distinctly as I did right then.

The stark opposition.

How when I was with Logan, I felt consumed.

I felt like I was being burned alive as I sat in the seat next to him.

Each breath.

Each movement.

Each stolen glance.

Well, the thieving was all on me.

As hard as I tried not to look at him, I kept peering that way. At the chiseled cut of his cheekbone, the rugged set of his jaw, and the strong profile of his brow. His sharp nose and his full, plush lips.

The way he looked feral as he drove, a sleek beast, a panther that was pure stealth as he hunted.

The man was art in the seat, one hand on the wheel while the other tapped out a controlled dance on his thigh.

Questions burned on my tongue. I wanted to ask him so much. About his life and how he was and if he'd found love—even if it'd drive a stake through my heart.

I wanted to ask him if it'd been worth it.

I stole another peek.

My spirit twisted.

I supposed it had. The proof was in the wealth and the arrogance. Greed and power his only friends.

It's what he'd wanted, wasn't it? To prove something? Have it all? No caution to what it would destroy when he did.

The game he'd played last night confirmed he'd become the man I'd worried he would all along. Those sorts of tables were as crooked as they came. Illegal. Dangerous. The highest stakes cast because the men who sat at them got off on the risk.

If I were the one making bets, Jarek had at least one thing right— Logan had most likely stacked that game. He'd never exactly played fair, so I shouldn't have been surprised.

His mind was too sharp. Quick to add and calculate. He'd arrived at a sum before anyone else had the time to process the cards they'd been dealt.

Flashes of memories flooded my brain, the way he'd yank me into a deserted room.

"*What are you doing?*" *My breaths were short, and my pulse sped. His hands were in my hair.* "*I need to kiss you.*"

"*Someone will see us.*"

"*Don't worry, they're distracted.*"

I clutched his shirt. "*What did you do?*"

Green eyes gazed down at me. "*I fell in love with you.*"

His mouth crushed against mine.

Sheer obliteration.

I clung tight to him like I might not ever have to let him go.

"*None of it matters. None of it but you,*" *he murmured against my lips.*

"*Then take me away from here.*"

His hold tightened on my face. "*One day, Aster. One day.*"

I was shocked out of the memory when the calloused word broke through the daze.

"Don't."

His big hands flexed on the wheel, both wrapped around the leather as if it were the only way to keep them tamed.

"Don't what?" I fumbled and blinked.

He shot me a glare. "Don't look at me like you have the right to know. Like you have the right to look inside me."

Tears burned my eyes.

"Are you happy?" God, I had to be a masochist. Why would I ask him that? Give him the pain that was woven in the question?

He laughed out the darkest sound. "I have everything I need, Aster."

Sorrow pinched my face, the sword he'd swung meant to kill. Still, I gave him more of my truth. "That makes me glad."

He scoffed. "Don't sit there and pretend like you care."

I did. I did.

Way too much.

We whizzed by the sign that said the airport was a mile away, and I looked at my fingers that were clenched on my lap, dread coming up as quickly as our destination. "What are you going to do now?"

Speculation tightened his expression. "I haven't decided yet."

"Please, let it go, Logan. Jarek isn't the same person he was then."

I hated that it came out an appeal, the words a thin plea, but this might be my only chance.

"He was an arrogant prick who underneath was nothing but a pussy. Doesn't seem to me like much has changed."

Except for his title.

His power.

The fact that Jarek had never let go of what Logan had done that night.

If there was one person Jarek wanted to destroy, it was Logan Lawson.

I was terrified it might already be too late now that Jarek had discovered where Logan was.

My head spun with worry as Logan came up quick on the small airport. My breaths shallowed out, alarm filling me like the swilling of a coming storm.

He skidded to a stop at the curb. I sat there in the silence for a moment, trying to formulate what to say. How to make this right. I had so little. I squeezed the door handle. "Please...just...be careful."

"Not my style."

I looked at him. "Please."

Disturbed confusion knitted his brow. As if part of him wanted to trust me and the other wanted to kick me from his car. "Maybe it's time someone stopped giving him a pass."

With a lump in my throat, I pushed open the door and started to stand, but I paused halfway out. I peered at the man as if I might be able to claw my way through the debris and make it back to him. "I knew you once."

Sadness flashed through his expression. "Yeah. I thought I knew you, too."

Then it was gone, and he was grinding his teeth as he faced forward in clear dismissal.

I climbed the rest of the way to the sidewalk, hesitating for a second before I let the door shut between us. It'd barely clicked before he was peeling out from the curb and roaring away, the tail of his black Maserati fishtailing before he disappeared in the distance.

I watched him go.

It was like the cutting of a fresh wound.

This agony a blister that would never heal.

The bet had only exacerbated it. Left it raw and throbbing.

When the sound of the engine finally faded, I forced myself to turn and walk through the automatic doors that led into the airport. Fighting the dread, I headed toward the wing that housed the private hangars at the far-left side of the building.

I stumbled to a stop when the wall of windows came into view.

A fuel tanker was being moved away, and there was an empty spot where our chartered jet had sat last night.

Disbelief burned through my system. That asshole had…*left* me.

Logan was right. He was a pussy.

My teeth gritted. A crush of despair and a slur of insolence.

Hatred and disgust.

What was I going to do? I had sixty dollars, a phone charger, and a tube of lipstick in my clutch.

Jarek saw to it that I had no funds at my disposal. I was given an allowance to shop and play the pretty part of a woman in my position.

Beyond that, I was at his mercy.

Which meant I would have to call my father, swallow what little pride I had left, and make up some vapid story about how I'd gotten to this ski destination and become stranded.

Ask him for a way to get home.

So, so long ago I'd lost any semblance of what *home* might mean.

Because there was no sanctuary there. No respite. No comfort.

Swallowing it down, I moved for the ticket counter so I could inquire if there were any available flights, my hand shaking as I fumbled into my clutch to get my phone.

Only it rang the second I pulled it out.

My stomach soured when I saw his name on the screen. A burst of spite filled me to full.

"Jarek." I wished his name didn't tremble when I said it.

"You answered." His voice was a sneer.

Barely controlled hatred whipped through my chest like a windstorm. I tried to keep it subdued. To act like the dutiful wife I was supposed to be.

"You thought I wouldn't?"

He scoffed. "I thought you might be busy."

Anger broke through a fissure. One that'd been forming for years. "What is that supposed to mean?"

"Don't play coy, Aster. Don't act like last night didn't play out exactly how you intended it."

"Are you serious right now?"

"Or was it planned all along?" he pressed. "Make me look like a fool? Cheat me?"

Ire escaped my lungs, scraping up my throat in a clap of disbelief, resentment thick in the hiss of the words. "You think *I* set that up?"

I heard the clanking of ice in a glass. It wasn't even eight, and I knew he was drunk. "Maybe not, but I know you wanted it. Did you enjoy fucking him? You are just a whore, after all, aren't you?"

Pain lanced through my spirit, wrapped in a bow of malevolence. The horror he'd wielded. The sorrow he'd inflicted. And I'd had no choice but to go along with it.

Moisture burned like poison at the backs of my eyes.

Tears that welled from the loss.

The injustice.

The loneliness.

"You are the one who all but sold me."

He laughed a disgusting sound. One that crawled over me like chills of revulsion. "You're mine to sell, no?"

Bile ran the length of my throat, and I finally cracked. "Fuck you."

Before I let him get in another word, I ended the call, and I clutched the phone in my hand like smashing it could grind the last seven years into dust. Short clips of air jutted my shoulders, and waves of dizziness spun my head.

What had I done?

I was supposed to go crawling back to Jarek to smooth things out for Logan, and I'd likely made it worse.

Stifling the meltdown, I forced myself to look up at the monitors, at the departing flights for the day, because I had to get it together.

They bleared over, the times and destinations morphing into lines of nothingness.

My phone buzzed, and I managed to read the text through the blur. One from my father.

> **Papa: Where are you? I was informed you did not arrive home on Jarek's plane this morning.**

I should make something up. Ask him to get me home. Crawl back on my hands and knees to Jarek and bargain my soul.

But I was frozen.

Unable to do it.

There had to be a better way.

There had to be.

I swallowed down the fear. Everything that had bound me my entire life.

What had kept me small and broken.

What had shaped me into a person I didn't want to recognize.

What had chained me to a life I hated.

I let my fingers tap out a response. One I knew was a gauntlet. One that made Logan's recklessness of last night look like child's play.

> **Me: It seems your underboss has lost me in a bet.**

Then I turned and ran out of the airport.

Chapter Five

Aster

I T WAS FUNNY WHEN YOU CROSSED A LINE IN THE SAND AND there was no turning back. When every excuse, rationalization, and justification of why you *couldn't* twined together to form a knot of why you *should*.

Of why you *had* to.

Why you had to take a chance because you could no longer exist in the nothingness.

It didn't mean it wasn't the most dangerous thing I'd ever done.

It didn't mean it probably wasn't also the most selfish.

But I had a plan.

Kind of.

One that had started as a tiny seed and had grown so quickly I felt its sprouts touching every part inside me as I slinked down the sidewalk. I kept myself close to the exterior walls of the shops and restaurants that lined Main Street, like if I stayed twenty steps back, this recklessness could be concealed.

My heart galloped like the frenetic sprint of a spooked horse as I tried to wind my way through the crowds that flocked along the walkway, ducking my head without losing sight of the man who strode ahead of me as if he didn't have a care in the world except for that moment.

Logan Lawson wasn't hard to find. I'd searched him, and a slew of results had populated, and I'd had the driver drop me two doors down from his office where I found he practiced as a financial planner and investor.

I wasn't shocked.

He loved to gamble other people's money.

Apparently, their hearts, too, because mine was way out ahead of me as I trailed him.

I tried to gather it up and keep it from getting squashed as I watched him hold a child's hand.

A little boy skipped alongside him, and the child would turn to beam up at Logan's face every couple feet, then Logan would crack up at whatever he said.

Light and carefree.

As if he didn't sense the way my world had imploded.

The child was all caramel hair and adorable smiles and deep, expressive dimples.

Questions spun. Churning devastation.

Was this his child?

His son?

Was the reason he didn't take me back to his place last night because he had a family waiting for him there?

Sorrow surged, and I did my best to gather it up and tuck it down because I couldn't allow myself to go there. To the what-ifs and should have beens and the grief over all that had been wasted.

But reliving the pain would not get me anywhere, so I slipped along behind them at a safe distance.

Safe.

The thought was hysterical. I didn't think I'd ever been in more danger than right then. Hadn't brought more peril upon anyone than I had with this rash decision to take a chance.

And if I was going to take a chance, then I was all in.

Logan and the little boy dipped into a café on the right. I peered through the frosted glass at the two of them where they got into line.

I was an idiot. A fool. Because I stole through the door, hovered at the edge of the bustling room, and prayed I didn't stick out like a blot of red in the winter snow.

They moved forward a couple feet as the line moved, close enough that I could hear them over the dull drone of chatter that filled the café.

"I can get hot chocolate and a doughnut because I'm so good and I got all the As and because I'm your *favorite*, right, Uncle Logan, right?" The little boy emphasized favorite. A sweet shot of manipulation.

Was it wrong I swayed with relief at the child calling him uncle? That my hand came out to the wall to steady myself as I was slammed with an inundating wave of reprieve?

That in itself was a thousand shades of wrong.

That the idea of Logan being married made me feel like I would vomit.

Like I said, selfish, but I didn't know how to stop it.

Logan ruffled his fingers through the child's hair.

Affection poured from the man.

A tenderness I'd been convinced had gone missing.

"Oh dear, young Gage, do you forget you're with the coolest uncle of all time? Come on, man, you shouldn't even have to ask. I am the raddest of the rad, after all. Are you trippin'?" he teased.

A giggle slipped from the boy. "No tripping here, I got really super steady feet because I do the ballet classes with Mommy. See?" He did a little jig in his checkered Vans. "And I already know you're pretty rad. Just don't tell Uncle Jud I said so because I'm not picking no favorites. Never, no way. That's not even nice, and I don't want to make Uncle Jud sad."

Awareness spun.

Gage had to be Trent's son.

Trent who was Logan's oldest brother. The brother who was going to take the entire family away from Los Angeles where they would build a better life. I'd wondered too often where they had gone.

Logan tsked, his demeanor easy playfulness, the hard, rigid lines from our last two interactions nowhere in sight.

"Uncle Jud is just jealous he's not as awesome as me."

"You'd better watch it if Uncle Jud even hears it. He's gonna give you a one, two, three kapow." Gage threw a punch at the air.

"Pssh…Uncle Jud is the one who'd better watch it. He might be big, but he knows I'll take him down."

"Because we're speedy quick and sly as a dog, right, Uncle, right?"

"That's right, little man, that's right."

Then the boy sobered into seriousness. "But we love everyone the same. Because we're family and we got to stick together no matter what."

Logan chuckled, a soft swell of love rippling from his mouth.

I didn't know how I remained standing.

The way my spirit clutched, and affection tried to become the reigning emotion.

"That's right, Gage. Because we're family, and we stick together. No matter what." He touched Gage's chin.

I swore the barista swooned as the customer in front of them took his coffee and walked away.

Oh, wait.

It was me.

Get it together, Aster. Otherwise, this was going to be a suicide mission. My mangled heart no longer fit to beat.

Logan tossed the barista one of those cocky smiles that could melt a glacier. "Good morning, beautiful. It seems we need a hot chocolate *and* a doughnut. Large black coffee for me."

Her smile was edged in interest as she punched in the order, her eyes raking him with a wash of familiarity. "Sure thing, Logan. Anything else I can get for you?"

"My uncle is pretty cool. You want to marry him? He doesn't got a wife and my daddy says it's a sad, sorry state of affairs, way he's out tappin' about everything that walks."

Logan choked and moved to clamp his hand over Gage's mouth. "Um, you'll have to excuse my nephew. He's a pathological liar."

Gage squirmed out of his hold. "Liar? Lies are bad, Uncle Logan. Don't you know nothin'?"

The barista laughed while she eyed Logan over the counter. "It does sound like a sad, sorry state of affairs."

I might have wanted to stab her in the eye if it weren't for the fact that I was still getting pummeled by swells of relief brought on by the details this conversation had brought to light.

Logan wasn't married.

Wasn't tied.

And I was the stupid, stupid girl who wondered if he'd never moved on.

Chapter Six

Logan

"WE'LL SEE YOU TONIGHT, YEAH?" TRENT PRESSED like he thought I was going to swindle my way out of tonight's duties as he helped Gage into the backseat of his white Porsche Panamera.

The kiddie wagon.

It cracked me up he drove it half the time considering my oldest brother was the scariest motherfucker I knew.

Covered in tats. Deathly quiet. Sight of him caused grown men to stop in their tracks.

Old MC before he'd left that life behind. Now, he ran Absolution, a club across town.

But I doubted much you could fully purify your blood of those kinds of metals.

Oil and leather and perversion ran through our veins.

Ruthless depravity.

Mine flowed differently, though.

Greed the fix my body craved.

It was funny that I hadn't given a shit about any of that until having it had become something I needed to prove.

"Dude, come on, have you ever known me to miss a good time?" I grinned.

Trent all but rolled his black eyes. "Yeah, man, I'm sure spending a Saturday night at a kids' dance performance is exactly what you had in mind."

I pressed my hand to my heart, all dramatic like. "Trent, you wound me. You know my niece and nephew are my world. Isn't that right, Gage?" I shouted it a little louder to get Gage in on the antics.

"That's right, Uncle. Families got to stay together, no matter what," he hollered back from where he was strapped in his seat, kid cute as fuck as he kicked his little feet.

"See?" I drew that one out.

Trent grunted. "Sure, sure."

The truth was, Gage was my life. He was the one who'd given me a reason to move. To put one foot in front of the other. A purpose when Trent had needed me to have his back, to stand in and help him raise his son when he and Jud were trying to get their new businesses here in Redemption Hills off the ground.

Holding him for the first time on the day he was born? I could still distinctly remember that moment.

The way it'd felt.

The way something had thawed.

Cracked.

And I'd smiled for the first time in six months.

My teeth gritted as a slew of the memories I'd repressed slammed me from out of nowhere.

I could thank Aster Rose Costa for that.

Girl had fucking crushed me, and now she had me stumbling all over again.

I forced myself to keep the grin plastered to my face as Trent tossed Gage's backpack to the floorboards.

"Just be sure to leave the rest of the teachers alone, yeah?" Trent razzed as he closed Gage's door.

"Of course...that is if they can keep their hands off me. Impossible, I know, but I'll do my best."

Trent shook his head, though his eyes glinted with amusement. "That ego is going to bite you in the ass one of these days."

"As long as she's cute, I don't mind."

"For my own sanity, I'll pretend I didn't hear you say that."

Laughter rolled out of me, and I clapped him on the shoulder. "You know you love me."

"Barely." He fought a smile.

"I'll see you tonight," I promised.

"Seven," he reiterated.

"Yes, Daddy." I winked.

Since the dude had basically raised me, doing the best he could even though he was nothing but a kid himself, trying to keep me out of the clutches of our piece-of-shit father, I doubted much that he'd ever stop looking at me like I was five.

I didn't think there would have been a thing either he or Jud could have done to stop that spiral, though, the fact our father had manipulated each of us into who he wanted us to be.

Our father had been the president of a brutal MC back in LA. Iron Owls.

The club had been steeped thick in every sort of crime, and before they could even drive, Trent and Jud had been seeded deep.

Roots getting tangled in ugliness.

They'd tried to protect me from it—from the hooks that sank in and drained out innocence and life before it filled it back up with death and immorality. I figured they'd been so wrapped up in surviving, it was easy for me to slip into the debased, even before I'd realized it myself.

"Later, man. Be good." Trent gave me a jut of his chin as he moved to the driver's side of his car.

"Always," I said as I backed away.

I couldn't help the twinge of guilt over what had gone down last night. He would flip if he knew my vices. If he knew the thirst that could never be quenched.

It was the one sin I'd never let go.

It was who I was. Who I'd been bred to be. The numbers came easy. Manipulating them came easier.

Because I'd never again allow anyone to own me. Control me. Would never allow anyone to look at me as less than because I would be the one to dominate.

But I'd always done it in ways that it wouldn't blow back on my family.

I wasn't sure that was the case this time.

They pulled from the curb, and I watched them disappear down the road. The second they were gone, that antsy feeling was back full force. The sense that something was off.

No doubt, it was the traces of Aster Rose that clawed under my skin and made me feel like I was coming unhinged.

How many times had I had to stop myself from going back there? From trying to convince her that she belonged with me?

But I'd never forget what she'd said that night.

The look in her eyes.

"I hate you."

I'd known she meant it.

That it was all for naught.

A goddamn waste.

And here I'd let her come in and stir up my life again. Let her feed the vengeance.

It felt like I held two fistfuls of white-hot coals in the palms of my hands.

The sick, twisted truth that I wanted to hurt Jarek Urso.

That I'd wanted to keep her like some kind of aberrant prize.

Or maybe I'd just wanted to torture myself.

Turning on my heel, I moved back up Main Street. I drained the rest of my coffee and tossed the cup into a bin, working my way toward my office that was half a block up from my apartment since I needed to check in on a couple accounts.

No rest for the weary.

I tried to clear all thoughts of her from my being. To pretend last night had only been a wicked dream.

Instead, I needed to focus on what I'd been given.

Gage.

Trent and Jud's joy at finding the good life.

Their amazing wives and kids.

It was all we'd ever wanted for each other, and I'd done my best to find my own satisfaction in that.

Not to mention what I'd worked to become. The power I'd gained so no one could look at me like I was garbage again.

Still, I itched.

I sensed the crawl of something unfathomable at the base of my neck, whispering in my ear and tickling down my spine.

I glanced behind me into the mass of bodies that were out to enjoy Saturday morning.

A puff of frustrated air gushed from my nose.

I was losing it.

I pushed the key into the lock of the office building and let myself into the quiet, stilled space. I walked past my office manager's desk and into my office at the back.

I tossed my keys and my phone onto the black, metal desk, and I moved around to the chair and sank into the soft leather. I breathed out a sigh of irritation.

That was the second before every bit of oxygen was suddenly sucked from the room when the door opened.

I sat back in my chair and forced myself not to shoot to my feet when I saw her standing in the doorway.

Disheveled.

Gorgeous.

Hopeful.

The sight of her stopped my heart in my chest.

My teeth gnashed as a fist of greed tightened my stomach.

It felt like I got smashed in the face all over again.

There she was in that same black, slinky dress, one that I was sure would be emblazoned in my mind for the rest of my life. That white coat tucked tight around her. Not to mention she appeared five feet taller in those silver heels.

For a flash, every dark place in my mind went light.

There was something that had shifted since she'd gotten out of my car earlier. Something that had rearranged in those agate eyes. Determination and heat fired from the depths.

It plundered all logic.

Because I was slammed with a swell of relief.

Because she shouldn't be here.

Because she needed to go.

Last night had been a mistake. I'd been playing with the type of fire that should have long since been put out. Seeing Gage's sweet little face had only reiterated that.

I couldn't drag my family into that type of sordid mess.

I couldn't seek the revenge I thirsted for so desperately.

I couldn't touch her.

No matter how fucking bad I wanted to.

Aster stared down at me with her chin lifted the slightest bit. That fierce bravery wobbling with the fear written underneath.

I set my elbow on the arm of my chair and rested my temple on my fingers like I was bored to death while the buzz of energy nearly lit me in flames.

"What are you doing here, Aster? Aren't you supposed to be on a plane to LA right now?"

"You won me, didn't you?"

I almost choked. Instead, I forced out an incredulous chuckle. "Honestly, I never took you as the type of woman who could be bought."

Her face paled in a regret so stark I thought she might sink to her knees. One that made me want to hurtle over the desk to get to her.

She seemed to gather it, to reclaim that ferocity, and she strode forward and sat down on one of the chairs that faced my desk. "I have a proposition for you."

"Really?" I asked, completely droll while my spirit screamed.

What the hell was she doing?

She blanched and shook and seemed to have to force out the word. "Yes."

Old spite flooded out with my response. "And why would I ever do you a favor?"

Hurt trembled her mouth. "I'd hoped it would be mutually beneficial."

Send her packing.

Send her packing.

I sat forward and asked, "How so?"

Her honeyed voice shifted to a plea. "You get to shame Jarek, and I have a place to stay."

"A place to stay?" My brow cocked in disbelief.

"Yes. Let me stay here, with you." Her fingers curled into her bag, her throat bobbing as she swallowed.

"You want to stay with me?"

Her tongue stroked out to wet her lips. "I can't go back there, Logan."

Ironic, considering she'd chosen him over me. Considering that was the life she'd wanted.

The truth that I would never be good enough.

Old rage I'd carried for too many years pushed me to standing, and I stalked around to the front of the desk.

The air shivered as I moved to stand in front of her.

She sat back like she could protect herself from the proximity while I rested on the edge of the desk.

Attraction blazed.

A connection neither of us had been able to resist.

Something I'd felt once in my life and thought I'd never experience again.

And there it was, sparked back to life by this girl who was my one true threat.

Her breaths were hollow, and her eyes whispered over me like I was the one thing she'd been missing.

My dick hardened at the sight.

A haze of lust permeated the room.

Like a fool, I reached out and took her by the chin, my thumb tracing that mouth that could drive a decent man to depravity.

I wasn't exactly a decent man.

"You should go home, Aster. It's where you belong." It was laced with a warning.

"I never belonged there. You know that." Her words were soft snares.

Pain banged through my being. "Don't fucking lie to me."

Her eyes dropped closed, and her chest heaved as she looked away for a moment before she looked back at me. "I need a place to stay, Logan. I can't go back there. I can't."

Rage burned through my spirit. For her. At the thought of what put this desperation on her face.

I couldn't trust it.

I'd seen it before.

Had fallen for it before.

If my father had been a master-manipulator, she'd been the queen.

My voice dropped to a growl. "You want to stay with me? When I hate you?" It was true. I hated her. Hated her for how much I still loved her.

That she still held the power to fuck me up.

She pinned the fakest smile on her face, like this was a win-win. "You won me, Logan. Let's show him what that means. What he gambled with. When my father realizes what Jarek has done? What he's been doing? He'll set me free."

She sat forward a fraction. "I think Jarek has turned, Logan. I know it." On a ragged breath, she touched her chest. "I know it. I just have to find a way to prove it, and I need a place to stay while I do."

"And when they come for me? Like you said?"

"I'll make sure that doesn't happen. My father…he owes me this." Her knee was bouncing so hard I knew she was trying to convince herself.

"What does he owe you?"

Crestfallen hope singed her expression. "A chance."

Without giving her a warning, I dragged her to her feet, spun her around, and pressed her back to the desk.

I pinned her to the hard, unforgiving metal.

Shock filled her gasp, and those fire-agate eyes flashed with flames that could sear me through.

She'd ruin me.

She'd ruin me.

I already felt myself coming apart.

I couldn't let her go there. Couldn't let her get under my skin.

Still, the words wheezed from my lungs when I bit them out. "How can I trust you?"

She stared up at me, dark chocolate hair spread out on my desk. Her face so goddamn pretty she made my chest feel like it was going to cave. Her heart ran at an erratic, frenzied rhythm. Her spirit a wail. "I give you my word."

My eyes squeezed tight.

Her word? She'd given me a million of them.

Promises that had slayed.

I needed to toss her lying ass out onto the street. Let her fend for herself because there was no time in history when she'd actually needed me. Still, the question gritted out, "What do I get out of it?"

"Anything you want. Everything I have." I saw the flash of grief before she squeezed her eyes closed, as if she were searching around in herself for resolve. For a way to take it back.

Because I think we both knew this wasn't going to end well for either of us.

Then her lids fluttered open, and I had to stop myself from falling all the way down into their hidden depths.

I shifted to plant my hands on either side of her head, and I angled down, so close our lips nearly touched. The words were quiet threats. "And what if I don't want anything you have?"

Her hand curled in my shirt, a plea, poison, I didn't know, I just knew I could feel her sinking her nails right back into my soul. She lifted herself an inch and brought us chest to chest.

"You said you loved me once. If it was true? If it was real? Then do this one thing for me. Let Jarek's debt become mine, and I will be the one who makes him pay."

Like a fool, I eased lower, let my fingers toy with the necklace around her throat as the flames lapped and leapt and consumed. The demand was out before I could stop myself. "My rules, Aster."

She stalled for a moment before she offered me a wary nod. "Okay."

Chapter Seven

Aster

"**M**Y RULES, ASTER."

My chest was tight as the powerful engine roared down Main Street as what I'd agreed to ran through my mind on a circuit.

"*My rules.*"

Every cell on my body was edged in agitation.

What had I done?

What had I agreed to?

Could I really pull this off?

And at what cost?

Because if I couldn't convince my father…

It was an endless cycle of dread and hope.

Dread and hope.

I glanced at the ferocity that vibrated Logan's profile.

Hope.

It was such a reckless, heedless emotion. One I'd long since given up fighting for, succumbing to the reality of what my life would be.

But there it was, blooming like a poppy.

Quickly.

Rising up through rocky soil to become something beautiful.

The thought itself was something I should fear. It wasn't like Logan was sweeping in to rescue me, not that I wanted a hero. But I guessed I'd always wanted a partner.

A friend.

A lover.

A home.

And that's exactly where we were headed—Logan's home, when it could never be home at all.

Knowing he hated me, and I hated what he'd done, the choice he'd forced me to make. I hated that every plan and promise we'd made to each other had been squashed.

I needed to remember nothing remained but tragedy and debris.

My desire for freedom and Logan's thirst for revenge.

I peeked his way again, unable to stop myself. At the strength in his jaw. At the sharpness of his nose and the shrewdness of his eyes.

My fingers itched with the urge to reach out and trace the shape.

To restore.

To remember.

To renew.

If he was beautiful then, he was devastating now.

Every line of him was hard and severe. Wide shoulders and defined chest that led to a trim waist. Tall and almost thin, though from the feel of him earlier, I knew the muscle hidden beneath his clothes was rigid and packed.

Rippling with strength and intimidation.

The fitted suit he wore over his chiseled form only amplified that truth.

He glanced at me.

Energy cracked in the dense air.

Those green eyes sharpened with a threat. "You're doing it again."

My brow furled in question.

He released a cruel chuckle that skated over my skin, a harsh, seductive caress. "Looking at me like you have the right to know."

"And you act like I'm not going to wonder."

Pushing out a sigh, he let the words fall as if they were trivial. "It was a long time ago."

"Yet it feels like yesterday."

Only an eternity had been woven in between.

He shrugged a nonchalant shoulder that weighed a million pounds. "Yesterday...a lifetime ago...it doesn't matter, does it, Aster? Not when it can't be undone."

"But you haven't forgotten." I didn't know if it was a question or a plea.

He came to a quick stop at a red light, and he whirled on me. A gasp rocked from my lungs when his hand curled into my upper thigh. The flesh burned hot when he dug his fingers in and squeezed. "Do not toy with me, Aster."

My mouth went dry, and I gulped on the scorching air. On his anger. On his hurt. "I'm not."

His hand moved to my face, his thumb on my jaw, far too gentle for the darkness that reigned in his eyes. "Such a sweet little liar."

The light turned green, and he skewered me with that gaze for the barest flash that felt like he could see through to the marrow. Penetrate and cut me down to nothing.

Then he turned and accelerated through the intersection, that powerful body slung back so confidently, but there wasn't anything casual about it.

Fierceness radiated from his pores, spilling free like brutality.

Suffocating.

Compelling.

I didn't know if I felt hollow, wrecked and ravaged and laid to waste by that single glance, or if for the first time in seven years, there was a part of me that felt alive.

That blooming of what I shouldn't allow to take root.

I forced my attention out the window. I had to be careful. Guard myself, or I wasn't going to come out of this better on the other side.

This was my chance. I had to use it right. I couldn't allow myself to be crushed any more than I already had been.

I'd been caged for so long. Held in chains of torment and pain.

If I was going to stretch my wings, then I was going to fly.

We crawled along the busy stretch. The silence that rained between us was heavier than stones.

The street was filled with tourists, the snow on the ground and coating the rooftops a draw for those who had flocked here for a winter escape.

We traveled only a short distance before Logan made a quick left into the side drive of a large building that sat close to the street.

It was seven or eight stories, I would guess, modern, yet it still exuded a warm, cabin-esque vibe. Dark woods and even darker panes of glass that glinted against the frosty rays of sunlight that blazed from the clear, blue sky.

The first floor housed a steakhouse and a couple boutique shops, and I could only assume there were apartments on the floors above.

We followed along the drive lined by snow-covered shrubs before Logan pushed a button on his visor and a gate opened for us to enter a parking garage in the basement. He whipped down the short slope. The sun faded behind us, dimming the atmosphere to a hazy glow of yellowed lights that illuminated the dank space.

In an instant, it felt as if the walls had closed in.

As if I had been sentenced and was being led into punishment.

But that's what this was, wasn't it?

Punishment?

Because there were few things that hurt as badly as looking at the man I loved with all of me and never being able to admit it. Few things that hurt as badly as the loss that had eclipsed my heart in vacant shadows.

My heart throbbed.

I thought maybe he was being punished, too.

He pulled into a spot reserved for L7E, put it into park, and killed the engine. For a second, I stared ahead, fidgeting because I wasn't sure where to go from there. I hadn't planned beyond this, but I refused to believe it was a mistake.

"That's your cue to get out." Logan's voice was hard.

Fumbling, I rushed to unlatch the door and stepped out into the frigid cold. Goosebumps crawled up my legs and burrowed beneath the dress. Thank God for the jacket, but it did little to shield from the cold that seeped all the way to the bone.

Logan was already there by the time I shut the door. He reached out and grabbed both sides of my coat, drawing the lapels up close to my chin.

My eyes widened in shock, and my stupid, frozen heart thawed at the gesture. At the energy that whispered and called.

A swift, unspoken claim.

"We need to get you inside and get you warm."

My eyes flicked all over his face, searching for an answer.

The man heard the silent question for what it was.

"I take care of what's mine." He repeated what he'd said last night, the words a seductive threat that would ruin me if I let them.

The man was luring me into a gulf of contradiction.

No right, and no wrong.

No up, and no down.

I was subject to this division that would cut me in two.

He set his palm on the small of my back. "This way."

The murmur was a crack of incongruity.

Whiplash.

My head spun with the push and pull as he guided me toward the elevator and punched in a code. The doors swept open, and a bluster of heat radiated out.

A sigh got free as I stepped inside, and I stuffed my hands into the coat pockets. I made to move away, to put as much space between us in the confined space as possible.

God knew we were already too close, balancing on a quickly fraying rope that would hang us both.

But no, Logan looped his arm around my waist and drew me closer.

It swamped me in his aura.

Clove and cinnamon and corruption.

My throat tightened and my stomach flipped, and I wondered if I'd willingly set myself a trap. If it really were a mistake after all because I was pretty sure the only thing I was doing was providing him with the ammunition to destroy.

Placing myself in Logan's massive, manipulative hands.

I had been there before, hadn't I?

He punched in another code, and the elevator lifted us upward. It came to a stop on the top floor.

The doors whooshed open to an elegant foyer. There was one double door to the left and another set to the right.

He nudged me toward the left, his voice a controlled rumble. "This way."

I gulped for clarity. For surety. Praying this was right.

I hoped I hadn't just traded one horrible situation for another.

But I'd already made this bed. Had given this man my word.

I wouldn't go back on it.

So I sucked it up and followed along beside him. He slipped a key into the lock and swung open the door to his apartment.

"This is it."

I came to a standstill just inside.

Logan released me, clicked the door shut behind us, and strolled deeper into his home.

So callously.

So arrogantly.

Energy buzzed.

A hum in the air.

He peeled himself from his suit jacket and tossed it to the back of a chair. He eyed me the entire time, watching me as if I were a new piece of the décor.

I tore myself from the trap of his gaze and busied myself with taking in what he had become.

I was used to pretentious things. To riches and wealth. They'd always meant little to me, and they were supposed to mean even less to us, but I guessed I should have recognized his weakness all along.

It was in his blood.

Inevitable.

And nothing else mattered but his rise to the top.

Not even me.

Here, the proof of that greed was exuded in this pretension that was purely masculine. Everything was both rugged and sleek.

Rough and dark.

As if a high-rise loft in New York had been juxtaposed with the presidential suite at a ski resort.

To the left was a bank of floor-to-ceiling windows that overlooked the quaint city that rambled on below and the mountain peaks in the distance. To the right was a massive fireplace that roared of overpowering warmth, the lapping of flames heating the smooth, black-stone floors.

The living room was filled with oversized suede furniture with a plush rug in the middle. It was fitted with comfy blankets and pillows intermixed with abstract statues and artwork.

The kitchen ran the opposite wall from the entry. Everything was chunky wood, frosted glass, and thick cuts of stone. A large island separated the two spaces, and six short stools sat facing the kitchen area. There was a small nook with a round table set that overlooked the forest at the back.

There was a hall that ran the wall on the right and another set of double doors that sat on the far left on the other side of the kitchen.

"Welcome home, Aster." He cracked a grin. It wasn't nice.

It was strange, looking at him then, at this cruel, harsh, bitter man up against who I'd witnessed earlier. The easy playfulness with which he'd interacted with his nephew.

I wondered which side of him was real.

Or maybe they both were, and I just brought out the worst in him.

"So, what now?" I threaded my fingers together.

His expression shifted to something unreadable. "That's up to you, isn't it? You're the one who came to me. It's on you to figure out what you want. What you're willing to fight for. If you're brave enough to see it through."

His head cocked at that. His words seemed both an encouragement and a challenge.

A question.

As if he were daring me to prove there was anything left of who I used to be.

I wanted to demand the same.

Beg him to show me.

To answer...why.

Why did he have to do it? He'd promised me. Promised. And here we were, seven years later, shells of who we'd hoped to be.

"It might end badly."

He moved for me.

Dark energy vibrated out ahead of him, wrapping me in a greedy warmth I shouldn't take comfort in. He touched my chin. The gentlest caress. The deepest wound. "It already did."

For a moment, he gazed at me as if I were the light before he stepped away, breaking the connection.

The distance amplified the emptiness that would forever live on in me.

"This way," he grunted as if he were suddenly ambushed in annoyance.

His shoes echoed on the floors as his lithe body moved. He headed for the hall on the right. There were three doors that ran along the left side.

He opened the first. "This will be you."

Warily, I peeked through the doorway into the guest bedroom. I wasn't sure what I'd expected when he'd brought me here. If he'd hide me away in some high tower or make me sleep like a dog on the floor.

Or maybe...maybe chain me to his bed.

I shoved that morbidly appealing thought out as quickly as it'd come, my teeth clamping down on my bottom lip as I eased around him and into the room.

Severity blistered from his body, shocking through me when I barely brushed his arm as I passed.

"Make yourself at home." It sounded like a lie.

I swiveled back to face him, the man so gorgeous where he held the knob and looked at me like I was poison from the doorway.

"You're going to make me regret this, aren't you?"

"It seems fair since I'll be regretting you for the rest of my life."

Hurt pierced me through, and I sucked in a shattered breath.

A stake of regret moved through his devil smile.

"Logan—"

He blinked long. The stark pain in his expression was enough to cut me off. When he opened back up, his features had turned stoic.

"I have some things I need to take care of. Do try and not get into any trouble while I'm gone?"

The last tweaked with something that sounded close to a tease.

It pinched my heart in old memories that spun.

His carefree smile. The soft mischief in his eyes as he'd look down at me beneath the comfort of the night.

"You are nothing but trouble, aren't you, Aster Rose?"

A giggle got free, my chest so tight with love I thought I would burst. *"Am I worth it?"*

Adoration filled his gaze. *"You're worth everything. Anything."*

I wondered if he saw it play out in my mind because his jaw clenched before he shut the door without saying anything else.

I blew out the strain toward the high ceiling before I turned to study the room.

The bedroom was decorated the same as the main area, all dark woods and heavy linens and masculine lines. There was a big window with a reading nook on the far side, overlooking the forest in the back, pines covered in snow that reached for the icy sky.

It was beautiful.

A clash of comfort that beat against the frigid cold.

It reminded me of the man.

Ice and fire.

Comfort and torment.

Everything I shouldn't want and everything I wished I still had.

Warily, I picked up my clutch and forced myself to dig out my phone that I'd set to silent before I'd gone in search of Logan.

My nerves rattled so intensely I couldn't keep my hands from trembling.

Spindly pricks of dread scraped my flesh and panged my chest in a clench of fear.

There was no question my actions were reckless.

Being here was in direct defiance of the promise I had made. A promise that had nearly killed me, but one I had no other choice but to make.

Barely keeping it together, I looked at the screen.

Seventeen missed calls.

Air wheezed from my lungs, and I did my best to steel myself, to find that internal fortitude, tapping into where my spirit shouted for freedom.

It was a conversation that couldn't be avoided.

One that everything relied upon.

His blessing or his curse.

I guessed that had been the entire story of my life.

Resolved, I turned it off silent. Immediately, it began ringing again, as if it'd never stopped.

I accepted the call.

"Hi, Papa," I whispered as I put the phone to my ear, knowing I'd likely incited a shitstorm with my text earlier this morning.

"Aster...where are you?" Fear burned through his hardened voice. "I've tried to call you a hundred times."

"I'm safe."

Silence pulsed for a short beat before I heard him swallow. "Tell me what is going on? I tried to call Jarek this morning to no avail, and now my daughter is missing."

"I'm not missing, Papa. I am right here."

"And where exactly is that?" His voice deepened with the question.

I paced, my heels snagging on the high pile of the thick carpet. My head dipped low as if my father could feel the weight of my plea. My heart clanged in fits of desperation when I let go of the words. "Papa, I need you to listen to me."

More silence.

This time baited. Harsher than it'd been.

"Who do I need to kill?" he finally offered.

I would have laughed if it hadn't been a horrible, terrible reality.

A reality that had destroyed the last seven years.

Could it be changed? Could it? I prayed and prayed that my father could be swayed.

"No one, Papa. No one, please." I hated it. Hated this ruthless world. Hated that I still loved my father despite his barbarous ways.

"I need you to spare someone." That, I begged, my pulse chugging as I croaked the anguished request. A request that would likely send him over the edge.

"Who?"

Gulping, I forced it out. "Logan Lawson."

I heard his teeth snap.

The old disgust.

The violence that coated his carefully constructed response. "You promised, Aster Rose. You gave me the Oath of Life."

"I know, Papa, I know, but I…"

Tears sprang free, and a sob ripped up my throat before I could contain it.

"Tell me where you are, and I will come for you." Panic whipped from him.

"I'm safe, I'm safe. But I need you to do something for me. Allow one request."

"And what is it I'm allowing you? For Logan Lawson to live when you went against the one thing required of you?" Rage thinned his words.

One thing.

My life.

Every last piece of me.

My pulse wavered and shook. "Yes. Yes, Papa. And I need you to allow me to stay here. Just for a little while."

Until I figured out how to prove to my father that Jarek wasn't loyal. That he was no good. That he would hurt the family in the end.

And if I could prove it?

Maybe...just maybe my father would see me as my own person. See me as someone who could stand for herself. See I didn't need him to pick a husband for me.

I was his *daughter*. Not his possession.

"You know I cannot do that, mia vita. This is where you belong, and the last place I would allow you to stay is with that boy."

That boy.

"I have never belonged with Jarek." The blasphemy was out on a whoosh of air that I should have dammed. But I couldn't stop it, the flashflood of hatred and hurt.

"He is your husband." My father sounded offended in his defense.

"And why is that?" Hurt shot through the words. I gasped in a shocked breath.

How could I say it? Release it? Not when it meant breaking the promise I'd made that day.

When I'd given Logan a chance at life at the cost of my own.

Tears kept falling, racing in a torrent of grief. I looked to the ceiling and tried to suppress the sorrow that surged from the secret places. To hold it back.

I had to be strong. I had to convince him there was a reason I was doing this.

But I had to be smart about it. "I need a break, Papa."

A permanent one, but I couldn't tell him that.

"I need to breathe. I need to heal. I've never had that chance."

"Aster Rose...your responsibilities are here." I heard the undercurrent of it.

I was a treaty.

A covenant.

A bond.

"You call me your life, yet you treat me like a possession, Papa. Like I'm merchandise to be bartered with. What about what I need?"

"You agreed." It was a warning.

"I know, but things have changed, and if you love me—"

"You know that I do." He said it with such force it shook the walls.

"Then give me this time."

"He is the very reason, Aster. Do you not remember the disgrace he brought this family? He *killed* my brother. He betrayed me. He stole my greatest treasure. And *he* touched you."

Yes, he'd touched me. In the most beautiful of ways.

"And now you dare ask me to leave you in his care?" He hissed it, venom in his disbelief.

"Yes."

For good or for bad.

Yes.

"I need closure, Papa. Do you not understand the pain I've endured? Please. Give me this time. And I'll…I'll find out what happened to the twin stones." The faulty promise was out before I could stop it.

The twin stones that had been at the heart of it all.

An albatross.

A heavy sigh left him. A moment of silence followed. A chasm of dread.

"I do not trust this. Not any of it," he finally mumbled, though some of the anger had drained.

I nearly dropped to my knees.

"I'm not asking you to trust him. I'm asking you to trust me," I rushed.

"Aster…you do not know what you're asking of me." His tone was underscored with his own contrition. His own obligations.

"I do."

"Jarek will be more than displeased."

"He wagered me in a game last night, Papa. He lost. He should at least suffer for that."

"Disgraziato," he spat.

It was my only chance. The mistake that Jarek had made and the idea that I might be able to uncover what had happened to the stones.

Except that idea was moot.

Logan had sold them.

Had told me himself.

God, I was playing a fool's game.

But I had to try.

"Please, Papa, give me this chance. One month. Until the new year. I'll find out where the stones are in that time. I promise."

Hesitation poured through the line, and I whispered, "Please, Papa."

I could feel the sag of his shoulders. The giving in. "One month, mia vita. One month is all I can give."

"And Logan will be protected? His family?"

He sighed. "You ask more of me than I should grant, but I give it because I do love you. Jarek will be ordered to stand down."

"And what will you do about Jarek?"

"I will speak with him."

"Papa, I fear he needs more than speaking to."

And I feared more I'd just told my father the greatest lie. I wasn't asking for one month.

I was asking for my life.

Slipping off my heels, I wiggled my toes into the plush carpet and exhaled a long breath of the fear I'd been holding.

I couldn't believe my father had agreed.

Couldn't believe it.

More tears fell.

These ones were of relief. For once, I felt like some of the chains I'd carried had been lifted.

I allowed myself to relish in it.

Freedom.

For the first time in my life, I was standing up for what I wanted.

Fighting for myself.

I didn't think I'd ever felt a more overwhelming relief than knowing I could breathe.

That I could sleep.

Logan and his family were safe, and Jarek wasn't there to control me.

To watch me.

To touch me.

Revulsion curdled in my stomach, the same sickness I'd lived in for years.

The vile man had demolished me in a single strike, yet day after day, desolation had built upon that tragedy.

They say time heals wounds, but every time I looked at Jarek, it felt like I was being ripped open anew.

At the nightstand on the right side of the bed, I plugged in my phone, then I moved to the dresser opposite the bed that had a large television sitting on top of it, and I pulled open the top left drawer.

Photo albums.

My heart palpitated in my chest. Part of me wanted to pry. To dig deeper into the ambiguous, confusing man that Logan Lawson had become.

The other part of me knew I couldn't stomach it.

It still stung too badly. Prying would only be asking for more pain.

Staying here, in his space? It was going to hurt enough.

I shoved it closed and opened the middle drawer.

Inside was a stash of journals, stationary paper, and pens. But next to them was a clear bin filled with the little paper stars.

Memories of us.

Why had he kept them?

God, this was brutal.

I slammed it closed before I looked too closely at his intentions.

I opened the drawer on the right. A soft smile tugged at my mouth when I found it was stuffed with toys. My mind traveled to the face of the little boy.

Gage.

To the adoration that had shown in Logan's eyes. The sweetness. The care. The mischief.

All the things I remembered.

And I wondered—wondered if pieces of that man existed.

My reckless, beautiful boy.

Heaving out a sigh, I moved to the row of lower drawers and opened the first.

Old tees.

Success.

I didn't know how much longer I could stay in this dress.

I grabbed the first black tee and held up the massive thing that would swallow me whole. The print on the front softened the blow of all the words he'd cast at me since he'd crashed back into my life.

It was from Star Wars. His old obsession.

It had Yoda on the front, and it said, *Yoda best uncle.*

Affection left me on a soft laugh.

I could only picture that little boy giving it to him. Could only picture Logan peeling off his fitted suit to put it on.

I pressed it to my face like it held the pieces of this mystery of a man.

Like the fibers might be woven in his complexity.

The dark and the light.

The wicked and the kind.

I just hoped they both existed when it came to me.

I moved into the bathroom and slid out of the dress and let it drop to a heap on the floor.

Tingles spread.

Comfort taking hold.

I washed my face, then found an extra toothbrush in the cupboard so I could brush my teeth.

By the time I pulled the shirt over my head and looked at my mussed reflection in the mirror, I felt like a new woman.

A free woman.

And to my reflection, I made a brand-new promise.

I will never go back.

Half an hour later, I eased out the bedroom door and down the hall. My footsteps were quieted, filled with the instinct to remain concealed when I was the only one there. Silence hovered thick, like when Logan had gone, he'd left the weight of his presence there, ominous and tranquil.

As if you could be lured into the comfort of it all when you were stumbling into a trap.

I padded barefoot through the living room. The smooth floor was surprisingly warm as the fireplace continued to cast its luxury across the rambling space.

I walked into the posh kitchen and searched for a glass in the cupboards above the countertop. I found one and moved to the sink where I filled it with tap water and brought it to my lips.

The main door suddenly burst open behind me. Surprise had me whirling around and the glass slipped from my hold as I went.

It shattered on the floor.

Shards scattered while my arms drew up in front of me like I could protect myself from any attack.

Which just so happened to be an attack by a woman who had to be in her late sixties. She skidded to a stop just inside the apartment looking just as shocked as I felt.

Humiliation crept to my cheeks at my overreaction.

But it was basic instinct. The fear that Jarek would come for me.

I frantically tried to regain my composure. "I'm so sorry, you scared me."

The woman's smile was sly. She was stocky and short, though clearly her strength hadn't lessened with age as she carried the bags inside.

"Don't you worry your pretty face about it. My husband used to tell me I garnered quite the reaction when I came into a room. I was a looker, too, you know, when I was your age. The man always did have to be right."

Her smile widened. "You stay right there, now, and I'll come rescue you. I heard we were going to have a pop of company for the next little bit, so I figured I'd better get to the market and get the refrigerator stocked."

"That's very nice of you," I mumbled.

She waddled the rest of the way in and piled the bags on the island. "Gretchen is my name, cooking is my game. Well, and cleaning and shopping and keeping that boy out of the messes he makes. He might look put together, but that's all me."

She tsked like Logan was nothing but an unruly little boy.

"Is that so?"

"Mmhmm...he's lucky he has me, that one." She eyed me up and down.

I tried not to flush, considering I was standing there in nothing but that tee that hit me mid-thigh.

"Looks like he's lucky to have you, too." She winked at that before she moved to a hidden pantry at the right end of the kitchen and came out with a broom and dustpan.

"I'm thinking *lucky* is not the way he would describe it."

She chuckled low. "That boy wouldn't know what's good for him if it knocked him upside the head, which I have half a mind to do most of the time."

"I guess he's not the only one you have to pick up messes after around here. If you can just hand me the broom, I can do it."

"Nonsense. What's your name, sweetheart? I think you and I are gonna be friends."

"Aster."

She froze at that, a wash of curiosity coming from her as she stopped to peer closer at my face.

A bout of nerves had me shifting on my feet, and I dropped my chin in a rush of insecurity.

Why was she looking at me like that?

"What the hell is going on in here?"

I jumped again when a deep voice hit the air, and I landed just to the left. A piece of broken glass pierced me on the bottom of my right heel.

A shriek tore from my mouth. Forcing myself not to move, I squeezed my eyes closed and gripped the counter behind me as if it could ground me.

I hated that Jarek wasn't here, and he still had me on edge.

The problem was, I knew firsthand the types of atrocities he inflicted, and as much as I wanted to cling to my father's promise, I would never forget the nineteen-year-old girl who'd lain bloody and weeping at his feet.

When I felt the movement, my lids peeled open, Logan a tether that widened my sight as he strode deeper into the apartment, dropping the bags he held on his way.

"Are you injured?" he grated through clenched teeth as he rounded the island. Some kind of venomous worry twisted his expression into hardened anxiety.

"I'm fine," I forced out. That gaze dragged over me like hot stones, narrowing on the shirt I wore before it went traipsing the rest of the way down my legs.

"You don't look so fine to me. I thought I told you not to get into any trouble while I was away?" There was the tweak of that tease at the end of his words.

Exasperation huffed from my chest. "I didn't realize water counted."

Gretchen tsked and waved the broom at him. "Are you just going to stand there staring? Where are your manners, young man?"

He pasted on the brightest smile I'd ever seen. All teeth. "What manners are you speaking of?"

She grunted at him in playful disappointment. "The ones your momma would have wanted you to have."

"Well, excuse me," he mumbled.

"Don't give me that *excuse me* bit until you get over there and help this poor little thing who is bleeding to death in your kitchen."

She waved an exaggerated hand my direction.

Logan rolled his eyes. "Bleeding to death? Hardly."

Still, he took a step my way and murmured, "Don't move."

It stole air. Stole reason.

I pressed myself deeper into the counter like it might protect me from the power of it.

Gretchen clucked her tongue as she started sweeping up my mess. "My, my, some gentleman you are."

Low laughter tumbled from his chest, and he didn't even glance at her when the words filled the air, his gaze locked on me. "Gentleman? I thought you knew me better than that?"

She pushed by, whisking the broom over the broken fragments on the floor. "I do...which makes me wonder why this beautiful, nice girl would bother herself with the likes of you."

"Nice?" He said it like insinuating it was obscene. "I'm not so sure about that."

Dark amusement played through his features, and his gaze was taking me in again, slower this time, so painfully intense I felt it like an undulating wave.

He edged forward. "Hmm...we wouldn't want a beautiful girl to bleed to death in my kitchen, now, would we? It might make me look bad."

I was in his arms faster than I could prepare for it. Shock raked up my throat when he tightened his hold around me, the smell of him overwhelming as he pulled me against his hard, packed chest.

Clove and cinnamon and corruption.

"Logan, put me down."

"No." He turned and started in the direction of the double doors to the left of the kitchen.

"You take good care of her...if you don't, I'll be using this broom here for different purposes. Don't think just because I'm old I'm not creative." Gretchen shouted her threat from behind us.

"It's becoming clearer each day that my housekeeper is a psychopath," he grumbled below his breath.

Logan carried me into the wispy dimness of his room. The blinds were pulled, and the light from the main room whispered in behind us.

My eyes tracked the space.

There was a monstrous bed on the far left, and a TV nearly the size of the wall hung on the opposite side.

A fireplace was in the corner next to a sitting area with two chairs and a couch facing each other under the window.

It was cozy but somehow...hollow. As if a vacancy echoed back.

He headed into the bathroom and flicked on the light.

I blinked against the intrusiveness then squeaked when he plunked me down onto the counter.

"You've been here for less than three hours, and you're already making trouble."

"I think we're in plenty of trouble, Logan," I whispered.

I let a little of our truth seep in.

On a grunt, he rummaged through a cabinet next to the sink. He returned with tweezers, a cotton ball, antibiotic cream, and a bandage. He eyed me as he set everything on the counter. "I always told you that you were worth it."

My heart fluttered.

The man so different.

So much the same.

I pushed out some of the strain, trying not to look at him, but unable to tear my attention away.

Unable to resist the energy that crackled in the atmosphere.

An old connection that searched for its union.

I had to be careful. So careful. But still I was whispering, "Thank you."

"For what?"

"For doing this for me."

A scowl scrunched his brow. "Who said I was doing it for you?"

My throat was tight. "Whatever the reason...thank you."

He didn't respond, he only hooked me with those eyes as he slowly knelt.

I heaved a sharp breath when he grabbed onto me by both knees. Fire raced my veins, that *connection* finding a place to take root.

"You cut yourself." It was a soft accusation.

A frown pulled tight, and the words whimpered free, barely audible with him touching me the way he was. "It really wasn't that big of a deal."

He eased back on his haunches, and his left hand glided down the back of my calf to draw my leg out so he could inspect the bottom of my foot.

He dragged his finger down my heel. "It is a big deal. I already told you I take good care of what's mine."

My stomach bottomed out, and I tried to ignore what he insinuated. The way it felt for this man to touch me. The way I ached.

He inclined his head low enough that it concealed his face, but I could feel the intensity that blazed from his being, the way I used to feel him. A lifetime ago when life had belonged to us.

He twisted my foot then used the tweezers to pull the glass from the cut. I hissed at the sting, then I couldn't breathe at all when he leaned in and blew over the flesh.

His breath was heated, and it swarmed me as if he were a scorching, summer wind.

A torrid, unrelenting flame.

I curled my hands tight around the edge of the counter to stop from doing something absurdly stupid like running my fingers through his hair.

My love for him throbbed with agony.

"Does it hurt?" he asked as he dabbed the cut with a cotton swab.

"It always has." The confession wheezed past my dried lips.

I could feel him swallow. The way his shoulders went rigid.

He angled his gaze up to take in my face, his words as broken as the shards of glass. "Who is it you belong to, Aster?"

It was the same thing he'd asked me last night, only this time, he wanted a different answer.

I knew it. Felt the possession in the way his big hand curled around my ankle.

"You." It trembled from my mouth.

At least for a little while, I did.

Because he'd chosen to do this for me. I just hoped whatever reason he'd done it for didn't destroy me in the end.

"Good girl." I could barely hear what he'd said, though I felt the caress of it skate up the inside of my thighs.

Need boiled in my belly, pouring out to touch every nerve ending as he cleaned the small amount of blood from the cut and applied a bandage.

"There," he murmured.

"Thank you," I said again, pushing it around the lump that had taken my throat hostage.

Everything was thickened.

The air and his words and the severity of his gaze.

Then he pressed his face to the inside of my calf.

I gasped.

"Do you want me to ruin him, Aster? Is that what you want me to do?"

Anxiety clouded the desire. My heart thudded at a furious, wicked beat. "I just want to be free."

Hatred clawed through his expression. Only part of it was directed at me.

Logan suddenly pushed to his feet.

Menacing.

Beautiful.

Terrifying.

He lifted his hand and touched the necklace I wore, as if the star had branded him, too.

"Do you love him?" His voice dropped low as he shifted his attention to the ring I hated that I wore around my finger.

"No." I couldn't stop it from bleeding with pain.

"So you did it for what?" His words became blades.

"You left me without a choice."

He pressed his face to my neck. I nearly drowned. Fell. Dug my nails into his back.

I forced myself to hold tight to the counter before I let myself go.

"There's always a choice, Aster." He pulled back, hurt a whorl that eclipsed the light in his eyes. "There's always a choice."

"And you made the wrong one." I shouldn't have said it, shouldn't have given it to him, but I was swept into his arms before I could think through the implications of what I'd done.

His nose was at my jaw. "Did I?"

I wondered if he didn't know. If he didn't understand. Or if the only thing that had really mattered in the end was the greed.

"I hate you. You'd do well not to forget it." It sounded of pain. A rush of regret. Hurt that slayed.

My arms curled tighter around his neck. "I hate you, too."

I guessed we were both good at telling each other lies.

Maybe it was the only way either of us would survive this captivity. The only way we'd make it through the torment of wanting something you could never truly have.

Because he could never know what his actions had caused. The dominos that had been set in motion. The promise I'd made the one thing keeping him alive.

He carried me into the main room.

Gretchen looked up from where she was dumping a dustpan of glass into the trash. "See, manners. It isn't so hard, is it?"

He grunted at her. "Keep it up, Gigi, and your days here are numbered."

She cracked up. "That's cute, young man, considering this place would fall down around you if I weren't here to keep it in order. Besides, I know how much you love me."

He grunted again. "You really know how to bust a man's balls, especially one who signs your paycheck."

"Pssh. I'd do it for free since I love you right back."

I felt the wobble of affection at the corner of his mouth, rising beneath the rage that simmered in the bare space.

I tried to ignore the way his body felt pressed against mine as he carried me through the main room and back into my bedroom. Tried to pretend my skin wasn't shimmering with the vestiges of his touch when he sat me on the edge of the bed.

He started to turn and leave, though he paused when I called behind him, "You're happy here?"

Logan glanced back. "My family has always made me that way."

"I used to."

He tapped the doorframe with his knuckles. "Yeah, but you stopped being her a long time ago."

Grief cut through the middle of me, and I choked over the regret that wanted to get free when he walked out without saying anything else.

Fisting the comforter, I fought the moisture that burned at my eyes. I had to keep it together. Stay focused and stay the course.

This wasn't about reconciling with Logan. There was nothing that could heal a wound that went that deep.

More than that, there was no way to undo what had already been done.

This was about my freedom. About recovering my life. About finding new direction.

I jolted when a minute later Logan strode back in. He carried the bags he'd dropped onto the floor and placed them next to me on the bed.

A frown pulled to my brow. "What's this?"

"Do you plan to wear that dress forever? Or that tee? Not that I would mind all that much." He cocked a grin at that.

Wings fluttered in my chest.

Crap.

I swallowed hard. "I guess not."

"Then you'll need more clothes." He moved to the doorway then paused to look back at me. "What do you need on Jarek?"

Gulping, I forced myself to focus on the mission. "Everything. Anything. I just need to prove to my father the snake that he is."

A difficult task when I'd been raised by a brood of vipers. Crimes expected. Cruelty required.

In the end, it would be Jarek's loyalty that counted.

"That should be easy enough."

"I'm afraid there won't be anything easy about this."

Jarek would kill anyone that threatened his position in the family. My father had no sons, and his brother was dead thanks to the man in front of me, which meant Jarek was next in line to take his place as the boss once he passed.

He would be none too keen when he found out my intention was to take that from him.

If I knew him well enough, he'd think at any time, I'd come crawling back, and I doubted he'd say much to my father, considering he was the one who'd made this dirty, messy bed.

I prayed that and my father's promise would give me time.

"Are you okay with that?" I pressed.

Logan shrugged too casual a shoulder. "He took what was mine. It seems only fair I take it back."

He started to duck out only to pause, hesitate, then stare back at me as if he wasn't sure about what he was getting ready to say. "I have a family thing tonight. Be ready at six. Pick something a little more... practical?"

Confusion bound, but I nodded quickly.

Dipping his head, he stepped out and shut the door.

I dug into the bags.

Jeans and tees.

Sweaters and a coat.

Boots.

A few more dresses as beautiful as the one I'd worn last night.

Toiletries and makeup and undergarments.

I tossed the lid off a box to find a silk night slip.

It was white and covered in the soft innuendo of stars woven into the material.

My spirit clutched.

Like a fool, I pressed it to my nose and stared at the door where he'd just been.

Little Star. Little Star.

Damn him.

I had to be careful, or he was going to ruin me all over again.

Chapter Eight

Aster

I EMERGED FROM THE BEDROOM AT SIX, WEARING BLACK LEATHER pants, a purple sweater that was slinky and loose but hung just right, and a pair of knee-high heeled boots.

I had a heavy gray wool coat draped over my arm and a handbag that was mostly empty slung over my shoulder.

If there was something to be said about Logan Lawson, he had really good taste.

Coming to the end of the hall, I stalled.

My nerves rattled.

Logan hadn't given me a whole lot to go on other than he had a *family thing*.

A family thing.

Anxiety bristled beneath my skin. Like, with his brothers? Their families?

The little boy's face tickled the back of my mind. The sweetness. The way Logan had looked at him.

Undoubtedly, the child, Logan's entire family, was a huge piece of his world.

I got it.

I just wasn't sure why he wanted to share it with me.

The only thing I knew was I felt his attention like a landslide when I stepped out from behind the seclusion of the hall and into the main room.

Logan looked up from where he stood at the end of the island typing something on his phone.

The man was so disgustingly gorgeous in his fitted suit.

Intimidating.

Jaw-dropping.

Those eyes flashed as they took me in.

Copper and green.

Stony.

Malachite.

Though tonight they were far from opaque.

They glinted in the flames that leapt in the fireplace.

Scorching rocks that could sear me through.

Fiddling with the hem of my sweater, I glanced down at what I'd chosen. "Is this okay?"

"It will do." His tone was grit.

He pushed from the island and came my way.

A slow prowl, a monster testing its prey.

He stopped a foot away, and he tipped up my chin, deceptively soft. "They say the devil is so beautiful you wouldn't be able to look at him if you saw him in his original form."

My insides quaked. I was pretty sure he had our roles reversed.

"And you have a hard time looking at me." Still, I let him have the perception.

I ached that he was right there, so close I could touch him, though I knew how dangerous it would be if I did.

He leaned closer, his presence destroying all sense, his voice a rough scrape he released at my ear. "The fucking problem is I can't seem to look away."

A whimper crawled my throat and chills flashed across my skin.

He inclined closer. "Is that what you are, Aster? The devil? Here to tempt me? Lead me into sin?"

"Ironic since that's what I'd always thought about you."

When it'd come to Logan Lawson, I'd always done the exact opposite of what was expected of me.

His thumb caressed the length of my cheek, the hard, chiseled angle of his jaw clenched.

In restraint.

In disgust.

I couldn't tell.

"Maybe because we both were born in the pits of Hell." It left me like some kind of surrender. Or maybe it was an out for both of us. A reason for the pain.

He kept sweeping the pad of his thumb along my jaw.

Back and forth.

Back and forth.

"We were supposed to escape it together." That time, his words gritted with spite.

The bitterness I couldn't seem to get over boiled inside. I almost demanded to know how much he'd sold the stones for. If he understood what it'd cost.

Instead, I let the resentment bleed out. "It seems like you're doing pretty well for yourself to me."

It was me who had been left behind.

I could hear the grinding of Logan's teeth. "You don't know anything about me."

He was right.

I didn't.

Not anymore.

All except for this connection that still felt so alive.

Except for the torment, the mischief, the loss, the sweetness that I saw play in his eyes.

He suddenly straightened and moved away from me so quickly

that I stumbled forward a step, not even realizing I'd given myself over to his hold.

A shattered breath heaved from my lungs as he moved for the door, the man ignoring that every second of this push and pull was wrecking me.

"We need to go. My brothers will have my ass if I don't show on time."

"Both of them will be there?" I asked on a worried breath.

He chuckled out a rough sound. "What, are you scared?"

Um, his brothers were terrifying, but that didn't have anything to do with it.

"Maybe it would be better if I stayed here."

He was back to touching my face, his voice this low, growl of a promise that shook me to the core, even though it was clearly meant to be a tease. "Don't worry, Aster, I'll protect you. You keep forgetting I take care of what's mine."

Logan whipped his car into the parking lot of a—my head jerked around to read the sign—Christian elementary school.

I could feel the confusion claw its way across my face as my attention jumped back to Logan.

Seriously, what in the world was happening?

He didn't even glance at me as he drove through the packed lot in search of an open spot, which by the looks of it, we were going to have to park along the street.

Apparently, most of Redemption Hills had shown for whatever this *family thing* was.

I'd thought it would maybe be a dinner. Or more than likely, a deal...the dirty kind dealt in dingy backrooms of seedy clubs or maybe in upscale basements like last night.

My chest squeezed as I watched the droves of families weave their way across the lot toward the main buildings, bundled in their jackets and scarves, their cheeks pinked and excitement filling their eyes.

Logan drove around the side of a building to another lot around back where he finally found an open spot tucked between a minivan and truck.

When he killed the engine, a swath of silence took over the cabin, and the man stared out the windshield at the flurries of snowflakes that fluttered from the darkened heavens.

Tension stretched thin.

Questions that swelled and taunted.

Old hopes and long-dead dreams.

It was insane being so uncomfortable with a man who had once been my refuge.

Finally, he glanced over at me, his tongue sweeping his lips in a rush of agitation, as if he'd just then thought better about bringing me here. "My niece and nephew have a dance performance to kick off the holiday season."

It was December 2nd.

Clarity moved through my consciousness, this whole thing coming to make sense. Except for the part of why he'd brought me with him.

"Okay." I stared at him, my response not quite a question but begging him to fill in the blanks.

"My family is the only thing that matters to me. Everything I do, I do for them. I will sacrifice anything for them. Reject anything that might bring them harm…or crush it before it has the chance." A warning lit behind it. His chest vibrated like he was dealing with his own dread.

I knew his statement was his truth.

"I understand."

"Do you?" That ferocity pierced me in the heart.

I swallowed down the disquiet.

"I do."

Because he was supposed to be mine, and I'd been living that stark, gutting truth for the last seven years. Sacrificing it all to protect the one that mattered to me.

He gripped the side of my face, so out of the blue my mouth dropped open at the blaze of his palm against my skin. "And here you are."

I guessed the reality of what I was asking of him had finally penetrated his hardened exterior.

I gulped the trepidation down. "My father promised time. Promised he would allow me this. Here. With you. I have until the New Year. Thirty days. He told me he would order Jarek to stand down."

Logan let go of a disbelieving sound. "You don't actually think that pompous prick takes orders from anyone?"

"From my father, yes." My spirit shook, hoping it was the truth. "Why don't you take me back to the apartment, though? There's no reason to drag your family into this."

Logan leaned farther over the console. All menace and power, the words razors that cut through flesh. "Is it wrong I don't want to let you out of my sight?"

"You don't have to protect me."

His hand spread farther across my cheek. "I might hate you, Aster, but I see your fucking pain. I know you've been hurt. So don't fucking tell me you don't need protected, even if what you need protected from is yourself."

My breaths were ragged when he suddenly pulled away and climbed from the car. I was still stuck in the same spot when he opened mine and extended a hand to help me out. "Come with me."

I obeyed, tried not to whimper when he pulled me against the hot, hard planes of his body as I was struck with a blast of frigid cold.

He balanced me on the slick, frozen ground. "Are you good?"

No.

Not even close.

I gave a quick nod, and he returned his hand to the small of my back as he guided me to the main doors.

Logan dug into the inside pocket of his suit jacket, pulled out two tickets, and presented them to the man accepting them at the door.

"We'd better find our seats." Logan took my hand and hauled me inside. He wound us through the crowd, and I struggled to keep up as we moved across the lobby and through another set of double doors into a multipurpose room.

The second we stepped inside, the overhead lights dimmed, and people rushed to find a place to sit.

Metal chairs had been set up in long rows, and one aisle ran down the middle leading to a stage at the base of them.

Strings of twinkling white Christmas lights were strung from the ceiling, casting the huge room in a festive ambiance. Decorated trees lined the walls, carols played overhead, and a buzz of excitement filled the air.

Every once in a while, I could hear the squeal of a child from backstage.

Logan's hand twitched on my back, as if he felt the sting of it, too. But I knew he didn't come close to understanding what that pain really meant.

How I had to guard myself from getting swept into a fantasy I would never get to live.

A speaker squelched, and a spotlight lit the black curtains that shrouded the stage that was elevated by three feet.

An older gentleman walked out in front of them, a microphone in his hand and a smile on his face.

Logan continued to lead me down the middle aisle as the man began to speak.

"Welcome to this year's holiday performance. For those of you who don't know me, I'm Gary Murphy, the owner and director of the school, and I cannot tell you how excited we are to have you here this evening. The children have been working incredibly hard to put on this wonderful show for you, and I know you are going to be wowed."

Everyone clapped.

Anxiousness tightened my lungs as Logan moved all the way down to the front row before he ducked to avoid the spray of a spotlight as he angled for two remaining seats about five chairs in.

My head was lowered like I could hide, too, and I almost breathed out in relief when Logan plopped me onto a chair and slipped onto the one next to me on the left, only that breath hitched in my throat when I saw who sat on the other side of him.

Trent Lawson.

I'd caught sight of him only for the barest flash this morning when I'd been following behind Logan, but I'd ducked out of view so I wouldn't be discovered.

The man had always been terrifying. A cold current running through his blood and hardening his nearly black eyes. He came with a reputation.

A ruthless one.

Tatted from head to toe, the colors swirled out from beneath his clothing to cover his throat and hands.

Only now, those hands held a newborn baby tucked in a swaddled bundle against his chest.

Every cell in my body shivered. I tried to rip my attention away, but my eyes traced the precious form, my spirit aflutter, my heart in my throat.

Finally, I managed to jerk my eyes from the child only for them to tangle with Trent's.

Obsidian eyes were wide with shock.

They turned to daggers when he focused them on Logan.

"*What the fuck?*" he mouthed.

Discomfort blazed.

I wasn't surprised by the *warm welcome*.

I knew my name.

I'd worn it like royalty, when really, it'd been nothing less than a cattle brand. Burned into my flesh. Nowhere to go, nowhere to run, not until the day I was slaughtered.

"What's up, man? You look happy to see me," Logan whispered back like a razzing to his brother. "Do you remember Aster Costa?"

He hugged me to the side of his chest like we'd remained the best of friends. "A real long time, right?"

"Not long enough." The grunted words left Trent on a growl.

Nervousness chattered my teeth, the freezing cold from outside dropping by thirty degrees.

This was bad.

Still, Logan just smirked the biggest smirk I'd ever seen and sat back in the chair, looping his arm farther around my shoulders and kicking an ankle onto the opposite knee like it was the most natural thing in the world.

Arrogance rolled from him in waves.

Crashed into me as heat.

I itched, shifted on the hard metal chair.

He pressed his nose into my hair and breathed out, "Relax. I've got you."

"This is a bad idea," I mumbled back.

He laughed a cocky sound. "All of mine are, Aster."

He pointed at the older man who was still giving his welcome, Logan's voice held just for me. "That's Gary, Eden's father."

A question furled my brow.

Logan almost laughed like he was just catching up on the fact I knew nothing about anyone he was talking about.

"Eden is Trent's wife."

"Oh." My lips formed it almost silently. There I sat, taking in the details as if I were the unwelcomed, second wife at her first family dinner.

Gary continued his introductions. "I just want to say how much we appreciate everything you do for this school and this community. We couldn't do what we do without you. Most of all, we couldn't do it without my daughter, Eden, our show director and producer."

An affectionate chuckle left him as a blonde head peeked out from between the part in the curtains and waved.

The crowd cheered and she ducked back in.

I peeked back Trent Lawson's way. My pulse thugged when I saw who sat on the other side of him.

Jud Lawson.

Logan's other brother. He had always been a beast of a man, but different than Trent. Softer, maybe, easier to laugh, though it would be a mistake to believe he wasn't every bit as savage.

It took me a second to notice he had his hand twined with another on his lap. A woman sat beside him, her attention rapt on the stage.

"Now, without further delay, enjoy the show…" Gary waved toward the curtains and the spotlight blinked out.

A second later, it flashed back on to the curtains sweeping open. It revealed a set made of painted cardboard, a winter wonderland of white paper confetti and silver stars that were strung from the rafters.

"Here we go." Logan murmured it at my ear as if I were in this with him. As excited as he.

I shouldn't be.

I should guard myself.

If I were smart, I'd get up and leave.

Because I thought maybe I was in more danger than ever when my spirit lightened in a wash of Logan's joy when Eden showed from the right side of the stage, wearing a black tutu, tights, and pointe shoes.

A row of little angels followed her out.

They spun around, trying to hide their giggles and shy giddiness as they looked out on the audience in hopes of seeing their families.

People oohed and aahed as Eden led the children through a simple dance.

Mostly the Lawson brothers who shouted and cheered when an adorable little girl with two-black buns on the sides of her head came forward and did an off-balance pirouette.

"Go, Juni Bee," Logan shouted. "That's my girl."

He tapped my thigh, whispered close to my ear, "That's Juniper, Jud's wife's daughter. His too, really, even though not by blood."

"She's beautiful."

"Prettiest girl in the room." Then his voice dropped, turned wicked, wrecked me in an entirely different way, "Except for you."

I wanted to beg him to stop. To tell him I couldn't deal with this. That this push and pull was killing me. The gravitation and the disgust. The hatred and the echo of a star-crossed love.

The little girl giggled and blushed and skipped back to the line before three drummer boys joined the group on the stage, marching and beating toy drums.

My spirit did that erratic thing when I saw Gage, the same boy from earlier today, so proud as he drummed to his own beat.

I tried to hold back the rush of affection I felt just witnessing the scene.

An outsider who wouldn't last dipping her toes into the impossible.

This was so incredibly foolish.

So perfect and so uncomfortable.

So right and so wrong.

I had to wonder if it was just another way Logan had in mind to punish me. If he wanted to toss in my face what I'd missed.

Didn't he get it?

I already understood I'd missed out on everything.

The loss was profound.

Deep and dark and perpetual.

One class would go out only for another to enter, the performance a mesh of ballet, carols, and small acts.

Each time, Logan seemed to draw me closer. As if in the whimsical fantasy, in the enchanted darkness, he'd forgotten that we were supposed to be enemies. As if he'd slipped back to the time when loving him was a sin but the only thing I'd ever done right.

The show was endearing. Filled with simple joy and Christmas spirit. I did my best not to get swept in the simple triumph of it. In the sweet innocence.

Impossible.

It was bottled in my chest like a shaken concoction. A chemical reaction.

Logan and family and regret.

Hope and warmth and joy.

It grew thicker and thicker with each minute that passed.

It was funny that I'd all but forgotten that Christmas was less than a month away, that it hadn't mattered, not any of it, not until right then.

"Sweet, isn't it?" he murmured, though it was tinged in sadness, and his hand slipped free of my shoulder only to thread with my fingers on my lap. He squeezed so hard I had to wonder if he needed to make sure I was real. "That right there, Aster. That's what I was talking about. That's what matters."

He glanced at me.

I got stuck there.

In the man who right then looked so familiar.

My heart panged, and by the time the children piled out onto the stage with their teachers, Eden and her father in the middle, all of them taking a bow, tears clouded my eyes.

The crowd was on their feet for a standing ovation.

I was on mine, too.

Luckily it was expected because there was no chance I could remain sitting. I doubted I could remain standing there, either, not when the overhead lights flipped on, and I suddenly felt as if it were me who was standing in a spotlight.

Once the applause wore off, Trent and Jud both looked between me and Logan.

What did Logan expect me to do now?

Play along that we were old friends?

That we'd kept in touch?

What did they even know about us?

Discomfort shifted my feet as I stood under the force of Trent's glare and the uneasiness of Jud's watch.

Logan wrapped his arm around my waist and cinched me close, his smile all easy cockiness and no shits to give, as if the man had stepped into a different persona in front of his brothers.

But I felt the undercurrent of severity in his hold.

"All I've got to say is my niece and nephew are superstars. I mean, we know they get it from me, but still, superstars. Both of them are going to grow up to be just like their uncle Logan. Awesome knows awesome." Logan grinned wide as his ridiculous claim flooded out.

Trent gently bounced the infant against his chest, kissing the top of her head as he sent a grunt at his youngest brother. "In my worst nightmare," he grumbled.

Logan cracked up, pulling me tighter like I was his lover and not his enemy. "Hey now, that's just rude. Why you gotta be so mean? I've obviously rubbed off on your kid. Did you see him up there? You know he didn't get that shit from you."

He pressed a kiss to my temple right after he said it.

My knees knocked. Clammy discomfort clashed with the warmth.

What the hell did he think he was doing?

Trent's gaze followed Logan's attentions, his eyes narrowing in speculation. "Aster Costa. Have to say, I'm surprised to see you."

We weren't friends.

We weren't even acquaintances, really. I'd known him from a distance and his reputation and the love Logan had for him.

That was true for all Logan's brothers.

Both the two still living and standing in front of me and the one they'd lost.

Logan laughed again and shook me around. "Seriously, can you believe it? I ran into Aster here last night, and I thought she should stick around so we could catch up. What luck, right?"

He sent me an overzealous smile.

"Hmm," was all Trent managed as he lifted the baby higher and pressed his mouth to her head.

Jud cast a cautious glance at Trent before he rounded him and came my way. Nerves shook the ground below before a surprised squeak left me when he suddenly curled me in his massive arms.

At first, I wanted to fight him, but it took only a flash to recognize his embrace was kind, though somehow filled with reservation. "It's good to officially meet you, Aster."

"You, too." I had to force the words out around the lump in my throat.

He tugged the woman who'd sat next to him up to his side.

She was stunning, curvy with a black bob that touched her shoulders. She wore a fitted sweater dress that went all the way to her ankles, a slit up to the knee on the side.

Jud slipped his hand around to her waist, his other going to the tiny bump that barely showed on her belly. "Aster, this is my wife, Salem."

She stepped forward and shook my hand like we were going to be the best of friends. "It's really great to meet you."

She gently smacked Logan's chest. "Tell me what you're doing with this guy?"

"Hey, now, hey. Is that any way to treat your favorite brother-in-law? So rude. And here I thought you loved me."

Laughing, she curled her arm around his waist. "You're lucky I do, that's for sure."

Her smile was playful when she shifted her attention to me. "This one, I tell you, you have to watch out for him."

"Oh dear Salem, what is this nonsense you say? We all know there's no looking away from me." Logan gestured at himself, all tease and arrogance.

The undercurrent of the vapid grin he sent me knocked my knees again, one that promised he was right there, that he wasn't looking away from me, either, that he knew this was difficult, but he was asking me to do it with him, anyway.

The why was what I didn't get.

Why not just hide me away for thirty days? But the newfound glint that speared me from that gaze made me wonder if he were contemplating how much it might cost to keep me.

"Ah, here come our superstars." He gestured toward the side of the stage.

Trent's wife, Eden, all but floated our direction. She held Juniper and Gage's hands.

"Holy cow, that was amazing!" Logan shouted as they let go of Eden and came bounding our way. "Like, seriously epic. I see Tonys in our future. Broadway, baby."

Logan shook his arms in the air like he was catching a dream.

"Right, Uncle, right? I was the best drummer in the whole wide world, right?" Gage bounded across the floor, words flooding from his mouth the entire way.

"Heck, yes." Logan swept him into his arms. "Seriously, so good. Or maybe it's a rockstar I see in our future. Those were some wicked drum skills."

"Wicked?" The little boy scrunched his nose.

My fingers tingled while my feet itched.

Trent grunted again. "Keep it up, man, keep it up."

"Prepare yourself." Logan grinned. "This one right here has entertainment in his blood. I can feel it, and you know I'm never wrong."

Trent rolled his eyes. "Never."

The little girl was right behind. She went for Jud, and he tossed her into the air then caught her. "There's my angel."

She beamed at him when he hooked her to his side. "What'd you thinks, Motorcycle Dad? Do you thinks I'm gonna go to Russia and do all the dances in the ballet?"

"Absolutely, Little Bee," he promised, pressing a kiss to her chubby cheek.

My head spun, my spirit abuzz as if I was tossed headfirst into the chaos of this close family.

Floundering through the fullness of it.

"Who's that?" Gage smiled at me with a tilt of his head.

"You're looking at one of my oldest friends, Gage. Her name is Aster." Logan watched me with something I couldn't decipher.

Energy lapped between us.

A tiny thread that weaved and grew.

If I wasn't careful, it'd become more powerful than the two of us.

This pull I needed to ignore.

If I were smart, I'd run up the aisle and disappear forever because I'd bitten off more than I'd bargained for.

Logan was already too much.

Toss the rest of his family into the mix?

I gulped and tried to pin on a smile when Logan's sweet niece piped in, "Oh, friends are the bestest and the most important in all the whole world except for the families. Is she your favorite friend, Uncle Logan?"

"She used to be. I keep wondering if there's a chance she might be again."

Redness flashed, climbed my chest and my cheeks.

This was bad.

So bad.

"Well, you look like a really good kind of friend to me, Miss Aster," Gage cut in. "Like the kind you get to marry when you get older and you love forever and ever. Just like I love Juni Bee to the highest mountain and I'm gonna marry her when I get big."

"But no kissin'. Blech." The little girl's nose curled in disgust.

A rustle of laughter moved through the adults.

Logan set Gage onto his feet and ruffled his hand through his hair. "Sorry to break it to you, Gage, man, but Juni here is now your cousin since her mom married your uncle Jud. You're going to have to pick a new wife."

"No way, nuh-uh, not a chance." Juni furiously shook her head.

Affection wrapped me. A stunning amount of it. They were adorable. So sweet.

"These two." Eden was suddenly in front of me, sweet amusement playing through her expression. "Aster, I'm Eden. I belong to this one."

She sent a sultry smile toward Trent.

"That's right, Kitten," he grumbled.

Apparently these Lawsons had no issues staking claims.

"It's really nice to meet you," she said.

"It's nice to meet you, too," I floundered, trying to hold it together. "The show was beautiful. I loved every second."

A squeal rang from behind us. "Um, hello, did you all see that? My babies made me proud!"

I swiveled to see a woman I recognized from the performance come racing up. She was dressed as a snowflake, which kind of fit her considering she was as pale as the snow, though her hair was flaming red, her face covered in a smattering of freckles.

"Yes!" Gage gave her a high five. "Auntie Tessa, did you see how good I did?"

"Oh, you bet, I did. You two made the show." She pointed between Juni and Gage. "Well, and of course my third-grade class, they were pretty spectacular if I don't say so myself."

Then she gasped when she noticed me, whirling around to take me by the hands. "Who are you? I'm Tessa...these bitches' BFF." She jutted her chin toward Eden and Salem.

Salem laughed. "Well, I guess we claim her."

Feigned horror rocked from Tessa's mouth while she squeezed my hands as if I were a part of their group when I'd never felt so much like the odd man out.

"Don't listen to her for a second. She loves me. Like, mad, mad love. So, who are you?"

Her eyes gleamed as she looked around me at Logan who stood so close I felt as if I were being sucked his way.

Pulled into his orbit.

Gravity.

I didn't have time to answer before Juni shouted, "She used to be Uncle Logan's favorite friend, Auntie Tessa, but not anymore, but maybe one day they can gets to be again."

I stood there shifting my feet, feeling as if I'd gotten hit by a landslide. An avalanche. This close-knit group a balm that could never soothe.

Because the loneliness ached and the vacancy echoed, and I realized, standing there in the midst of them, that I'd forced my way into a place I didn't belong.

"I, uh, think I need to use the restroom. I'll meet you at the car?" I asked Logan as if it wasn't a big deal, even though I was sure they could hear the undercurrent of panic.

I was itching to flee.

His eyes darkened.

Malachite sparks.

He frowned then murmured, "Sure. I'll see you in a minute."

Forcing a smile, I lifted my hand in a slight wave. "It was great to meet you all…and to see you again, Jud and Trent," I fumbled.

Then I turned and fled. Pushed up the aisle through the crowds still gathered.

The families that loved.

The hope that shined.

And I wondered…wondered if I would ever truly find it for myself.

I wound through, trying to keep my cool as I pushed into the restroom and locked myself in a stall. I pressed my forehead against the cold metal door in an attempt to squelch the fire that was eating me from the inside out.

Pain crushed my chest, and jagged breaths wheezed down my throat and into my lungs.

I hated it. Hated all that had been lost.

A tear slipped free, and I swatted at it, refused it because I wasn't weak.

This was about a new path.

A new *destination*.

It hovered out in front of me.

The tease of a dream.

The scrawling of beautiful words. Promises made in vain.

There is no place my heart won't find you. My North Star.

But where would it leave us in the end?

Stumbling out of the stall, I went to the sink and splashed water on my face. Then I forced myself to suck down the riot of emotions, and I slipped back out into the lobby.

I squeezed through the crowd, mumbling, "Excuse me," as I went, and I welcomed the frigid cold as I stepped out into the damp air. I tugged my coat tighter like it could shield me from it all, and I wound back around to where Logan had parked.

Winter clouds hung heavy in the night sky, though they'd parted near the moon that glowed from the heavens. Stars glittered in the crisp night like beacons that called through eternity.

I didn't flinch when I felt the presence possess me from behind, the beautiful torment that surrounded me like an embrace that could snuff me out.

"It's cold," he murmured, Logan's voice so low as he edged close.

He set his hands on the sides of my waist.

Tremors rushed.

A clash of ice and flames that tumbled down my spine.

My focus remained upturned, to the vastness that seemed so close, to the stars that glinted and shined in the sky.

Constellations written in mystery.

I felt as if I could reach out and touch them. Understand their meaning.

"Do you think it led us here?" I whispered into the lapping darkness.

Our old truth beat around us like a warning drum.

This man who had promised me that no matter where he went,

wherever I went, or anything that tried to come between us, he would find his way back to me.

Fate.

Destiny.

Our destination.

My North Star.

"I used to believe it," he muttered, "but it hurt too fucking bad when I discovered it was a lie."

Was it?

Because I felt myself being swallowed whole.

By his arms that wrapped around me like a fortress.

By the beat of his heart into my back.

By his spirit that held me like eternity.

"Your family is amazing." I pushed it out around the lump in my throat.

Logan held me tighter. "They should have been yours."

"Yes." Emotion clogged my throat, and I tried to swallow around it. "I think I made a mistake, Logan. Asking this of you. Bringing you into this."

His arms tightened more. "It's too late if it was."

"I would die first." My eyes pinched closed on the truth. "Before I let anything happen to any of you."

"No one's dying, Aster, no one except for your husband." He gritted it at the back of my head. Then he pushed away and rounded the car, clicking the locks as he went.

I stared at him over the top.

"It's already done, Aster. Just get in."

I shouldn't. I should end this now. Before it was too late. Because as desperately as I wanted my freedom, to be my own person, it was the moment I realized I wasn't sure I could handle losing Logan all over again.

Chapter Nine

Logan

Los Angeles, Eighteen Years Old

LATE AFTERNOON LIGHT FLOATED THROUGH THE WINDOW where Logan sat at the small kitchen table. His textbooks were spread in front of him, and his laptop was open to the report he was writing for his English 101 class. Not that he intended to do a whole lot with words. Numbers were his game.

He heard the rumble of a motorcycle approaching in the distance. A spot of excitement hit his chest. He was used to being alone, it didn't bother him all that much, but he had to admit sometimes the silence got to him.

It gave him too much time to think.

Too much time to ponder what life might have been like if his mother were still alive.

Too much time to contemplate the dynamic of his family.

More than anything, it gave him too much time to worry over his brothers, what danger they might find themselves in that day.

Logan knew Trent and Jud tried to hide the truth of who they were from him and Nathan. They did it out of love, hoping to guard them from the brutality of their day-to-day.

That didn't mean it didn't sometimes make Logan feel detached. Like he wasn't a part of who they were, as ugly as it might be.

The roar increased before Logan heard the bike come to an idle in the driveway of the four-bedroom house he lived in with his brothers. They'd moved there when Trent was twenty, when he'd stepped up and made the choice to take Jud, Logan, and Nathan out of their father's home and bring them there.

Away.

Separated.

Where it was safer.

Lonelier, too, because it was a world apart from where Trent and Jud spent most of their days and nights.

The side door opened, and Trent pushed through, donning his cut and worn boots and that darkly quiet ferocity forever hewn on his face.

Vengeance.

Cruelty.

Trent might not ever admit it, but Logan knew he'd been hunting their mother's killer since the day she'd been ruthlessly gunned down in front of their old house when Logan had only been nine.

His spirit curled in on itself when he remembered it. A crushing he was sure would never abate. He gulped around it when Trent jutted his chin his way. "Hey, man, how are you, brother?"

"Good." Logan eyed him in speculation. "What are you doing here? I thought you had business tonight?"

"Something more important came up."

Logan frowned. "What's that?"

Trent roughed a tatted hand through the short crop of black hair on his head, then he looked Logan straight on. "You."

Anxiety made a prickly slide down his spine, and he pushed his laptop back.

Trent hesitated, warred, then sighed as he crossed the kitchen. He pulled out a chair and flipped it around and sat on it with his arms rested on the back, staring at Logan like he'd become his sole focus.

"What's going on, man?" Logan hated that his voice wobbled. Hated that Trent thought him some kind of pussy. Like he wasn't strong enough to even know the monsters he faced each day. Not that he wanted to go on daily raids or murder sprees.

But he wanted to…belong. For Trent to trust him enough to at least confide in him.

Trent let his attention drift over Logan's homework before he cut a glance at Logan. "You're fuckin' smart, man. Smarter than any of us. Damned wizard with the numbers."

There was no missing the foreboding wound in it.

"That's no secret. We all know I'm the smartest, best looking of the bunch," Logan tossed out with a smirk, doing his best to ignore Trent's agitation.

Because seriously, what the hell was this about?

Trent checked on him, yeah. Made sure he was going to class. But Trent didn't need to worry about any of that shit. Logan was laser focused. Was set on coming out on top. He'd be rich, but he was going to do that shit right.

Trent rubbed his fingertips over his lips. It was a tell.

His oldest brother was disturbed.

"Yeah, and our father has noticed." It came out a low warning.

A frown took to Logan's face, and he almost shrugged if it weren't for the ripples of unease billowing off of Trent. "So?"

Trent grunted in frustration. "So, if he sees something that he can use for his benefit, that's what the bastard's gonna do."

Trent might have worn the vice pres patch for their MC, Iron Owls, but their father was the president. Which meant whatever their father said was gospel, no matter if Trent liked it or not.

Over the years, the animosity between the two had grown, but there was little Trent could do but his duty to the club. It was where his life was pledged.

Live to Ride, Ride to Die.

Once you took that oath, that was it.

You were an Owl until the day you were put in the ground.

Logan figured it was the main reason Trent had purchased this house in a family neighborhood clear across the city from the club's quarters. He was hiding both him and Nathan away, hoping their father didn't notice any talents that could be extorted.

Hell, he probably hoped their father had forgotten that they even existed.

Logan's knee began to bounce. "What does that mean for me?"

Trent's head barely shook as he rested farther on the chair and angled closer. "It means he found a way to use you. He promised you to a man named Andres Costa."

Logan blinked and his chest tightened.

He knew the name.

Trent's throat bobbed when he swallowed, irritation burning through his blood. "They want you working his books. Looking for ways to get their money into legitimate investments. Growing it."

It was pointed when Trent said it.

An undercurrent of a message.

A cold sweat broke out on the back of Logan's neck and fear took hold.

Trent was on his feet and kneeling in front of him in a flash. He gripped Logan's knee, angling his head up and forcing Logan to meet his eye. "I fought him on it, Logan. I did. Told him I didn't want you mixed up in this mess. You're too good for it. Too fuckin' good. He insisted you're a Lawson. That you are destined to patch in."

Trent drew in a shattered sigh. "Won't let that happen, Logan. I won't. I pushed back until we came to a concession that I still hate, but at least it spares you the cut. You'll be working at Costa's compound. Far away from the club. Where it can't touch you. You'll be safe there. It's where his family lives, and he does not allow violence to infiltrate those walls."

Logan couldn't stop the tremors that wracked his limbs.

Trent stood and brought him to his feet, holding him by the outside of both shoulders. "You just have to keep your head down low, Logan. Stay under the radar. Don't interact with anyone except to listen for instruction. You can't let this world get under your skin, man. You can't."

Trent's voice cracked on the last, and he gave Logan a soft shake. "Promise me, Logan, promise me you'll do your job, and it ends at that."

Logan forced himself to nod around the shock.

Trent breathed out in what sounded like pained relief as he pulled Logan to his chest and hugged him fiercely. "I won't let him destroy you, too. I promise, Logan. I promise."

Logan was nothing but nerves as Trent pulled his truck to the side entrance of a mansion in one of the wealthiest communities in the Greater Los Angeles Area. It was basically a compound, like Trent had called it, the walls almost as high as the security measures surrounding it.

From the front, it looked no different than any of the other estates that sat on multiple acres. Tall trees soared over the height of the walls, the gate ornate, the house within not visible from the street.

The truck idled at the curb as Trent clutched the steering wheel. His brother was clearly fighting a brand-new war.

"I'll be fine," Logan promised. "Don't worry."

Logan figured he'd make the best of it. Numbers were in his blood. He'd take every lesson he learned here and apply it to what he did in the future.

Make some extra cash, too.

He couldn't say he was bummed about that.

He could only be wary about who he was working for.

Trent stared at him, blinked, then sent him a tight nod. "Okay."

Logan gave him half a smile and climbed out. He hiked his backpack higher and moved to a narrow gateway where he was instructed to be at six p.m. He peered into the camera that stared back.

With his heart racing, a deep, thudding pulse that he felt all the way to his ears, he was buzzed through and led onto the grounds that made the Los Angeles Botanical Gardens look like a desert wasteland. In the distance was a house, so large it could have been a hotel.

Logan inhaled. He was sure he could actually smell money.

He felt a flash of excitement.

He quelled it, remembered Trent had warned him to keep his head down.

The man he followed led him through a set of doors on the far side of the rambling building. It was an area that appeared to be separated from the main living quarters.

He walked down the long corridor, his footsteps echoing on the marble floors.

There was a room on the right that made him slow as they passed by. The double doors opened to a massive room with grand ceilings and books lining each wall that were stacked to the sky.

Leather furniture filled the middle, and he wasn't sure if his heart stopped or sped so fast that he could no longer feel it when someone peeked at him from over the back of a couch.

The girl tried to keep herself hidden as she peered at him.

Her hair the darkest chocolate and her eyes the color of the molten sun.

Logan realized the promise he'd made his brother had been made in vain.

Because there would be no keeping to himself.

Chapter Ten

Aster

I PULLED THE NIGHT SLIP OVER MY HEAD. THE SOFT, WHITE material unfurled over my body and landed mid-thigh. I looked at myself in the mirror, blew back the dark brown bangs that had fallen in my face, and said a silent prayer for strength. That I could find my way through the turmoil.

That I could persevere.

That I could fly.

Tomorrow, I would form a plan.

Figure out how to prove to my father why I could never go back to Jarek Urso.

Dread scattered through me like the whisper of death.

I'd never caused it before. Been the precursor. But I knew what this might mean for Jarek.

Guilt threatened to claw. To rip open and infect.

A disease that turned my blood cold and my stomach sour.

I hated the violence. Hated it to my soul. But I had to remember Jarek was one of the greatest perpetrators of it.

Pulse fluttering, I blew out a heavy sigh, and I flipped the light off to the bathroom and stepped out into the bedroom.

The second I did, I froze, snared by the dark presence that whipped like a blizzard from the doorway.

My eyes narrowed as I stared at the man who might as well be a mirage.

Sanctuary.

Refuge.

Perdition.

The man who'd been little more than a boy when he'd captured me in that first, stolen glance.

I'd been obsessed, willing to break every rule to even catch a glimpse.

Now, I felt myself falling into the abyss of who he was all over again.

For good or bad.

Right or wrong.

None of it had ever mattered except for wanting him to be mine.

Still in his suit, Logan watched me as if he were bored, though I could feel the pinpricks of intensity that bristled beneath his skin. The white-hot energy that radiated from his being.

I fidgeted, wearing the slip, feeling so much more exposed than I had in the tee.

It was thin straps and thin material and a neckline that dipped low between my breasts.

Heat blossomed as I imagined him picking it out for me.

Tension stretched across the room. A dense, veiled pull that felt like a vacant ache, the heat of his eyes a beacon that shouted to me from the bowels of an obliterating storm.

"What are you doing in here?" I finally managed to press the words from my mouth while I took a fortifying step back.

As if I could protect myself from the lure.

The muted hum of a television droned through the walls from Gretchen's room, and the sound of the night howled through the mountain slopes and softly battered at the panes.

Everything else seemed magnified.

The shallow gasps of my breaths and the erratic hammer of my heart and the questions that raged through my mind.

Logan angled his head. A wicked smirk lit at the edge of his mouth as he leaned against the doorway with his hands stuffed in his pants pockets.

As if he held a secret that I wasn't privy to.

Attraction throbbed in my belly.

"Now, don't tell me you've already forgotten who you belong to?"

"This is a bad idea, Logan." It was my only defense.

"What's that?"

"You and me."

A roll of low laughter rippled from his mouth. "We were always a bad idea, but we did it, anyway."

I fidgeted. "And look where we ended up."

His head cocked.

The man so beautiful.

So gorgeous it was obscene.

"And why's that?" he pressed.

"I think it would be better for the both of us if we didn't go there."

He stepped forward.

Severity flashed.

A shockwave.

I couldn't breathe.

"I thought we were playing by my rules, Aster?"

I hugged my arms over my chest, and I gulped around the burn that crawled up my throat. "We are."

His prowl was slow and measured as he edged my way, as if the longer it took him to reach me, the harder my pulse would pound with want.

His breaths were jagged, his stare intense.

He gripped me by one side of the waist, hard enough to make me gasp, though his thumb caressed my hip bone in a soothing way.

Dangerous, dangerous seduction.

An edge had taken him over. As if he'd sensed my intention to leave, to save him from the same fate he'd been headed toward before. The softness from earlier this evening had constricted in possession.

"You're mine, Aster." It was a growl. I swore, his touch sank all the way down to my bones. Warming me from the inside out.

I shivered, and I tried to look away, but the only thing I could do was tip up my head to stare at him in the shadows.

His jaw was hard, his brow furrowed, his eyes intense. Every line carved in pained devotion.

"Please...don't play games with me."

He stepped into me, pressing me up against the wall, no amusement in his tone when he warned, "But the games are so much fun to play."

"Not when your heart is on the line." I forced the haggard words from my tongue.

The bare, cold truth.

He was going to hurt me, and I was going to hurt him, and I didn't think either of us could go through that again.

Still, lightheadedness swept through me when he touched my cheek. He dragged it down my trembling neck and over my collarbone, down, down along my side, all the way until he tickled my bare thigh, fingertips playing with the hem of the night slip.

I could barely see, could barely think.

Touch me.

They were the only words that made any sense. I bit down on my tongue to keep them subdued.

Shivers tumbled in a slow-slide, and he chuckled low, and his hand was coming up to press between my breasts on the exposed skin of my chest. Right over that organ that raged. "Whose heart is that, Aster?"

It was venom, it was a plea. He ran his knuckles between my cleavage.

Our gazes tangled.

Wild.

Needy.

Both desperate and disturbed.

"I think we both know it's mine." The confession was recklessly dangerous. I wished for a way to reach out and squash it before it hit his ears.

Darkness glowered from his frown, and the hand on my waist curled tighter. "Why are you here, Aster?" Logan's voice was gravel. "Why did you come back to me?"

"I don't know if I could have ended up anywhere else."

Tiny whimpers bled free when he let his palm travel down my quivering stomach before he was riding it back up.

His thumb lightly teased over my nipple, and my stupid hands clutched at the material of his jacket, holding onto his arms that I'd once thought a safety net.

"You're mine. I don't give a fuck who you're married to. You've always been mine." It cracked like a low, guttural threat.

Lust burst to life, rushing back to reclaim our sacred place.

Old, scarred passions ripping open, emerging anew.

I grappled to get closer.

Need welled up so fast that I had to bite down on my bottom lip to keep from begging for more.

"We can't, Logan."

He pressed his face into my jaw, let his lips travel the length until he was murmuring in my ear, "Oh, make no mistake, Aster. We will."

He stepped back and readjusted his jacket.

I sagged against the wall, heaving for the air that no longer existed.

His jaw ticked, and his stare was a flood of potency. "I have to attend to something. Do not leave this apartment. Do you understand me?"

"Where would I go?"

He was back in front of me, his thumb on my lips and his words in my ear. "Good girl."

Then he was gone.

Chapter Eleven

Logan

I T WAS HALF PAST TEN WHEN I WEAVED MY WAY THROUGH THE throbbing crowd toward the private booth tucked at the far back corner of Absolution. Absolution was the club Trent ran and owned, though a piece of that pie went to both Jud and me.

Our businesses were all tied. Bound together since the three of us were bound in blood and loyalty.

They earned the money.

I invested it.

Multiplied it and turned it over.

It was my calling. What I'd been bred to do.

What fed my addiction and destroyed the last vestiges of goodness inside me.

Lights strobed over the crowd, and lust stroked the air with an undercurrent of greed.

Tonight, a cover band was on the stage, the place packed and wild and hedged with a vibe of decadence.

I inhaled it like it might help me regain my footing.

Because I was tripping in a direction I couldn't allow myself to go.

I should've always known Aster Rose would be a dead-end, and I was pretty sure if I didn't get smart, that dead-end was going to land me six feet underground.

Things were already turning south in my brain. Leaving her there tonight? After walking in on her wearing that nightie? That shit had been one second from being impossible. How easy it would've been to slide my hands under the slip to get to all that sweetness.

To set my dick free and take her against the wall.

It'd been so fucking long since I'd been in that body, in that perfection, that I'd nearly walked right over that line.

Felt what she might give.

Topping it off was the memory of the way it'd felt sitting next to her at my niece and nephew's performance. Like she'd been there all along. Where she'd belonged. My mind raced with the possibilities that my brain knew better than to go to.

It'd left me shaken.

Hungry for things that really should sour on my palate.

I'd only intended to push her a bit. Tease her. Tempt her the way she was tempting me. Then I'd touched her, and all bets were off. I couldn't handle the way she'd looked at me with those fire-agate eyes.

The way she had to stop herself from letting the pleas drop from her tongue. I had nearly lost it right then, and I knew I had to get the fuck out of there before I did something stupid.

Like putting a wall between us was going to cure the need.

My cock still raged, and my fingers were itching with the desire to sink right in.

Mouth watering for any taste of poison she might give.

Funny since there was a huge piece of me that still wanted to tell her to fuck off.

This was the girl who'd destroyed me. One who'd left a hole so deep and wide it didn't stand a chance of callousing over.

It was just this gaping, festering mess that would forever hate what she'd done.

I didn't trust her.

Not at all.

And the really sick part of me didn't give a fuck. That part didn't care what she'd done or where she'd been. Her place was with me.

It certainly wasn't wise.

I'd known it in the hard panic that'd taken hold of my brothers when they'd seen me walk up with her like rolling in with a Costa was perfectly normal.

It was a line in the sand.

A beckoning of trouble.

A middle finger to the type of people who were not to be trifled with.

The kind of people we used to be, but it was a life that we'd left behind.

Permanently.

And now a Costa princess was in my penthouse apartment.

I shouldered through the crush to find my brothers were already waiting for me in our regular booth reserved for us at the very back of the club.

Trent sat on the right and Jud on the left, Trent sipping from the expensive scotch he preferred and Jud sipping from a foaming mug of his favorite beer.

It wasn't all that rare of a sight.

I slipped into the booth on Trent's side and cut them both an overzealous smile. "I'm here, boys. Let the party begin."

Trent grunted. "Think you know full well we didn't call you here for a party."

Right.

It was an inquisition. I'd figured Trent wasn't looking to chill when he'd leaned in like he was going to tell me goodbye after the recital and told me to be here at ten.

I rocked back against the booth like I hadn't dropped a nuclear bomb on them earlier tonight without giving them a reason for war.

"Why so glum? Tell me the honeymoons haven't already worn off?" I said it like it was a sad, sorry state of affairs. "Are your poor, tiny dicks shriveling up from disuse? It's an injustice, you know."

I cracked it the way I always did, rubbing it in like they were the ones going to be missing out for the rest of their lives when they'd tapped into what really mattered. "I warned you guys...but did anyone listen to their baby brother? *Nooo.* When are you all going to realize I'm the smartest of the bunch?"

Jud pointed at me from across the table. "Cut the crap, Logan. Don't think you're going to bullshit your way out of this one because I'm not buying that smile on your face for anything."

Trent went right for the throat. "Care to tell me why the fuck a Costa showed up at my kid's performance tonight?" he demanded.

I shrugged like it was no big deal. "Like I said, I ran into her last night and thought we should catch up."

Trent's brow lifted and his voice lowered, "You ran into her? Where?"

I knew I was going to get the rain of fury from my brothers. I respected the hell out of them, but in this instance, I was having a really hard time finding any fucks to give. Still, I tried to play it off like I wasn't in deeper than I'd ever been. "A friend's house."

"What friend?" he pressed.

I sighed. "A client of mine. No one you would know."

"Why was she there?"

"Not really sure." At least it was some version of the truth because really, what the hell was that prick Jarek doing there? "A few acquaintances and I were having a friendly game of poker, and lo and behold, there she was."

Nothing but a perfect dream wrapped in black silk.

My dick stirred again.

"*Friendly?*" Trent pushed.

"Just wagering on a little good fun."

Jud groaned.

They didn't exactly approve of my playing. I did my best to keep it on the sly most of the time, but there'd been instances when I couldn't turn over a car as quickly as I'd like, and they'd get a whiff of what was going down.

"Shit," Jud rumbled, scrubbing a meaty palm over his face. "Want to tell us what was on the table?"

"Things might have gotten a little dicey." I eased in the confession.

"How so?" Jud asked, eyes narrowing as he lifted his beer to his mouth.

I paused, hesitated, then let the truth bleed out. "I might have won her."

"The fuck?" Trent spat.

They stared me down like I'd lost my mind. Why I bothered pretending I hadn't, I didn't know because I knew I'd stepped into a world I'd do better to pretend I never knew existed.

We all three eased back when the server showed with my regular drink.

The second she was gone, Jud sat forward, his elbows propped on the table and his face in his hands. "This is a joke, right? Tell me it's a fucking joke, Logan."

His giant arms were bound in muscle that flexed and bunched. Like he was coming up on a battle that would require him to fight to the death.

I prayed to God it wouldn't come to that.

Because it didn't matter if I knew agreeing to her staying with me was the right thing to do, didn't matter that I knew she needed help, her being here was going to come at a cost.

Problem was, I still didn't know how steep that might prove to be.

Blowing out a sigh, I scratched at the back of my neck in discomfort. "Not a joke."

Anxiety gusted around the table, quiet taking hold for a moment.

My throat worked, and I forced myself to lay it out because there was no use in trying to keep any of it from them.

We had each other's back, whatever messes we found ourselves in. And when it came to us Lawson Brothers, we always seemed to find plenty of it.

I let myself feel it. The weight of what I'd done. The decision I'd made. How it might impact us all.

Aster's face flashed through my mind. The way she'd begged me to let her stay. The way the pain in her eyes was greater than the fear of what standing up for herself might be.

The way it had me itching to go on a murder spree.

I doubted much weighing any of the risks now would make me change my mind.

None of it would make me take it back.

Still, I was letting the disquiet come out with the explanation. "There was a big game at one of my most affluent client's places. He likes to play big. High stakes. All-in kind of shit. Played a couple times at his table over the last few months. I didn't know what I was walking in on last night, but I found myself sitting across from Jarek Urso."

"Fuck." It heaved from Trent in a bout of horrified shock. He scrubbed a tatted palm over his face, like it might flush out the mistake he'd undoubtedly believed I'd made.

"Yup."

Trent eyed me seriously, like he was calculating those days, trying to make it add up.

"You have history with her?"

Shallow, disheartened laughter rumbled out. "You could say that."

Shame bound my spirit.

All the warnings Trent had given me to lay low when it came to the Costas. The way I'd promised again and again that I would. That I was keeping my nose clean.

Never had I let my brothers in on what'd gone down with Aster. Not after everything that had happened. Not with the choices I'd made that started a domino effect that I couldn't undo.

I didn't even know how to give voice to the loss.

Guilt bottled tight in my chest.

Agitation buzzed from Trent. "How deep, Logan?"

My eyes dropped closed. "Really fucking deep." I opened them, bitterness getting ground up in the clench at the back of my teeth.

"But she ended up with Jarek?" Jud issued it like he was processing it, too, though his voice was tinged in understanding.

"That's right."

"Shit," Trent said low.

"And last night you ended up sitting across from her husband at a shady table at one of your client's places," Jud added like fact, scratching at his beard.

I was sure by the look on his face that he'd come to the quick conclusion that revenge was the sum I'd been aiming for.

"That is correct, brother." I swallowed around the landslide of jagged rocks that tumbled down my throat. "He and I were the last men standing. His stack was depleted fast."

I drove my fingers through my hair. "I just wanted to push him. Shame that motherfucker. So when he pressed to go all in, I called for his girl instead."

My girl.

Jud all but groaned, flopping his big body back in the booth. "You are a twisted fuck, you know that, Logan?"

A short shot of laughter rumbled out. "Made me crazy, her standing there with him."

I hadn't even acknowledged it then. The way I'd wanted to climb right over that table, put a bullet between his eyes, and take back what was mine.

"I thought I'd prove a point. Get him on his knees. But I didn't think for a second he'd bite. But I already knew the bastard was a snake, so I'm not sure why I was surprised. Asshole lost, obviously. Let's just say Aster was not pleased by me trying to claim my prize."

"Tell me she knocked you clean flat." Jud cocked a smirk.

I smiled with a rough chuckle. "Girl wanted to claw my eyes out, that's for sure. She ran upstairs instead, saying she wasn't going anywhere with either of us."

Sweet savage that she was. Fierce and defiant and soft and pliable.

My throat thickened. "The prick took off after her. He put his hands on her, so when I stepped in and distracted him, she bolted. I found her walking her ass through the frozen forest. Long story short, she asked for a place to stay until she can figure out a way to get free of him. I agreed."

All in a night's fun.

"And you agreed to help her? After this chick, *who you never should have touched in the first place*, broke your heart?" Trent added all kinds of emphasis in the areas that stabbed at my guilt.

"When you put it that way, it makes me sound like I'm the fool here." I cracked it like a joke.

"*Sound* like it?" Jud arched a brow.

"What's her end game?" Trent cut in.

I gave a halfhearted shrug. "She wants out."

"Out from under Jarek or her father?" Trent's jaw was working like mad. He'd always considered himself the protector of the family, like because he was the oldest, it fell on his shoulders. He'd forgotten our father's blood ran through all of us.

Vengeance.

Cruelty.

Greed.

Unease twitched the muscles at the back of my neck. "Not sure how far she wants to take it. She just said she needs to prove to her father that Jarek has turned on the family."

Dread poured out of him like a sieve.

"This could get messy."

I took a sip of my drink. "It always does."

"You trust her?"

My spirit shook. "I shouldn't," I admitted.

Trent eyed me, seeing way down deep the way he always did. "Think the most important question here is what your end game is, man. Why are you doing this? You want a revenge fuck, or does it go deeper than that?"

A disorder burned through my body.

Possession.

Hunger.

It all rose from a well to swill with the loss.

"I'm going to fight for her. The way I should have then."

The truth of it plowed through me like a cry for victory.

"Is she worth it?" Jud's voice was soft, filled with empathy.

I ran my finger around the rim of my glass, staring at it while I contemplated, my mind flashing through a thousand memories.

In all my rage, I'd almost forgotten how the girl'd been so fucking sweet.

"I might regret it, but yeah, I think she is."

Jud gruffed an incredulous laugh. "Chances are you will, man, chances are."

My exhalation was heavy. "I don't see how there's anything else to do."

"So that's how it is then?"

"Yup."

Chuckling, Jud lifted his beer. "To the love-fucked. Believe me, brother…" He looked between me and Trent. "Trent and I would be there in a heartbeat if it were our girls. Get it. Just fucking be careful. Watch your back. These people are not to be toyed with."

Trent took a sip from his tumbler, lifted his, too. "And know we're always here. No matter what you need."

I ducked into the hallway that read *Employees Only* and headed for the exit that would dump me in the staff parking lot.

Milo, one of the original bouncers here at Absolution, the guy more family than employee, stood guard at the door.

If Jud was a giant, this motherfucker was a goliath. Covered in tats and scary as fuck.

Dude rarely said a word, his demeanor quiet and subdued, though I was pretty sure he would take a bullet if it was required. God knew the number of pricks he tossed to the curb on a nightly basis.

"Logan, Sir, how are you tonight?"

"Same ol', same ol'."

I didn't see the point in telling him I itched. That I'd had one drink with my brothers and the only thing I could think about was getting back to my apartment.

To see that she was there. Whole.

"That's all we can ask for, isn't it?"

"Yup."

He opened the door. "You have a good night. Be safe out there."

"I plan on it," I said as I stepped out into the fat tufts of snow-flakes that flitted from the sky, and I stuffed my hands into my pockets to ward off the chill. Rays of glinting lights streaked through the frosty, damp air, the snowflakes falling in a slow cascade, casting the lot in a globe of white.

Absolution was set in an old warehouse on the industrial side of town. Most everything within a five-mile radius was locked-up tight for the night except for the chaos that roiled within its walls.

The lot was deserted, and the sound of the band and voices seeped through the bricks and vibrated the ground. I moved over close to where I'd parked my car before I glanced around to make sure I was alone. When I found that I was, I blew out some of the tension, leaned against the wall in the shadows, and dug into my pocket to pull out my phone.

I dialed the number then pressed it to my ear.

It rang three times before the groggy voice answered, "What the hell, it's almost two in the morning."

"Calling in that debt, Dean."

Dude owed me after not making good on a lost bet—I'd figured his connections might serve to be more valuable than the hundred-grand he'd lost.

I might play hard, but I played smart.

Rustling echoed from the other end of the line, and I heard a door snap shut before he exhaled heavily when he shut another. "What is it you need?"

"Information."

"On who?"

"I want everything you can get on a man named Jarek Urso."

I could tell he was fumbling around on his desk to find something to write on.

"U-r-s-o. Los Angeles," I continued. "Birthdate is May 12, 1993."

"And what do you want to know?"

"Everything. Everything he owns. Every investment. Every connection. Every sin he's committed and every debt he owes. Where he puts his dick and where he dips his dirty fingers."

It wasn't like a man like that would stay faithful.

Air puffed through the line. "And what do you want with this guy?"

"What do you think?"

Reservations left him on a strained sigh. "Why do I get the feeling I would have fared better giving you the deed to my house?"

"Don't worry yourself, Dean. It's off the books."

Off the books was what I did.

"Right," he grunted.

"Just get me what I need."

"I'll get everything I can. I'll call you tomorrow."

"Thank you."

"As if I have another choice."

He hung up without saying anything else. I tucked my phone into my pocket and moved to my car, started it, put my hands to the vents and welcomed the heat. I tried to gather my emotions before I headed back to my apartment where I'd lived for the last year.

I rubbed my hands over my face like it could break up the disorder. Give me some clarity.

I didn't know if I saw the flash of darkness or felt it.

The depravity that curled through the air.

I dropped my hands and peered into the hazy white light where the vapid shadows hovered like an army of wraiths at the edge of the lot.

I swore I saw something.

A shift.

A shape.

I didn't know, but the only thing I could do was open my car door and climb out into the soft fall of snow.

A feeling took me over.

Possession.

The need to protect.

I saw it.

A silhouette that disappeared around the side of the building.

"Hey!" I shouted, "Hey, stay right the fuck there."

I took off in that direction.

A gust of wind howled through the evergreens, swishing and churning through the towering spikes that touched the heavens, and I thought I heard the clatter of footsteps retreating in the distance.

I hustled along the side of the brick building in the direction of the disturbance. It was chaotic. An upheaval that shuddered in the frozen air.

I ran headlong into it, overcome by the need to hunt down any fucker who would do her harm. Hurt her. Stop it in its tracks if we were being hunted.

I rounded the corner only for that whooshing in the trees to become the air whooshing from my lungs when a rod slammed into my stomach.

Pain shattered through my body.

I was hit so hard my footing failed, and the ground came up quick under me. My face impacted the pavement before the rod struck my ribs.

Agony flash-fired up my side.

I clawed to get up, to get to my feet, to face this piece-of-shit who lurked in the darkness.

The voice was at my ear. "It's the only warning you'll get."

Then he shoved off and ran into the cover of the forest.

I managed to climb to my feet. The sky and ground spun. A whorl that became one. The pain almost dropped me to my knees again, but I forced myself to stand, swiped the blood from my mouth, and shouted into the distance, "Pussy. Next time, show your face."

I felt the hatred that blistered back.

I bottled it. Took it down. Made it mine.

Then I stormed back to my car and got inside.

Chapter Twelve

Aster

I STARED OUT AT THE ENDLESS WINTER NIGHT THROUGH THE frosted panes of my bedroom window. My fingers reached out, tracing the cold. My finger looked so odd without the ring that I'd removed.

Everything felt foreign. The crush of emotions and the tangling of need. A contrast of sensations that'd left me up pacing half the night.

There was a time in my life I'd dreamed in color.

In vivid hues and lush textures. In laughter and song.

I used to believe in truth and light. In faith and beauty and the goodness of humanity.

I'd once dared to trust in love. Dared to believe that we would end up where we were destined. Our paths leading us to the exact point we were meant to be.

I'd dared hope for a family.

All of it had been sparked by a connection that was real and true and had stolen the breath from my lungs every time he came into the room.

Until one day those colors went dim. It was the day joy was sucked out and darkness set in.

I'd exchanged the safety of his arms for the torment of everything I had lost.

Exchanged a blossoming of hope for a lifetime of loneliness.

I'd done my best to shut it off because it was too painful to experience each day.

I attempted to harden myself to stone, but as far as I'd gotten was a hollowed-out numbness. For years, I'd drifted through memories that never quite felt real.

As if I'd conjured them as a way to survive the hand I'd been dealt.

And there those dreams were—sparked to life.

Lit by a touch. A glance. A whisper.

I was a fool, but there was no way to stop the way my blood pounded. The way my nerves sizzled every time he was near.

Blowing out a frustrated sigh, I turned from the window and paced the room, hugging my arms across my chest as if it could guard me from it. Block it the way I'd learned to do because if I kept up this way, I was going to get crushed, and this time I doubted I'd be able to make my way back to that dented form of comfort.

Comfort.

I almost wanted to laugh because I'd never been so *uncomfortable* in my life.

I ached.

My body shaky and trembling.

Caught in a wash of old desires.

Alive, something vital I could physically take into my grasp.

I was just terrified of what reaching for it might mean.

Turning, I paced the opposite direction of the room. Through the dimness, my reflection again caught in the panes of glass that overlooked the frozen earth.

My skin was flushed. My eyes wild. My stomach in knots.

Logan had been gone for a couple hours, and the reaction he'd left me with hadn't waned.

Want.

I wanted to be touched.

The truth of it rushed like slippery warmth down my spine and poured like flames into my belly. A hot, boiling river that throbbed between my thighs.

God, I was a fool.

A fool, but there was no stopping the visions that flashed. Every memory I'd suppressed rushed to the surface, rising so high I thought it would suck me under.

Where I'd drown in the dark, toiling waters of temptation.

He'd ruin me there.

I knew he would because there was no changing the finish-line. I might one day be rid of Jarek, but I would never be free of my name.

Blowing out a sigh, I forced myself to move to the massive bed where I crawled under the heavy, plush covers, and sank down into the over-the-top luxury that hugged me like a dream.

I pressed my eyes closed tight.

I prayed for sleep to consume me.

For the memories to fade.

No such luck.

Malachite eyes.

They flashed like strobes behind my lids.

Brighter than life.

Darker than destruction.

There was no escaping the vision of him, either.

His body pressed against mine. His hand on my breast. His kiss on my mouth. The words he'd whispered.

If only for one night…

Another roll of desire whisked beneath my skin, a drip of honey on my tongue.

Sweat gathered across my flesh.

I flopped around onto my stomach, pressed my face to the pillow, and groaned.

With all of me, I tried to will it away.

It throbbed and grew.

Flinging myself onto my back, I tossed off the covers in search of cool.

It only caressed and murmured.

Crap.

I pressed my eyes tight in a vain attempt at blocking the onslaught.

Wave upon wave of the need I'd repressed.

Seven years.

Seven years.

No longer dormant.

Lying there, I swore I could actually feel the soft press of Logan's thumb turning my nipple to a hardened, sensitive peak. Could hear the growl in his throat. Could sense the need radiating from his pores.

It was a battle I couldn't win, and my fingertips were running over the same breast where he'd touched me, where he'd stoked that fire that I was afraid could not be doused.

Alive.

Every nerve.

Every cell.

I panted a soft breath as I gave over to the sensation. To the fantasy of a man I had no business fantasizing about.

Visions of those green eyes spread through my mind like tendrils that sank in and took root.

Beautiful depths and darkened hollows.

In that moment, I was no longer Jarek Urso's wife, nor was I Andres Costa's oldest daughter.

I was his.

His.

A phantom touch slipped down my belly, and I bit down on my lip to suppress a moan when I let my fingertips follow the perception. My knees angled and my feet slid up to plant on the bed.

Everything shook when the silky material of my gown slipped high, and my fingers crept beneath my lacy underwear.

My fingers dipped lower. Brushed over my engorged clit.

Chills raced.

A forewarning of bliss.

I stopped fighting the need and let my mind drift away to a better time.

To the places where we'd hide away, where he'd love me in the shadows and beneath the night.

Where the heavens watched down over us like a vigilant embrace.

Our time secreted away.

Forbidden but right.

I whimpered as my thumb circled that throbbing bud, and I held back the tiniest cry as I pressed my fingers into my body.

The air crackled. The room shook. The oxygen grew thin.

I froze when I was hit with the awareness.

With the distinct sensation that I was not alone.

Heart battering at my ribs, my eyes snapped open to find the dark form standing just inside the bedroom door.

My throat closed off as his presence swept over me like a drug.

I prayed I was hallucinating, that I'd been foolish enough to invite the memories into the here and now and they were messing with my head. But I was sure there was no way I could make up the reverberation that rumbled the ground when he clicked the door shut behind him and edged my way.

Each step measured.

Purposed.

His foreboding shape was silhouetted in the middle of the room, the man smoke, as if he were both solid and didn't exist.

I pressed my knees together like I could pretend he hadn't just walked in on me touching myself to the echo of who we once had been.

It didn't matter—I could feel the searing of his gaze.

Fire burned me alive.

I wanted to die.

To turn to vapor.

To exist in his hands.

Everything was silent except for the ravaging of my heart, the blood that whooshed through my veins, and the rasps that panted from my mouth.

Finally, I managed to push the jagged words from my lips. "What are you doing in here?"

Even though I couldn't make out his face, I could feel the piercing of his eyes as he stared at me where I writhed on the bed.

"I needed to see you."

I shivered at the possession in his statement.

"Why?"

"To know that you're whole. That you're here. That you're mine."

My throat nearly closed off. "Logan."

It was a plea that had no clue what it was begging for.

"Do you want me to leave?" There was a tremor in his question.

I couldn't make the right answer form on my tongue. Not when my mouth had gone dry, and I could barely squeeze oxygen into my lungs.

The atmosphere thickened.

Dense.

Every cell combustible.

Hinging on tonight.

When I didn't answer, he stepped forward into the milky rays of moonlight that slanted in through the window.

I gasped when I saw him. There was a deep cut that had split open his bottom lip and blood and grime saturated his shirt.

"You're hurt." I shot upright as horror filled my spirit. I couldn't do this. Couldn't bring him danger.

He gave a harsh shake of his head. "It doesn't matter."

I tried to swallow, to stop the spread of flames, the crackle in the air. "How can you say that?"

"Because I'm here...standing in front of you right now."

My feet were still planted on the mattress, my knees bent, the slip bunched up around my thighs. My hand was fisted in the material over my stomach.

Logan came to stand at the end of the bed. He winced once as he moved, guarding his side as he gritted through the movement.

He stared at me through the lapping shadows as if I might be a figment, too. As if he'd drifted through that same vacancy for the last seven years, the two of us floating through the nothingness that kept us separated.

My pulse raced my veins, so hard I was sure it was palpable. He reached out and trailed a single fingertip from the outside of my knee to my ankle.

Searing.

Scorching.

Inciting.

He angled his head, his profile so strong it verged on obscene, though his voice dropped to a grumble of agony. "Were you thinking about him?"

A wise woman would lie, one who held an ounce of self-preservation, but my head shook. "You know that I wasn't."

Logan leaned forward, and his breath whispered across the inside of my thigh. My heart bucked involuntarily in a bid to reach the one who'd left me adrift.

"Who then?" It was the roughest scrape of a demand, green eyes slicing through me with the sharp edge of a knife.

Everything shivered, and I tried to swallow, to regain some semblance of control when I'd slipped off the edge.

I squeezed my eyes shut to shield myself from the power of this man.

"Say it." It cut through the air. Logan towered over me. His frame was rigid, hard, and held in some kind of restraint.

Hesitation rippled from my body and ricocheted against the walls, then the confession came tumbling out. "You."

A growl rumbled from his chest. "Good girl."

The mattress dipped when he set a knee onto the mattress, and I was pretty sure the entire Earth tipped from its axis when he began to slowly crawl up the bed.

Gravity shifted.

Setting me on a path for a new destination.

My North Star.

I was a fool.

A fool, a fool, a fool.

But I trembled in anticipation as he crawled up close to me, pressing me back to lie flat as he came.

He planted his hands on either side of my head, and my legs dropped open to make him room as he hovered there.

As if he both would consume me and couldn't bear to touch me at the same time.

He just pinned me with the brunt force of his presence.

Heat blazed in the empty space that roiled between us. Never had my body ached in such a way, desperation taking over.

I was a second from begging him to drop down and press his heavy weight against me.

Allow me to feel.

Make me remember.

"This is a bad idea, Logan." A moment's clarity somehow busted through the haze.

Gone in a flash when those green eyes glinted in the rays of moonlight. "You were the best idea I've ever had."

His words were hardened, strained with regrets and wounds.

Time was held in that moment.

The seconds gone stagnant.

My orbit this man.

It was torture.

It was bliss.

"And we still ruined each other in the end." The words fell like an appeal from my lips.

Logan almost smiled, his gorgeous face staring down at me, wicked and right. "Who said it was the end?"

It sounded of a warning.

"Logan." My heart crashed against my ribs like it could claw its way to meet with him. His raged back.

His eyes dragged down my body until his hot gaze landed on my underwear. Then he swept back up to my face.

"Finish." The command was a whisper of seduction, so low and lethal I would have thought I'd made it up except for the fact I couldn't look away from the movement of his lips. The way his teeth grazed the plump flesh when he formed the word, the way his tongue just peeked out at the end.

"Logan, please." My chest jerked, and my fingers twitched.

I wanted to beg him to do it. To put me out of my misery.

But I was chained.

Tied.

Shackled to his potency.

"Let me see you finish, Aster. Go back there…where you were…with me. Finish."

My tongue swept over my dried lips. "Logan. Please."

"Who do you belong to?"

My thighs trembled and my pussy throbbed.

So heavy and needy I had to stop myself from lifting my hips to rub against his pants.

You.

You.

It shouted from my soul.

Even though it didn't come from my mouth, I knew he saw its truth in my eyes.

"Who, Aster? Who do you belong to? I need you to say it."

I saw the flash of grief. What was at stake.

The confession rolled out without permission. "You."

Because this time, it wasn't about some stupid bet or deal.

It wasn't temporary.

It was yesterday.

It was today.

It was forever.

It was the bare, violent truth.

Dark satisfaction flashed through his expression, the angle of his fierce jaw rigid, his eyes glinting with dominance.

"Finish, Little Star."

My spirit thrashed.

Panged and danced and sang.

My stupid, tattered heart grew wings.

Emotion gathered so fast I was afraid it would seep out through my eyes.

He leaned down, but only his breath touched my ear. "Are you wet, Aster? Are you wet for me? Is it me you've been thinking about all these years?"

Tremors rocked me head to toe. "Don't make me admit that."

"You don't have to." His voice was close to cruel. Temptation. A tool. "I already smell you. I already feel you. I already know you."

"Let me hate you." I begged it.

"No," he grunted back.

I gulped, and a fresh rash of chills lifted across my skin when he leaned down and ran his breath along the length of my jaw, his lips fluttering the barest fraction away.

A tease.

Torment.

"Close your eyes, Aster. Go back to where you were. Just for a minute. Let me watch you."

I was afraid if I went there, I'd take him with me, or that maybe I'd never make it back.

But the lust was too thick.

His presence too full.

And my hand was splaying across my stomach, slipping beneath the lace, my fingers sweeping across my clit, rubbing as I closed my eyes and tried to pretend we were in a faraway place. That we'd made it out. That our promises had been kept.

That he hadn't done what he'd done, and it hadn't cost what it had.

I knew he went there with me. That he saw the same thing. Our hearts and minds and hopes alike, even though they'd been scattered like toxic waste between us.

I knew it from the harsh pants that roughed from his throat.

I knew it with the hard thunder of his heart.

I knew it with the whisper of his tongue.

"Beautiful. So fucking beautiful. I'm going to lose my mind."

A whimper wheezed from my lungs as I kept stroking myself. As I felt his aura surround.

Every inch of him hard.

Those eyes flashed before he eased back a fraction so he could get a better view.

I got caught in the flames. Lost to an inferno of greed that whipped through the air.

It melted my inhibitions and scorched my sanity.

The air sizzled.

Crackled.

Seethed.

He took me by the knees and spread me farther.

A groan rumbled in his chest and climbed his throat as I rubbed myself faster.

Building.

Building.

His hands curled in tighter before he let go with his right hand and reached down and pulled the crotch of my panties to the side.

His tongue licked his plush, decadent lips. "Look at your cunt. I wanted to forget how perfect you are. Not for one day, Aster, not for one day."

"Please." My hips bucked.

"What do you need?"

"I need to feel you."

Without hesitation, he drove two big fingers inside me.

That was all it took to tear me apart.

An orgasm gathered from the inner parts of me, where I'd hidden him away, where I'd kept him like a dirty secret when he'd been the most beautiful part of my life.

And I split.

Rapture took hold. A perfect eruption that burst in my body.

And I was heading in that one singular direction where I knew I shouldn't go.

Soaring.

Shooting.

My North Star.

"Fuck. I feel it, Aster baby, I feel what I do to you."

I gasped and shook and arched from the bed.

"Tell me again." It was the rough scrape of a demand from his mouth.

I didn't need him to clarify. "You. You."

It has always been you.

A truth that would get him killed if anyone knew.

My eyes pinched closed as I was rushed with regret, overcome by the reality of my stupidity.

My recklessness.

Agony fisted with the bliss.

His hand was suddenly on my chin, squeezing tight, the word harsh and hard when he said, "Don't."

My eyes peeled open, and I blinked at the raw beauty that hovered over me. "I never should have come here."

He cracked an arrogant grin. "Oh, you're gonna come, Aster. Again and again."

A blush rushed to my cheeks, sweet, sweet heat, that swoony, goofy boy I'd once known cracking through the surface of who he'd become.

"Logan." My voice turned tender, and I reached up and traced the cut on his mouth. Anger burned from my soul—because I knew.

I knew.

Logan took me by the wrist and drew those fingers into his mouth. He hummed as he sucked.

That barely sated fire leapt.

He kissed the tips when he let them go.

"I'll kill him, Aster. I'll kill them all."

Without saying anything else, he crawled off the end of the bed and walked out, shutting the door behind him. He left me lying there, floating adrift, terrified the current would always lead me back to him.

Chapter Thirteen

Aster

Little girl dreams…

R EALLY, I SHOULD HAVE KNOWN BETTER THAN TO HAVE believed in them. Known better than to wish upon the stars when I could never rise high enough to touch them.

I'd been shaped and molded since the days I'd sat in front of my dressing mirror as a tiny child. Before she'd passed, my mother would brush my long, brown locks and tell me the order of my life as if it might be a fairytale rather than a horror story.

It hadn't taken me all that long to see it for what it was. To recognize something in our lives was amiss.

Perhaps that was why I'd buried myself in the pages of books. In fantasies and faraway lands where this one never existed, and I could be anyone I wanted to be.

I guessed I shouldn't have been surprised it was there that I first saw you. When I'd been nudged out of a love story that had my pulse racing and my heart in my throat when I'd felt the shimmery disturbance come whispering down the hall.

I'd peered over the couch to find you staring back.

As if you'd felt it, too.

The tall, beautiful boy with black hair and the greenest eyes.

Intrigue.

It sparked and glimmered and called across the space.

Christof nudged you to move along.

I should have let you go and forgotten that I'd ever seen you.

It was forbidden for me to speak to anyone who walked these halls. I really wasn't supposed to be here at all, but my papa knew my love for books, and my excursions to the library were our little secret.

I waited until you were alone because I somehow needed you to become my secret, too.

I peered around the door at you sitting so unsure at the desk with your backpack at your feet, awkward and confident at the same time.

You didn't belong there. I knew it in an instant. The same way I knew that I didn't, either.

"Why are you hiding?" you'd muttered, staring ahead without glancing my way.

I held your first words like one of those dreams.

"Because I have to."

Then you turned and studied me like I was a mystery. "Are you going to get into trouble?"

My head frantically shook. "No. I'm going to get you into trouble."

You'd smirked. "Do I look like the kind of guy who minds? I think I can handle it."

I should have warned you that you would.

But I'd wanted a different story. A better story. And I knew I wanted it with you.

My North Star, my North Star.

It was the first day I believed in you.

Chapter Fourteen

Aster

THE BAREST RAYS OF MORNING LIGHT ILLUMINATED THE bedroom window as I pressed my ear to the door and listened. My heart was a riot in my chest.

Memories of last night lingered like a bad, blissful dream. That sticky, heavy sense that everything was off, that my world no longer rotated the same way, the truth that nothing was going to be the same.

Before dawn, I'd woken drenched in sweat from a nightmare.

In fear.

In those old chains that wanted to drag me back to conformity.

As the day had broken on the snow-covered Earth, I'd come to the quick realization I couldn't remain that girl. Not anymore. The hardest part was I didn't want to hurt anyone on the road to finding my destination.

I didn't want to hurt Logan, and I didn't want him to hurt me in return.

I'd only secured that as an impossible feat by letting him touch me last night, proven by the last words he'd spoken before he'd strode out the door.

Now, I had no clue what to do. Every step I took seemed to lead me to a greater mistake.

Closer and closer to the man I should be running the opposite direction from.

Silence echoed back from within the apartment, and I carefully turned the knob, cracked the door, and peered out into the hall.

You know, all courageous like.

All was clear.

Inhaling a steeling breath, I tiptoed out, my footsteps quieted as I edged down the hall toward the main room.

I paused at the end of it. There was no sound other than the whooshing of the flames in the fireplace.

But I didn't need him making a sound to know he was there.

Awareness hummed in the air. A dense aura that held a life-beat. A pulse of possession.

I peeked around the corner.

Every cell in my body was drawn that way when I found him sitting at the small, round table in the nook on the right side of the kitchen.

He sat facing out, thumbing through his phone with a cup of coffee sitting in front of him.

The man was angled back in the chair, and he had an ankle hooked over the opposite knee, wearing another one of those fitted suits that made him look like a king.

My stomach stirred in hunger. My eyes raced to take in every inch.

His black hair was effortlessly styled, his scruff trimmed, that decadent scent coming off him in waves. Though this morning there was a small scab on his bottom lip and newfound violence in his posture.

It looked so damn good on him that it sent a tremor sailing down my spine and shivering out to my fingertips.

I wanted to touch.

He looked up when he felt me there.

"Are you hiding from me, Little Star?"

His words struck through the years. A reminder of who we'd always had to be.

I fumbled out from around the corner.

His eyes skimmed down my body as if he were remembering the view last night. It didn't seem to matter that I'd pulled on a pair of pink sweats and a loose fitted, long-sleeved white tee and the thickest, fluffiest socks I'd ever worn.

He still looked at me like I stood there completely bare.

His gaze molten, the smirk that kissed his gorgeous mouth illicit.

"I think it's time you stopped hiding, Aster." He took a casual sip of his coffee.

I eased farther out, hoping my knees didn't knock. "Is it?"

He gazed at me from over the top of his coffee cup. Severity flashed. "Are you afraid of me?"

"Am I afraid of how much it hurts to be around you? Am I afraid that this is a terrible idea? Am I afraid of what's to come? Yes. But am I afraid of you, Logan?" My head barely shook. "No."

Maybe I should be. Maybe I should be terrified of it all. But it was with him where I'd always felt safest.

I looked anywhere but at him as he stared me down as if he were searing holes into the places where my secrets lie.

"Coffee?" Warily, I glanced at him.

Not even that was safe.

Because my belly flipped and my stupid heart fluttered.

The man was dangerous to my sanity.

"Of course. Let me get—"

"I have it." I made a beeline for the pot that was on the opposite side of the island, and I busied myself with pouring it into a mug that was already set out.

Two of them.

My stupid fluttering heart went and panged.

He'd set one out for me and one for Gretchen.

This hard, dangerous man with this soft side that made me melt.

I peeked back at him, wondering if he were the same. If the years hadn't hardened him.

If there was any part of the boy left who I'd fallen in love with.

I poured in some creamer and fiddled with the spoon, procrastinating as I hovered by the island.

He pointed at the chair across from him. "Sit."

I hesitated for one second more before I shuffled across the floor and sank onto the chair. Taking a sip of my coffee, I studied the man I was still trying to recognize.

"Do you sleep in that suit?" Okay, so it wasn't of the utmost importance, but I had to ask, and it seemed like a pretty good distraction from what was bristling between us.

A bolt of amusement rocked from his mouth, then he sat farther back so he could track my movements, that smirk turning wicked. "Wouldn't you like to know."

Did he have to toy with me?

Clearly, he did.

Relished it.

The way his eyes traced the redness that flushed up my chest to my cheeks when that thought sent my mind tumbling right back where I kept trying to keep it from going.

"But I guess that would only be fair considering I know exactly what you wear when you're sleeping." A taunt and a tease.

"I think I should pass."

He sat forward. "I think you *are* afraid."

My teeth clamped down on my bottom lip, and I wrapped my hands around the steaming mug. "Yes."

He pressed forward. "I would never hurt you."

I looked up and met his stare head on. "You already have."

Lines of regret cut into his hard, chiseled face. So gorgeous. Too much.

"Aster…"

I tried to look down. To look away. But he still surrounded me. If I listened closely enough, I could hear the fierce rhythm of his heart, the way it'd once woven with mine, the man a ghost that would forever beat in my blood.

And here he was, alive and real and ruining me all over again.

He inhaled a heavy breath. "I think we need to discuss some things."

Unease squeezed my ribs. I peeked at him. "We probably should."

He took a sip of his coffee, every edge of him intense. The question left him like the topple of stones. "You want to leave Jarek? Permanently?"

Fidgeting, I inhaled a shaky breath. "You know I do."

"And what will your father think about this?"

There was bitterness there. My father the root of it all.

The evil.

The injustice.

Although Logan had fed right into it.

I gulped around the knot laced tightly in my throat. "Like I told you, I spoke with my father yesterday, and he's giving me thirty days."

I watched the way every muscle in his body flexed.

"And what do you plan to do with thirty days, Aster?" The question was icy.

"My father thinks I need time. Time to myself. Time away. *A vacation.*" I left out the defective promise I had made. "He agreed, and he promised Jarek would stand down and leave both of us alone until then. He thinks it will teach Jarek a lesson for being so reckless."

Hatred burned across Logan's flesh, and I could almost feel the throbbing of the cut on his mouth. My chin lifted farther, my attention on his wound. "But it won't, will it?"

Logan sat back, malice in his posture. "I doubt there's any lesson that prick could learn."

"I'm not going back to him, Logan. I just…" I paused, looked away, tried to gather my thoughts before they came rushing out on a flood of words. "I need the time to find a way to prove to my father that Jarek has become disloyal. That he is wrong for the family. Wrong for me."

A blister of rage bludgeoned the air.

And here we already were, right at the heart of it.

"Yet, you agreed to marry him." It wasn't a question. It was an accusation.

As if I had a choice.

I bit back the words I wanted to spit.

Tremors ripped beneath the floor, and I had to plant my hands on the table to steady myself. To keep my chair from vibrating with the shame. The hurt. The pain. The anger.

All of it swept into a snarl of regret.

I couldn't look at him when I admitted, "Yes."

"So why leave, Aster? It seems to me it turned out exactly how you planned it." Disgust twisted his voice.

Clearly, he was having second thoughts about what had happened last night. About the promise he'd made when he'd walked out the door.

There were too many things I couldn't say. Too many things that couldn't be taken back. Too many things that would destroy him now.

A fist slammed down on the table, and I sucked in a shocked breath. I squeezed my eyes shut as I fought the impact of his fury.

"Why?" It cracked through the room.

Guttural.

Grieved.

A single tear streaked free.

It wasn't of fear.

It wasn't of weakness.

It wasn't of anything but the loss that neither of us could take back.

Every secret I could never give him.

I lifted my face because there was no use hiding from him. Not when he was there, potent and powerful. Angel and beast.

"Because there is only so much one person can take."

I wondered if he had any idea I'd taken it for him.

Based on his expression, I believed, no. He'd just been a reckless fool.

Greed had infested and taken control. Clouded who I'd once believed him to be.

Something moved through his being.

Something barely held.

Something barely contained.

"Has he hurt you?" Logan's question was almost emotionless.

Almost.

Except his green eyes turned a deadly shade of black.

A flashfire of visions banged through my mind.

Pain. Blood. Shattered on the floor at his feet.

Begging.

Begging.

The knot in my throat throbbed, blocking off the truth that ached to become his.

I wanted to look away. To drop my gaze.

But I just sat there, shackled by this rage, by this lure, by the past that had caught up to Logan and me so quickly, neither of us knew how to stand in it.

The eye of the storm.

Right here.

Right now.

And there I sat, staring at the face of my glorious, dark defender.

My beautiful, sweet boy who'd loved me like loving someone was simple.

His chair suddenly scraped across the floor and, one second later, he had me torn from mine with my back pinned against the wall, so fast I could barely process the action.

Then everything stilled.

The only movement was my pulse that screamed through my veins and the savagery that radiated from his body.

Air wheezed from his lungs, and every muscle in his powerful body vibrated as he pressed closer.

He reached out to take me by the jaw so he could tip my face up to meet the vengeance in his. His hand was shaking. Shaking and shaking.

"Tell me, Aster."

"It doesn't matter."

"It doesn't matter?" It was venom.

"I'm already leaving him."

Logan had one hand pressed to the wall to hold himself up. With the other, he scratched his fingertips along the edge of my face, as if he had the urge to claw his way in. His head tipped to the side and the violent words cut into the dense air. "I told you last night. I will kill him, Little Star. I will."

Agony lanced through my being and ripped me wide open.

"You don't want that kind of war."

"It might be the only thing we can find."

"The only thing I want is my freedom."

"Yet you gave yourself to me."

He'd always been my heart's direction. I wasn't sure there was anywhere else I could have gone.

Still, I needed to play it off like the only reason I was here was because of the bet. Like this twisted fate hadn't drawn us together.

Magnets.

Gravity.

"Only because it bought me time. Because he'll honor the bet," I forced out.

The curl of Logan's smile with his split lip was full of ire. "I think we both know that's not true."

I tried to hold back the welling of emotion. The moisture that burned. But I couldn't. Couldn't.

Not when for the first time in seven years, I felt it.

Hope.

Beauty beneath the betrayal.

And I found it in the man staring back at me.

Logan's trembling thumb traced my cheek. "He can't have you back."

The words cracked.

Everything sizzled.

The man was a short-circuit to my mind.

"Thirty days," I forced out. It was a reminder of our deal. It was all I had to give. I might get free of Jarek, but I'd never be free of my name.

That old possession burned through those stony, green eyes.

"Thirty days." When he whispered it, I knew it was a lie.

"I'll find the proof you need, Aster. I'll find it and set you free."

My smile was sad.

Because that's where he was wrong. Because my heart, it would always, always belong to a man I couldn't keep.

"Aster." His breath turned needy.

Hypnotic.

He dropped his forehead to mine.

My lips parted, held by those eyes that looked at me with distrust and devotion.

I was sure it was the exact same way I looked at him.

I jolted when I heard the rustling come padding into the room.

Gretchen came up short when she saw me pinned beneath Logan. I squirmed to get free. Logan didn't budge.

"Oh."

She was wearing a bunch of pink curlers in her hair and a matching muumuu and slippers. She'd even taken the time to smear thick, pink lipstick onto her lips.

"Well, it seems I'm interrupting."

Logan exhaled a heavy breath before he tore himself away.

I didn't mean to whimper.

Impossible.

Not when I felt the vacancy like a blade cutting through flesh.

He pasted on a grin and straightened his suit jacket. "You're not interrupting anything, Gretchen. It's fine. Coffee is ready."

I ran my hands up the sleeves of my shirt like it could chase away the chills that rushed in to take the place of his heated presence.

Gretchen's gaze narrowed. "Sure looked like I was interrupting something to me."

She shuffled into the kitchen. "But hey, what does an old, senile lady know? Not worth much but cleaning up the messes made during the things I was *not* interrupting."

She went to wiping up the counter that didn't need to be cleaned.

Logan grunted. "We were only having a discussion."

"Huh, that's weird, I wasn't aware you could get pregnant from having a discussion."

I nearly choked.

Disbelief filled Logan's laugh. "Clearly, you are either senile or blind, Gretchen. Tell me you haven't forgotten the act, or are you actually having trouble seeing that we are fully clothed?"

He gestured at himself.

"Don't think I couldn't tell you were about to take that thing out of your pants." She waved at his tented crotch. That time there was no stopping it.

A bolt of laughter busted free of my mouth.

It wasn't funny.

Not funny at all.

But I couldn't help it.

Logan rolled his eyes in affectionate annoyance. "Only in your dreams, Gretchen."

She huffed. "Hardly, young man."

He chuckled, then he straightened out his jacket. "I need to go."

Then he moved back toward me, like it was his right, his duty.

His fingers found my chin. "Are you okay?"

The words clotted in my throat because I wasn't sure I ever really would be.

Still, I nodded.

"Okay. I'll see you later."

Then he strode out without looking back, leaving me there gaping behind his retreating form. I didn't realize I was staring at where he'd disappeared until Gretchen's voice broke through the disorder. "Lord a'mercy, he really was about to take it out."

I whirled back around, tried to tamp all the emotions back into place. "He was joking."

Laughing, she poured herself a cup of coffee. "Um, that boy *is joking* about every minute of his life. Right up until the minute you walked into it."

At that, she eyed me suspiciously.

I wrung my fingers. "I guess I bring out the worst in him."

"The worst?" She hummed like it was absurd. "The harsh? The truth? The real? All that pain he's got buried so deep he has the whole world charmed into thinking it doesn't exist? Sure. You might bring all those things out in him. But what I'm sure it's not is the *worst*."

Chapter Fifteen

Logan

THE DOOR RATTLED SHUT BEHIND ME, AND I STORMED TO the elevator like there was no air left in the building, and I had two minutes to escape.

Sounded about right.

Because if I stayed in that apartment with her for one second longer, my lungs were going to fail.

Thirty fucking days.

Bullshit.

I knew as I rode the elevator down, with the way everything twitched and my spirit screamed, there would be no letting her go.

Whatever it took.

I'd been a fool last time, but I'd been a kid.

A fucking kid who didn't have a clue.

She might have betrayed me, but that didn't mean I couldn't read what was written underneath, that I couldn't see all the secrets that writhed in the depths of those fire-agate eyes.

A fire she kept raging like a fortress.

The girl shrouded in old pain.

I wanted to reach into her soul and rip them out.

It only made it ten-thousand-times worse after what I'd walked in on last night.

After what I'd given in to.

I wasn't sure what the hell else I would have been expected to do, though.

After what had gone down outside Absolution, I'd been compelled to check.

It'd made me sick to think that bastard might have weaseled his way back to her and manipulated her into leaving.

Or worse.

The piece of shit was lurking in this city, that was for sure. Scum hiding in the shadows. Waiting for the opportune time to steal back what had never been his to take.

My car rumbled to life when I pushed the ignition button. The leather was cold, and the air was icy. I blasted the heater to compensate, and I pulled out of the garage and headed toward the mountains.

I took to the two-lane road that the last time I traveled it, I'd had no idea what was waiting for me. How my life would change in a split.

No warning.

And I was determined to find out why.

How the fuck Jarek Urso had ended up there.

Thirty minutes later, I was pressing the button at the security gate outside Haille Manchief's home. It beeped and the voice came through. "Ah, Mr. Lawson."

"Oz," I said back.

He chuckled. "He's not going to be surprised you wish to speak to him."

"I doubted that he would be."

"Come in."

The gate buzzed and swung open, and I wound up the curved drive and came to a stop in front of the massive stairs. I hopped out and started up them. Oz opened the door before I made it to the landing.

"How is it problems follow you wherever you go?"

I roughed out a laugh, tossed a smirk in his direction. "I'm just appealing that way. Everything is drawn to me. You have seen me, right?"

He scoffed a teasing sound. "More like a magnet for trouble. I haven't had to draw my gun in years, and the last two times you came around, things got interesting."

"What can I say? I'm an interesting kind of guy."

Oz laughed. "You're something, all right."

With a grin, I shook his hand as he welcomed me inside. The man was all affable smiles while his attention still seemed to travel everywhere, constantly on guard.

The guy took his job seriously, that was for sure. But it was no secret men like Haille Manchief traveled in dangerous circles. They had shady friends and even darker enemies. No doubt about it considering mine had been sitting across from me just a couple nights ago.

"Right this way." Oz gestured down the hall, and he led me into a sweeping library where another mammoth fireplace roared.

The man himself was behind a desk at the far end of the room. He stood with an amused grin. "Logan Lawson. Welcome. I have been expecting you."

I strode that way, reaching over to shake the hand he extended. "Haille. Thank you for having me."

I sank onto the seat opposite him and crossed an ankle over my knee, trying not to fidget, to act like this visit didn't feel like it was the most important I'd ever made.

A chuckle rumbled from him as he sank into his plush chair. "You know my door is always open to you. You've made me a lot of money, so in my book, that means we're very good friends."

The arch of his brow was pleased and intrigued.

"It's my job, and I do it well."

"So humble."

I shrugged. "I see no reason to be."

He laughed a rumbling sound. "No, not when you're as good as you."

Rocking back in his chair, he studied me with a sly grin on his face. "So, what is it I can do for you?"

Apprehension gushed through my veins. I sucked it down and attempted to play it cool.

"I need to know how Jarek Urso ended up sitting at your table two nights ago." That shit came off hard, anyway.

Amusement played through his expression, his red cheeks puffing out. "I figured you would."

He was far too pleased in my discomfort.

The twisted, sadistic fuck enjoying someone else's pain.

I could see it written all over him. He was excited by the idea of Jarek and I actually fighting to the death.

May the best man win.

I intended on it.

I toyed with the seam of my pants, canting a glance at him when I asked, "I suppose it was clear enough he and I have a history?"

"Blatantly."

"And did you know this when you invited him into your home?" There was a challenge behind it. Haille might hold the money, but that didn't give him the go to toy with me.

"No, I got word from a connection that there was a very hungry player...someone in trouble who needed to flip his circumstances quickly."

I let that seep in.

I'd already known it—had smelled the desperation oozing from Jarek. He was backed into a corner, and I just needed to figure out exactly what that slime had done.

Give it to Aster.

Set her free.

He cocked his head. "I couldn't think of a better opponent than you."

"You knew I'd win." It wasn't a question.

He almost shrugged. "You usually do."

And he got his cut.

It was our agreement.

If I won, his cut was double what anyone else paid to play at his tables. It didn't hurt me since I almost always came out on top, and he brought the highest rollers. The ones who had the most to lose.

Thing was, most of them didn't care all that much if they did.

But a man like Jarek…one who had a knife to his throat? They're the ones that got in over their heads.

Do or die.

Last chance.

Last ditch.

And I was going to be sure to see to it that it was his.

"What happened after I left?" I asked.

He cracked a smug grin. "He said he was going to ruin me."

Clearly, Haille loved the idea of someone trying.

"Where is he now?"

He gestured toward the door on the far side of the room. "Oz has eyes on him. He left yesterday morning but returned in the afternoon with three men. It appears he may be…disgruntled."

Disgruntled was likely a gross understatement.

"Judging by your face, I would say you already knew he had returned?" Haille rocked back in his chair, eyeing me like he was gauging my next move. Like he might want to wager on it.

"I had a feeling." I itched, fighting the fury that simmered deep.

He laughed.

"Do you know where he's staying?" I pressed.

"Downtown at the Shillhire."

The Shillhire was an upscale hotel about a mile down from my place.

Fucker.

He wanted to play dirty?

Fine.

I was ready to get filthy.

"That's all I needed to know. Thank you for your help, Haille. I appreciate it."

"Always."

Then his smile shifted as I started to stand. "I think the more intriguing question is what happened with you and the girl after you left?"

I rebuttoned my coat. "I took her home. Where she belongs."

Then I turned and walked out.

Chapter Sixteen

Aster

I LIE ON MY STOMACH ON THE BED WITH A BLANK JOURNAL I'D taken from that drawer that I'd slammed closed when I'd first found them.

Part of me wondered if Logan had stashed them there for a day like this, the way they sat there unused, waiting for a brand-new story to fill their pages.

For me to rip them out and fold them into a newfound hope.

Litter them between us so he could find his way back to me.

My hand flowed across the page, my concentration set on trying to decipher a feeling. To capture a memory. To walk into a better future.

Logan promised he would find proof, but in the end, this was my fight.

Something I had to do.

A reckoning between my father, Jarek, and I.

I'd drawn Logan into the middle of it, right into the most dangerous place he could be.

I didn't know if it made me selfish or weak.

Greedy in my own, demoralized way.

Or maybe my heart wouldn't allow me to believe anything else than he'd found me and I'd found him.

A crash course.

A collision.

One destination.

The words poured over the page as they sought to find new meaning.

New purpose.

As a new strength built from the reservoir where it had always lived.

I jolted when my phone rang out from the nightstand, my heart thrashing with a bid of nerves before I smiled when I saw the name on the screen. Reaching over, I tugged it free.

"Hi."

"Oh my god, Aster Rose, what the hell is going on?"

My sister Taylor hissed it beneath her breath from the other end of the line. It might as well be the opposite side of the Earth with how out of touch I felt.

I pressed the phone tighter to my ear, glancing around as if I were doing something salacious, when that honor usually landed on Taylor. There was no shucking the instinct to check my back, to make sure no one was listening, that I could actually have a private conversation with my baby sister without someone running back to report to my father or Jarek.

The sound of a vacuum running from the other side of the apartment echoed through the door, the same as it'd basically been for the last three hours.

Gretchen was a machine.

"Give me all the details," she pressed. "I'm literally dying."

"I hope that's not true," I said, my voice wry.

Taylor harrumphed at me. "So literal."

"That is what it means."

"You're so no fun." I could almost see her pouting through the phone. It made me smile.

"What are you talking about? I'm a blast."

"You'd better be *having* a blast." There was the innuendo I was waiting for.

"Uh, let's see, my worthless, piece-of-crap husband bet me in a poker game, and I was won by my ex..."

The one who still owned my heart, the one who I'd first believed hated my guts and was only in it to torture me, but now...

"The really freaking hot one?" It was a high-pitched whisper.

"That's the one." I saw no point in denying it.

She squealed. "Oh my god. I cannot believe you're with him. This is the best thing I've ever heard."

"Is it?" I deadpanned.

Because it was exhilarating and terrifying and possibly the most reckless thing I'd ever done.

"Well, it is if you've gotten up in the good dick because we know Jarek isn't giving you any of that."

"Taylor," I hissed as I sat up. "What is wrong with you?"

"Well, have you? You can't keep the good stuff from me."

A heavy sigh filtered out. "Believe me, none of this is good."

Except there was a glimmer of something good that hadn't been there before.

A chance.

A way out of a life I hated leading. One my sister was most likely heading toward. Nineteen and ripe for my father to find her a *good* husband that would make him a *good* ally.

Half the time I thought he chose to be blind, and he allowed himself to believe he was doing us a favor, saving us from heartache when the only thing he was doing was bartering those hearts.

"Oh, I bet it's good." She giggled.

"You don't even know him."

"Um, you realize you whisper his name at night in your sleep, don't you? Last summer when we were on vacation in the Mediterranean on that boat? I had to listen to it all night long. *Oh, Logan. Ohhh, Logan.*" She moaned his name.

Embarrassment flushed my skin. "I do not."

"Um, yes, you so do. Thank God your actual husband wasn't there because it probably would have incited a murder spree."

Worry filled my chest.

I could only imagine the type of anger that would incite in Jarek if he'd heard me calling for the one I belonged to in my dreams.

He'd likely not mention it, though. Admitting it would be a blow to his ego.

"I mean, who could blame you because Jarek," Taylor continued. "Ew and gross and I literally just threw up in my mouth. And besides, I found your keepsake box when I was fourteen. There were letters and pictures in there. I know exactly what he looks like and Oh. My. God. He is delicious." She rambled all of it so fast I almost missed the middle.

"Wait, you did what?"

My letters.

I'd hidden them in the floorboards in my bedroom at my father's house, as if I'd buried my heart and my hope and my dreams with them.

My love and our secrets.

Because it had no space to flourish with the confines of the walls that had been built around me.

I could feel everything about her soften.

"It's okay, Aster. I know you love him."

My spirit trembled. "I don't."

I couldn't admit it to her. Tried to deny it to myself.

Because I couldn't allow it to sink in and take hold.

Those words were dangerous.

They desolated and destroyed.

"Then why are you there, with him? One call to Papa, and you'd be on the first flight home."

I hesitated, warred, wasn't sure if I should be honest with my sister or just lay it straight. I scooted over so I could sit on the edge of the bed. "I can't stay with Jarek anymore, Taylor."

Silence fluttered through the line.

Worry from her side.

Agony on mine.

She lowered her voice even farther. "You mean, like you're getting an apartment across town, or you intend to *leave him*, leave him?"

Women in our family didn't do that. When it came down to it, we didn't make any real choices of our own. The fact my father had granted me this time was a miracle.

Defiance lined the words, old pain and disgust and hatred bleeding into the claim. "It means he won't ever touch me again."

"This isn't going to end pretty, Aster." Her voice went timid, and the mischief drained away when she pressed, "That's why I've been trying to find a good time to call you in private. I heard Jarek freaking out in Papa's office yesterday morning, talking about a pact that had been broken. Papa said something I couldn't hear, then Jarek stormed out. I overheard Camden telling Lorenzo that he took off…I think he went back to wherever you are."

Bile lifted in my throat.

Jarek would do anything to protect his unstable position. He was also a narcissist who would never admit he was the one who'd gotten himself there.

He'd pin the blame on me.

Pin the blame on Logan.

I pushed to standing. Every part of me was at war as I paced. Finally, I let out the plea, "I think I need your help, Taylor."

"Anything."

I hesitated, then whispered, "Are you still seeing Dominic?"

"If you mean getting some of those yummy O's on the sly? Then why yes, yes I am."

It was always, always on the sly because our father would kill her if he knew.

Dominic *literally*, and not in the way she used it.

"Before he does anything, he needs to get confirmation that Jarek is out of the city and there is no one guarding the house. If it's clear, then I need him to get something for me out of Jarek's office. There's a large safe at the back of the closet."

Taylor actually squealed. "Like…a covert, ninja mission in the middle of the night?"

She clearly hadn't fully grasped the severity of what our family did.

"Kind of like that."

"How do we get into the safe?"

"I think I might be able to figure out the combination."

Jarek was almost superstitious in the way he used numbers. I prayed it would come out in my favor. I gave her the options of what I thought it might be.

"He'll have to shut off the alarms to get inside," I continued, "and no one can know he went in there."

"What do you need?" Her voice dropped with the scandal, so on board.

It was wrong dragging her into this, but I didn't have a lot of options. If I was going to do this, I needed evidence, and I was pretty sure I knew where to find it.

"There's a fake bottom in the safe, and there's a leather case in there that has a lock."

I'd seen Jarek bring it in and out of his office many times over the years.

"What's in it?" she whispered.

I hesitated, then said, "I don't know exactly, but I'm certain it's my freedom."

Taylor sobered, her voice sincere, "We'll get it. I promise. It's not right, what Papa does. The way these men treat us. Like we're objects to be sold. I won't do it, and I'll stand beside you when you walk away. It's time we make a stand. Fuck 'em."

She was right.

Fuck them.

My phone buzzed, and I pulled it away to look at the text that had come in.

> Logan: Be ready in an hour. Wear the red dress I bought you.

I didn't know how he'd gotten my number, or when he'd added his contact information to my phone, but a tremor of anticipation rolled down my spine.

A need that glowed like a beacon from the abyss where I'd tumbled.

I should tell him, *no*. That all of this was a bad idea, and I would leave and do it on my own.

But rather than climbing out of this pit, rather than letting him go and setting him free, I was only dragging him deeper.

I stood in front of the full-length mirror looking at my reflection. I'd donned the red dress. It had the deepest, plunging neckline I'd ever seen, halfway down my midriff where it nearly touched my belly button. It exposed the inside curve of my breasts that were covered by the thin, silky fabric.

A slit ran up the side to the top of my thigh, ending only a second before it became obscene.

I'd paired it with the black strappy stilettos that had arrived with the rest. My hair was down, done in fat, full curls that bounced around my shoulders and landed in the middle of my back.

I felt beautiful.

Sexy.

At least I shivered at the thought that Logan might see me that way. That maybe it was what he'd envisioned when he'd picked it out.

I blew out a sigh as I glanced at the huge round clock that hung on the far wall of the room.

Two minutes.

They passed like stagnant honey, sweet and deploring, like as the seconds dragged, they begged me to come to my senses.

But as I waited for Logan to arrive back home to whisk me away to wherever we were going, I felt the faint vestiges of who I'd once been skim through my consciousness.

For a moment, I remembered what it'd felt like to hope. When I'd woken each morning with a blaze of excitement in my belly. When I'd loved to be touched by a man who'd touched me in a way no one else but he could do. Before I'd realized the true meaning of what losing something you loved meant.

I drew in a deep breath to contain it, to hold it back before it busted free.

Then that control was slipping when I heard the two slight knocks on the door before it drifted open.

Logan stood there.

The master of my universe.

The one who made me question it all.

He wore the same suit he'd been wearing this morning when he'd left.

He didn't need to change.

He was the most striking man I'd ever seen.

Then.

Now.

Forever.

Black hair effortlessly mussed, his jaw shadowed by his short, trimmed beard. Everything about him was potent.

Provocative.

A temptation that felt impossible to resist.

A lure that called and pleaded and tempted from the doorway.

He leaned against the doorjamb and let his eyes rake over me as if that was what they were made to do, as if looking at me supplied him with the necessities he needed to breathe.

His nostrils flared. "I imagined you in that dress, and my imagination didn't come close to doing you justice."

Redness flushed, and I spread my palm down the bodice as if it could smooth out my emotions that were racing wild. "Do you like it?"

Foolish girl, inviting the pain.

I didn't know how to stop.

Logan straightened to his full height and took one step forward. Overpowering. Mind bending. Every single thing I'd once thought right.

"Do I like it?" His voice was close to a growl. "I'd forgotten what beauty really was until I found you standing in that basement."

Heat flashed.

"Logan…we need to be careful."

"Fuck being careful."

He prowled my way. Every step he took sent a reverberation across the floor.

His hand landed on my hip, and he angled down to get in my face. "And for the record, there is nothing *careful* about the way you look."

I stared up at him. "What if I asked you to be?"

Careful with me?

Careful with us?

Careful with this whole situation?

His mouth tipped into a wicked smirk. "You asked your father to stay with me, Aster. You didn't just throw caution into the wind, you kicked it out the fucking door. And if he gave you thirty days?"

He spread his hand out over my cheek. "Then we're going to use it."

My insides trembled.

A landslide.

A toppling of stones.

Then he stepped back and stretched out his hand. "Do you trust me?"

Reservations clashed with the faith I'd once had in him. Faith that he would always stand up for me. That above the money, the greed, the desires, he would always hold me highest.

I wanted to believe he would hold me there again.

I accepted his hand without giving him an answer.

A thunderbolt raced my flesh.

Every touch.

Every time.

"Where are we going?" I asked.

"Dinner." He said it simply, but there was an undercurrent in his tone that lifted chills on the nape of my neck.

Nerves that warned I was slipping into the unknown. When Logan told me he had a plan, it meant there would be action.

He wasn't going to stand idle.

He was all in.

I worried that might be the greatest risk of all.

I whispered, "Okay."

"Good girl." He leaned in and pressed his lips to my forehead when he said it.

A soft sigh.

A humming of need.

The faintest smirk when he stepped back.

"We should go before we're late."

He led me out into the main room, helped me into my coat, and pressed his nose to the back of my ear. Inhaling, he murmured, "I think you have me hypnotized, Aster Rose."

Without question, that was reversed because I walked along beside him to the elevator, leaned into his side as we rode it down, and relished in the feel of his arm linked around my waist like a leash.

Tension bound and built and blinded in the confined space.

A silence that screamed a million things.

Need and regret and far from pure intentions.

When the doors swept open, he guided me to his car and helped me into the passenger seat. He leaned in and reached over to buckle me.

It stole my breath all over again.

He slowly eased back, and his gaze tangled with mine as he went.

If he kept this up, I was going to succumb right then.

He rounded the front and slipped into the driver's side, and he pulled out of the lot and onto the road. It took all of three minutes for him to be pulling into the valet in front of an upscale steakhouse attached to a hotel.

He was out and to my side in a flash. Opening the door, he extended his hand. I took it, felt the flames that licked up my arm and set fire to my insides.

I sucked in a stealing breath.

I was in trouble. So much trouble.

Leaning closer as he led me inside, his voice was a rough scrape at my ear, "Trust me, Aster."

I wanted to. God, I wanted to.

But how did we make it past all that had been tainted? Past the ugliness?

Would there be anything left beyond it?

"Lawson," he told the hostess.

"Right this way."

She led us to a small table in the middle of the restaurant. It was covered in a black, draping tablecloth and adorned with a large white bouquet of fresh flowers with candles in the middle.

"Aster." He said my name like a secret as he pulled out my chair, and his hands caressed my bare shoulders as he slipped off my coat.

"Thank you." It barely made it to a whisper when he helped tuck me into the table.

He situated himself across from me. Severity played in his green, hypnotic gaze.

The dangerous kind. The kind that promised I wasn't going to make it out of this unscathed.

He was up to something.

"Wine?" he asked.

"Please."

A bottle or three.

When the server showed and introduced himself, Logan ordered us a bottle of Malbec.

"You look nervous."

"And you look suspicious." I said it with a bough of anxious curiosity.

That smirk danced around his delicious mouth. "Is that so? Suspicious? Surely not me?"

It would be a whole lot easier if he didn't affect me this way.

"Nothing but a common criminal." I didn't know if it was a tease or a plea.

A deep roll of laughter punted from his mouth before his eyes narrowed. "I should hope you could recognize one."

It was almost a taunt.

Almost pain.

All except for the truth of it.

"I suppose I should be able to."

I sat back when the server presented our wine, and I managed a weak, "Thank you," when he poured me a glass.

"I'll be right back to take your orders."

I took a shaky sip, and I let the dark, fruity flavor coat my tongue and throat as I swallowed and contemplated what to say.

"How deep does it go?" I finally hedged.

Logan was angled back in his chair, so casual the way he was, though there was no missing the ferocity that rolled through his body. "What are you implying, Aster? I'm as straightlaced as they come."

A grin cracked his gorgeous face.

All faked easiness.

I leaned forward. "If you want me to trust you, you need to be honest with me."

He blew out a sigh, chewed at the inside of his cheek, tapped his fingertips on the table as he studied me. "The gambling and some not so on the up and up investments. When we left LA, we left the rest behind."

Then he shocked me when he leaned over the table. His palms were planted on the top, and his tone shifted from mild to lethal. "But I have a feeling that is about to change."

Unease stirred in my chest. "The last thing I want is to cause you trouble, Logan."

He roughed out a disbelieving sound, though there was something soft about it. "Oh, sweet Aster, you have been a lifetime of trouble, haven't you?"

Hurt underlined his words, and I fidgeted, took another sip of my wine, and fiddled with a piece of my hair when the server returned.

We ordered our dinners, and when the server walked away, Logan lifted his glass in my direction. "To a new beginning."

My teeth clamped down on my bottom lip. "And which new beginning is that?"

His smile was too dry. Too casual, though it radiated with an intonation of hate and power. "The one where Jarek Urso never touches you again."

"I can drink to that." The words wobbled free on an outpouring of my own determination.

Logan sat forward. There was something furious in his demeanor. "Drink to it? I can promise it."

My throat thickened. "Logan…"

"I promise you," he said again, words a growl. "He needs to be reminded of his place. Trust me, Aster."

It was underlined with implication.

Worry burned through my being as I watched Logan from across the table as the server placed our salads in front of us.

"Is there anything else I can get for you while we await your entrees?"

"We're fine." Logan didn't look away from me as he dismissed him.

Under his stare, I felt the ground tremble.

The whirring of the air.

I took a bite of my salad to distract myself from the magnitude of it.

As if the entire world was focused on me. My skin flushed.

That was right when a tacky, clammy awareness crawled over my skin. I looked up, over Logan's shoulder, toward the bar on the far side of the restaurant, compelled by the tension that bound the air.

Black eyes stared back at me.

Jarek.

I gulped as fear crashed through my being, and my body heaved forward in shock.

Revulsion.

Loathing.

A sickness I couldn't escape.

The fact that no matter where I went, Jarek would be right there.

My attention snapped back to Logan who looked as if he were about to go on a rampage. As if he were barely keeping it together.

"Did you know he was here?" It was a rattle of terror.

He gave me a tight nod. Did he have any idea the danger he was putting us in?

"So you brought me here?" The accusation was fueled by fear.

"I told you to trust me, Aster."

My face pinched. "How can I trust you when you're parading me around like bait?"

"Don't fool yourself into thinking you're not already the end-goal, Aster. You are the cup and the crown and every jewel that has ever existed."

The blood thudded heavily in my veins.

"If you want me to help you, you have to trust me."

Every line in his face was hard.

Every cell bated.

A tremble of foreboding in the air.

From across the room, I could feel Jarek tremoring, too.

It felt like I was being ripped between the two of them.

Logan pushed back his chair a fraction and patted his leg. "Come, sit on my lap, let me feed you."

I gripped the edges of the table. "Are you insane? What do you think you're doing?"

"I'm simply reminding him of what he can no longer have."

"You are trying to start a war."

"What I'm doing is trying to set you free. And if a war is what it takes, then so be it." The words were clipped, his expression fierce, the inevitability set deep in the wells of those green eyes. The browns and golds swirled from their depths.

Entrancing.

Enticing.

He patted his leg again. "Come here, Aster. My rules, remember?"

I'd almost forgotten the power I'd left him with.

I guzzled the entire glass of wine in search of courage, and I pushed from the chair.

Jarek never averted his caustic stare, and I could feel the lances of anger blistering through the room. It clashed with the stupid need that suddenly welled up in me as Logan sat there watching me like I was his.

Possession seared through his gaze as I slowly moved his way, but it was different than the way Jarek viewed me.

Logan looked at me like I was the treasure.

The reason.

The destination.

My breaths were jagged as I eased around to his side, and I settled down onto his lap, angled across him so both my legs draped off to one side.

Warmth spread fast, goosebumps a flash that sizzled along my arms and skated to my nape. Logan curled an arm around my waist, and I curled both of mine around his neck.

I was inundated with his aura.

Clove and cinnamon and corruption.

I knew that's what he was set on.

He would see to it that even if I walked away, I would never be the same.

"Good girl," he whispered in my ear.

Rage flooded the atmosphere.

My heart raced. Pounded and shook.

It was such a risky game.

Shaming Jarek.

Logan showing off his prize.

Needling a knife that just might end up in our backs.

A rustle moved through the restaurant, and eyes shifted our way, peeking, and others outright staring.

"They're all looking at you," Logan murmured in my ear. "The most gorgeous woman in the room. In the city. In my universe."

Shivers tumbled down my spine.

"What they're thinking is this is horribly inappropriate." My response was barely a gasp.

The roughest chuckle scraped up his thick throat, coating me like a covetous caress, and his voice dropped even lower. "No, Aster, every man here wishes he were me right now. Including your husband."

That was a growl, and he shifted me so that my legs were under the table, hidden by the cloth, though my body was still angled, my side pressed to his chest.

His chest that was big and warm and vibrated with bristling strength.

He reached into the basket and tore off a piece of bread, and he angled in so his lips were right next to mine when he balled it and slipped it into my mouth.

It was warm and soft, and I felt it like the soft lick of his tongue.

Then he slipped his hand under the table, his palm on my bare thigh where he slid his hand up under the slit, riding the bare flesh.

I gasped and curled deeper into his hold.

Logan ran his thumb along the top line of my inner thigh.

Back and forth.

Back and forth.

Shivers raced and greed rushed and desire pounded through my bloodstream.

It twisted me into a needy bow. Every cell rode a razor-sharp edge. Anticipation a slow burn that singed my skin.

"Logan." The plea was out before I could stop it. "This is a bad idea."

He leaned in to whisper in my ear, "No, Aster, men are the most reckless when they're angry. When they're pushed up against a wall. I'm merely showing Jarek where he stands. Most of all, he needs to know you no longer belong to him."

I was the reckless one considering I could almost forget Jarek was even there.

I was losing all semblance of control.

Conceding to every brush of this man's wicked, wicked hands.

Falling deeper into his darkness where I'd never find my way out.

And still, I let him continue, let him knead his fingers into my thigh, let him press his mouth to my neck as I peered over his shoulder at Jarek who was incensed.

A short fuse that was at its end.

His bastard jaw clenched, and his hand wrapped so tightly around a tumbler I was sure it would bust.

Logan shifted to send a smirk Jarek's way.

Gauntlets and games.

This was so messed up. So wrong. And still, I remained on his lap like I was chained.

So foolish because I could run, but I couldn't get away.

Jarek tossed back the rest of his whiskey before he shoved to his feet and tossed some cash onto the bar. His stare remained locked on us for one brutal beat before he stormed out and into the lobby of the hotel.

"This is wrong," I whimpered, still holding onto Logan. I was worried if I let go, I would float away.

"Is it? Or is this exactly what you wanted?"

"I don't know what I'm doing, Logan."

"Men are motivated by three things, Aster. Money, women, and power. He'll have none of them left when I'm finished with him, and you, Little Star, will be mine."

My arms curled tighter, though the words climbed free of where I wanted to keep them locked. "Thirty days, Logan."

It was all we had.

We were nothing but a time stamp.

One that might cost him everything.

Anger vibrated along the hard flesh beneath his suit.

My mangled, tattered heart flapped in the wind.

He let his arms fall to his sides. "You can get off my lap now."

Shame burned through my body when I finally pulled away. Cheeks hot, I fumbled back to my side with a slick of humiliation burning me through.

I just couldn't pinpoint what brought on the shame.

The server showed up with our meals just then, and I edged back, embarrassment tinging my cheeks.

What had I let him do?

Degrade me?

Is that what this was really about?

A show of hand?

A vendetta he would do anything to avenge?

Did he hate me that much?

I stared at my food.

"Eat, Little Star," Logan said, no emotion in his voice other than the inflexibility of stone.

My head dipped, and I at least found the self-preservation to make one request. "Please, don't call me that."

Leaning forward over the table, he brushed the hair back from my face and set his palm on my cheek. "I wish I could stop."

Chapter Seventeen

Logan

I HANDED OFF MY CREDIT CARD TO THE SERVER TO PAY THE ridiculously expensive bill for the dinner Aster had barely eaten. The girl hadn't cast me a glance while she'd picked at her food, while I'd sat there like my guts were getting chewed up and Aster was the one who was going to spit them out.

Thirty days.

Thirty fucking days.

And she had every intention of leaving me.

I wasn't sure what had come over me. I didn't plan this dinner with the intention of pulling the stunt that I had.

I'd just wanted the show.

To send a clear message to Jarek that we were not deterred. That we were not afraid.

Then I'd pushed it to a place I shouldn't have let it go.

The possession that had wound through my being. The urge to hold her that had twitched through my fingers.

I blamed it on that dress.

The all-consuming need I'd had to touch her in front of him. To prove to him that he could never have her again.

Or maybe I'd just been trying to prove it to her.

Maybe prove it to myself.

No doubt, I was playing with fire. I knew it. Risking everything. But I'd known it the moment I'd made that wager.

All in.

So yeah, it'd pissed me off when Aster had reminded me that she wasn't.

Standing, I moved to her side. "Let's go."

Aster stood, and I helped her into her coat. I did my damned best not to lean in and inhale the flesh behind her ear. Not to press my nose into the curls that I was dying to take in my fist.

This girl was going to wreck me.

She'd done it before so I wasn't quite sure why I'd convinced myself she wouldn't do it again.

Still, I allowed myself to pull her hair free of the coat, being the *gentleman* that I was, my nose just brushing into the fall.

Hyacinth and magnolia leaves.

I pressed my hand to the sweet spot low on her back and guided her out into the frigid cold night where I stood there with her like she was mine as the valet pulled my car into the rounded drive.

He hopped out, and I tipped him then helped Aster into the passenger seat. The car was low, and she had to slide in, and the slit of her dress opened to reveal the delicious expanse of her upper thigh.

My mouth watered.

She looked up at me like she'd physically felt the smack of lust.

I touched her exposed knee. "Aren't you the perfect tease."

I couldn't hold it back.

The anger that bottled in my stomach and spread out to infect my chest where it became a lash from my tongue.

She was leaving me.

She was leaving me.

Pain made a thousand stab wounds in her expression.

In the barest flash of time, she stared at me with a torment so deep I wondered if she could meet me at mine.

My spirit screamed.

Then she ripped her attention away, taking the oxygen from the air when she did.

The atmosphere darkened, clouded and dimmed, and her breaths turned short and uneven.

Fuck.

I was such a prick, but I felt myself unraveling.

Losing control.

Aster Rose was driving me to the point of insanity.

The whole goddamn problem was I didn't know how to stop myself when it came to her.

She didn't budge when I shut the door, didn't move when I rounded the front of my car to the door that remained open. I went to slide in, only I got snagged on a rush of scalding hatred that blistered through the frozen air.

I looked up to catch the figure staring out from behind a drape in a window four stories up.

I cracked him the biggest grin.

Jarek looked like he wanted to bust through the glass to get to me.

Fucker.

I hoped he did.

I slipped onto the heated seat, shifted into gear, and gunned the accelerator. My Maserati skidded out of the drive and onto the main road.

Aster stared out the passenger window, so still it would be easy to miss the way every cell in her body oozed with hurt.

I didn't.

I could feel it.

Sense it.

The way I'd always been able to do.

The knot in her throat. The way her shoulders hitched. The emotion that wept even though she tried to hold it like a secret.

Regret tightened my chest.

I was pretty sure my faulty plan had been too much for her.

I was thinking right then it'd been too much for me, too.

It took all of a minute to get back to my building. I punched the button to the gate and whipped my car into my reserved parking spot. I hadn't even gotten it into park when Aster tossed open the door and fumbled out, slamming the door shut behind her.

I killed the engine and jumped out.

She was a fiery flame that flew across the garage.

"Aster." I shouted it over the top of the car.

She kept going.

"Aster. Come on. Talk to me."

She spun around, her bag clutched to her chest like it were a shield. "Come on? Come on? Screw you, Logan Lawson." Agony convulsed in her throat. "You want to hurt me? Is that what all of this is about? Payback? Fine, you hurt me. You embarrassed me. You made me feel like a whore. The way all of *them* have always done. You win."

She whirled back around and ran for the elevator. Her heels clacked frantically against the concrete.

"Aster." I scrambled to catch up to her. "Would you wait?"

"No. Just leave me alone. I'll get my things and go. I'll figure this out on my own because I can't do this. I can't do this and clearly, you can't, either."

It was a rambled cry that hitched helplessly from her throat as she whirled back around.

It was right before her heel slipped on a patch of ice that had formed three feet in front of the elevator door.

My heart seized. "Aster!"

She yelped and tried to right herself, but she only sent herself hurtling the other direction, her arms flailing as her feet fully slipped out from underneath her.

She toppled backward.

I was running but I was too far away. I wasn't even close to getting there before she landed hard on her left side. The air knocked from her lungs on a huge oomph when she slammed against the concrete.

When I made it to her, I dropped to my knees. "Aster, oh my god, Aster."

I was over her, searching her face that was as pale as the concrete beneath her.

Every cell in her body was locked.

Her breaths and her blood and her tongue.

"Aster. Are you hurt? Tell me where you're hurt, baby."

Then a jagged, pained cry erupted from her chest. Her mouth split open, and her eyes pressed tight as tears streamed down her face.

"Aster. Fuck, are you okay?"

Another cry burst from her. She curled onto her side like she could protect herself from it all.

"Aster."

"Leave me alone. Please." She wept it, folding in on herself where she lay on the frozen, freezing concrete.

Carefully, I scooped her up. "I can't."

"Please," she gasped and choked. "Leave me alone."

I held her against my chest. "I already told you I take good care of what's mine."

"I'm not yours. I'm not. I'm not." Each word was obliterated pain. Her mouth was open with a sob when she buried her face in my shirt. "I'm not."

I tightened my hold, lifted her higher, and pressed my lips to her temple. "You're wrong. You have always been."

She burrowed her face deeper into my jacket.

Aster wept.

My heart cracked in half.

"I've got you," I promised as I carried her to the elevator door. I managed to punch in the code, and thank fuck, it was already right there, the doors opening with a gush of warmth.

Aster shivered when we stepped inside, and I held her as the elevator whisked us to the top floor. My arms tightened around her as I carried her to the door and let us into my apartment.

It was dark inside except for the fire and the single light over the sink where Gretchen was doing dishes. She spun around. Her eyes widened and worry filled her face. "Oh, dear lord. What happened now? You are some kinda mess, aren't you, sweet girl?"

She started our direction.

"I've got her." I sent Gretchen a look that made her stop in her tracks. I continued across the floor.

Gretchen hesitated. I knew firsthand it went completely against her nature not to help.

"You let me know if you need me. I'll be right here."

"I know, Gretchen. I've got this. Just go to bed," I instructed as I carried Aster the rest of the way into my room.

She continued to tremble and shake, her head burrowed so deep in my jacket I got the reckless sense that she might be able to build a home there.

That right there was where I was going to get destroyed.

I was the sucker in this fool's game.

But it didn't matter. It didn't fucking matter. Nothing did except for her.

It was dim within my room, a chill in the air, winter pressing at the windows. I set Aster on the edge of my bed. "Sit right there."

I moved for the fireplace and flicked the switch. Flames leapt to life. I wound out of my jacket as I made my way back to the woman watching me through the flames.

Wary.

Hurt.

But her breaks? They were bone deep. Wounds I couldn't see but knew without question were there.

Her shoulders slumped but that fierce bravery she'd always worn fired from her eyes.

I believed her wholeheartedly.

She would find a way to do this on her own. Walk away if it meant her freedom. If it meant mine.

If it meant we wouldn't have to hurt each other all over again.

Staring at her, I knew it was already far too late for that.

The first time I'd seen her, I'd known I'd never set my eyes on anything more beautiful.

The girl was better than any flower or rainbow or piece of priceless art hanging in a museum.

Aster Rose was my poetry.

Kneeling in front of her, I tried to keep my shit together. "Tell me if you're hurt."

Aster's voice was thin. "I think you already know the answer to that."

My ribs clamped around my heart because this pain had little to do with her fall. Still, I searched her, eyes racing as I hunted for any injury. Her coat was wet, and her dress was ripped on the left side. I lifted the tattered fabric a fraction. Aster flinched, and I cringed when I saw the trickle of blood above her knee.

Pushing to standing, I stretched out my hand. "Come here."

Aster wavered, her attention dipping toward the ground, her profile so goddamn gorgeous I had to stop myself from leaning down so I could run my lips along the length of her defined jaw.

"Please, let me help you."

Agate eyes met mine. A burn of hope and a glimmer of dejection. She set her hand in mine.

Energy lapped, a warm buzz that eclipsed reason and sight.

I pulled her to standing. She winced again.

"I'm sorry that I upset you."

"It's not even that." Her head barely shook.

It was everything.

Everything that felt insurmountable.

Old wounds and a new trauma that somehow felt unavoidable.

And still, something I would hold.

I took her chin between my fingers and tipped up her face.

So she would see.

So she would understand.

"I regret every instance I have ever hurt you."

At my confession, her expression deepened.

I let my fingertips flutter down the length of her neck as I rounded her, and I grasped her coat so I could slip it down her trembling arms. I tossed it to my bed before I reached out and gathered the bulk of her hair and tucked it over her shoulder.

I inhaled.

Hyacinth and magnolia leaves.

A new beginning.

A fresh start.

Aster shivered.

Everything slowed, and I swore I was tripping into a dream.

When my fingers found the top of the zipper, Aster's spirit stormed the room.

"Why does it have to hurt so bad?" It was a breath of agony.

I angled down so my mouth was at her ear. "It hurts because we didn't end up where we were supposed to. Because there has been a piece missing in each of us. An ache that can never be filled."

Old wounds throbbed and moaned in the bare space that separated us.

My mouth found the cap of her shoulder and ran the length to the back of her neck. A kiss that really didn't exist.

Chills flashed across her skin as I slowly dragged her zipper down. It sparked like shocks in the night.

The fabric slipped off her shoulders, and I let it go so the dress pooled at her feet.

Aster was frozen, like she was terrified to move, though her entire body was vibrating so violently I was afraid with one wrong brush, she would burst into flames.

She stood facing away in her underwear, the fire illuminating her curves, her perfect shape, the piece of my heart that had gone missing. An outline that had crusted over with that unrelenting pain.

"I want to hate you," I murmured at the nape of her neck. "I want to hate you, Aster. But I remember it…it didn't matter what you said, I read what was in your eyes."

Coming around to her front, I let my eyes roam her body.

Her small, round breasts.

Her flat, quivering belly.

The contour of her full hips.

The fear I'd felt when she'd fallen slammed me anew when I saw the huge welt on her upper thigh, red and abraded with the promise of turning black and blue. Blood oozed from the abrasion in the middle of it, and a tiny rivulet had run down and was smeared near the top of her knee on the outer edge.

"I'm sorry I caused you to fall. This was my fault."

My fault for being a dick.

"Wait right there."

I moved into the bathroom, grabbed a bandage, and dampened a cloth under hot water. I snagged a T-shirt from the closet before I strode back into the sorrow-addled room that fizzed with something else.

The girl the gravity in the space.

An orbit.

An obligation.

A destination never meant to be.

I climbed down onto my knees in front of her.

An illogical offering.

I pressed the cloth to the wounded flesh.

She whimpered, then swallowed and held onto my shoulders as I wrapped my left hand around the back of her leg so I could properly clean it.

"I'm sorry." The grunt of an apology scraped my throat like dull razors.

I glanced up to catch Aster staring down at me.

In confusion.

In regret.

In that old, magical awe that had once made me believe that I could be the type of man who could deserve the kind of girl I'd once believed her to be.

It was the same look that'd had me on my knees then, too.

"What are you sorry for, Logan?" I didn't know if it was rejection or a plea.

Hesitation held the words before they left me like a twisted admission. "That nothing turned out the way it was supposed to. That I didn't fight harder. I promise that won't happen this time."

The last was gravel. The coarse scraping of determination that infiltrated body and mind.

Her eyes dropped closed for the barest moment, and she sucked for cleansing air before she opened them again. Torment rained down, a misery that flooded a drought-stricken desert.

"Would you have changed it if you could have? If you knew it then, would you have stopped it? If you could go back and know everything, would you still have done it?"

Vulnerability trembled through the words.

The woman laying herself bare and asking me to do the same.

A rock got lodged in my throat.

Buying time, I focused on cleaning the dried blood from her abrasion and the line down to her knee. Meticulously, I applied the bandage, my movements careful.

Then I stood, keeping my eyes on her face as I eased my T-shirt over her head and dragged it over her beautiful body.

Then I fisted the hem in my hand and jerked her my direction.

Aster gasped as she jolted forward, and her fingers drove into my dress shirt like she might never let go.

My mouth found that sweet spot at her jaw, right where it curved up to meet the lobe of her ear. "I would go back and change everything. Losing you. Losing Nathan. I was blind. A fool."

Grief clamped around my heart.

"Was it worth it?" she pressed, like she didn't know how to believe me.

"You already know it wasn't. I would have given up everything. I would have burned the world down to get to you."

"Why didn't you?" The question trembled from her mouth.

My hand found her face, my thumb tracing the angle of her cheek. "I did. I burned it all to the fucking ground, Aster, and you already know what happened when I got there. You were no longer mine."

Those eyes found me in the whispering night. "I thought you said I've always belonged to you?"

It was a challenge.

My hands slipped low, gliding down her sides and molding to her hips. I yanked her so close every inch of her was pressed against me. "Is that what I should have done? Taken what was mine?"

One hand curled into her hip while the other slipped up her spine until I had a fistful of her hair. I angled her head to the side, and my lips grazed the length of her jaw.

Inhaling her sweet, exotic scent.

Potent.

Powerful in a way I shouldn't let it be.

But she had always been my weakness.

She looked up at me with torment in those agate eyes. She barely shook her head. "I was already ash."

There was a confession in it.

It didn't matter.

I already would have been too late.

Rage tightened my chest, and I struggled to draw her close, to erase all distance.

Every mistake.

Every wound that had been inflicted.

"Tell me what happened while I was gone."

When the only objective I'd had was finding my way back to her, when I'd found her, and in one moment, my world had been decimated.

"I hate you, Logan Lawson, and I don't want to ever see you again."

Her fingers sank beyond my shirt, burrowing into soul and flesh. "I can't."

My arms wrapped around her. Tight. Like I could forever lock her to me.

Aster whimpered, pressed her face to my shirt, and exhaled. A ragged breath of surrender.

Moonlight streamed into the bedroom.

My little, fallen star.

One that'd burned out.

Slipped through my fingers.

I swayed her, danced with the girl that used to be mine.

Thirty days.

We stayed like that, in the silence for the longest time, before I whispered, "Was it real?"

She pressed her lips to my sternum, like it was her spirit's way to my thrashing heart. "It was the only real thing I've ever known."

So, I held her the way I used to do. Under the cover of night. In a place where no one knew.

She let me as our souls shifted.

As we sank deeper.

Against my chest and under my skin.

As a promise changed.

Time passed, minutes, hours, I didn't know. But Aster sagged, and she let me hold her weight.

Her burden.

She drifted, like for the first time in years, her trouble had gone light.

So, I took it.

I swept her from her feet and into my arms. She sighed as she curled hers around my neck, and I carried her out into the sleeping house and into her room where I laid her in the center of her bed.

Agate eyes fluttered open. A murmuring of affection. A haunting of old hope. It was dimmed by the years of cruelty that had separated us.

She stretched out her hand. "Stay."

I hesitated, then I kicked off my shoes and undressed down to my briefs and undershirt.

She lay on her side, her head on her pillow, and she stared at me through the shadows.

She sighed when I climbed in and laid beside her.

Reaching out, I brushed the hair from her face. I leaned in and pressed my lips to her forehead, her temple, her chin.

Then I spread my hand across the side of her face as I pressed my wandering lips over the soft curve of her mouth. They barely moved.

It was the softest caress.

A promise.

An oath.

The truth.

"You're mine."

Chapter Eighteen

Logan

Los Angeles, Eighteen Years Old

"WHY ARE YOU HIDING?"

Logan felt the smile pull to the edge of his mouth when he murmured it to the wind. His eyes remained upturned toward the starless, Los Angeles sky, though every fiber of his being was tuned into the presence that hovered behind the wall of an outbuilding.

He sat on a bench in the rambling gardens, lost in a maze of foliage and trails that stretched out far beyond the pool behind the mansion.

In the place that had become his sanctuary. In the place where they met.

"I have to," she whispered back, the way she always did.

He fought it, but his smile grew. "Are you going to get into trouble?"

Aster Rose giggled, a slight flush rushing her soft cheeks as she stole a glance around to make sure they were in the clear.

With the way the sight of her punched him in the gut, you'd think it was the first time he'd ever seen her. How his stomach flipped and his chest tightened.

"No. I'm going to get you into trouble." She gave him the same warning she gave him every time. Like she was waiting for the day he would turn her away.

Logan smirked. "Do I look like the kind of guy who cares? Besides, I'm pretty sure it would be worth it."

Her cheeks were red as she nibbled at her bottom lip, this shy, bold girl who had twisted up his mind and become his best friend.

She felt like more than that, though.

Like she might be everything.

Like there was a reason he'd been consigned to this place of depravity and greed.

Where nothing cost too much and where one misstep could cost you everything.

Where he worked his magic into corruption.

For the last six months, Logan had spent his evenings and well into the night forging false documents, making dirty money look clean, and investing in places where it would grow.

He'd made himself valuable. He knew it. Andres Costa had said it himself. The man had filled Logan's pockets with portions of what he'd earned. Promised him more if he kept performing the way he had.

Logan had tried to keep his nose to the paper and his fingers out of the wickedness, just like Trent had warned him to do, but that was hard when you'd become an integral piece of it.

But he knew what he was doing with Aster Rose was more dangerous than any of that.

He'd never even touched her, but his mind was all over her.

He pushed to standing when she gave him the go, and he took a furtive glance around, too, before he slipped behind the building hidden by high shrubs and bushes, out of sight of the guards and cameras.

Not that there was a whole lot of attention on this area.

Andres Costa's concern was keeping threats out. Well, that and his daughters in.

Aster slipped down onto a patch of grass. Logan sat beside her, and he fought the urge to reach out and touch her sweet face when he did, tried to ignore the way his heart raced and his blood pounded.

Sure, he'd been with girls before, but this one…this one had him losing sleep and acting rash.

Dangerous ideas and reckless acts.

He wasn't even supposed to look at her, and there they were, sneaking out to meet each other whenever they got a chance.

When he'd found the piece of paper folded into a star where it'd been tucked under the logbook he often worked in, his heart had sped, the way it did every time she left him a secret message.

Nine, was all that it said.

Prime time for his *dinner break*.

"How are you?" Aster murmured, peeking at him like maybe she felt the way he did, too.

"Good, now that you're here."

Her lips pursed. "That bad?"

Logan shrugged. "It's fine."

"You hate what my father is making you do." It wasn't a question, just soft understanding.

Really, it was his father wielding the command. Two men who were radically different and basically the same.

At least Aster's father seemed to maintain some semblance of humanity.

He blew out a sigh and returned his gaze to the hazy glow of the city sky.

"I think the problem is that it doesn't bother me as much as it should." He'd grown to like the feeling he got when he saw the numbers double. The pride he felt when Aster's father rewarded him. The fact he'd lost any twinges of guilt over what he was doing somewhere along the way. "It's better than the alternative, that's for sure."

Aster frowned. "The alternative?"

Logan plucked at a blade of grass, warred with the confliction he felt over Trent and Jud's role in the family. "Way better than what my brothers do," he admitted.

He glanced down to catch the sorrow carved in her expression.

Her wide, knowing eyes and the pained sweep of her plush, full lips.
"They don't have another choice?"

"Sometimes we're bred from the beginning to become something we don't want to be." He mused it quietly toward the heavens.

He knew neither of his brothers had ever wanted to follow in their father's shoes.

He'd formed them into the shape and then shackled them to his truth.

Trent and Jud might try to shield him from every sordid detail, but he listened close enough that he knew—he saw—he recognized the upper hand.

The callous manipulation.

He startled when she set her hand over his, and he suddenly found it difficult to breathe.

"And sometimes we have to stand up and fight for what we know is right in spite of it."

"And how do we do that?"

Logan's gaze swept her way when he asked it, his eyes tracing the pretty curve of her jaw as she turned her focus upward. He got the sense neither of them knew how to admit their innermost fears while looking at the other.

"We take the chance when it's presented to us. Refuse the heartache when it's demanded of us. And we make sure to never surrender to the greed. It's what drives these men and what has ruined them."

His spirit fluttered at her words, and Logan shifted his hand so their fingers were threaded together.

Energy crackled.

This feeling that rushed up his arm and settled in his chest.

"Are you going to refuse it, Aster?"

He'd heard the rumors. The rumblings that Aster had newly been pledged to Jarek Urso, to be married on her nineteenth birthday which was less than a year away.

Jarek's father was one of Andres' closest allies.

The marriage would make them family.

"I'm going to figure a way out of it, Logan. One way or another,

I will find a way. I won't be forced into marrying a man I don't love. I don't care who my father is." Her voice was pure determination.

The pad of his thumb ran circles on the back of her hand.

"You're so brave."

She choked a tiny sound. "No, I'm terrified. So terrified of the alternative that I'm willing to fight to keep it from happening."

Her smile was soggy when she looked at him.

His chest tightened in a fist.

He had to tear his attention away and return it to the sky before he did something more reckless than he was already doing.

A soft giggle left her. "Why are you always staring at the sky when you can't see anything?"

Her curiosity burned on the side of his face.

His lips twitched at her question. He realized then why her covert messages came in the shape they did.

"Even if we can't see them, the stars are there, waiting for us to find them. To look beyond the smoke and distortion to the beauty obscured just on the other side of it. And if you look hard enough…"

He took their woven hands and lifted them, pointed with his index finger at the tiny shimmer that broke through the dingy sky. "See right there? That little star? It always shines through the haze."

"Can you find it every night?" Her voice was the rasp of a whisper.

He tightened his hold on her hand. This girl who shined the brightest of them all.

Through the ugliness of her world.

Through the atrocity of their calling.

Maybe he really could rise above, be better than it all.

"I think I'd find *her* anywhere," he murmured, turning his gaze on her.

Redness flashed on her cheeks, and she peeked his way.

The air shifted.

Flames raced over his skin.

Because Aster crawled to her knees and eased over to straddle his legs.

He sucked for a breath.

Inhaled too deep.

Hyacinth and magnolia leaves.

She touched his chest over his shirt, where it pounded out of time.

Her expression turned to awe.

He took her precious face in both his hands.

Agate eyes flashed and danced.

Sparked and begged.

Their connection fierce and unseen.

"Little Star," he whispered.

Then he kissed her.

Kissed her soft and slow.

And he knew she was worth any amount of trouble she might bring.

Chapter Nineteen

Aster

"WHAT DID DOMINIC SAY?" I WHISPERED AS I glanced out into the hall to make sure it was clear before I clicked my bedroom door shut.

Taylor's voice was held, too. "He scoped out your house. Jarek is definitely not there."

I blew out a heavy sigh. I could certainly attest to that.

He was here.

Lurking.

Watching.

Waiting.

"But of course, the prick has someone posted there. Sketchy much?" She scoffed it.

I almost laughed. "Taylor, Jarek is the definition of sketchy."

"Um, he's the definition of a lot of things. Skeezeball. Douchemonger. Fuckface. Shall I go on? *Shudder.*"

I could practically see her convulsing with revulsion when she said it.

"I think I got you."

She giggled.

It'd been three days since I'd heard from my sister. Three days since Logan had curled up beside me and held me all night. Three days since he'd whispered that I was his, and he would do anything to protect me.

He'd murmured it would be fine, the way he used to do, though there had been an undercurrent to it that hadn't existed in the man before.

He promised he was already digging. That he would find a way to free me of my chains.

One way or another.

I'd awoken to his side of the bed cold.

We'd tiptoed since, unsure of our standing.

His caresses were real but restrained, his gaze sure but his steps faltering, as if he were waiting for me to decide because both of us had so much riding on this fine, undelineated line.

I forced myself to focus on Taylor. "Does Dominic know who it is? Family or hired?"

"Definitely hired. Tatted dude on a bike who looks like he slits throats on the daily and gets a kick out of stomping on kittens with his boots."

MC.

Nerves rattled through my being.

Those connections went deep.

My father tended to hire them to do the family's dirty work—all depravities accepted as long as you were willing to pay the price.

It was also what brought me Logan.

A boy I never should have noticed but whose spirit had called out to me.

I paced as anxiety clamored beneath my skin. "Crap. I don't know what I'm going to do."

"Um, dude? Do you think so little of me? Your baby sister has this handled."

"What are you talking about?"

"I'm getting whatever is in that safe."

"No—"

"Yes, absolutely, yes. I will find a way to get in there. Dom is trying to figure out a plan in exchange for a little *dom* play."

"Ew, Tay."

She cracked up. "Don't knock it until you try it. Unless you have?"

She sounded way too excited by the prospect.

My entire life was submission. I'd pass.

Logan's rough voice skated through my mind. The rasping scrape of a command.

It became clear in a flash, if he demanded it, I would gladly get onto my knees.

"Let's just stick to the subject."

"You're no fun."

"I'm a blast, remember? A total blast."

"You will be when you're happy. When your heart gets set free. I promise it." Her entire voice changed, my careless sister so intuitive beneath her crass.

"Give us a couple days to figure something out, okay? We'll get it. Somehow, we will get it."

"Just be careful. I couldn't stand it if something happened to you."

"Pssh, do you think I'm scared of a little biker?"

Exasperation heaved from me on a sigh. "I'm scared that you're not."

Tinkling laughter rolled from her, then she sobered. "I have one question for you, Aster. Are you afraid, right now? Are you safe?"

Emotion tightened my throat. "I'm afraid I've never felt safer in my life."

Silence held for a beat before she whispered, "There's our answer. Leave it to your baby sister to get the rest of this shit taken care of."

∞

Two days later, I was sitting at the round table in the kitchen, hand sweeping over the little sheets of paper I'd ripped from the journal, trying to process these feelings I wasn't sure how to deal with. It had always been what I'd done, escaped into my thoughts and tried to process them on a page. Left messages from my heart and prayed the right soul would receive them.

That I could be heard.

Found.

The door buzzer rang.

So lost to the memories of this very day from years ago, I jolted back to the present. I didn't know if it was a problem or a simple variant of self-preservation.

Gretchen was at the kitchen sink, and she dried her hands on a towel and started in that direction. "Oh, there they are. It's about danged time."

She sent an excited glance my way.

"Are we expecting company?"

Worried, I looked down at myself.

I was wearing sweats and another of Logan's tees.

I loved the feeling of him surrounding me.

Holding me.

Even when he wasn't there.

Clearly, I was getting too comfortable in this new, temporary skin.

"That we are, sweet thing."

"Who?" I wondered if I should make a beeline for the seclusion of my room.

"Well, it's a special day, and they want to make sure Logan knows it," she answered without really answering at all.

It was a special day.

One I'd held like a treasured secret.

A small thrill rose from the depths, and I stood as she opened the door.

Gage and Juniper darted straight into her arms.

"Nonie G...where have you been my wholes life? I've been missing you." Juni wrapped herself around the old lady's leg, both arms and legs.

"Right here waitin' on you to come visit me."

"Well, I'm here now and that's what counts. We got the busies because we got a new baby comin' and there's the most work to do." The little girl almost huffed.

Gage squeezed Gretchen around the waist. "Did you miss me, too?"

She touched his chubby cheek. "Now tell me how it would be possible not to miss the likes of you?"

Gage shrugged. "Uncle Jud said I'm nothin' but a handful, always makin' messes, and I know you don't like the messes, nope, not one little bit, so I wasn't so sure."

Affection rang from her deep laughter. "Oh, sugar pie, you can make all the messes you want."

My spirit sang while I hovered across the room like a voyeur.

Gretchen opened the door wider and gestured with both hands to whoever was still in the hall. "Well, get in here with that."

She stretched out her arms, and a second later, she was cradling Trent's tiny baby girl and cooing down at her.

I did my best to avert my gaze.

Not to get too close.

But there I stood, vibrating with the joy that bloomed in the room.

Eden shuffled in, pushing a stroller stuffed full of bags. "I think I need about six more arms if I'm going to juggle all of this."

The woman looked a little frazzled.

Her gaze swept around Logan's apartment. It froze in surprise when it landed on me.

I didn't mean to itch, to fidget and act like I'd been caught doing something illicit, but crap, here I still was in Logan's space like it was where I belonged. A *friend* he was only supposed to be catching up with.

But if things were different, I would belong.

With Logan.

Forever.

Not for thirty days. Thirty days that were already dwindling fast.

"Aster." Her smile warmed in this welcome that I shouldn't take on for myself. But I couldn't help it. The springing of affection that developed at the sight. "It's so great to see you again. I wondered if you'd be here."

My smile was unsure. "It's really nice to see you, too."

I glanced at the children, at the stroller, back at her.

"Salem has an ultrasound today, so Juni is hanging out with us while Salem and Jud are at their appointment," she explained. "I might have bitten off more than I can chew."

"That's what you have me for," Gretchen said.

"Oh, hi! I remember you. You used to be Uncle Logan's favorite friend but not anymore. But are you his favorite, favorite now?" Juni bounced my way, all black pigtails and cherub face. "Do you live here now? What's your job? If Uncle doesn't want to be your favorite friend, do you want to be mine? My mommy said I'm a really great friend."

Light laughter rippled from Eden. "That's a lot of questions, Juni Bee."

"I just wonderin'." She shrugged.

My laughter was a slip of discomfort. A crush of awe. "It's fine. I'm not quite sure what I'm doing here, either," I admitted.

Gretchen waddled past, gently bouncing Baby Kate.

"She's twisting your uncle up in a thousand knots, that's what she's doin'. I've never seen that man strung so tight. About to blow, if you ask me."

She winked at me.

Redness flashed.

Eden giggled. "Gretchen."

"I just tell it like it is, honey. No need to beat around the bush, and we can be mighty sure Logan has been doing some *beating*."

My hand pressed to my mouth to stop the crack of surprise.

Wow. She really wasn't one to keep her tongue tamed.

I kind of loved it.

I kind of loved her.

I kind of loved it here.

And with each day that passed, I knew it was going to become more and more difficult to leave this sanctuary.

Gage ran over and grabbed me by the hand. "It's Uncle Logan's birthday so we have to make him feel extra, extra special in the whole wide world right up to the highest mountain, so we came to decorate for a surprise and then we have a super special surprise party for him at our house tonight. It was all my idea. Do you want to come?"

Warily, I glanced at Eden.

More of that warmth flooded from her smile. "She's absolutely invited, but only if she wants to."

"Do you? Do you want to come?" he asked, beaming up at me with that smile.

The vacancy throbbed, while a hardened place within me melted.

I squeezed his hand back. "Well, I'm not sure what I'm doing tonight, but I'll definitely try to make it."

"Try harder," Juni said, propping her hands on her hips.

Eden shook her head. "This one is testing out how far she can get away with the sass."

It was pure love when she said it.

This family so close.

So right.

Affection bound me tight. "If there's any way for me to be there, I will be, Juni."

"Promise?"

"Yes." Why it wobbled, I didn't know, but making an oath to this little child felt monumental. Like I was pledging something I didn't have the right to pledge.

Claiming something that wasn't mine.

I didn't even know if Logan would want me there. This was already hard enough.

Perilous.

My stomach clutched.

I'd die before I'd put these babies in danger. This family.

I had to believe Jarek wouldn't be so foolish to go against my father's direct orders, though. He had to stand down. Give me this time. It was the only reason I felt comfortable staying here while I figured out what I was going to do.

Eden's smile shifted, as if she held the power to read every reservation that'd flash-fired through my mind. "Us Lawsons, we stick together. Through the good times and the really, really terrible times. And believe me, we've had some really terrible times."

She reached out and touched my hand like in doing so, she was tying me to them.

A connection.

Binding me to the promise that those who loved you fought for you.

A reassurance that I didn't need to be afraid.

"God knows them boys find themselves in plenty of trouble," Gretchen tsked.

Juni grabbed my other hand. "You got to come because we're gonna finds out if I get a baby brother or baby sister. My mimi said it's a double trouble party. Do you know my mimi? She's the best Mimi in the whole worlds."

"No. I don't."

"Don't worry. I'll introduce you. You don't got to be shy." Juni nodded emphatically.

"Well…now that we've properly scared the poor girl away." Eden lifted her brow in apology.

"Nonsense. This one's tough as grit." Gretchen gestured toward me with the infant in her arms.

"Hardly." I feigned a giant smile.

"I'm pretty sure you're tougher than you think." Gretchen eyed me differently that time. Intuitively. As if she knew more than she should. "Hard in all the right places…soft where it counts."

Unease lifted in a show of red, and then Eden cleared her throat. "We'd better get to this or we won't have it ready before Logan gets back. Trent is making sure he's occupied until five."

She started taking bags from the stroller and piling them onto the island. They were full of craft and party materials.

"I get to do the balloons!" Juni shouted as she scrambled onto a stool so she could reach.

Gage hauled me that direction. "Do you want to help me make the invitation? It is going to be the coolest in ever and ever! Right, Mommy, right?"

He looked to the woman who gazed at him in absolute adoration. So thick I felt as if we were wading through it.

"That's right, my sweet boy."

"Let's do it!" He fist pumped the air.

Eden put out the materials.

Balloons and streamers and a giant poster board.

And we set to work.

To work on this special treasure. A mark in time. Logan Lawson's birthday.

The memory something I'd cherished, held like a dream and stored like a shrine.

The man my holy place.

My whisper of hope.

That space that was now a void that ached to be filled.

Chapter Twenty

Logan

"**WHAT THE FUCK IS UP WITH YOU, MAN?**" With my hands stuffed in my pockets, I leaned back against the wall of the elevator and eyed Trent.

Dude stood there wearing black jeans and a worn black leather jacket and unlaced motorcycle boots, trying to hold back a Cheshire smirk from his mouth.

It wasn't working.

He laughed under his breath and stared at the elevator floor.

A grin taking hold, I shook my head. "You lightweight mother-fucker. Are you drunk? Tell me you haven't gone weak on me."

He'd shown up at my office two hours ago and insisted we head out to grab a birthday beer or two.

I hadn't complained much except for the fact I'd been dying to get back to my apartment.

I just wanted to look at her.

See her face.

Be in her space.

Pathetic, much?

Felt like we'd been orbiting each other for the last five days since the night something had changed.

The change had been in me, I imagined.

Like the wounds she'd inflicted no longer fucking mattered. The only thing that did was her.

Still, I'd held back, waiting on her because I was certain the girl hadn't yet caught up to me.

She wasn't getting it.

What made things worse was Dean had come back with squat. The only thing he'd found were a few indiscretions that weren't anything we could take back to Aster's father, considering most of them had been done in the Costa name.

Chuckling low, Trent scrubbed a palm over his face and cut me a glance. "Not even close, bro. Who do you think I am?"

"Then what the hell is so funny?"

"Nothin'."

Nothing.

Right.

He laughed again.

"Why are you acting like a giggling schoolgirl with her first crush?"

He shrugged a shoulder with a damned red face.

What the hell?

The elevator dinged open at my floor, and I went striding toward my apartment, trying to hide how anxious I was to get inside. I swung open the door.

"Surprise!"

A crash of voices lifted in the air. Gage and Juni. Eden and Gretchen and poor Baby Kate who'd gotten spooked by the sudden shouting.

Aster.

Aster who was there hovering to the side.

Unsure of where she fit.

My stomach flipped and my chest squeezed tight because she was right where she belonged.

My eyes took in the scene, affection twisting at my mouth.

So damned sweet.

Helium balloons were floating everywhere, streamers strung along the ceiling, and a confetti explosion had laid waste to the room.

Gage and Juni held a big poster board, one of them on each side, their precious faces full of excitement and this crazy amount of joy as they came running for me.

Or maybe that's just what they hit me with.

Joy.

"Happy birthday, Uncle Logan! Happy birthday! Do you like your surprise?"

"What? This is amazing. How could I not like it when I have the best niece and nephew ever?" I scooped them up the second they got to me, and I squeezed them tight while trying not to crush the poster board they held between them.

Because I did like it.

Fucking loved it, actually.

I loved that it felt like coming home.

Like today mattered when it'd ceased to hold meaning a long-damned time ago.

Trent clapped me on the back before he wound around me and went striding for Eden.

No wonder he'd been acting like a freaking weirdo, and it didn't have a thing to do with my birthday surprise, either. Dude never could wait to get his greedy paws on his wife.

"Look it, Uncle, look it!" Juni and Gage waved the poster around, but it was up so close I couldn't read what it said. I pulled back a bit so I could read the words constructed of crayon and child-like handwriting.

Birthday Bash for Logan.

6:30.

My house.

Be there or be a square.

Laughter rumbled. "Tell me you aren't planning me a party?"

I said it like it was absurd.

Juni threw her little arms in the air, and she screeched like it was the best thing in the world, "Yes! You guessed it!"

Then she got serious. "But you gotta share the party with my baby brother or sister because we're gonna finds out which one we gotta get. It's a double trouble party."

"That sounds like a fine plan to me…as long as we know who's really the most important one here, of course. I mean, we know who that is, right?"

I squeezed them both again, bouncing them as I did.

They cracked up.

My spirit soared.

"I even got you a present, Uncle!" Gage curled his arms around my neck as I carried them deeper into my apartment.

"No way."

His sweet eyes rounded. "Yes, way."

"I can't even wait to see."

"Well, you gots to," Juni piped in. "Party isn't until six-thirty."

Laughing, I set them onto their feet.

I moved for Eden, picked her up, and flung her around. "Looking gorgeous today, as ever. Tell me you've gotten sick of his grumpy-ass, and you've finally seen what's right in front of you."

Trent grunted.

I cracked up.

I only did it because Trent was the most possessive bastard I'd ever met.

That shit was hysterical.

Like I'd ever touch his wife.

Maybe I understood it then, though, or maybe subconsciously I had all along, since I was stealing a peek at Aster who still hovered on the outskirts, so damned gorgeous as she shifted on her feet like she felt out of place, like she didn't belong, when I'd never seen any one person look so right.

And I knew I'd claw a fucker's eyes out, too.

I should have then.

More than anything, I was sure I was going to have to do it now.

Still, I tried to ignore her and went to Gretchen and tossed a kiss to her temple, then I brushed my fingertip down Kate's plump, pink cheek. The little, black-eyed girl was the most adorable thing I'd ever seen.

She made this gurgling sound and wrapped her tiny hand around my finger, and I swore I was done for again.

Then I looked up at Aster.

She had backed away. Her arms held over her chest like a cross. Like she couldn't handle it. Like she was terrified of it.

Still, when her agate gaze tangled with mine, she mouthed, *Happy birthday, Logan.*

Her pain, her love, her regrets ran along the tether that pulled between us.

Sparks of light.

A prodding of purpose.

A pressure that compelled us in the direction we'd been destined for.

I wanted to go to her. Wrap her up and hold her and kiss the fuck out of her until she no longer wore that look in her eyes.

Gage grabbed me by the hand and gave me a good tug. "You have to hurry and get ready. We only have one hour which is only really super short. You don't want to be late because being late is bad."

I sent him a big smile. The kid was a stickler for the rules. "Right. On it."

"Whew. We did it." Juni gave him a high five, like they'd been stressed.

Juni looked up at me. "And don't worry, Uncle, Aster is going to try reallys hard to come as long as she don't got nothin' else to do."

I looked at the woman who swarmed me like a remedy.

Filling holes and cracks and vacancies.

I glanced at Juni.

"Don't worry, Juni. She'll be there."

What if time and distance held no meaning? What if it held no standing or claim? What if we had made a million mistakes and those mistakes led us astray and we got lost and wandered for years?

And what if, after all of it, we ended up at the very same place?

I squeezed Aster's hand where she hesitated beside me. Her breaths were shallow and her apprehension thick. Vapor puffed from our mouths as we stood in the frozen darkness outside Eden's modest house that was lit in Christmas lights in one of the older family neighborhoods in Redemption Hills.

"It's so small." Most would take it as an insult, but Aster whispered it like wonder.

Like the sight of it stole her breath and filled her heart to overflowing.

I got the sense the girl gazed upon her dream home. One on a poster tacked to a wall or on an inspiration board that would never come true.

Out of touch. Never tangible. A flatlay that could never come to life.

I turned around to face her, still holding onto her hand as I cocked her a grin. "You probably shouldn't announce that when we get inside. Someone might think it's rude."

She choked out a disconcerted laugh. "That's not what I meant."

I stepped forward, brushed back a lock of her hair, and tucked it behind her ear before I rested my hand on the side of her face. "I know, Aster."

She gulped. She was so damned pretty I couldn't look away. I let the pad of my thumb brush along her cheek. "Eden lived here before she met Trent and Gage," I explained. "They're building a larger home just on the outside of town. Jud and Salem are building one on the property next to them."

From over my shoulder, she looked back at the house. Her voice was a thin mist. "They're so sweet."

She blinked while still staring that way. "This afternoon was…"

"Crazy? Chaotic? Wild? I already saw the proof of it explode in my house. Poor Gretchen is going to be battling glitter for the next six months." I let it go as a tease.

She whispered, "No, Logan. It was wonderful."

My chest tightened, and I stepped back and gave her a gentle tug. "Just wait until we get inside."

Aster remained rooted, and her eyes dropped closed. "I'm not sure I should go in there."

I touched her chin, urging her to look at me. "Why not?"

This time, the laughter that left her was dejected. "I think I've intruded on your family enough."

I gave her a slow smile. "I don't think you've intruded on my family nearly enough."

I tugged her again.

Her heels dug in. "Logan."

I edged forward, inhaled her scent, her beauty, her bravery, and I slipped my arm around her waist and tucked her firmly against me. I crossed that invisible barrier we'd been treading for the better part of a week.

She shivered and shook.

My cheek brushed hers, and my mouth went to her ear. "My rules, Aster."

I didn't give a fuck if I was playing dirty. Using our agreement to my advantage. Some things just needed to be done.

I soothed the sting by stepping back, taking her hand, and dragging her toward the walkway with a playful smirk lighting my mouth. "Besides, it's my birthday. You wouldn't want to go and hurt my feelings by missing my big surprise party, would you? Especially after all the work you put into creating that epic invitation with my niece and nephew?"

"Never." She almost smiled, almost got swept up in the feeling.

The tease and the play.

The hope and the joy.

Because I could already feel it radiating from the walls of the simple house as Aster hustled along a step behind me as I hauled her toward the door, then I felt it explode when I opened it to the crush of people gathered in the cramped space.

I felt it to my soul when a chorus of voices went up with a loud, "Happy birthday!"

I grinned, pulled my girl up to my side, and slung my arm over her shoulder. "That's right, the one you've all been waiting for is here. Let's get this party started, baby."

By the streak of excitement that impaled me right then?

I was sure I was stepping into the best night of my life.

I grinned back at Aster, then I pulled her in with me.

Chapter Twenty-One

Aster

IF IT HAD BEEN CHAOTIC BACK AT LOGAN'S APARTMENT EARLIER, it was madness inside Eden and Trent's home.

A home filled with smiling faces, warm welcomes, and genuine embraces.

People were crammed into the small space, although no one seemed to mind the close quarters.

The entry room was a tiny square with a couch and a loveseat in the middle facing a TV against one wall. Bookshelves filled with pictures and trinkets and at least a gazillion pieces of artwork that clearly had come from Gage's precious little hands were proudly displayed on every other flat surface.

An archway on the left opened to a kitchen with a breakfast nook where a ton of people were hanging out, and there was a hall on the opposite far side of the room that I assumed led to the bedrooms.

It was simple and modest and felt like falling into my favorite dream. A dream I'd cached away, where I'd buried it beneath my family name and my father's expectations. A dream I craved to slip into but was terrified to take the first step.

Logan did it for me.

He grabbed my hand again and, with a gentle tug, he pulled me deeper into the fray.

Juni and Gage came streaking through the crowd. "You're here! You're here! You're here!"

Gage got there first, and Logan picked him up the way he had earlier, his smile so free as he hugged the child to his chest. He scooped up Juni in his other arm. His joy became profound, all the rigid hardness that seeped from his pores giving way to an easiness I'd almost forgotten existed.

Close to how it was that first night at the recital.

But different.

Not so reserved. The man turning over the top as he tussled with Gage and Juni, swinging them around like rag dolls.

"Now who's your strongest uncle?" he demanded to know, his tone playful.

"Uncle Jud!" Gage cackled when he said it, clearly knowing he'd given the wrong answer, and Juni giggled adorably when she shouted, "Uncle Trent!" at the same time.

Logan feigned the biggest gasp.

"What? How dare you? And it's my birthday? What is this madness? You know I'm the strongest of the Lawson brothers. Trent and Jud just look big. But your uncle Logan is pure muscle."

He squeezed them tighter as if to prove it.

In it was care. Every movement done with caution so neither of them would be hurt.

"You'd better watch it, or Uncle Jud is gonna take you down!" Gage shouted as he scrambled around, trying to get his little arms around Logan.

From where Jud was leaned against the back of the couch next to his wife halfway across the room, the giant man lifted a beer in the air and shouted over the din of voices and the music that played at a low volume. "That's right, Gage in the Cage. You pin him for me, then I'll be over to take care of the rest."

"Wow. Just wow. Why do you always gotta be so violent?" Logan taunted just as Gage was climbing over his shoulder and jumping onto his back.

Jud cracked a grin and tucked Salem closer. "Someone has to take care of punks like you."

Horrified offense took over every line of Logan's face, clearly faked, all while he was being climbed like he was a jungle gym in the middle of a playground.

"I'm wounded."

Jud scoffed with a smile. "I'll show you wounded."

I tried to hold a laugh, not to get too comfortable, but it was really hard to do when it felt as if I'd stumbled into a safe space. Where it was joy and light and life. Different than anything I'd ever experienced. Better than anything I'd ever imagined.

Logan tossed a soft smile my way and slowly set the kids onto their feet. "All right, all right, everyone off, Uncle Logan needs to make the rounds."

"I'll destroy you later." Gage giggled the words as Logan flipped him around onto his feet.

"I'm sure you will." Logan laughed, ruffling his fingers through the child's hair before he turned to me and stretched out his hand. "Come on. Let me introduce you to everyone."

Uneasiness climbed through my consciousness, that reminder that I didn't belong, that I shouldn't get too comfortable, that this was absolutely reckless, coming here like this. But it felt too good to let Logan slip his fingers through mine, to act as if I were his and he were mine.

Casually, he led me to Jud who stood and gave me a bear hug the second we approached.

Welcome.

Salem, whose blue eyes twinkled and danced with this mischief that was still somehow kind, pushed up from where she had been leaned against the couch. She reached for my hand and squeezed. She was different than Eden, a little harder around the edges, I guessed, as if she'd been through more than any one person should be expected to.

Her hair was black and pin-straight where it brushed around her shoulders, and she gave off a naturally sexy vibe that somehow came off sweet.

"So, you're still hanging out with this guy, huh?" It was a tease of affection.

Logan gave her a giant hug. "Yeah, yeah, you know you love me the most. Just keep pretending."

Stepping back, he pointed at her belly. "Tell me I'm getting another niece because the last thing we need around here is another Lawson boy to bust my balls."

"Hey, I bust your balls, Uncle Logan." Juni was clearly offended.

Her mom covered her ears, but not nearly in time. Laughing under her breath and shooting daggers at Logan, she glanced at her daughter. "Don't listen to anything that comes out of your uncle Logan's mouth, Juni Bee. He's a terrible influence."

Logan stretched out his arms. "What are you talking about? I'm a great influence."

"Hardly," Jud grunted before he took a swig from his bottle of beer.

Chuckling, Logan reached over and ran his hand over the back of Juniper's head. "Fine. That was a bad word, Juni, I'm sorry. You probably shouldn't say it again even though it was completely valid."

The last he tossed out with a grin at Salem.

She scowled at him, though I was pretty sure it was riddled with affection.

"It's okay. You're forgiven. But you still gotta put some dollars in the swears jar. My mimi already gots it half full." Juni's tone was pure disappointment.

Logan dug into his wallet and pulled out a five-dollar bill. "How about you do it for me the next time you go to your mimi's?"

Juni snatched it. "Or I might keep it. Payback."

Logan's mouth dropped open. "For what?"

"For your birthday." She gave him a look that said, *obviously*.

"I have to pay you for my birthday?"

"It was a lot of hards work, Uncle."

Amusement pressed at my chest.

Logan laughed. "Little swindler."

"Seems she learned from the best." Jud winked at me when he said it.

Redness flashed.

Clearly, they'd heard how Logan and I had *run* into each other.

Logan slipped his arm around my waist, his heat so sweet, his mouth so tempting. "Come on."

"It was nice to see you both again," I murmured, overcome, swept away, unable to keep the smile from taking to my face.

A real one.

Not forced or faked.

Because I wanted this. To celebrate Logan's birthday with him. With his friends and his family. To experience what it would have been like if life weren't so cruel.

If it didn't steal our hearts and souls.

Crush every part of us that was good.

If it didn't make us *choose*.

Logan introduced me to a few people around the room. His office manager. A couple friends he golfed with. A mechanic named Brock from the custom bike shop, Iron Ride, that Jud owned.

He led me to three intimidating men drinking beers in the corner. They had their massive, tattooed arms crossed over their chests and gave off the vibe any one of them could be currently standing outside guarding Jarek's house.

Logan fist bumped each of them. "I can't believe you're here and my brother actually thought to give you the night off. It's a Christmas miracle."

"Birthday miracle," the first one said. A gleam lit in his eyes when he looked at me. "Guess there are a ton of birthday miracles going around considering you walked in with a woman that looks like this. I'm Sage, beautiful."

A blush hit my cheeks. "Aster."

Logan curled his arm around me, and I thought he was going to pop off a razzing insult, but he tucked me close and muttered, "You're right, Sage, it's a fucking miracle."

My heart thrashed.

Then he gestured at Sage with a smile. "Sage is Absolution's general manager, the poor bastard who is tasked with keeping Trent in line."

"You know it." The man was all easy grins. "Place would go down if I wasn't there to make sure that shit didn't go sideways."

"And these two monsters are Kult and Milo." Logan tilted his chin at the other two men. "Head bouncers at the club."

"I could have guessed that," I said with a soft smile as I shook their hands. "Nice to meet you all."

I startled when a little hand threaded into mine, interrupting the introductions. I looked down to Juni bouncing at my side. "Oh my gosh, I almost forgot the most important thing, Miss Aster, I gotta do the introducing to my mimi."

She jerked at my hand. I glanced at Logan. He smiled.

Smiled this smile that sailed through me with the force of a knife. Impaling me deep.

Tenderness.

So much of it I didn't know how to stand.

"You'd better go then," he said.

Flustered, I fumbled away from him, somehow feeling attached, like a band was stretched taut between us and it only tightened with each step I took. It wasn't as if it was all that far because Juni hauled me around to the other side of the couch.

Gretchen sat on the right with a giant margarita in her hand. She'd ridden over with Eden to help her get set up and to give her an extra hand with the kids.

Next to her was an older woman, close to her 80s, I would say, her aged face filled with mischief and warmth.

Juni hopped the rest of the way over to her.

"Well, who do we have here?" the woman asked.

"Mimi, this is Uncle Logan's old favorite friend but not his favorite anymore, and her name is Miss Aster, but she had to come because we likes her so very much and she helped us get the party ready."

"Huh," was what the woman said as she eyed me up and down. Then her smile turned sly. "Sure looks like you're Logan's favorite friend to me."

Gretchen smacked her knee. "Oh, Maria, you should see it, this one has that boy wrapped around her little finger. I keep having to tiptoe around the apartment before I come across something I don't want to see."

She actually waggled her brows all while tipping half of her margarita out onto her lap. "Ooops."

She giggled.

"Don't want to get a look?" Mimi was aghast. "Now that is one hiney I wouldn't mind getting my peepers on."

She knocked her shoulder into Gretchen's, giggling, too.

My lips pressed together.

These two were drunk.

"Well, now there's our double trouble." Logan's voice came over me from behind.

I swore Mimi blushed while a shiver raced down my spine. "There you are, you sly dog."

Logan chuckled low, then he bent over and kissed her cheek. "Good to see you, Mimi."

"That's Maria, to you." She winked at him as she patted his cheek.

Oh my god.

I felt the giggle threaten at the base of my throat. I tried to cover it with my hand.

Logan peeked back at me. My brows lifted. He grinned.

Mimi's expression turned soft. "Happy birthday, Logan."

"Thank you."

"Oh, I think it's gonna be good, alright." Gretchen lifted her margarita. It sloshed over the side and onto her hand.

"Sheesh, for someone who doesn't like the messes, you sure is makin' plenty of 'em, Nonie G." Juni shook her head.

I laughed.

Logan stood, pushing to his full, towering height.

The man took the one step it required to erase the space between us, then he was slipping his arm around my waist, tugging me right to his chest. He leaned down so close I was almost scared and really excited that he was swooping down to kiss me, but he came up short, his breath mine. "Oh, it's definitely going to be good."

Stepping back, I tried to straighten myself out. To thwart this new energy that buzzed between us.

Logan introduced me to more guests, always calling me, *His Aster*.

He leaned down and kissed me on the temple.

I tried to keep it together.

To remember.

But tonight, I couldn't seem to stop myself from slipping into his fantasy.

From tripping his direction.

Thirty days.

Thirty days.

I tried to chant it.

Claim it.

I needed to remember it because I was setting myself up to get ripped apart.

This was so much more dangerous than any deal I had made that fateful morning when I'd come crawling back to Logan's office.

This?

This was real.

"Oh my god, you're here!" A screech came from somewhere within the kitchen as Logan stepped through the archway.

A red head bobbed through the crowd, the woman literally jumping so she could see over the heads. She came winding through, wielding a bottle of champagne.

Logan leaned toward my ear. "You're in trouble now."

Oh, I was already there, but I felt it coming like a hurricane when the woman I remembered as a snowflake from the recital was suddenly throwing her arms around me like I was her oldest friend.

She squeezed me and shook me around. "I'm so happy you're here! I wasn't sure if you'd be since this guy over here usually has his big head shoved so far up his ass he doesn't know up from down. I mean, I've seen his horrible decisions, but for once, I can see he has his head on straight."

"Um..." I stammered.

Logan gave her a light punch on the shoulder. "It is my birthday, Tessa. Think you could cut a guy a break?"

"Nope, she's bustin' your balls, too." Juni blazed by as she shouted it.

My hand pressed to my mouth.

Chaos, I tell you.

Logan blinked. "Wow. Some party this is. Even my adorable niece has turned against me. And here I am, the smartest, best looking, richest guy around."

I cringed at the last.

Tessa cocked her head. "Well, if you actually tacked nice and humble onto that list, you might be worthy of the celebration."

"Ouch." Logan touched his chest.

"I'll *ouch* you."

"But I just want you to love me." Logan stuck out his bottom lip.

Amusement pulled through the atmosphere.

Giggling, she sidled up to him and slid her arm around his side, hugging him tight as she looked back at me. "Okay, fine. This one right here is pretty amazing, and he's smokin' hot if I don't say so myself. Like catch the house on fire hot, if you know what I mean."

She puffed that out of the side of her mouth toward me like it was a secret.

"Now we're talking." Logan bobbed his head in encouragement.

"I've heard it's all due to the fact he has a really big..." She paused, her blue eyes wide and emphatic. "Ego. A really big ego."

She cracked up like it was hysterical.

He kissed the top of her head, though he growled like I couldn't hear, "Keep it up, Tessa, and I'm putting you in the shower under cold water. I'm trying to impress the prettiest girl here, can't you see?"

"You wouldn't dare," she gasped. "She is really pretty, though. I think we should keep her."

Rattled, I shifted my feet.

She lifted that bottle. "Champagne?"

"Oh, most definitely," I said.

She moved in, wrapped her arm around my waist, and led me deeper into the kitchen. "Don't worry, Aster, we're going to be the best of friends. I know these things." She knocked her hip into mine. "Mad love. Mad, mad love. Just wait and see."

So it turned out Tessa was kind of insane. Crazy and fun and impossible not to like.

Because it was all genuine. The care she showed for everyone around her. Even if she didn't know someone, she made them feel like she did.

Especially me.

I sipped at my flute of champagne while she danced in the kitchen with Eden in some kind of horrible ballet/break dancing routine to the beat of "SexyBack".

Nothing like a little JT.

Tessa scattered the crowd crushed in the space and did the worm across the floor.

I didn't think I'd ever laughed so hard in my life.

Didn't think I'd ever felt so perfectly right when she popped back up and took my hand and spun me around.

Didn't think I'd ever felt so free than when she slung her arm around my shoulders like we were a pair, the woman talking to Salem who'd joined us on the other side, Eden in front of us, this whole thing so casual, no pretenses.

As if I could be a part of them.

Jud, Salem, and Juni were ushered into the middle of the mayhem and were presented with a bouquet of black helium balloons.

Jud helped Juni pop one.

Blue confetti fluttered out.

"A boy! We get a boy!" Juni shouted, and she threw herself around her mom's neck, hugging her tight. Jud wrapped himself around both of them. He leaned down and kissed his wife, and I saw Salem's eyes were filled with tears.

He kissed them away, murmured something none of us could hear.

So tender.

So sweet.

I had to look away.

My eyes tangled with Logan's where he leaned against the counter three feet away next to Trent.

Malachite.

Stony green that sparked with flecks of gold.

His hands were in his pockets, and he had an ankle crossed over the other. This sexy casualness rolled from him in waves that tied my stomach in a needy knot.

Hot and blinding.

But it was his expression that did me in.

The soft affection that played and danced, the tiniest tweak of a warm smile kissing the edge of his mouth all mixed with old understanding.

My spirit lit.

Caught in his energy.

In this gravity.

All while my brain kept warning I was being a fool.

Heedless.

I could feel the tendrils of my spirit weaving into the fabric of these people, and when I pulled them loose, they were going to snap.

Break.

Still, I mouthed, *Happy birthday*, as he gazed over at me.

That time he did smile. This slow satisfaction taking over the gorgeous, defined angles of his face when he mouthed back, *The best*.

I jolted when Eden was suddenly in front of me, her voice a little panicked. "Can you hold her for a second?"

I didn't have time to refuse before she set Baby Kate in my arms.

I froze, and my heart rose to my throat. The knot was so huge it clotted off air.

I tried not to look, not to turn my attention down on the precious little face that stared up at me. Her eyes were so dark they were nearly black, her cheeks pink and her nose tiny, her mouth curled in the sweetest, crooked smile.

My chest clutched, and my arms shook, and I held her to me probably a little too tightly, scared that I would hurt her. That I would harm her.

Emotion burned, a flashfire through my veins, and I knew I was messed up.

Scarred with no hope of recovery.

I couldn't even hold an infant without having a panic attack. Without wanting to hold on tighter while simultaneously wanting to jerk my arms away.

Eden returned, laughing under her breath. "Sorry about that, I needed to refill the ranch dip."

She took her daughter back without the knowledge that in the one minute I'd been holding the child, I'd been scourged.

Because being here? In this town? In this place with this man?

It ripped off the scab of everything I'd fought for years to suppress.

It'd been the only way I could survive.

To refuse and forget.

But there was no forgetting when I stood under the force of Logan's eyes.

Tessa suddenly grabbed me by the hand, yanking me out of the void of despair I was sinking into. "Come dance with me!"

A smile forced its way to my mouth when she shimmied in front of me like she was seducing me onto the makeshift dance floor.

She twirled me around and around until I felt dizzy.

I laughed. Awkward at first, but then hard and free. My breaths were harsh, but they finally filled my aching lungs.

Tessa leaned in closer. "There, that's better."

A frown pulled to my brow. "What?"

"That smile. That's the one I was looking for." Her response was soft, knowing, and I wondered how it was possible that these people I'd known a handful of hours knew me better than anyone knew me back home.

That they saw through the barriers.

The veil.

"Mad love." She shouted that above the music as she twirled me again. Another roll of laughter erupted.

Logan was suddenly there, big and towering, his jaw hard and his eyes soft. He glanced at Tessa. "I think it's time I cut in."

She pouted and gathered me in an overbearing hug. "What? No way. I just got to meet my new BFF and I'm keeping her forever."

"Tessa." He gruffed it with a slough of affection.

She pouted harder, pushing out her lips in a ridiculous way, then she laughed and pushed me in his direction. "Okay, fine, since it's your birthday. But I love her and she's mine, and if you screw this up, I will kick your ass."

Logan grunted.

I tried not to laugh.

Tried not to cry.

Tried not to get crushed by the care of this family.

Everyone had taken me under their wing. They'd shown me their love and protection as if I were one of them. The problem was they had no idea even if I wanted to stay, even if Logan wanted me to, I couldn't.

Thirty days.

Thirty days.

On top of that, I didn't understand Logan. What he'd done, the choices he'd made, up against the fierce look in his eyes when the man took me by the hand.

Our hatred, our hurt, at odds with this twining of want there was no chance of escaping.

I felt it build as the man walked backward facing me as he pulled me out of the kitchen and into the living room where it was even more crammed with people.

The mood had gotten a little rowdy.

Voices raised and laughter flowing.

The music had been turned up a notch, enough that it covered the conversations and lifted everything to an elevated hum.

In the middle of the throng, Logan pulled me into his arms and crushed me against the hard, rippling planes of his body.

He had one arm banded around my waist. His other palm was

splayed wide, gliding up my spine until he was slipping it under the fall of my hair. He took hold of the mass of it in a fist.

A surprised squeak whispered through my lips.

Strength vibrated through his body.

Chills skated across mine.

"Logan." I didn't mean to plead his name the way I did, but it was getting harder and harder not to beg for what every part of me wanted.

He grunted and somehow tucked me even closer. His voice was a rough scrape against my ear. "I've been waiting hours to get you alone like this."

"Are you jealous?" There was no stopping the tease because the sulking woven in his voice was ridiculous.

Adorable and ridiculous.

This rigid, intimidating man who could be so goofy and sweet.

"Tessa was hogging you."

"Hogging me?"

"Yes. Hogging."

I glanced behind me then back to him. "Well, she is really pretty."

"Aster." His voice deepened to a growl. "Don't make me punish you."

His hand tightened in my hair, giving it a little yank to tug my face back to meet the warning in his gaze.

I giggled.

Clearly, I was losing it, letting go, getting caught up in the swell of giddiness that swept through my being.

"Are you laughing at me?" Logan grumbled.

"Maybe."

Another giggle, only that one morphed into a needy moan when he pressed his face to the edge of my jaw. He ran his nose along the sensitive flesh, slipping up to my ear and back down to my chin.

Twice he did it, whispering, "You're mine," as he went.

It was a mind-altering caress.

One that made me forget what I was supposed to be fighting for. One that made me forget the danger and the risk and what was at stake.

One that made me sigh and press my face into his chest when he began to lead me in a gentle, slow sway.

We danced at half the beat of the music that played.

Like the song belonged to us.

This moment in time carved out for what might have been.

"Aster." Logan muttered it like praise at the side of my head where he had his nose buried in my hair. "Never in a million years would I have thought two weeks ago that on my birthday I'd be given a gift such as this. Never thought I'd get to hold you again. Never thought I'd get to touch you again."

"It's not a gift, Logan, it's a burden."

He edged back to gaze down at me. "No, Little Star. Don't you get it? You are worth fighting for."

My heart banged.

The energy crackled.

The people around us began to blur as Logan and I sank into each other.

The world faded, and the only thing I was aware of was the thunder of his heart and the erratic pound of mine. The feel of our bodies pressed tightly together.

His lips gently brushed my cheek, hit the edge of my eye, and ran up to my temple.

My fingers curled into his shirt.

"Aster."

It was a call.

A claim.

We'd drifted, slowly moving across the room. The sounds of the party quieted the barest fraction, the same as the lights.

I almost had to blink to orient myself to the fact that Logan had pulled me into a hall that ran off to the far side of the living room.

I hadn't even noticed he'd lifted me off my feet until I realized my toes were barely grazing the floor where he had pulled me into the darkness.

It was in the darkness where my love for him endured.

Words I would never say.

But the truth of it screamed through my veins.

He pressed my weight to the wall.

His big body towered, eclipsing reason, sight and judgement and prudent thought.

There, it was only the feel of his hands that slipped down my arms and the harsh pants that jutted from his lungs.

"You're going to ruin me." Logan raked it like a curse, and he suddenly pinned my arms above my head.

I didn't care.

I just felt.

Whimpering, my hips bucked toward him.

He was pressed so tightly against me that the movement had me rubbing against his massive erection that strained the fabric of his pants.

Lightheadedness swept the fears from my mind, and a dreamy daze took me over.

A bluster of desire so intense I wanted to weep.

I'd almost forgotten. I'd almost forgotten.

I sagged in his hold.

Surrendering.

"Fuck," Logan grunted, then I was off my feet again. He whipped me around and pulled me into a dark room. He shut the door and pinned me to the wall beside it.

The party echoed from the other room. It felt as if we'd been elevated. Lifted above reality. Above circumstance. To the place where only Logan and I existed.

The barest light seeped through a window, only enough to illuminate the carved lines of his immaculate face.

In the wisps of shadows, he looked like a demon, an avenger, my sweet destination.

His hand spread farther out over my cheek, and he tightened his hold on my jaw. Malachite eyes flashed in the bare rays of light.

"Say it," he demanded.

"I'm yours." There was no hesitation. No holding it back. The confession was out without thought of consequence.

The second I said it, Logan dove in. His hands were on both sides of my face when his mouth covered mine.

His lips were soft but the kiss was rough.

Heat flashed, racing my flesh, dumping into my stomach to boil in my belly.

A whimper broke free, and he kissed me deeper, his tongue stroking into my mouth in a bid of possession.

It wasn't sweet.

It was a plundering.

A claiming.

A raid.

A vengeful man who wouldn't stop seeking retribution until everything that had been stolen was returned to him.

I kissed him back.

Frantically.

Desperately.

My hands in his hair. On his face. Digging into his shirt.

I wanted to touch him everywhere.

He groaned when I made it under the fabric, and I raked my nails down his chest.

He kissed me harder for a second before he slowed, his lips plucking over mine in a gentle push and pull.

Logan whispered over the swollen, lust-bitten flesh. "Do you remember me, Aster? Do you remember me?"

I choked over the pain that threatened to rise. "I wanted to forget."

Big hands gripped me by the hips, and he lifted me from the floor. On instinct, my legs wrapped around his waist.

He rocked against me, his cock huge and hard and scorching hot.

A searing.

A burn.

A tattoo forever imprinted on me.

"Do you?" he pressed, his fingers digging into my flesh as if he could uncover the truth in me.

"I remember. I remember."

He was rocking harder then, friction and fire, and I was so spun up, so lost, that I was gasping.

Pleasure rose like an eruption.

Like dammed water springing from dry, dead earth.

So much. Too much. Not nearly enough.

I clawed at his shoulders. "Please."

"What do you need?" he rumbled as he kissed a path up my neck. "You."

The door banged open, and the light flipped on.

I choked.

Logan froze where he was dry humping me against the wall where my legs were still locked around his waist.

Horrified, I whipped my attention to the doorway.

Mimi slapped her hand over Gage's gaping eyes before she shuffled him around and told him to go to the kitchen.

She turned back to us with a grin on her face.

"You sly dog."

Gretchen peered over Maria's shoulder. "Oh, lord a'mercy…he was about to take it out, Mare."

With both hands, I covered my face. I didn't need to worry about my knees being weak from embarrassment since Logan still had me pinned.

Awesome.

"You could shut the door," Logan said, his hands planted on either side of my head as he glared their way.

"Now what would be the fun in that?" This from Mimi.

"We were kind of in the middle of something." Logan raised his brow.

"Not anymore…this old girl needs to get home. My dogs are a barkin', and it's way past my bedtime. You promised to give me a ride, doncha remember?" Gretchen slurred.

"Call an Uber." Exasperation filled his tone.

"I can't find my phone." She hiccupped.

Logan shook his head. "You're fired, Gretchen. Totally, completely fired."

"Fired? Not even close, young man. Just a smidgeon tipsy, is what I am." She pinched her fingers together.

I pressed against his chest. "We should take her home."

The bubble had burst.

My lips burned and my spirit singed.

In the glaring light, it was very, very apparent this was a horrible idea.

I'd let myself get lost. Allowed myself to forget.

And that was the most dangerous place I could be.

Logan sighed in their direction. "Cock blockers."

He helped me to my feet.

I swayed to the side, and Logan steadied me. "Are you okay?"

So definitely not okay.

I gave him a shaky nod.

He led me back into the main room, and he kept his fingers threaded through mine as we told everyone goodnight.

Eden, Salem, and Tessa hugged me forever. They told me how great it was that I was there. How we were all going to have so much fun together.

I fought the welling of emotion that burned at the back of my eyes.

This was what happened when you got careless. When you touched upon things you couldn't have.

Window shopping for what you could never afford only made you long for the unattainable.

The whole time, I tried not to stumble through the lust that still smoldered between Logan and me. The way his fingers twitched, and I could feel the desire vibrating beneath his skin.

When we stepped outside, snow was flitting from the sky.

I lifted my face, welcomed the cold, and hoped it could put out this fire.

Logan helped a stumbling Gretchen across the street. She cracked up about every three steps.

I tried to climb into the backseat, and she pushed me away. "Pssh, get your cute butt in that front seat next to your man where you belong."

She flung herself into the back and let out a huge sigh as if it'd been the longest day of her life.

Warily, I climbed into the front as Logan did the same.

We both shut our doors, and he started the deep, rumbling engine.

Nope.

There was no dousing this fire. There were only flames.

The tension was so thick, I couldn't breathe as he drove through the sleeping city streets.

There was no oxygen in the silence. No relief in the miles we traveled.

It only compounded with each second that passed.

He peeked at me, stroked his tongue over his lips.

I wiggled in the seat.

Logan whipped into his parking spot in the basement garage.

He jumped out, and I did the same.

He moved around to the back of the car so he could help Gretchen to the elevator, and we rode it up.

That dense, deep silence followed us.

I tried to inhale.

To stop the shaking.

To pretend as if I hadn't just crossed a line that I never should have crossed.

The first night in my bed? That had felt like a dream. As if it hadn't happened. Tonight? It felt all too real. As if I were touching the same boy I'd fallen for all those years ago.

Logan let us into the muted light of his apartment.

Gretchen started for the hall. "Whew, I thought I was gonna blow in that car with y'all. Barely made it out alive." She lumbered away. "I'll be in my room. There's a good chance I might need a little privacy, so whatever you do, do not come a knockin.'"

In exasperation, Logan rubbed at his forehead. "We're going to have to find her a boyfriend."

I would have laughed except I could only focus on my next breath.

On not being consumed.

I shuffled my feet. "Well…goodnight," I finally managed, and I ducked my head and started in the same direction Gretchen had gone.

"Not so fast." Logan's voice stopped me in my tracks.

I peeked back at him. He was so gorgeous it was unfair.

So powerful in his suit, every inch of him hard, rippling with sinewy strength.

I waited.

Spellbound.

"I think we have some unfinished business."

Then he turned and walked into his bedroom.

And I was the fool who followed.

Chapter Twenty-Two

Logan

I LOOKED BACK FROM WHERE I'D FLICKED THE SWITCH FOR THE fireplace that now cast my bedroom in a red-tinged glow.

Aster Rose hovered just inside my doorway. She wore a plush gray sweater that crisscrossed in the front, creating a deep V between her breasts. It was tucked into a pair of tight leather pants, high-heeled boots that came up to just above her knees.

She looked like a fucking seductress standing in my room. Like temptation. Like every-fucking-thing that had been missing in my life for the last seven years.

She fidgeted.

Twitched.

Unsure.

Oh, but we could be certain of one thing.

She wanted me. She fucking wanted me.

Even knowing what felt like insurmountable obstacles separating us, she wanted me.

The problem was, my head didn't know how to keep up with my heart that was already pounding out ahead of us.

My mind full of questions while the rest of me just didn't give a fuck.

The only thing that mattered was the feeling that coursed through my veins.

This steely determination that I was going to take back what was mine.

I wound myself out of my suit jacket and tossed it to the couch.

Aster throbbed.

I saw it. Felt it. The way her entire being flared. I could taste her sweet breath that ensnared me like an echo. I could feel the filaments that curled between us like silky bonds around our wrists.

I toed off my shoes, unbuttoned the cuffs of my shirt, and rolled them up my forearms. She watched the action like she was committing it to memory. Or maybe like she was going back. Back to where we belonged.

Lust battled with the anger that stroked inside me.

With the war the sight of her incited.

The truth that she was mine, but she didn't quite know it yet.

"Come here." It cracked through the quiet, dense air.

Air wheezed from her lungs.

"I don't think this is a good idea," she forced out.

"Tell me you're not aching, Aster."

She whimpered out a frustrated laugh. "That's the whole problem, Logan. I've been aching since the moment you burst back into my life, and I don't know how to handle that."

I saw the dread written on her face.

Her fear.

Her belief that after this, she would have to leave.

"Come here, Aster." I said it softer that time.

I didn't know which of us was the gravity. Which one of us compelled the other because I knew right that fucking second I would follow her anywhere.

She approached like she was walking on a sea of black ice littered with cracks, and she was afraid she might fall through.

One misstep and it would be over.

While I was going to teach her how to disappear into the moment.

Then I was going to keep her there forever.

Rich locks of brown hair flowed around her precious face. Her eyes were alight, flames dancing in the depths. She tiptoed across the floor. She came up within a foot of me when she paused, and her chest shuddered, and the tiniest, neediest breath escaped her full, pink lips.

Then she slowly climbed down onto her knees on the rug. As something locked inside her broke. "Logan. I'm not sure I know how to stand any longer. I've been doing it alone for so long."

"Fuck me." It slipped from my tongue as sure as I was slipping into a dream.

Her throat worked as she looked up at me, as she sucked every last drop of self-restraint from the air.

Hers.

Mine.

I wasn't sure.

The only thing I knew was I heaved a breath as heavy as stones when she whispered again, "Logan."

She leaned up and pressed her cheek to the inside of my thigh, rubbed herself there, eliciting an inferno that scorched through my insides.

A whirlwind of heat.

I reached out and traced her lips with the pad of my thumb, urging her to look up at me.

Flames leapt.

Danced and played.

Ready to consume.

"Aster."

It was praise.

Affection.

A threat.

"Was I always destined to end up right here?" Her voice was a wisp. Short rasps of uncertainty. "No matter where you went, would I find you there? Or is it all a horrible coincidence? A stroke of bad luck? Or maybe...maybe it's a punishment?"

"Little Star. One tiny star hidden in a vast cosmos. The only one I can see."

She choked out a pained sound. "Even if I can't see you, I'll know you're there, and I'll find my way to you."

She repeated the promise I'd made her that night.

A promise that whipped in tattered shreds around us.

Taking her by the chin, I lifted her face farther. She looked up at me with this expression that slayed me through. "Did you believe it, Aster? Did you believe what I told you then?"

Her throat bobbed heavily when she swallowed, and her eyes filled with the mist of old-broken dreams. "I believed you."

"But you didn't wait for me." The words cracked.

Blinking, she forced out the confession. "My heart did."

The air thinned, and my blood thundered. This manic crash that wanted to tear its way through.

"Did you feel it?" she asked. So quiet. So unsure. "Did you feel my heart through the space, even when you couldn't see me?"

My hand splayed over the side of her face. "Every day, I thought I was losing my mind, Aster, the way every road wanted to end with you. Every fucking minute I wanted to come to you. Find you. To listen to the call of your voice that forever echoed in my ear."

Shifting, she pressed her mouth to my palm, kissed it gently, lingered there for the longest time.

She held my hand to her face like her haggard breaths could heal our wounds.

I eased down onto my knees, took her face in my hands, and stared at her through the lapping shadows. "Did you feel it? Did you feel me?"

Tears slipped from her gorgeous eyes, the moisture seeping into the webs of my fingers.

"You are the only thing, the only one, I've ever felt."

"Aster." I leaned forward and pressed my mouth against hers.

Aster inhaled like it was the first time in years she could breathe. Then her hands spread over my chest and up around my neck.

I kissed her slow. My lips in a constant press and pull with hers. Soft laps and tiny flicks of tongue.

Without breaking the kiss, she fumbled through the buttons of my shirt.

The first.

The second.

She moved faster the farther she went.

She gasped a little sound when she got the last one free, and she pressed her palms to my bare chest and ran them up over my shoulders to push back the fabric.

I was quick to wind out of it, needing to feel her heat, the touch of her hands, the raking of her eyes.

They flew over me like a storm. Like annihilation. This one single girl who held the power to destroy me. She'd done it before, under the covenant of a thousand secret kisses, so I should have known better right then.

But yesterday didn't matter. This moment was the only one I could control.

My skin was unmarred except for the single tattoo that ran up my side from my waist to my ribs.

She whimpered when she saw it.

GREED.

Aster edged back a fraction, and she glanced at me once in question before she turned to watch as she ran her fingers over the ink.

"It stole you from me." I could barely hear her heartbroken words over the crash of her heart. The pound, pound, pounding that ravaged and shook.

She was wrong.

"Everything I ever had belonged to you."

Everything I'd ever done had been done for her.

Every lie told in her favor.

She looked back at me. "Our worlds have always been against us."

I set my hand on the side of her face. "Then let's burn it down."

She leaned forward, and she was kissing along my bare chest, over that rampage that beat against my ribs, over the hatred that churned in my soul, over the word that had cost it all.

Greed. Greed. Greed.

Who I was bred to be.

What my father created.

I'd stolen. I'd manipulated. I'd contrived.

But this time…this time, the gain had taken new shape, and I wouldn't stop until she was mine.

My hands drove into her hair as she kissed lower, and I lifted as she went, until she was dipping her tongue along the band of my pants.

I almost came undone right there.

Lust buzzed in my ear. Stampeded like gasoline as it sped through my veins.

Every muscle in my body went hard.

It was a greedy sound that rumbled up her throat when she undid the button and pulled down the zipper.

The sound reverberated through the room. Banged the walls like a promise.

"Aster."

It was a grunt.

She was heading in a direction she wasn't ready for.

Aster sat up so she could push the tips of her fingers under the material. "Please. Just let me touch you. Let me feel you. I know it's temporary but—"

I cut her off by closing my hand up around her throat. "Don't fucking say it."

It killed the words right there, and her eyes rounded in fear.

I knew she wasn't afraid of me, but she was terrified of what I might do. The lengths I would go. I'd promised her freedom and I fucking meant it.

All the way.

"Please," she said instead, sagging forward with her mouth finding my chest again. She worked her way down in frantic, frenzied kisses. "Please."

She left a trail of flames. A fire in my gut. A burn across my flesh.

I grunted when she made it down to my hip bone on the left, and she followed the line of it with her tongue as she pushed my pants and underwear down to the middle of my thighs.

My cock sprang free and bobbed against my stomach.

Hard as fucking stone and set on possession.

"I want you so fucking bad, Little Star. Do you have any clue? Any idea the times I thought of you? Imagined you?"

"I hope as many times as I thought of you." It was a whimpered confession.

She leaned over and licked my head right over the slit before she returned those gorgeous eyes to me. "I can't believe I'm looking at you like this. On this day."

My chest tightened.

I wanted to suppress it. Shun what she was referring to. Like either one of us could forget that night.

A moan got free as she curled both her hands around the base of my dick, and I reached out and pressed my thumb between her plump, wet lips. I pushed it in and drew it out. "Are you going to fuck me with that sweet mouth?"

She stroked me once, from base to tip and back down again.

Pleasure built like a summer storm.

One fucking touch and this girl had me shaking where I knelt.

"Do you want me to?" It came out with a tremor of her soul, and the barest, smallest tease. "It is your birthday, after all."

I touched her face again, my voice a low growl. "Don't you dare do anything you don't want to do, Aster. Not now. Not ever."

Not with me.

Not with that bastard I was going to put in the ground.

"I have never stopped wanting you."

Then she was slipping her gorgeous lips around my cock and sucking me into the well of her mouth.

I nearly came with the feel of her. At the pleasure only she could bring. This girl who was everything.

"Fuck, Aster, baby...I love your mouth."

I could feel her smile around my length, then she licked up to my engorged head, sucked long and slow before she was consuming me all over again.

My hips jutted and jerked.

Bliss threatening to take me whole.

I was not going to last.

Not with her hot mouth and her sweet heart and the old dreams that could no longer be repressed.

"I can't believe I'm with you like this. Could die right here, baby. So good. So fucking good." It mumbled from my mouth on a slow slide as she sucked me up and down. She took me deeper and deeper with each pass until the tip of my cock was gliding to the back of her throat.

I grunted as she took me whole.

She stroked me in sync.

My hands were fists in her hair, guiding her harder. Faster. Deeper.

"Good girl." The affection fell from my lips. "You're perfect. So perfect."

I sat up high on my knees, my hips thrusting as she took me as far as she could, the girl close to gagging, and there was something about it that fully set me off.

The way she hummed and moaned, the reverberation vibrating me to the bones. It wound me straight to the point I was going to blow.

Pleasure raced my spine, my balls fucking tight.

She grabbed me by the ass with both hands and gave herself over. Let me lead this frantic rhythm.

I took her in long, deep strokes.

She urged me faster.

I split apart.

Prisoner to this girl's mouth and hands.

But it was her heart that had always fit me just right.

Aster whimpered as she swallowed around me while I sat there on my knees jerking.

Completely fucking shattered.

I choked a needy sound as I slipped out of her mouth then tucked myself back into my pants while Aster continued to kneel there, pressing her thighs together.

I saw the flash of a war in her eyes, the way a part of her wanted to run, escape what she should already know had been coming all along.

I had her scooped up and tossed to the couch so fast she yelped.

"Think you're going somewhere?"

Her eyes were wide and round as her gaze roamed over me where I stood hovering over her, while I took in the delicious sight of this girl writhing in need on my couch.

Her tongue stroked her lips that were still wet, and that was all it took.

I was hard again.

"I should." It sounded of submission. "I should go, Logan. I should leave this city before it hurts any more than it's already going to. Before I bring trouble to your door."

I tsked and trailed a fingertip over her knee. "I thought I told you that you're worth the trouble? Besides, did you really think I'd let you walk out that door without making you come?"

Her hips jutted from the couch in a needy plea.

"There's my girl."

My girl. My girl.

She'd know it soon.

I dropped back to my knees, and I grabbed her by the ankle and unzipped one of her boots.

Her breaths were shallow as I dragged it off. I turned to do the same to the other.

Both of us were held in this feeling in the air.

Dense.

Dark.

Desperate.

Different than the night when I'd touched her in her bedroom.

That had felt like a hallucination.

This?

This was a fucking promise.

"Logan." She whimpered that, a low sound in the back of her

throat as she lifted her ass from the couch. I pressed my face there, to the front of her leather pants over her pubic bone. I took her by the outside of both thighs when I did, and I spread her wide so I could run my nose over the length of the seam.

She jerked. "Please."

"What do you need?" It was a rough scrape against the heated air.

"You."

"When did you stop needing me?" My fingers moved, only they hesitated at the top button of her pants.

"Never. I never stopped."

I ripped the row of buttons open, and Aster mewled in anticipation as I dragged the tight material down her gorgeous legs.

Full hips and lush thighs.

I wound them off her feet, leaving her in her sweater and a matching gray satin thong.

She looked so perfect sitting there.

Her lips parted.

Her eyes wild.

Her heart hammering.

A fucking fantasy I'd long since forgotten to dream.

I pressed my finger to the little thatch where she was wet between her thighs.

"Even if you lied with your mouth, I'd know you want me, Little Star. Look how wet you are. You're drenched, aren't you?"

I ran my finger up and down, up and down, pressing the fabric deeper between her lips with each pass.

She rasped. Lifted her hips from the couch again. "You're teasing me."

"You deserve it, don't you think?" It was close to playful as I dipped the tip of my finger beneath the edge of her panties and dragged it along the sweet spot where her thigh kissed her pussy.

She gulped for air. "Is that what you want? To punish me?"

I pressed my nose to the spot my finger had been, my words a low breath. "No, Aster, I don't want to punish you. I want to give you the world. I want to chase down every dream you've ever had and give it

232 | A.L. JACKSON

to you. Kill everything that threatens it. I want to fuck you. I want to keep you. I want to feed you and love you and protect you. I want to live for you, Little Star."

Aster gasped, then her hips bucked high when I ripped her panties from her body. I had my mouth on her faster than she could protest. Before she could say the words I hated.

Thirty days.

Thirty days.

Fuck that.

Fuck Jarek.

Fuck her father.

I fucked her with my mouth, instead.

Drove my tongue deep into her cunt.

Aster fisted my hair in both hands. "Logan."

I licked her everywhere I could taste her. Tongue thrusting into her pussy before I lapped up to suck her throbbing clit into my mouth, scraping it with my teeth.

Aster moaned and jerked. "Please, Logan. Please. I want to feel you. All of you."

I edged back to look at her. "You want my cock, baby?"

Her head nodded frantically against the back of the couch.

"No. Not until you know you're truly mine. Not until I have you, heart, body, and soul. Not until you get that I'm not letting you go."

I dipped back down between her thighs, hoisting her up so I could lick between her cleft, tongue stroking her asshole because I was going to take that, too.

Aster was an earthquake in my hands. Vibrating. Shaking. A tremor that would bring down her walls.

I slipped higher until I was back to sucking at her needy clit, and she was begging me all over again.

I pushed two fingers deep into her body, rubbed her in that place that had her losing all sanity. I pressed down on her lower stomach at the same time.

"Oh god, Logan...how...I didn't think it was real...thought it was a dream."

"It's real, Little Star. It's you and me."

She came apart right then.

Beauty in my hands.

I led her through, as she tightened and quivered and floated toward the sky.

I held her there, whispering, "You're mine. You're mine."

I was going to keep saying it until she understood it.

She slumped down, gasping for breath.

I eased my fingers out of her, then sat up higher so I could kiss her mouth.

Soft and slow.

Tender.

Because I saw the panic in her gaze, rising up from that place that had been broken apart.

"Wait right there."

Pushing to standing, I moved into my bathroom where I started a bath in the massive tub because I was intent on taking care of this girl. On showing her what she deserved. Who she was and what she meant to me.

Maybe I shouldn't have been surprised that when I walked back out to get her, Aster Rose was gone. I knew she was afraid.

She had to learn to trust this.

To trust me.

And how would I ever fully trust her if she never stayed?

Chapter Twenty-Three

Aster

WHAT WAS I DOING? WHAT WAS I DOING?
I couldn't stop shaking as I scrubbed my face with cold water in my bathroom.

Every choice I made seemed to bring me closer to disaster. But I couldn't stop. Not when I was with Logan. Not when he was bringing it all to the surface.

The loss.

The grief.

The fear.

The hope.

The love I had to stop from raging on inside me.

Choking over a sob, I turned off the faucet and rubbed my face with a hand towel until it was almost raw, as if I could wash away every scar. Blot out every stain.

Or maybe find some way to bear a different name.

I suppressed a wail of agony that bubbled up in the towel.

Or maybe it was a war cry.

Tonight…tonight the shackles were too heavy and the only thing I wanted was to break free of them.

I dropped the towel and stared at my reflection in the dusky mirror.

My cheeks were red.

My lips swollen and bruised.

But my eyes were too wide. Too wild. Gone to a place where I shouldn't have let myself go.

To him.

I felt shattered.

Broken into a million pieces.

Pieces that I was never going to mend or reclaim because every touch he stole belonged to him.

Tears blurred my sight, and I stepped away and forced myself to focus on pulling on the night slip and a pair of new underwear considering mine were tattered on his floor. I was a fool to think covering myself would shield me from the hope that kept trying to sprout.

It was dangerous.

Dangerous to my heart.

Dangerous to the man that I loved.

But how could I stop it when he touched me that way? When he held me that way? When he looked at me as if I were a treasure?

I froze when I felt the shift in the air, the intensity that lapped, the energy a cloud that hazed common sense.

Logan appeared as if he'd been summoned. Vapor that'd become whole.

He towered behind me in the doorway of the bathroom, the man staring at me through the mirror where I faced away.

He wore the same expression I needed to hide from.

Feral, savage possession.

Bridled violence to be unleashed at any moment.

A veil of protection shimmering around him to reach out and cover me.

He took a step forward.

Warmth skated through the cold air. It curled down my spine like an illicit embrace.

Wrong. It was so wrong. So wrong that I moaned when he stepped even closer. He reached out, pulled my hair aside, and pressed his mouth to the spot where my shoulder met my neck.

"Do you think you can hide from me, Aster?"

He reached around to touch the star that dangled between my breasts.

"I think I should run from you. Before something happens we can't take back. Before it's too late."

"It was too late the moment you stepped foot in that basement."

"Logan."

Big hands banded around my waist, and he slowly turned me, his gaze fierce and unrelenting.

The scariest part was he already knew who he was dealing with. He wasn't going into this blind.

"You are worth it." His words were a crack in the dense air.

And I realized it then…he didn't care. He didn't care about the cost.

He would pay it all, but that was a consequence I would never survive.

Expression hard, he hoisted me up. A tiny peep of reserve whisked from my lips.

Still, I wrapped my legs around him with a breath of surrender, the same way as I did with my arms, the same way as my face pressed to his pulse that thudded and boomed.

I tried one more time. "We shouldn't do this."

His arms tightened around me. "My rules, Aster. My rules."

I clung to him as he carried me out of the guest room and through the apartment. He didn't slow until he was kicking his bedroom door shut and carrying me to his massive bed. He pulled the covers down and laid me in the middle.

My spirit clutched as he loomed over me at the side of his bed.

The man was so gorgeous he made it difficult to breathe. His profile sharp, every chiseled line powerful. Cut in stone. Harsh and hard.

But then he smiled. He smiled soft and slow as he reached out and fluttered his fingers along the curves of my face, and I could see all the way down to the boy who'd once dreamed so free.

"There. Right where you belong," he murmured.

I couldn't do anything but take his hand and press it to my cheek. "I always wished that."

"It was always the truth, Aster. We were always supposed to be together. We just got lost along the way. I mean, come on, look at me…" He stretched out his arms and cracked a giant smirk at that. He still was without a shirt, his chest wide and shoulders muscled, his waist trim and his abdomen packed with rippling strength. "Have you seen me? Like you could forget all of this."

His tease filled the air and sweet amusement had me biting down on my bottom lip, a lightness taking hold as he gazed down on me like he was looking at eternity.

"I never forgot."

His smile slowed, and he unbuttoned his pants and let them drop to the ground. He kicked them free of his ankles. He stood there in nothing but a pair of black underwear, and I swore, it had me blushing like the teenage girl I'd been when he'd first touched me.

Redness heated my cheeks, and I buried my face in the pillow, but not far enough that I couldn't peek out with one eye.

"You are so beautiful," I mumbled because I didn't know how not to give him that.

He climbed onto the bed and slipped under the covers. He pulled me against him, tucked my head to his chest, and gently stroked his fingers through my hair.

I was a fool for feeling so content.

Thirty days.

Thirty days.

I hated my life was a trap.

He shifted so he could press his mouth to the crown of my head.

"I missed you." He issued the words for the first time.

They flooded through my bloodstream like liquid.

Molten warmth.

Profound and sad and the bitter, ugly truth.

I curled in closer, and I whispered my lips across his ribs. "I missed you, too. So much."

And after this, I was only going to miss him more.

His arm tightened farther, and he pulled me so close I was almost draped across his chest. I could see the torment carved in the lines of his face when I peeked that direction.

"Tell me what it's been like." His brow twisted when he asked it.

I winced. "You don't want to go there."

"Maybe that is exactly where we should go, Aster. Maybe it's time."

"And what if it hurts too much?"

What if it destroyed us? What if it sent Logan to a place he could never come back from?

He pulled my leg over his waist. Every muscle in his body twitched. Bristling with strength. Flexing with greed.

He reached out and threaded his fingers through my hair, and he tipped my chin back with his thumb. "And what if we can't move on until we do?"

I hesitated for a moment, looking at this man who watched me as if it didn't matter what'd happened.

A promise that he'd hold it.

The grief and the pain.

I thought maybe he was wondering if it were possible I could hold his, too.

"Do you want to know what it was like, Logan?"

It was torment.

It was sickness.

It was chains.

It was floating through a vast nothingness that had no end.

But I could boil it down to one thing.

"It was lonely. It was living through an emptiness so deep and dark. A hollow vacancy that went on forever."

A sound of commiseration puffed from his nose as he held the side of my face. "Meaningless."

I dipped my head in a slight nod.

Malachite eyes roamed my face, though in the darkness, they'd come alive, the gold incandescent.

"What was it like for you?" I was scared to ask it. The times I'd wondered where he'd gone and what he'd done. If he'd ever looked back. If it was worth it.

"The same but different. Focused on what didn't matter. The money. The gambling." He hesitated for a beat before he grated, "I fucked about anything that walked…"

I cringed with his forwardness, but he was right, I needed this, too. His honesty when we'd had none of it.

His thumb brushed back and forth beneath my chin. "I was looking for a feeling, Aster. For one person who could spark that feeling inside me…even if it were only a mere fraction of what I'd felt with you." He wavered, his thick throat bobbing when he swallowed. His fingers sank deeper into my hair. "And it's not like there was anything wrong with any of them, nothing except none of them were you."

My heart squeezed in pain, the words shards when I pressed them from my lips, "While I lay beneath Jarek numb, wishing I could just disappear."

"I hate him." Rage howled through his body. Barely contained.

"So do I."

Logan ran his fingers from my shoulder and down my arm. Chills lifted, sweet, sweet dread. His hurt so thick. His voice was gravel when he spoke. "I can't believe you don't have his children."

Tears sprang in my eyes, and my throat tingled with the emotion that wanted to flood out. I fought to suppress it, to hold it in, giving him at least a piece of our truth. "Our housekeeper…she has a daughter who is a nurse practitioner. I meet her in a parking lot every three months, and she gives me a shot."

"Jarek doesn't know." It wasn't phrased as a question, but there were a million of them in his eyes.

Still, I choked over the idea. "No, Logan. He would…"

I trailed off, unable to express it.

Agony screamed through my body. Fists, boots, the grip of a gun.

Each blow came harder than the last, powerful enough to shatter bone, to shatter courage, to shatter sanity.

A cry tore free, torment and pain, torment and pain. I rocked, tried to hold myself, to protect.

The vile voice whispered like it could be a balm in my ear. "Don't cry, Aster. This is what was meant to be. You'll see. You'll see."

"I will never allow it, Logan. I will never put a child in the same position my father put me and my sister in. I will die first."

Shifting, Logan rolled us until I was on my back, and he was hovering over me. He planted his elbows on either side of my head to prop himself up, his wide chest shuddering.

Anguish.

Affliction.

Grief.

It was so heavy.

So absolute.

A chasm that was broken between us, where our hopes had fallen through and were smashed at the bottom.

I could barely handle the way his voice broke in sorrow when he asked, "Is that why? Is that why you did it?"

Green eyes roved over me as if they were searching for something to believe in when they'd lost all faith.

"Yes." It was the scrap of a sound that I pressed from my tongue. Sometimes a lie was nothing but compassion.

Logan recoiled like I'd driven a blade through his ribs. Misery wracked through my being.

Then his forehead dropped to mine on a pained gasp, and he was mumbling, "I'm sorry, I'm sorry," over and over again.

Agony cleaved through my spirit.

I tried to hold it. To keep it from cutting both of us in two.

"We were born into those lives," I managed.

"And I was supposed to take you from it. Together, we were supposed to find better lives."

In the dimness, my fingertips found the tattoo inscribed on his side. I didn't need to see it to know where it was, to remember what he'd written on himself like a brand.

"Who bought them, Logan?" My voice warbled with the question, as if maybe I could understand. My promise to my father had never been a real intention. But somehow, after everything, I needed to know.

The twin stones.

The reigning crown jewel.

Two stones that perfectly matched, their settings made of clasps that interconnected and made one matching stone. Each hung from rhodium necklaces.

Necklaces that had been passed down from my grandfather to my father.

Necklaces that fools had fought over for generations.

Necklaces that set together were said to be worth thirty million dollars, even though they could never be sold at auction. Their existence was a rumor that had been true, only sought by thieves and cheats and swindlers.

Necklaces that had cost us everything.

GREED.

Logan was the last known to have them in his possession.

He froze for the barest moment, the only movement the sticky awareness that skimmed the surface of his skin.

He averted his gaze when he grated, "You know I can't tell you that."

Tears blurred and burned.

I didn't know why it hurt so bad.

"When?" Sadness poured out.

Logan hesitated, warred, his teeth gritting when he forced out, "After I came for you. It was the only thing I had left."

"I did. I burned it all to the fucking ground, Aster, and you already know what happened when I got there. You were no longer mine."

"Your brother died the night you left me." It rushed out on a breath of sorrow. I didn't know the details.

It was the same night I'd barely survived myself.

Logan and I strewn across the earth.

Separated.

Cleaved in two.

His entire being wept. Obliterated pain reverberated through the low hung words when he rasped, "That night cost me everything."

"I hate it...I hate what this life has caused."

And I wanted to drown. Slip away and disappear. But Logan gathered me up in his arms and pressed a kiss to my mouth.

"Don't look back, Aster. Not right now. There are too many things between us we can't undo, and we have to focus on what we can change."

I worked to swallow the sorrow. I'd lived in the chains of agony for so long. Now they rattled. Clanged and clashed.

"What is the one thing that would turn your father against Jarek?" he pressed.

My father considered Jarek the son he'd never had. Dethroning him would take the greatest disloyalty.

I blinked through the hopelessness that wanted to enfold. "I'd need to prove he was stealing from him or keeping something from him that would hurt the family."

"And you believe he is?"

"I don't believe he's ever been truly loyal." My eyes fluttered over the intensity that rippled over Logan's face. "There's always been something there, Logan, something at odds with my family."

"I won't stop until I find out what that is." Logan paused, lost in thought. "That night, I think Jarek set me up. I've always believed the whole thing was a setup."

Hope blazed, burned against the helplessness. "I never believed you were the one responsible, Logan. He knew...I know he knew about us. He knew I was going to leave. But it will always be your word against Jarek's, and you know whose side my father is going to take. He truly thinks him a son."

"I will find a way."

"My sister is trying." I hadn't told him about it. I hadn't been sure what I could trust him with.

Logan frowned.

My tongue swept out to wet my dried lips. "There's a safe in Jarek's office at our house. I don't think he knew I saw that there's a fake bottom when he was slipping something in one time, and he always seems more secretive and on edge when he opens it. My gut tells me if there's something to find, we'll find it in there."

"Let me do it." He nearly flew off the bed.

I grabbed onto him like there might be a chance I would never have to let him go. "No, Logan, you can't go back there. It's a miracle my father agreed to this at all. If he catches wind of you digging into family matters…"

"He wants me dead." It almost sounded as if he were trying to make a joke, as if he hadn't stolen something that many fools had fallen for.

"The real miracle is you're not."

I wasn't laughing at all, my voice taking on a grim tone.

There was sorrow there. A confession. I didn't mean for Logan to see it, but I knew he did. The way his expression shifted and changed and took on new understanding.

He brushed his fingers through my hair.

Softly.

Gently.

An apology.

It was also riddled with an aching question. "When you first came here, you told me I'd left you without a choice."

His eyes roved over me as if he could sift out the answer.

My mind spun back to that day.

Weeping. Weeping. So much pain. My hand grasping at my father's. "Anything. Anything, Papa. Just promise me you'll spare him. Promise me, and I'll do what you demand."

"Maybe that statement was wrong, Logan…because I had a choice, but there was no other choice I could make." The admission clotted in my throat, emotion so thick I could hardly speak.

Logan tightened his hold, confusion and dread rushing from the words. "You told me once that we have to take the chance when it's presented to us and refuse the heartache when it's demanded of us."

I traced my fingertips over the thunder of his heart. Over the proof of life that beat at a constant, steady drum. The soft words tried to stick to my tongue when I let them go. "I did, Logan. I refused the heartache."

Because living in a world where he didn't exist had never been an option I was willing to entertain.

"Aster…"

"Please, Logan. Leave it at that. I can't do this. Not yet."

Logan pressed his forehead back to mine, his breaths drawn in pain. "You're never going back there, Aster."

"I know you want me to stay—"

"Do you want to stay? With me?" He cut me off.

"Logan." It was torture.

"Do you?" he demanded.

Tears slipped from the edges of my eyes and into my hair. "I've never wanted to be anywhere but by your side."

"Little Star." Logan's thumb ran the angle of my cheek.

"But I would never put you in the position—"

That time when he cut me off, he cut me off with a kiss. An earth-shattering kiss that rattled me to the core.

One that sank down deep into my bones.

Flooded cells and infiltrated marrow.

He kept himself propped on his hands and knees while he dipped down to capture my mouth, as his tongue stroked and his lips possessed.

He left a foot of space between us everywhere else.

My spirit wept in the middle of it.

Called out to his.

Begged for a way.

My hips did the same, jutting from the bed in a bid to meet with him.

He splayed his hand over my heart. Tension bound the air. A fierce intensity that refused to let me go. As if he'd called me there, and now that I'd arrived, neither of us could escape this connection that had haunted us since the day we'd met.

"Say it, Aster. Say it."

It didn't take a lot for the truth to scrape between my lips. "I'm yours."

Always.

Forever.

For just a little bit of time.

And still, it wasn't enough.

For a moment more, he kissed me, soft and slow, tender in this domination.

Then he heaved out a sigh of restraint before he slumped down onto the mattress on his side.

The man sent me a gentle smile when he pulled me against him, and he wrapped me in his arms so we were nose-to-nose, breath-to-breath.

I settled down to rest my head against the banging that rioted in his chest. My fingertips fluttered over the rest, exploring the divots and lines and dense, corded muscle. "Happy birthday, Logan."

He pressed his mouth to my temple. "Is it wrong if it feels almost as good?"

"No."

Because any day he was holding me? It was.

Chapter Twenty-Four

Logan

Los Angeles, Nineteen Years Old

LOGAN CHECKED TO MAKE SURE HE WAS ALONE IN THE OFFICE before he worked to open the carefully folded star that he'd found tucked between two books on his desk.

Seven, was all it said.

To him, it shouted a million things.

I miss you.

I need you.

You're worth every risk.

It's your birthday and I cannot wait to spend it with you.

Warm excitement dripped like honey into his bloodstream.

He couldn't wait to see her. Hold her.

Aster Rose had become the minutes that counted in his day.

The reason he would fight, steal, cheat—anything to find a way to set her free.

She was his soul's destination.

The three hours passed like oppression. Every second the building blocks of a fortress that endeavored to keep them apart.

He ran his thumb over the star he'd returned to his pocket.

Let it soothe.

When it was finally time, he all but sprinted out of the office, so eager to get to her that he could hardly think straight. He stepped out into the last vestiges of daylight and into the labyrinth at the back of the property. Glittering rays of light slanted in through the drooping branches of the trees that concealed the grounds in obscurity.

The ground below him was soft and damp, and with each step that he took his pulse beat harder.

Anticipation.

A newfound greed.

Aster Rose.

It was all he wanted.

He slinked under the cover of the trees in the direction of their meeting place, keeping low, angling down, his breaths coming shorter and shorter the closer he got.

It was then that he heard the voices.

One hard and condescending.

The other soft. The poetry of his heart.

"Is there a reason you're acting this way? You already belong to me, no?"

"Not if I have anything to say about it."

Hatred squeezed Logan's chest in a fist.

Keeping himself concealed, he peered over a hedge of shrubs.

Jarek Urso had Aster backed into a corner where she'd been following along the trail she'd taken from the house.

A riot of fury burst in every cell of his body.

A thirst to destroy.

To defend.

To fight for the one who he'd offer everything.

Jarek laughed a disgusting sound that rippled through the fading light. Arrogant and vile. The asshole was dressed in slacks and a button-down, his hair black, shaved on the sides and curly on top.

He was only a couple of years older than the two of them, though his overinflated ego made the prick think he was the ruler of this world.

The problem was, if this wedding happened, one day he would be.

"I think we both know you have absolutely nothing to say about it."

Jarek grabbed Aster's hand.

Jerking it free, she tried to back farther away. "Don't touch me."

Revulsion and terror twisted through her features.

Logan knew she was doing her best to remain brave. To stand her ground when some asshole thought he could have his way.

"You'd do well to learn from the start not to fight me."

"I'll die before I ever let you touch me."

Low laughter rolled from Jarek. "We'll see about that."

Without warning, Jarek flew forward, fisted a hand in her hair, and yanked her head to the side.

Aster shrieked in surprise.

In pain.

In fear.

Logan was on him before the bastard knew what hit him. He grabbed him by the shirt, spun him around, and slammed a fist into his pompous face.

In the back of his mind, Logan realized he'd likely sealed his fate.

Death's signature scrawled on the dotted line.

He didn't fucking care if it meant this girl might have the life she deserved.

Jarek's head snapped back, and blood spurted from his nose.

Howling, he bent in two.

A second later, he rebounded and came rushing at Logan. The prick hit him at full force, wrapping his arms around his waist and knocking both of them to the ground.

Jarek had the upper hand, straddling him as he let his fists fly.

One.

Two.

Three hits landed on Logan's face.

His jaw, his eye, his cheek.

Pain ruptured over his skin.

But Logan sensed it like fury.

Like a madness that would take him over.

He struggled to get his arms free where they were pinned under Jarek's legs, while Jarek landed another hit to his temple. "Do you have any idea who you just fucked with, you stupid cunt? You're dead."

Logan got his right arm free and grabbed Jarek by the wrist before he could land his next blow.

Logan twisted.

Hard.

"I'm dead? I don't think so, fucker."

Jarek wailed, bending to Logan's crushing fist. He slid off the side onto the ground, on his knees with his arm bent behind him.

Logan didn't let go as he climbed to his feet.

Logan kept Jarek's wrist at the harsh angle. Not quite hard enough to break it, but enough to feel like that was exactly what was happening.

Jarek tried to get loose, asshole sniveling when Logan tightened his hold, the words curling off his tongue in a rash of hot hatred. "I'm pretty sure that's going to be you when Aster's father finds out you tried to touch her before you're married. That's forbidden, isn't it? He'll have your balls strung up before he puts a bullet in your head, won't he?"

It was the one fucking saving grace in the whole mess. That tiny spec of humanity Aster's father possessed. It made Logan irate that once Aster was married, it gave this piece of shit the go ahead to do whatever the fuck he wanted with her.

Like some alliance gave this monster the right to touch on this beauty.

"She's mine. Mine to do with what I please, and I'll fuck her when I want."

Logan couldn't help it. Jarek's wrist snapped.

He screamed in agony.

A guard shouted in the distance. "Jarek?"

Jarek raged as he stumbled to his feet, protecting his arm against his chest. "You're dead."

Aster laughed a maniacal sound. "And my father will kill you. Logan has become invaluable to him. To the family. See what happens if you touch him."

She was reaching. Logan might have been an asset, but he didn't hold the position Jarek did.

Still, hatred flared in Jarek's eyes.

The guard suddenly broke through the foliage. It was a man named Toban who often accompanied Jarek when he visited the compound.

Toban's gun was drawn and pointed Logan's direction.

Aster stepped between them. "Put your gun down."

"What happened?" the man demanded instead.

"I fucking tripped." Jarek spat it in Logan's direction rather than at the guard.

He'd tripped, all right. Logan wished for a way to make sure he didn't get back up.

Toban's attention jumped between them. There was no missing the hostility that fizzed in the space.

Finally, he slowly lowered his gun while his eyes narrowed in concern. "Are you okay, Sir?"

"Just meet me at the car, Toban." Jarek never looked at the man since he was glaring at Logan.

Chaos spun through Logan's being. The urge to end it right there. Do or die.

Except he could feel terror radiating from Aster. Her sweet spirit crying out in horrified desperation, at the truth they would never be together if Logan touched him again, the truth that it might already be too late.

Toban hesitated. "Are you sure, Sir?"

"Yes."

Jarek stared Logan down while Toban retreated through the garden toward the front. A sneer curled his face while Logan stood there wanting to go back to tearing the asshole to shreds.

Aster spun and got in Jarek's face. "I want you to leave."

"I don't give a fuck what you want."

She pulled out her phone, all kinds of fierce bravery. "Fine. Then we'll take this up with my papa."

Jarek tried to bottle the fear that flashed through his expression, and his teeth gritted when he spat, "I'm leaving."

He started to walk, only he grabbed her with his other hand, dragging her close by the upper arm. "But don't think I'm finished with you."

It curled through the air.

Logan almost went for him again.

Jarek lifted an arrogant chin like there wasn't blood smeared down his face, stepped around Aster, and leaned in toward Logan as he passed, "Or you."

Then he disappeared into the shrubs.

Logan sagged.

Aster rushed for him, taking him by the hand and hauling him into their secluded spot. "Oh my god, are you hurt? That asshole."

"I'm fine." It was pure frustration.

Aster touched the bruises that were undoubtedly forming on his face. Tenderness wept from her fingertips.

Logan's raging heart slowed the barest fraction.

"Thank you," she whispered.

Logan met her eyes. "I would die for you, Aster Rose."

She took his hand, and her voice shifted to a plea. "I know. And that's why I'm asking you to live for me, Logan. There is no point in any of this if you're dead. We have to be careful. We have to be smart about it."

"I want to end him." Logan gave voice to the violent impulse that still boiled in his blood.

"No, Logan, we have to do this together, or neither of us will ever be free."

Logan exhaled a long, heavy breath, and he let his forehead drop to hers. "Is that what we're doing, Aster? Setting ourselves free?"

She ran her fingertips over a swollen spot on his jaw. "Yes, together."

"Whatever it takes." He murmured that as he held her gaze.

The air shifted as the last of the daylight drained away. Darkness wisped over the heavens to take its place.

"Yes," Aster whispered. Her lips were an inch from his, their noses touching, their spirits joined.

Logan's hands slipped around both sides of her neck, and he exhaled his greatest confession near her mouth. "I love you, Aster Rose. I love you so much."

He'd never said it before.

She gasped before her fingers curled in his shirt. "I thought I'd never get to experience it, Logan. The kind of love that makes you feel as if you're soaring. As if you're flying. But I do...I feel that love for you."

Logan gave on a groan, and he jerked her toward him and kissed her like he'd never kissed her before.

Desperately.

Madly.

Wholly.

His hand spread over the back of her head while his other took her by the hip and dragged her close. So close he could feel her soft curves pressed against the straining muscles of his body.

The kiss was hungry and impatient.

As impatient as her hands that worked under his shirt and the words that whispered from her lips. "Please, Logan. Please."

"What do you need, Little Star?"

"You. I need you. All of you. I need you with me. I need you standing beside me. I need you inside of me."

Logan moaned as they toppled to the soft ground. Their kiss grew more frantic as Logan wound himself between her legs.

Aster's hips rose to meet with him, rubbing, begging, her breaths shallow and her heart pounding so hard that he could feel it like a plea against his chest.

His hands rushed to feel her everywhere, her face, her breasts, riding up the outside of her bare leg and pushing up the skirt of her dress. In a frenzy, her hands fumbled with the button of his pants as he pulled her underwear aside.

She freed him, and they both were gasping for air when she had him poised at her center, the head of his cock pressed to the hot, needy flesh between her thighs.

He looked down at the girl who stared up at him. His lungs were close to failing.

"Are you sure?" he managed on a ragged breath.

She wrapped her hand around the back of his neck and lifted her face so their noses touched. "Take me."

He pushed into her, swift and deep.

She cried out as her body bowed from the damp earth. He covered it with a kiss, and Aster dug her blunted nails into his back, held onto him tight as she whimpered, "Take it all."

Maybe he should have been gentle, but he moved in frantic, urgent strokes, driving into her while she fought to meet him thrust for thrust.

Her fingers burrowed so deep he was sure she drew blood, the same as he knew he'd drawn hers.

He shifted so he could touch her, his fingers rubbing at her clit.

Their gasps filled the air as their devotion filled their hearts as he recklessly fucked her beneath the stars that never quite shined, though his little star would never dim.

She burned so bright he knew he'd been singed. Seared. Scarred by her light.

They came apart together, like the bonds that held them shattered. They soared and flew. Stumbled through a faraway paradise that only belonged to them.

They clung to each other as they floated through the aftershocks. They both searched for the missing air, their chests heaving with fractured juts as they clung to the other.

Then Logan choked out a shocked, affected breath.

Because he loved her. Loved her in a way that he hadn't believed possible.

She blinked up at him, her expression soft and awed. "Happy birthday, Logan."

He let go of another disbelieving shot of laughter as he pecked a tender kiss to her lips. "Best birthday ever."

Her demeanor shifted to worry. "How can you say that after what happened?"

Fingertips barely brushed over the welts on his face that he'd almost forgotten existed.

He edged back so he could meet her gaze. "Because I'm here, with you. And with you is the only place I want to be."

She cast him a soft smile that hit him like wonder. "That's the only thing I want in my life, Logan, is to find a way to be with you. I'll convince my father. Somehow, I will."

She offered it like an oath.

He took her hand and pressed her knuckles to his lips, then he tucked their joined fingers against his heart that battered in his chest. "We'll find a way, Aster. No matter what happens, I'll always find my way to you, Little Star. There is nothing in this world that could keep me away from you."

She cupped his cheek, her voice a low promise. "My North Star. My direction. My heart's destination."

He smiled down at her, then he gently resituated her clothing, glancing up at her when he did. "I'm sorry if I hurt you."

"You would never hurt me."

He sat up, tucked himself back into his pants, and shifted so he could lean against the building. He situated her between his legs and pulled her back to his chest. Then he dug into his pocket and pulled out the necklace he'd had hidden there, not saying anything as he leaned forward and slipped the chain around her neck and fastened the hook at the back.

He glanced over her shoulder at the little star charm that rested just above her cleavage. It glinted and shined in the bare light that seeped through the leaves of the trees.

She touched it, her voice a thin strand of surprise. "Logan. What's this?"

"Do you like it?" he whispered against her ear.

"I love it, but it's your birthday."

He pulled her closer, wrapped her up, and mumbled into the night, "And you, Aster Rose, are the only gift I want. My Little Star. Even if I can't see you, I'll know you're there, and I'll find my way to you."

∽

It was late when Logan pulled into the drive of the small house he shared with his brothers.

He was almost surprised to find both Trent and Jud's bikes parked beneath the carport since they spent most nights at the clubhouse. Nathan's bike sat on the other side of them in its normal spot.

He killed the engine and sat in the silence for a moment, gripping the steering wheel while a thousand emotions raged inside him.

Even with his face throbbing from the cuts and the blows, he couldn't remember a day in his life when he'd felt better.

When he'd felt more alive.

Logan knew tonight, he'd found his true purpose. He had to believe he'd been set on this path for a reason—that he was bound to collide with a girl who'd become his hope just like he'd become hers.

Like the two of them had been called to meet at this very time and place.

Their soul's destination.

Joy riding on his face, he climbed out of his car and strode up to the house.

He put his key into the lock of the side door and let himself into the kitchen. He almost stumbled when he walked in and found all three of his brothers sitting around the table drinking beers.

"Ah, there's the birthday boy," Jud said, lifting his bottle as Logan stepped farther into the kitchen and shut the door behind him.

Trent had been wearing what could have been construed as a smile until he focused in on Logan's face. He was out of his chair and on his feet in a flash. "What the fuck happened to you? Who did this?"

Trent was already halfway to the door, booted feet thudding with retaliation.

Fuck.

Logan hadn't anticipated an encounter with Trent. He'd figured he'd be able to slink into his room the way he did most nights, patch himself up, and no one would have been the wiser.

Jud got to his feet, too, hand in a fist around his bottle and murder written on his face. "Just need a name or two and Trent and I will be on our way."

"It's fine." A war went down inside of Logan. He had to be careful. Like Aster had said. He couldn't mess this up before he even figured out how he was going to get Aster out of there.

"It doesn't look fine to me." Concern moved through Nathan's expression, unease billowing from him in waves as he slowly stood from where he'd sat. "Are you okay, man?"

It was funny that Nathan was Trent's twin. They basically looked like replicas of the other in that kitchen, yet Nathan's vibe was the opposite. Anyone could see Nathan was the softest of the Lawson Brothers. Quiet and reserved. Working at a local hardware store. One-hundred-percent outside the business.

Logan had heard their father tell another Iron Owl that Nathan couldn't hack it.

That he was a pussy.

A weak link.

The way Logan saw it, Nathan was likely the bravest of them all. Standing his ground. Living his life right.

Logan forced himself to crack a smirk like the altercation hadn't been a big deal. "Yeah, stopped for gas on the way back. Couple of pricks thought they'd scored themselves an easy target."

"Looks like they scored to me," Trent spat.

"Nah, man. Fuckers got what was coming to them. Not to worry. It's all taken care of."

Logan silently swore one day that statement would be true.

Jud frowned, then laughed. "Well, shit, man, here we came to take you out. Show you the town for your birthday. Find you a sweet girl to sit on your lap. And you stroll in busted to shit."

Unease stirred.

He hated keeping secrets from his brothers, but there was no chance in hell he could dish about what was going down with Aster. The mess he'd found himself in, a mess he wanted more than life, the truth that he didn't want any other girl.

He only wanted her.

And if Trent found out he'd gone up against Jarek Urso?

Dude would lose his ever-lovin' mind.

"Honestly, a beer or two here with you guys sounds about right tonight."

"Hell, yeah." Jud squeezed his shoulder, strolled to the refrigerator, and pulled out another round. He passed one to each of them. Everyone twisted their caps and lifted them to the center of the kitchen.

"To our baby brother who's sure as hell not a baby anymore." Jud gave the toast.

Everyone tapped their bottles together. "To Logan. Happy birthday, man."

Logan smiled, joy seeping all the way through because this was the only thing that mattered.

His brothers.

Their devotion.

And his girl.

It was on him to make sure all of them were safe.

The four of them sat around drinking through the night. Talking shit. Reminiscing.

And Logan thought for the first time in a long, long time, since they'd all suffered the most brutal blow, witnessing their mom go down in cold blood, that maybe, just maybe, things might turn out right.

The dull haze of morning appeared at the windows when they finally called it. Trent hugged him tight and whispered, "Proud of you, Logan. So fuckin' proud. Stay smart, brother. Stay safe. Want the world for you."

Jud hugged him just as tight. "Happy birthday, little brother. You amaze me, you know. So damned smart. You're gonna own this whole fucking place. Can't wait to watch you do it."

Logan nodded. Emotion clotted in his throat, close to overflowing. "Thanks, man."

Jud stepped back and squeezed his shoulder. "Mean it."

The two of them rambled off to their rooms, and Nathan remained there, watching Logan from where he was leaned against the wall.

Logan roughed a hand through his hair. "Well, think I'm gonna hit it, too. It's late."

Nathan hesitated, then quietly said, "Know you're in deep, man."

Logan froze before he swiveled back to look at Trent's twin. "What are you talking about?"

Logan attempted to play it cool, to play it off, like he didn't have a clue. Like his limbs weren't shaking so hard the bones clanked.

"You think I don't see you come in here every night with that look on your face? You're fucking flyin', man. And you know I want that for you. For you to find that happiness. To get that love I see blazing in your eyes. But you can't do it with a Costa. You're gonna end up in the ground and put the rest of the family there, too."

Agitation gathered as sweat at the nape of his neck.

How the fuck did he know?

"I'm not." It tremored from his mouth.

Nathan sighed without any anger. "You are, man. I know you are. You can't wait to get there every day and you come home later and later every night. Not sure how Trent and Jud bought that bullshit you fed us when you walked through the door, but you and I both know it's exactly that—bullshit."

"Nathan…" He drew it out like a plea.

Nathan pushed from the wall and came toward Logan. He set a hand on his shoulder, looked him straight. "I'm just scared for you, Logan. I mean, I'm fucking terrified every day for all three of you. But what you're doing? An Owl moving in on a Costa? One who's already pledged to another? You're signing over your life, man."

A heavy sigh pilfered from Logan's lungs.

"You're right, Nathan. I'm signing over my life. Because that's exactly what she is. My life."

Chapter Twenty-Five

Aster

IT WAS SURREAL WAKING IN THE ARMS OF A MAN YOU WERE supposed to despise and know you'd never felt safer.

Knowing you'd never felt more alive than you did with the steady thrum of his heart beating against your ear.

The blankets were down around his waist, and every inch of him was bare except for his underwear. His skin was warm and smooth, glowing like bronze beneath the streams of early winter light that bloomed at the base of the window in a show of brilliant golds and blazing oranges.

His breaths were long and deep, even and sure, as sure as his arms that still held me the way they'd held me the entire night—as if they were created for me.

For security.

For surety.

A promise to see me through the night where he would continue to love me in the light.

I knew it.

I felt it in the way his pulse sped at my touch. In the way his chest expanded each time he looked at me. In the oaths that fell from his tongue. The way even in his sleep, he seemed aware, as if his body gravitated to each movement of mine.

Every shift, tucking me closer.

Each breath, drawing me nearer.

It terrified me. Terrified me because I couldn't fathom ripping myself away. Couldn't imagine having to leave this sanctuary that had come to feel like a home.

It was getting harder and harder to deny that I hadn't stumbled into where I belonged.

I knew I was falling.

Sinking.

Going under.

And I wasn't sure I'd ever break the surface again.

Just thinking it felt like a risk. For both of us. For our hearts and our minds and our physical safety.

It wasn't just our hearts on the line.

Jarek was a monster, and my father was the overlord of it all. But I'd seen his compassion before. Both times it had been given to me out of the love he held for me, as twisted as it was.

Hope sparked in that secret place I'd kept like a dream.

What if...what if my papa could understand? What if he really saw? In his harsh, traditional eyes, could love ever count?

I angled so I could peer up at Logan's face—so perfect I had to wonder if he were real. Wonder if I'd gotten so lost in the loneliness—in the vacancy—that I'd conjured it all.

That game.

The bet.

My plea.

This man, who through it all, through all the pain I had caused him, still promised to stand by me.

Fight for me.

As if he felt every question ripple beneath my skin, those stony green eyes blinked open in the rays of sunlight that streaked into his room. It was the gold flecks that glinted and flamed.

Severe and without shame.

He didn't hesitate. He pulled me on top of him until my chest was pressed to his. That was all it took for my breaths to jolt. For my heart to hammer and the blood to pound like chaos through my veins.

One touch from this man and I lit.

A needy rasp flooded from my mouth when I straddled him. The slip I wore bunched up high on my hips, and on instinct, I rubbed myself against him, his dick hard and huge where it was pressed against the thin fabric of my underwear.

Tiny pinpricks of bliss flickered. They spread like the splay of fingers around my waist and pooled low in my belly.

I whimpered a needy sound. Rocked over him again. I needed more because when it came to him, it would never be enough.

Logan curled a hand in my hair as he met me, his hips barely lifting from the mattress. He spread his other palm out over my bottom to guide me in the slow, seductive rhythm.

In the hazy, iridescent light, our bodies rolled.

Hitched and bucked. The sounds that wheezed from our mouths was close to silent, bated in the thickened, dense air.

It felt as if another chink had come loose somewhere. The reservations holding me together were steadily, quickly, resolutely breaking apart.

Soon, there would be no foundation.

Just a freefall with no chance of survival when we struck the bottom.

We'd hit it, I knew we would. But the falling felt so good.

The pleasure that built and buzzed.

The whooshing of the blood in my veins.

Logan held me by the back of the neck, our noses close to touching, though he didn't bring me any closer. He just rocked against me again and again while he watched me with this look that I knew would do both of us in.

"Logan," I finally whimpered. Needing more.

"What do you need, Little Star?"

"I need you."

He shifted us so his cock was no longer against where I needed him most, but his fingers were there instead, slipping beneath the edge of my underwear.

My walls clenched around his fingers when he drove them deep.

I moaned.

Whimpered.

Rode his hand.

Harder.

Rising up on my knees and grinding back down.

His hold tightened on the back of my neck. "Do you like it when I fuck you with my fingers, Aster? Wait until it's my cock. Do you remember what that was like? How I fit you?"

This time the moan that rolled up my throat was desperation.

"Please." My nails scratched at his chest, clawing for a way inside, while my mind raced with all the inevitabilities.

We were going to end up a broken pile of rubble.

Toppled stones. A house of ruin.

Logan flipped me onto my back.

I gasped when he shoved his underwear down and freed himself.

He fisted his shaft and ran his hand up his long, thick length.

My entire body arched from the bed. "Please."

He dropped down closer, and he rested on one forearm while he continued to stroke himself with the other. His mouth was at my ear. "I've wanted to hear you beg for so long."

"Is that what you want? To punish me?" I asked him the same thing I'd asked last night.

Because this was torture.

"No, Aster. I want to touch you. Please you. Make you feel the way only I can. I want to worship this body the way it deserves to be worshipped. Take you hard and soft and every way in between. Give you the pleasure only I can give." He gritted the words between clenched teeth.

"I'm going to send you to the stars, and then I'm going to keep you there because when I finally have you, I'm going to make you come again and again. And you'll beg me, Aster, I promise you, you'll beg me…but I will be more than happy to oblige. But not until you know. Until you understand. You are mine, Aster. Mine."

A needy whine rolled from my tongue.

Logan pulled the crotch of my underwear aside and pressed himself against my center.

I cried out at the tiniest flare of relief.

At the heated, hard, velvety flesh of his dick where he rubbed himself through my lips.

It was pure sensation overload.

I was slick and wet, and he slipped through me like a perfect, miraculous tease.

Friction and torture.

Friction and torture.

Because I wanted all of him. To let go.

The tip of his head was engorged, fat and throbbing, driving me mad where it hit me each time he rubbed it over my clit.

I met him, rocking and grasping and pitching in a bid to get closer.

"Logan." My nails scraped down his bare back. Pleasure raced and gathered. Tingles that swelled and spread.

Rising.

Lifting.

Taunting.

Ragged grunts tore up his throat, and he dropped his forehead against mine as his hips snapped in a frenzied play of pleasure.

Rutting and jerking.

Giving in his restraint.

"Aster, what you do to me. Do you understand? Do you have any idea what you mean?"

His thrusts became rigid, faster and harder.

Bliss built.

Built and built, until I broke.

Euphoria.

It scattered and blew as the orgasm ripped through my being. A shockwave that rushed like wildfire. Consuming. Destroying.

And still, it was not enough.

This man who was too much.

Overpowering.

Everything I'd ever wanted.

He thrust twice more before every muscle in his body bowed in ecstasy, and he was quick to push up the slip I wore.

He came on my lower belly, my name a low, searching moan. "Aster."

I writhed below it, aftershocks rocking me through, my hips still pleading.

My eyes grew wide when he swirled his fingers through the spill of his body then he pushed them back inside me. He drove them in slow and deep three times, then his mouth was at my ear, "Soon."

I was gasping when he withdrew then pushed off the bed. "Wait right there."

What the hell was he doing to me?

He strode for the bathroom, so freaking tall and wearing nothing but his underwear, his shoulders wide and his back rippling with taut, packed muscle. His ass was round and perfect, and I was sure this man was set on complete annihilation.

He glanced back at me from the doorway. "And don't even think about taking off, Aster. There's no use in hiding from me. I'll just come and find you."

"But what if I get you into trouble?" Old murmurings rocked loose, a tease and our heart's greatest secret.

Pure devotion was embedded in his smirk. "Do I look like the kind of guy who cares?"

Chapter Twenty-Six

Logan

TUESDAY MORNING, I WAS IN MY CLOSET GETTING READY so I could head into the office. I could hear Aster on the other side of the wall, moving around in the kitchen.

It brought a wistful smile to my mouth because I had to wonder if maybe I just felt her.

The energy that rippled through the air.

A soft, lulling whisper that tremored along the floors and climbed into my spirit.

I got the sense that I'd sank into who she was and had become a part of her being.

But it'd always been that way with us.

Held by an attraction that pulled and pressed and compelled.

A gravity that neither of us could resist.

Three days had passed since I'd dragged her into my room, and I hadn't let her go since.

During that time, I'd reminded her again and again that she was precious. A fucking treasure, but she still hadn't quite accepted what that meant.

Each night, I held her in her sleep. Held her through her fitful dreams that incited a fury inside me that I could barely keep restrained.

A fury that one day I would unleash on the monster who had the girl a prisoner to the type of nightmares I still didn't understand.

Where she'd sweat and whimper and beg to be set free.

I'd whisper in her ear that it was going to be alright. That I'd die before I let anyone get to her.

I knew that was part of her dread, too.

She believed her being here put me in danger.

It did.

I wasn't a fool.

It was a calculated risk.

And she was worth any cost.

I strode back through the bathroom and grabbed my suit jacket from where I had it draped on the back of a chair, and I headed out the door.

I slammed right into her presence.

Aster was barefoot by the island, slathering butter over a piece of toast. Her hair wild and pulled into a reckless knot on her head. A black sweatshirt draped off one delicious shoulder, and she wore these tight leggings that made her ass look juicy and ripe.

A growl got free.

I wanted to devour her.

Take her.

Hold her.

Keep her.

She felt me staring, the way she took a cautious peek my way and the sweet, bashful smile tweaked at the edge of her gorgeous mouth.

"Holy shit. I must have died and went to heaven because there's an angel in my kitchen."

I gave her the cheesiest line I could find because I wanted to see the blush rise to the surface of her skin. I ate up the way she fought the amusement as she stood there shifting on her cute little feet trying to act like I didn't affect her.

"You think you're some kind of charmer, huh?" Her teeth raked her bottom lip like she could hold in the giggle.

Fucking loved that sound.

Aster happy.

"The most charming there is. Have you even met me? I mean, I'm so charming, that's Prince to you." I let go of the same sort of tease I would have in a group of my favorite people. When I was playing outrageous because outrageous and carefree was the only way to keep myself from taking a swift trip to Los Angeles so I could go on a murder spree.

It was the one city Trent had made me swear an oath never to return to. An oath I'd broken because I'd promised this girl I would always find my way back to her.

I beat down any kind of bitterness that tried to sprout when I thought back to the devastation that return visit had spawned.

The hatred I'd held for years. The hurt. This agony that I'd thought would go on for the rest of my days.

I wondered when looking at her had stopped hurting quite so bad.

When a piece of me understood she'd had little choice, even when the woman was still keeping me protected from the details. But she was going to have to figure out I wanted to hold them all, no matter how ugly they might be.

Trust me, the way I needed to trust her.

Fully.

Wholly.

Without reservation or question.

Fuck, I wanted it. To look at her and never again think of what she'd done.

To never again feel the pain of the blade she'd driven into my back.

Right then, I shunned it all and edged up behind her. I wrapped my arms around her waist like it was the most natural thing in the world.

She leaned against me with a slight laugh, peering back at me from over her shoulder. "Prince, huh? Wow, someone sure thinks a lot of himself."

I rocked my erection against her ass because if Aster Rose was around, that shit was going to be hard. "Give me a couple minutes, and you'll be thinking a lot of me, too."

She giggled again, and I held her, my face pressed to the side of her neck, her face tipped up to mine. I rocked her there for a second, just relishing in the feel of what was always supposed to be.

Her phone pinged on the counter.

She jumped a little before she reached for it and read her text.

"Who is it?"

I'd already seen it, but I held the chuckle that wanted to rumble out.

She lifted her phone, though there was a frown knitting her face.

Tessa: Coffee (okay, fine, mimosas) at O'Malley's at noon! Half day shenanigans, baby. Your presence is required.

She pushed her phone aside like it might actually be a bomb.

"You don't want to go?" I rumbled it at her ear. "You don't need to worry...she's only half insane."

Aster almost caught onto the lightness, but I still felt the way she warred.

"What is it?" I asked, urging her closer to me.

I felt her eyes trace the message again, and her heart slugged a missing beat.

"You're afraid you don't belong?"

Her head shook. "No, Logan, I'm afraid to get attached."

So yeah, my spirit soared.

I pressed my mouth to the sweet spot behind her ear, my words low when I told her, "Get attached."

"I'm not sure that's a good idea."

"I think it's a fantastic idea."

Stepping away from her, I slung into my jacket and pressed a kiss to her cheek.

"I have to go. See you later, honey." I sent her the biggest smirking grin I could conjure.

Choking out a laugh, she shook her head. "You're ridiculous."

I took her by the chin. "I'll be whatever you want me to be, just as long as you know you are mine."

Because it was time both of us found a way to move on from the chains that had bound us to our pasts. Time to move on from the separation. Time to move on together.

∾∾

It was a little before two when I ducked out of my office and wound down the sidewalk in the direction of my favorite coffee shop that was half a block away. I inhaled a deep breath of the frozen, misty air, relaxing so I could let the jumble of numbers unwind where they were twisted in my brain as I strolled down the sidewalk.

I was fucking good at my job, but truth be told, it could be a bit of a drag, especially considering there were so many things I'd rather be doing right then.

Like exploring every inch of Aster's body. Or hell, just looking at her would do.

Hedge funds and investments and fucking obnoxious clients freaking out if their stocks dipped even the slightest amount after I'd already made them filthy rich had started to grate.

I thrived on the high-risk.

Excelled at the hazardous.

Took chances that paid off big and had my roster stuffed with millionaires who held grandiose ambitions of becoming billionaires.

For years, I'd even delved into the shady, dipping my fingers into places I never should have let them go.

It seemed no matter how much money people had, it was never enough.

It was what had driven me for years because I didn't see much sense in going after anything else.

Greed.

It was instinct.

It was justice.

It was taking for myself when the world had stolen what should have been mine.

And no, there wasn't a thing wrong with being comfortable, but there was something about it now that left a bitter taste in my mouth. Or maybe it was the singe of Aster's fingers when she'd tremble them over the word like it were inked in venom that had left me questioning everything.

The bell rang above me when I tossed open the café door, and the heavy aroma of fresh brew filled my nostrils.

My favorite times were bringing Gage here. We used to come often when I'd taken care of him in the evenings, the two of us a pair, the kid the one single pure thing I'd had in my life. It'd felt like something innocent to share. The one good thing I could give myself to, even if it'd stung.

It felt different today when I stepped inside, though, like so much had gone good, and I wasn't quite sure what to do with it. It was funny how I always wore a smile, but for the first time in a long-damned time, this one felt real.

I got in line, stepped forward when it was my turn, and tossed a casual hello at Sara whose smile lit up like seeing me was the highlight of her day. "Hey, there, stranger. Where have you been?" Her eyes narrowed in speculation as she took me in. "You look...different."

That smile filled my face. I guessed it was joy. "I feel different."

"Yeah?" Then she let go of a self-deprecating laugh as she punched in the same order I'd given her almost every day for the last three years. "Damn. Looks like I should have worked up the courage to ask you out sooner."

She peeked at me when she said it.

I pressed my card to the reader, a low chuckle riding out. "It probably was best you didn't."

"That bad, huh?"

"It was just *that* good with her."

She smiled this sweet, shy smile and nodded, like she completely got it. Which was exactly why I never would have touched her in the first place.

"There you go." She slid the cup my way.

"Thanks, Sara." I moved over to the counter so I could add some cream and sugar and a dose of that cocoa powder that Gage used to think was pixie dust.

I smiled some more as I sat at a small round table by the window and sipped at my coffee as I watched people meander by in the frosty day, loved that right now Aster was with some of the people who meant the most to me.

Eden, Salem, and Tessa were like sisters. A real kind of family that we'd been lucky to find. How desperately I wanted Aster to be a part of that, too.

I finished off my coffee and stood, tossed the cup into the recycle bin, and stepped out into the flurries that had started to fall. I headed back in the direction of my office, feeling so damned right that I didn't believe a thing could go wrong.

I slid my key into the lock at the front door of my office. My office manager was off today since her son had a half day at school, so I let myself into the empty waiting area.

I walked through it to my office at the back, and I pushed open the door to the darkened room.

The second I did, I felt it. A foul presence that hovered like a sickness. My pulse spiked, and I was wishing I hadn't left my gun in its locked case underneath the seat in my car.

I pushed my back up against the wall next to the door and inhaled a steeling breath, my brain calculating the best way to handle this. My hands twisted into fists as I prepared for a fight.

I reached in and flicked on the light, peeked into my office, then stumbled into the doorway as I took in the sight.

Rage crashed against the confines of my chest.

The place was trashed.

My desk was upturned, tossed on its side with all the drawers ripped open and dumped on the floor. Every chair in the room had been thrown in a heap on top of it.

The file cabinets had been ransacked. Papers strewn across the floor.

Three framed pictures had been torn from the walls and smashed on the ground.

My laptop was gone.

But none of that even mattered.

Only one thing did.

Aster.

Blood pounded through my veins. Sloshed and chugged and screamed for vengeance.

I swallowed down the bile that threatened to rise, and I dug my phone from my pocket and dialed Aster's number, flying back through the front door and out to where I'd parked my car in my reserved spot at the curb.

The whole time, I made that same promise all over again.

I took good care of what was mine.

My precious, perfect star.

And I would never let someone hurt her.

Not ever again.

Chapter Twenty-Seven

Aster

"**O**H MY GOD, TELL ME." TESSA WAVED WILDLY AT HERSELF as she tipped her head back and drained the rest of the mimosa from her champagne flute.

They were bottomless.

She'd obviously taken it as a challenge.

Or maybe she thought she was training for an Olympic sport.

God knew it was going to take some acrobatics to get her out of here.

We'd been at this pub for two hours, the group laughing and chatting, catching up. The children were spending the day with Mimi and Gretchen who were taking them to the park.

I took a small sip of my mimosa, this ridiculous redness flushing my cheeks while three pairs of eyes stared back at me in anxious anticipation.

I liked these women.

Too much.

Which was why it was really hard to sit there in their midst and pretend I was normal.

"There's not much to tell." There, that would appease them.

Tessa smacked her palm onto the table then pointed at me. "You are the worst liar in all the liars. Do you think I don't see this right here?"

Tessa leaned over the table and drew a big circle around my face.

Eden hid her laughter behind her soda water.

"And what's it saying, Tessa?" Salem's voice was droll, a low teasing with a shake of her head as she took a sip of her hot tea.

"Um, it's saying our beautiful Aster here has mad, crazy secrets, and they're really juicy, and it is her duty as our new BFF to dish the deets."

"I'm not sure how she's supposed to talk at all when you never stop." Salem sent me a wry grin as if to let me off the hook.

Tessa pressed her hand over her heart. "Don't make me kick you out of the Fantastic Foursome."

Eden groaned. "Fantastic Foursome? Really?"

"Um, hello, the Three Amigos just gained another amigo. This trio is now a quartet. That is unless I have to kick the rude one out."

Tessa sent Salem a pout.

Salem laughed, her black hair swishing around her shoulders. "I'd rather be rude than nosy."

"As long as Aster dishes, we'll be just fine," Tessa said. "So, let's hear it. Tell me what it's like with Logan. Is he wild in the sack, or does he not live up to the hype? Just how big is his dick because I accidentally saw Trent's once and Oh. My. God."

That time, I choked on my sip of mimosa. A stream of it dribbled out, and I swiped it with the back of my hand.

"Tessa." Eden scolded it like she was dealing with an unruly teenager.

"Um, what? Don't sit over there and act like you're complaining."

"If you're going to hang out with us, you're going to discover this one has zero filter." Salem jostled her shoulder into Tessa's.

"I'm getting the sense…" I drew out.

Tessa's blue eyes widened as if she'd been wronged. "Inquiring minds, people. Help a girl out."

"And that *help* she needs is a direct result of her going without an orgasm for five years. At least one she hasn't given herself." Salem quirked a pointed brow.

Tessa gasped in offense. "I do have a boyfriend, you know."

"Who is the biggest douchebag on the face of the planet, and whatever the size of his dick, it wouldn't matter because the moron has no clue what to do with it." Salem leaned toward me when she said it.

Apparently, this was a common topic of conversation.

"Karl's not that bad."

"Oh, he is that bad." Eden's nose curled in distaste.

"Wow, guys, wow. Where is the love?"

Eden giggled. "We're only saying this because of the love."

Tessa's demeanor shifted. "Then maybe you should support the decision I have to make."

Half of me felt like an outsider who'd stumbled into a private conversation, the other felt as if this was exactly where I belonged.

As if I'd been destined to be here, too. That North Star guiding me to my special place.

I couldn't help but be completely invested when Eden reached her hand over the table and took Tessa's. "I'm sorry. You know I didn't mean to put you on the spot like that. We just want better for you. We want you to find someone who deserves the amazing person you are, and that person is not Karl."

Tessa deflated the smallest amount, and she looked away, out into the booths that were mostly vacant at this time of hour.

"It's not that simple, and you know it." She wasn't looking at anyone when she let the whisper free.

"But fighting for what you need? Going after who and what brings you joy?" Eden squeezed her hand tighter. "You're right. It might not be simple, but it's worth it, even if it's messy."

"Life is always messy, especially when it comes to the things that mean the most to us." Salem's gaze shifted to me when she said it.

Unease quivered through me. It felt as if she were making a point to change the focus of the conversation.

I took a shaky sip of my mimosa and wondered why I'd agreed to this. I was a fool for trying to cling to what would never truly belong to me.

But I'd come...come because of Logan's encouragement. Because he wanted me to be a part of his life.

Because I wanted to be a part of it, too.

Hopelessness sank into my spirit when I thought of it. How hopeless all of this really was.

I mean, what was I thinking, sitting here as if I wouldn't be dragged back to Los Angeles, one way or another—either by Jarek or my father?

Consigned to a life I didn't want.

Eden and Tessa both noticed it, but it was Salem's words that held me like a trap. "I was from LA, you know."

It stalled me out, and a short breath left my lungs.

Intensity swirled through her expression, and the woman gazed across at me as if she were studying a familiar picture.

My hand was trembling so uncontrollably when I set the flute onto the table that the glass clattered against the wood, barely remaining upright.

I tried to breathe, to steady myself.

What the hell was this? An intervention? Were they stepping in to protect Logan from me? Would I blame them for doing it?

Wanting to protect him was the entire reason I had to guard myself from falling any further than I already had.

"You know me." I lifted my chin when I said it. I might as well face this head on.

Jud and Trent had most likely let their wives in on my identity, anyway. Why wouldn't they?

But somehow...somehow who I was felt like an ugly, dirty secret.

I almost choked on the lump that lifted in my throat. That was exactly what I felt like.

Dirty.

So much for the Fantastic Foursome. I really was a fool, looking for something I couldn't have.

"I do. I know your name," Salem said.

I wanted to melt. Disintegrate. Turn to vapor. Just disappear, whatever it took.

I looked around for an escape route.

Her head tilted to the side. "But you don't know me?"

The way she said it had me stilling, and I looked at her closer but without recognition.

"I don't…" I couldn't process what she was getting at.

"Carlo Molan. He was my husband."

Shock impaled me against the chair. The blood drained from my face, and a swell of lightheadedness set me off-kilter.

I knew his name although I'd never met him. Carlo Molan had been directly tied to my father. He'd disappeared years ago. I didn't know the details, how they worked together or what they shared because my father had kept me as ignorant of faces and names and places as he could.

He'd always shielded me like some kind of precious relic before he'd sent me barefoot and defenseless into a colosseum to be torn apart by raving wolves.

And this woman had come from where I had. My mind spun with possibility. She had a daughter and a child on the way and an amazing husband.

I couldn't process it.

"I didn't tell you that to make you uncomfortable, Aster." Salem leaned my direction. "I told you because I can see you sitting there feeling like you don't belong. Like you're not worth it. And when I came here, I was looking for a new beginning. A safe place when I was literally running for mine and my daughter's lives. And it took courage for me to get here. It was terrifying, but I knew I had no other choice than to fight for it."

She reached for me then, the same way as Eden had done to Tessa. She curled her hand over the top of mine.

Emotion shivered through my body.

Disquiet butting with the hope.

"And these people…these amazing people…" She glanced at Eden and Tessa before she turned back to me. "They came alongside me to help me do it. I was terrified of trusting them. Of letting them in. I'd believed there was no chance I could stay here. No chance I could make it our home. But I learned quickly it was where we belonged. I won't pretend like the journey of escaping that life was easy. But I know that I came here for a reason—for a purpose—and I know you have a purpose, too."

Her words infiltrated the cracks, sank inside to fill me up, and rose to thicken at the base of my throat.

Moisture filled my eyes. I fought it. Fought the tingling and the burn and the urge to reach for the three of them.

Eden touched my forearm, and her voice was soft when she spoke, "We know who you are, Aster, and it doesn't matter. We've all been in horrible situations. We've had to fight for our families and for their safety. For the love that found us here. And we want you to know we'll fight for yours, too."

Tears leaked free, hot and fast as they streaked down my cheeks. Frantically, I swiped them away. "I don't…"

Tessa leaned over so she could place her hand over Salem's who held me tight. Eden set hers on top.

"You do know."

It was a promise.

An oath.

I felt overcome. Overwhelmed. Held in this belonging.

"See…the Fantastic Foursome. Because you're all pretty fantastic. Even when you won't stop giving me crap about Karl." Tessa's words were light and soggy.

"Oh, we'll stop giving you crap when you kick Karl to the curb," Salem told her.

"Jerks." Still, Tessa smiled.

"You know you love us." Eden gave Tessa a goofy smile.

"Mad love. Mad, mad love." Tessa looked at me. "And we all have mad love for you, Aster. We knew it the second we saw you. The second we saw the way Logan looked at you and the way you looked at him."

"We're here for you, whatever you need," Eden promised. "Because life is so much better when you have friends on your side."

I choked over a small laugh, not sure how to handle their support.

"I just hate the idea of dragging Logan back into that world," I admitted.

Salem almost grinned as she sat back. "Those boys are no strangers to trouble. If you don't bring it, they're just going to find it somewhere else."

"Now that is the truth." Eden nodded.

"So *how* did you end up back here?" Tessa asked, voice full of the scandal.

I figured I might as well give it to her.

"Logan won me in a bet."

Eden choked on a shocked laugh, and Tessa's eyes widened with glee. "Shut your fucking face."

"It's the truth."

Incredulous laughter rolled from Salem, and she lifted her cup. "To destiny. However it brings us to where we belong."

"Is that what you think it is? Destiny?" My heart beat erratically.

My direction.

My destination.

My North Star.

"I think sometimes life cuts us a break and lands us exactly where we're supposed to be."

Her blue eyes gleamed with the promise.

That maybe…maybe that promise was mine.

And right then, I felt it sink in and take hold.

I used a napkin to dry the tracks of tears from my face. They all watched me as if they understood.

As if I weren't a burden or a threat.

In staunch, unflinching support.

"Now about Logan…" Tessa waggled her brows.

A giggle got free. "You know I haven't even slept with him since I got back here."

"Holy shit. That boy either is losing his touch or he is lost for you," Tessa said.

My phone rang from my purse before I got the chance to answer, and a grin split my face when I pulled it out to see Logan's name on the screen.

Affection billowed from my spirit.

There was no chance of stopping it.

"Ah, I see who's lost," Salem teased.

"I'll be right back." I waved my phone a little and stood from the chair so I could dip out of the bar to hear him. Or maybe I just wanted the privacy.

To confess to him what I could feel simmering all around.

This feeling that had bloomed. Or maybe it'd been seeded long ago, and these women had only fed and nourished it so it could grow.

"Hey," I rushed, my tone a little too excited when I finally stepped outside into the frigid cold and answered his call.

"Aster, where are you?" Panic steeled the sharp cut of Logan's voice.

Confusion knitted my brow. "I'm at O'Malley's with everyone. What's wrong?"

Ferocity radiated from Logan's being, palpable through the phone. Dread slithered down my spine, as cold as the snow that fell from gray, heavy clouds.

"Just stay put. I'm coming to get you."

I paced a couple steps down the sidewalk. My head was bowed in worry as I whispered, "What happened?"

Then the air froze in my lungs when I felt the ice-cold hand clamp around the back of my neck. Jarek squeezed tight, his voice a callus that scuffed in my ear. "Hang up the phone, Aster."

My hand shook.

Fear clouded my vision.

"Aster!" Logan shouted. "Do not fucking move. I will be right there."

"I said to hang up the phone. You should never have forgotten to do what I say. If you remember correctly, when you don't abide by my commands, it doesn't end well in your favor."

Horror skated across my skin in a slow slide of awareness. It spun with hatred and hurt and this rising determination.

A culmination of who I wanted to be.

Or maybe it was just who I had always been, and I was finally setting her free.

The one thing I knew for certain was I hated him.

I hated him.

The women's belief from inside filled me up like a fortress of fire.

Magnified the love that Logan had been pouring into me.

The truth that the fight was worth it.

I was worth it.

I'd known I was done with Jarek the morning I'd last spoken to him, but that was the moment I accepted I was finished with it all.

Jarek gripped me by the collar of my jacket and dragged me the few short steps down the sidewalk to an alleyway that broke between the two buildings. He shoved me into it.

I stumbled on the pitted, coarse pavement, trying to get my bearings.

My senses.

My strength.

I stood away from him, my shoulders heaving with the force of my haggard breaths.

With the force of the hope.

With the force of my love.

With the force of this conviction.

Jarek slowly spun me around. Every line in his face was contorted in disgust and loathing. As if I were the one who should be ashamed. It was a face that would be handsome if I didn't know every gruesome thought behind it.

"Such a whore. You've always been, haven't you? Fucking the one you don't belong to?" The look on his face intended to hurt. The bastard thought I should feel disgraced?

Screw him.

Lifting my chin, I hissed the words, "It seems you're mistaken, Jarek. I don't belong to you. Logan won me, remember? Because of your pathetic bet? Do you remember that? How pathetic you were in the basement? All those men who saw you sweating? Out of control?"

I let the insult wind into my voice. I knew it was a provocation. I knew it would piss him off.

I wanted to.

I wanted to make him feel small and tiny and insignificant.

The way he'd made me feel my entire life.

So I pushed it. "But don't worry. Logan has taken *good* care of me."

"You don't know a fucking thing," he spat as a furious hand cracked across my face.

The sharp sting burned my cheek, but I gritted my teeth and refused to cry out. Instead, I lifted my chin again and prepared to fight it out because I was finished being forced into who I didn't want to be.

That was right when a gun cocked at the back of Jarek's head.

The ground tremored beneath my feet.

My dark defender.

"The lady is right."

Logan's voice was a blade.

Chaos.

My soul's perfection.

Fury rustled through Jarek's being in a livid tremor. It rolled through him, head to toe.

Logan grabbed him by the back of the neck the same way as Jarek had grabbed me. He angled him down, bending him at the waist so Jarek was turned away from him.

Completely at his mercy.

I didn't feel a lot of that resonating from Logan right then.

Logan kept the gun pressed to the base of his skull as he leaned over him, and the warning ground from his mouth, "You can't stand losing, can you, Jarek? It's an embarrassment, you know, someone who can't accept that they've lost. That they're less. That what they want doesn't count because in the end, they don't count for anything."

It was cool, hard rage.

Logan's scorn was barely held in the violence I could almost visibly see illuminated on his flesh.

"But I guess you've always been a pussy, haven't you? Hitting a woman? She's right—you're pathetic."

Logan tsked like he was annoyed.

I heard it crack with the intent of death.

"She's for my pleasure." The words squeezed from between Jarek's clattering teeth. "She belongs to me, and she's coming home with me tonight. Where she belongs."

A sound of pain curled up my throat.

Malachite eyes flashed to me. A promise. He would destroy anyone who believed it. Anyone who intended it. I was his treasure, the same as he was mine.

Logan leaned down so he could let the derision cut at Jarek's ear. "For your pleasure? No. I give it to her, and she returns it to me. You were the ignorant fuck who wagered your wife. Now she belongs to me."

"You forget who I am." Jarek raged, though there was no chance of him breaking free of Logan's powerful hold.

Jarek's eyes latched onto me in a clawing of spite.

As if that would bring me to my senses.

Remind me of my place.

I wanted to spit in his face.

Fisting the back of his hair, Logan jerked his head higher.

Jarek writhed and flailed.

Logan leaned closer, and I could barely hear the words above the low strain of aggression. "No. I haven't forgotten. I haven't forgotten one single thing."

Logan hissed it near Jarek's ear. "Not one fucking thing. I think it's you who has forgotten what my family was bred to do. Our calling card. It was you who came to us when a job needed done. You'd do well to remember it."

"Fuck you, Logan. She's mine. She's always been. You'll see."

Logan tightened his hold. "You're desperate, Jarek. I can smell the stench of it coming off you. I bet you don't have anything left, do you? The way you came into that game like an arrogant prick? But I saw you sweating under it. What did you do, Jarek? Did you fuck up again? Lose it all? Only whose money was it you were gambling with this time?"

Jarek thrashed. "You have no fucking clue what you're talking about."

"I bet you went crawling back on your hands and knees to Aster's father like the neglected pup you are, didn't you? Did you beg him to take me out? Try to pin me as a threat to the family? It's funny, though, isn't it, that Aster is still here with me? He must finally be catching on to who you really are. Does he know you're here? Because the last I heard, you aren't supposed to be."

"Fuck you." Hot hatred spilled from Jarek's mouth. "It's you who took what he wants. Where is it?"

The stones?

That's what he was after?

Revulsion clawed at my insides.

Logan shoved him forward.

Jarek stumbled two steps before he tripped and landed on the ground. Logan moved to stand over him, and he kept the gun pointed his direction when he pressed his foot to Jarek's back to keep him pinned. "Nothing of mine is any concern of yours. Aster no longer belongs to you. My suggestion would be that you quickly drag your sorry ass back to LA before you can't."

Then Logan stretched his hand in my direction. "Come on, baby. Let's get out of here."

I reached for him.

He entwined our hands.

Energy raced.

Crackled with the connection.

He smiled at me. Soft and slow and knowing as he stepped over Jarek like he was trash.

My dark defender.

My soul's destination.

My North Star.

Chapter Twenty-Eight

Logan

ASTER THREADED HER FINGERS THROUGH MINE.

At her touch, warmth spread over my flesh and sank all the way to the marrow, thawing the freezing cold that had hardened my heart to stone.

All it'd taken was coming around the corner and finding Jarek's hands on her for my spirit to slip into depravity.

To sink into a hollow darkness where there was no conscience or remorse.

No mercy.

No grace.

But it was far from detached.

It'd felt like the loss and the hope and every regret I possessed had boiled down to that single point.

I wanted revenge.

I wanted retribution.

I wanted to set her free.

Her limbs shook harder and harder as I led her out of the alleyway and back onto the sidewalk. I could physically feel the adrenaline drain-ing from her body and shock sweeping in to take its place.

My teeth ground with restraint as I pulled her away from that piece of shit.

I had to focus on holding onto her so I wouldn't turn around and finish a job that should have been finished years ago.

Aggression seethed just below the surface of my skin, ripping and clawing for a way out, while this girl soothed it with only her touch.

Her breaths were shallow and hard, though her tongue seemed to be tied with a thousand things she wanted to say.

Once we got to O'Malley's door, I frantically turned her around, tipped up her chin, and searched her gorgeous face.

The panic I'd managed to contain in the alley spilled out. "Are you okay? He hit you. That bastard hit you."

Her head shook with the shock. "I'm not hurt. I'm fine. I'm fine."

I inhaled a desperate breath and pressed my forehead to hers. "I want to—"

Aster curled her hands in my jacket. "Just take me home, Logan. Just take me home."

Home.

I reached up and touched her face. "Okay, baby, I'll take you home."

I pulled Aster out of the way when the door suddenly flung open, and Salem and Eden stepped out. Confusion brought them to a quick stop when they saw me.

Tessa pushed out into the front of them, the girl all spastic with her arms flailing. "Aster, are you okay? It's been forever, and we were getting worried, and now…you're…here."

That time, she flung an arm at me. Tessa looked at me like I might be a hallucination.

I ran the pad of my thumb over the back of Aster's hand. "Seems I can't stay away from her."

Salem's brow was twisted, clearly calling bullshit.

She knew something was up.

"You all should head home." I issued it low.

Salem slipped her arms through Eden and Tessa's like she got it. "Tab is settled. We're out of here. Are you all good?"

I glanced at Aster and she looked back at me.

"I am now," Aster told her.

"Okay. Let us know if you need anything. Let's go, guys."

"Ahh, but mimosas…" Tessa slurred the whine and reached back for the pub's door while Salem held onto her other arm.

"Come on, miss drunky drunk. It's time to go."

"Thank you," I told Salem.

Eden stalled, clearly wanting to find out what was happening. I gave her a slight smile that promised I'd fill them in later.

I watched until the three of them climbed into their car and drove away, and I helped Aster into the front seat of mine and ran around to get into the driver's side. The urge to shift my car into gear and run the motherfucker down when Jarek staggered out from the alleyway was almost irresistible.

He glared at us.

I saw it there—he wasn't going down without a fight.

Aster's breath stalled out, her spirit whipping through the air, her chest beginning to jut as she suppressed the sobs that wracked from deep within her.

I took her hand. "He won't touch you."

Except he already had. I could have been too late.

Tears fell down her face. "Take me home."

I warred, watching out the windshield where Jarek climbed into a car and tore away.

"I want to end him, Aster."

"Please, take me home."

My gaze swept to her, to the fiery depths of those agate eyes.

Sparks and life.

There was something there. Something that hadn't been there before.

I pulled from the curb in a squeal of tires and torn intentions, flying toward my apartment before I did something that couldn't be undone.

The air in the cab thinned. Dense and dark and desperate.

Heart in my throat, I peeked at Aster. She itched on the leather seat. Her face was flushed from the cold, and her skin was hot from what had gone down in the alley.

She was so goddamn perfect in my eyes.

A dream.

My purpose.

My reason.

The only destination I'd ever wanted to seek.

"I'll do anything for you, Aster." It left me as a low threat.

The lengths I would go.

Fuck any consequence.

Tension bound. Built and shuddered and blew.

She writhed where she sat, angling to the side as her heart thundered in the space. "And I'll give you everything I have."

I wanted to possess it.

Take it.

My car skidded around the sharp turn I took, and I gunned it, flying down the road.

I glanced at her, and Aster stared back at me with giant, awestruck eyes.

Molten.

Lava that rushed, consuming every part of me in its path.

Energy pulsed.

A shockwave between us.

A coming storm that neither of us could avoid.

"Do you want it, Logan?" she asked, her voice a rough scrape that blistered over my skin as she reached out with her shaking hand and ran her fingertips down the edge of my face. "Do you want it?"

I gripped her hand and frantically pressed the back of it to my mouth. "I want it all, Aster. I never stopped."

I whipped into the drive of my building, quick to push the button to lift the gate.

The afternoon light dimmed to shadows when I drove into the basement and swung into my spot.

Killing the engine, I turned to face her. I did my best to keep my cool when possession burned a hole through the center of my chest. I framed her face with my hands and tugged her so close our lips nearly touched.

"I'm not ever fucking letting you go. Do you understand, Aster? Do you understand what that means?"

It came out low and thin, close to a warning.

Because I knew we were at a crossroads.

That once we got out of this car, nothing was going to be the same.

"I understand," she whispered.

The second she said it, I crushed my mouth to hers.

I kissed her like kissing her was a necessity.

Because it was.

My love for her a requisite.

Our tongues clashed, and our lips plucked and pulled in a bid of possession.

I kissed her until I was in pain.

Mind.

Body.

Soul.

Because loving someone this much?

It always fucking hurt.

Chapter Twenty-Nine

Aster

LOGAN WAS A CONTROLLED WINDSTORM. SEVERITY BUNCHED and bound his being, the man wrung like a tight cord.

A crated squall that whipped with energy and dark, dark light. Crackling and snapping where the barely contained gusts sparked.

He helped me out of the car, and he threaded his fingers through mine in a fierce hold as he led me to the elevator.

He said nothing as he punched in the code, though his touch said everything. I could feel the vibration of it. The compulsion that guided us to a better place.

The elevator sped toward the top floor, while our hearts panged and raced and our spirits thrashed in the confined space.

It felt as if it were lifting us to a new destiny. A destination that had once felt impossible.

But after today? After him?

I gulped as I looked at the rigid set of his jaw. This beautiful, beautiful man who'd changed it all.

One who'd given me a reason to look forward. One who reminded me I was brave. One who made me remember that I deserved a better life.

A life I wanted with him.

The elevator door swept open, and Logan tightened his hold as he led me to his door. He let us into the quivering silence that danced within his apartment. Afternoon light seeped through the windows, muted with the sky that was cast in dreary grays.

It held us in whispers of anticipation. In a need so severe it felt as if I were wading into a tortured paradise, where you'd either reach the stars or stumble into the pits of Hell.

Tension radiated with each step as Logan guided me across the room.

Malachite eyes melted to gold when he looked down at me. His tongue stroked over his plush bottom lip. "Little Star."

Just one glance, and he twisted me into a needy mess.

Or maybe that's what I'd been all along—a needy mess that only he could undo.

He pulled me into the duskiness of his bedroom. It was strewn in silvered hues and crystallized shadows. He shut and locked the door before he pressed me against the wall.

He planted both forearms on either side of my head, caging me in, consuming me with his presence.

His aura whipped and whirred, corruption and clove, talons that penetrated flesh and sank in to take hold.

Claws that would never let go.

I didn't want them to.

I wanted him to violate every part of me.

Keep me.

Wreck me.

Take me.

"Say it." His forehead dropped to mine, the action an achy plea. Harsh gusts of air wheezed from his lungs. "Say it."

I felt his teeth clench with the command. His heart pitch. His spirit possess.

"Logan," I whispered his name, overcome.

He angled back and hit me with the fierce strike of his eyes. "Say it, Aster. Say it and fucking mean it."

It didn't take much to understand what he meant.

What he needed.

And I knew it was my truth.

My spirit gave as my hands fisted the lapels of his jacket, and the words flooded from my mouth on my own plea. "I love you, Logan Lawson. I love you. I am yours. Today, tomorrow, and yesterday. Forever. I'm yours."

Logan growled.

Soul deep.

"Say it back," I whispered as my hands curled tighter. "Say it back."

Those eyes raced my face, tracing every inch. His voice became a rasp of conviction. "You think I don't love you, Aster Rose? You are the very meaning of it. You are the one who taught me what it meant."

He had me in his arms before my mind could catch up. His mouth captured mine. His kiss a bond.

He wound a hand into my hair as that kiss turned rash. Rugged and hard.

He stroked his tongue deep into my mouth to tangle with mine.

Passion stormed.

White hot.

Desperate.

An inferno that would lay us to waste, but I would be glad to live in the wake of his fire.

Logan tugged my body flush to his, friction and flames, and our heartbeats became frantic as new lifeblood beat through our veins.

A resurgence.

An awakening.

A dawning day where I'd stand in his light.

My dark, dark defender.

He climbed with me onto the center of his bed. He laid me there, and he hovered high as he gazed down.

"Say it again," I begged because I'd done without for too long.

A big palm cupped one side of my face, warm and right, and his rugged voice cracked with devotion. "I love you, Aster. I love you with this heart that had forgotten how to beat. Not until it remembered you. It belongs to you, Aster. All of it. It always has."

My fingertips stroked along the lines of his unforgettable face. "I think I've loved you since the moment I saw you. When I felt you at that doorway. It was the moment my heart came alive, and I've loved you every second since. I never stopped. Not once. Even when it hurt."

His expression deepened, understanding the confession for what it was.

My tongue swept across my lips as I pressed out the words. "Every day we were apart, I was missing a piece of myself, Logan. I was missing you. *You.*"

Grabbing my hand, he pressed my knuckles to his mouth. "Never look back, Aster. Never look back. From here, from this point on, it is you and me. Nothing else matters. Do you understand me?"

His voice grated with control, merciless in his demand. "Tell me you understand."

My throat grew thick. "Nothing else matters but you and me."

Logan jerked me up enough that he could peel off my jacket. "Fucking sublime. You in my bed. Where you belong. It's time, Aster. It's time."

It was all a seductive murmur that whispered from his full lips, and his eyes flashed to mine before a grunt left his mouth. "Everything I do, I'll do it for you."

My head spun, rushing to keep up with the tornado that was this man. The stark ferocity and the tender loyalty.

Everything.

Everything.

Leaning down, he kissed the edge of my mouth before he ran his lips along my jaw and up to my ear. "Now you know, Little Star. Now you know you're mine, and I'm not giving you back. Not this body or this heart or this mind. I'm going to own them all."

Shivers raced, and he continued his assault, kissing down my neck as he began to wind up my shirt. He edged back to his knees so he could pull it over my head.

My hair fell around my bare shoulders. Heat flushed, racing my skin as fast as his eyes devoured it.

With a growl, he tossed it to the floor. "A vision. You sitting there. Do you have any idea?"

He glided a single fingertip over the curve of my breast along the edge of my bra. "Fucking perfect, Aster Rose."

Logan dipped his thumb beneath the lace, and he watched my expression as he dragged his nail across my nipple.

Sensation streaked far and fast, and it tightened to the hardest peak.

I was already gasping, and he'd hardly touched me.

He gripped me by the back of the neck and dragged me forward for a kiss.

A kiss that altered reason.

One that changed standing.

One that shifted meaning.

Logan's mouth was hot, delirious fire. The darkest, deepest ocean. A magnificent sea where I would drown.

He kept flicking his thumb over my nipple while he kissed me into a messy puddle of desire, then he licked down my neck in a low, seductive path. He nibbled and sucked at my flesh as he went.

Down, down, down until he yanked the cup of my bra away and closed his mouth over my breast.

A tiny yelp escaped, and my fingers drove into the locks of his black, thick hair.

I held on tight as he sucked and licked and stroked me into a frenzy.

He reached around and flicked the snap to my bra so he could pull it all the way off.

"Logan...Logan...please." My body arched toward him. "Please."

"What do you need, Aster?"

"You. I've always needed you."

Since the day he'd brought the best part of me to life.

Severity flashed through his gaze. A possession so intense I felt it rumble the ground.

The man was an earthquake. A firestorm. Obliteration.

I wanted to be wrecked.

Destroyed.

For the two of us to reform and reshape as we rebuilt the pieces that had been littered between us.

I wanted to come alive under his hands and his body and his sweet, hardened heart that was littered with cracks.

I wanted to bleed into the secret places inside him that had always been reserved for me.

He slipped off the bed, and he tugged me by an ankle to the side.

"Logan." It was a wheeze, my hips bucking a fraction.

"I know what you need, Little Star. Don't worry, sweet girl, I'm going to give it to you."

He tugged off my boots. One then the other. They clunked to the floor.

The air shivered and flashed.

Logan's sexy grin went wicked when he leaned over me so he could reach the button of my jeans. He set it loose in the same second as he pressed his nose to my belly button.

He exhaled.

Flames lapped.

He kissed over my abdomen as he pulled down the zipper, whispering, "I'm going to give it to you, again and again and again. Forever, baby."

Tremors rocked through my body as he edged back so he could peel both my jeans and underwear down my legs. "Look at you, Little Star. Fucking glorious, the only one I can see."

I writhed, a naked, itching mess on his bed.

Those eyes grazed over every bare inch of my skin.

Etching.

Slaying.

Remembering.

"No one will ever touch you again, Aster. No one but me." He nudged my knees apart, and his jaw clenched tight when he drove two fingers deep into my body.

A moan rolled up my throat.

"I need you." I whimpered it as my hips jerked toward his touch.

"You have me, Aster. You just had to accept it."

Logan stepped back, and the man watched down on me as he stripped.

Slowly.

Purposefully.

He unwound from his jacket, then he ticked through the buttons of his shirt before he pulled it away to reveal those broad, muscled shoulders.

He toed out of his shoes and socks then undid his pants and stepped out of them before he shoved out of his underwear.

The man was a masterpiece.

Carved of an ethereal canvas.

Dark and wicked.

Beautiful and right.

My mouth went dry, and my insides shook.

"I'd forgotten what life looks like." The praise tremored from my tongue.

The man towered there as twilight seeped into the room, the barest rays of white illuminating his smooth skin. Every muscle in his body was rigid.

Flexing with strength.

"I never thought I'd want this way again, Logan. Not once. Not until I ended up here."

"Right where you belong."

I gulped.

I had almost forgotten.

Had almost forgotten what it felt like to be loved by this man.

The way he watched me.

All consuming.

Logan's expression deepened. Lines of fierce adoration. Strokes of grief and guilt. A shadowy mystery that glowed beneath absolute beauty. "I was a fool who didn't fight for you once, Aster. You need to know that won't happen again."

Joy sprang up from the vacant places. From the places I never thought could be filled.

Where old pain howled and promised I was nothing but a fool.

All while dread threatened to lay siege. To clot out the hope because neither of us knew what waited. How we would find the freedom to continue to love this way.

I wondered if he saw it, my fear, because he leaned over me and brushed his thumb across my jaw. The words left him on a rough promise, "You are worth the risk, Aster. Whatever it costs. I will fight for you. Live for you. Kill for you. Whatever it takes."

You are worth it.

You are worth it.

I didn't think I'd ever felt as cherished as I did then.

"Love me, Logan," I whispered desperately. "Love me, and don't you dare ever stop."

Logan's expression was sheer devastation as he slowly climbed up onto the bed.

Energy swelled.

Filled up the bare space that raged between us.

Logan's heart thundered.

Powerful and bold.

While mine wept and rejoiced.

I swore, right then, as he climbed to hover over me, that those two broken organs tangled and tied. Bound together to make something whole.

His expression churned through a million emotions.

Love.

Tenderness.

Joy.

Possession.

I traced my fingers along the contours of it like I could keep all of it for myself.

Like we could find it together.

Logan shifted so he could kiss over my fingertips, devoted and soft. Harsh and sweet.

"Aster Rose."

It was like coming home.

"This is it, Aster. After this, there is no letting you go. You're mine."

Throat thick, I gave him an erratic nod. "We fight together. We live together. We love forever."

Severity flashed through his expression.

The man took me in one rigid thrust.

It was close to a sob that tore from my throat when he filled me.

Tortured greed and frantic desperation.

My nails clawed at his back while pained pleasure shimmered behind my eyes.

It'd been so long.

So long.

"Mine," Logan rumbled where he pressed his face to my throat.

Logan's body consumed me, so big and full that the only thing I could breathe was him.

Grunting, Logan curled a hand in my hair, and he yanked it back farther so my throat was exposed and my chest arched from the bed to crush against his.

"Look at you, all spread out for me, this body taking me the way only you can. Fucking perfect, being in you."

He remained completely still as desire burned inside me.

"Logan." I whimpered it.

"What do you need, Little Star?"

"You, I've always needed you."

"You have me. Forever."

He kissed my throat before he pulled back and began to move.

He moved in slow, measured thrusts.

His gaze remained unrelenting, his stare ruthless as he took me.

He consumed me.

He claimed me.

He rebranded me with the mark of his body.

His lips were parted as he panted. He worked over me, all that lean, hewn muscle flexing in ripples of strength.

Every thrust was obsession.

Every drive possession.

Gasps wisped from my throat, and I lifted to meet him as I begged him for more.

His hips began to stroke faster.

Bliss prickled and teased, a whispered promise that hummed from the edges of eternity.

A song that grew louder.

A rhythm that climbed toward a crescendo.

He gathered me closer as if he could never possibly get me close enough. "You feel so good. So right. How's it possible, Little Star? How's it possible you do this to me? Do you have any idea? Did you know my perfection is you?"

He grunted it with each jut of his hips.

Friction flamed and fanned, and our hearts picked up the same rhythm as our bodies.

Jagged.

Erratic.

A desperate devotion that thrummed and churned and grew.

It built to a point where it was blinding.

Blind love.

Because there were no guarantees.

There were only our oaths and our truths.

It didn't matter what either of us had done in the past.

Not the scars or the betrayals or the grief.

It was only this.

Now.

So I fell into this man who I'd promised I'd never trust again.

A man who was supposed to be my enemy.

My lover.

My destination.

My North Star.

Pleasure blossomed in every cell.

It shivered and trembled and expanded.

It sizzled then blew.

Every molecule in my being ruptured.

There, beneath the savage loyalty that blazed in his eyes, I broke apart.

His name rasped from my lips. "Logan. Logan."

A moan of my spirit. A shattering of my soul.

I fractured into a million unrecognizable pieces. Splintered apart.

And I floated somewhere in that paradise that only existed in his hands.

Wave after wave.

Flood after flood.

Rapture.

Ecstasy.

Logan edged back and took me by both knees as he climbed onto his. He pounded into me, scoring himself deep.

Frantic.

Wild.

Unhinged.

I felt it when he came. When his bliss was mine. When every muscle in his gorgeous body tensed and he let go.

A guttural moan ripped up his throat as he poured into me.

Pleasure pulled every muscle in his chest and abdomen taut.

"Fuck, so good. So good," he muttered incoherently before he slumped forward.

Pants jetted from my mouth, and every fiber in my being vibrated with aftershocks.

It was a feeling that went bone deep.

Satisfaction.

Contentment.

This man who was everything.

How could I ever have believed otherwise?

Those arms wound around me, and his nose ran up my cheek until his mouth was at my ear. "You might be mine, but you, Little Star, own me."

Chapter Thirty

Logan

I BRUSHED THE HAIR FROM HER FACE AS SHE LAY ON HER SIDE staring at me.

Fire-agate eyes glowed in a slow simmer. Coals that glinted. This girl who'd thawed my frozen heart from the inside out.

I didn't think I'd felt more content, so at peace, than right then.

It might have been a bit illogical considering this girl was a boatload of trouble.

She'd always been.

And she'd always been worth it.

We floated in that peace, like we were back out under the stars in Los Angeles, held by their secret cover. By the sounds of the night and the whisper of the darkness.

I thought maybe our minds needed a minute to catch up to the place our spirits and bodies had gone, except I was sure my mind had known it all along.

There was a part of me that had to wonder if I'd always known we'd catch up to this day.

That it was always going to be her and me.

"There is no better place in this world than being in you," I finally murmured as I let my fingertips brush along the ridge of her mouth.

A breathy giggle rippled from between her swollen, plump lips, Aster's breath kissing my skin as she gazed at me like she'd found her way home. "And how do you know that, Logan Lawson? I'm pretty sure you haven't visited *every place.*"

She drew out the last, pure suggestion.

A tease and a play.

Joy rumbled in my spirit, and a grin split my face. Her mood was so light she might as well have been high. The girl was still soaring somewhere in the heavens where only this kind of pleasure could exist.

"Oh, I'm well-traveled." Playfulness weaved into my response.

"Is that so?"

"Yep. Been searching high and low for anything that could make me feel as good as you." My voice softened as I caressed my fingers down the edge of her face. "It was all made in vain because every road led back to you."

Those knowing eyes flashed. "Do you think it was inevitable, us ending up here? Together?"

My fingers slipped through hers, and I drew them to my mouth and murmured, "I think we should have been here all along."

"Why did you do it, Logan? Why did you go when I begged you not to?"

Sickness clawed at my insides at the thought of that night. That horrible night that had desolated and destroyed. The choice I'd made had been the domino that had begun to topple it all.

A cataclysmic fall.

Aster ruined.

Me ruined.

Our hope ruined.

Nathan ruined.

I struggled to breathe, and the blood thickened in my veins, slogging with regret. My thumb traced the apple of her cheek and ran beneath the hollow of her eye. "I thought it was my only chance to win your father over. A way to provide for us. For our family. I thought it was my only chance to prove to him that I could be good enough."

Her voice grew hoarse. "You were always good enough for me."

"But not for him. I never would have been."

She touched my bottom lip with all four fingertips. A tinge of sadness laced with the softness in her tone. "You still won't be."

"I know. But this time, I don't give a fuck."

Dread slipped into her expression. An ice-cold slick that made her shiver. I ran my hand over the chills.

"What matters is what you want, Aster, and whatever that is, that is what I'm going to fight for. We do it together."

Then I let a grin fill my face. "Unless what you want is to leave me, and well, I think we already established that's not going to happen."

I yanked her toward me. Aster squealed, and a thrill filled up my smile as I got that sweet, naked body tucked against mine. I pressed my lips to the top of her head. "I'm keeping you."

Aster laughed and sank deeper into my hold. Then she sighed as she curled into my chest, her voice twisting into a wisp. "I used to dream of it, Logan, of you coming back, storming the castle and whisking me away. And I never wanted to be weak, to need a hero, but I never could find my way out of those caged walls. I remained a prisoner, without escape, until you."

Affection tightened my chest. "You're the one who chose to take a stand, Aster. The one who decided it was time to fight. I was the fool who dropped you at that airport, thinking you'd leave me again. You're the one who was brave. The one who looked for a different solution."

"And I found it in you."

I edged back to meet her gaze. "Because we were supposed to do this together."

She pressed her lips against my raging heart. "You are the end of every road."

Her words resonated. All the way back to the nights when I'd held her like a secret. "I will always find my way back to you," I finished.

"We just took the twisted route." I felt her smile against my skin when she said it.

I rubbed my hand down her back. "A very twisted, fucked up route."

She burrowed in closer. "I wish I would have been stronger."

Pain squeezed my spirit in a gutting fist because I heard in her voice what she was referring to.

It was a loss that tasted sour on my tongue.

One I doubted would ever stop hurting.

One that a part of me would forever hate her for.

"It kills me that you made that choice. That you felt like you had to." I could barely grind out the words. I had to hold back the bitterness that still coiled inside.

Hot tears seeped onto my chest, and a sob suddenly hitched in her throat.

Regret slammed me. The truth was, I didn't have a clue what she'd been through. The desperation she'd felt. Right then, I knew her regrets might be as great as mine.

I rushed to shift her, tipped up her chin, and forced her to look at me. My thumb gathered as much moisture as I could. "Please don't cry, Aster."

Her eyes were wide. So wide that I could see all the way down to a void that radiated from within, where ghosts haunted, and wraiths foraged for the weak. "If I could go back, Logan, if I could go back and change it all. Stop you from leaving that night—"

She choked on the agony that poured from her mouth.

I grappled to get her closer, and my hold tightened on her face. My voice dipped with emphasis. "I thought we just said we were never looking back?"

Fat droplets escaped the edges of her eyes and slipped down her cheeks. An edge of hysteria screamed through her body.

Sorrow a stampede that stormed her spirit.

Her fingers dragged over my shoulder and down my arm, like she was trying to get me to understand. To see. "There's a piece of my heart that will always remain there, Logan. Broken and lost." Another sob ripped from her, and she pressed a hand to her hemorrhaging chest.

"And I don't want to leave it behind or forget it. I won't ever forget it. I won't."

Misery clutched and bound and tied us tighter than we'd ever been.

Wrapped our spirits and traipsed through our minds.

So much loss.

I dove for her, my arms fierce around her, pulling her as close to my chest as I could. My nose pressed into her hair and the words fumbled in a litany of our sins. "I'm sorry, Aster. I'm so fucking sorry."

My heart heaved with the velocity of our mistakes.

With the circumstances that I'd tried to control but had failed.

Her head shook, and she climbed up to straddle me, and I shifted all the way onto my back. My hands shot to her waist.

She was so damned gorgeous as she looked down on me.

Dark brown hair wild around her face. Her throat still trembled with the silent cries that twisted her mouth.

But I thought maybe—maybe a piece of her heart had been freed.

"I love you, Aster. Through it all, I've loved you."

Her tongue swept over her soggy lips. "And I'm terrified that my love for you is going to ruin us both in the end. That my being here…"

I flew up to sitting. I had one hand wound in her hair and the other linked around her waist. The words rushed out with a curl of severity. "This time, we're not giving up anything, Aster. We're not sacrificing or yielding or surrendering. We're taking what's ours."

This was the greed I was giving into.

And I wanted it all.

The sheet was twisted around her legs, and every inch of her exposed skin was bare.

Her heart beat at a ragged sprint.

Wrapping me whole.

Her head tilted to the side when she touched my face. "No surrendering."

My guts clenched.

Clenched with want.

With need.

With this devotion that made me weak in the knees.

She pushed me onto my back, and she stared down at me like she was searing this moment into her mind.

Her eyelids dropped closed as she savored it.

Then she dove forward, the oath frenzied when she whispered, "We're taking what's ours."

She kissed me hard, with a devotion that singed across my skin and embedded into my bones.

It was dizzying, being with her like this. Fully freed. Just her and me. Lost to each other. To the truth that we were where we were always supposed to be.

All it took was a brush from her and I was hard again.

She felt it, and a needy gasp raked from her lungs.

Desire filled her being and glimmered from her skin.

Aster pushed up onto her knees, fisted my dick, and aligned me with her pussy.

She plunged down.

Took all of me in.

Body and fucking soul.

My hands shot to her hips. "Shit. Aster. Yes. Do you have any idea how you feel?"

A wispy, dazed laugh ripped through the air. "I hope half as good as you feel to me."

She began to move, and I held her by the waist while the girl worked me over.

She glided up and down on my shaft. Her walls clutching my cock in a fist, and her tits bouncing with each pitch of her body.

Bliss.

Bliss.

Bliss.

I shot upright so I could get to that mouth, kissing her hard and wild while she rode me in her own form of possession. Writing herself on my being.

But she was already there.

Greed.

She just hadn't fucking known it.

I rubbed my thumb on her clit as I kissed down her throat.

I felt her wind, the sensation grow, her body burning up as the pleasure gathered quick. Two strokes later, an orgasm tore through her, head to toe.

Her pussy throbbed and squeezed as she moaned my name.

"I told you that you would be mine, Aster Rose. I told you I was going to own this body. That I was going to fill you up and take you over. This body belongs to me."

I went back to stroking her clit while her nails scratched and clawed at my shoulders.

She was feral.

Wild.

"Oh…Logan…please…I don't think…"

"Don't think, Aster. Let go. Give it to me. Everything you have."

That time, when the second orgasm hit her, she cried out, and the sound of her pleasure banged against the walls.

I came with a rush, holding her by the inside of the thighs to press her down onto me while my cock throbbed and pulsed.

A bomb of pleasure detonated.

Blinding as it blazed through my being.

Paradise.

My arms tightened around her as we both came down.

As we gasped and panted.

I edged back, and the girl smiled at me in this way that pierced me all the way through. I leaned forward and gave her the sloppiest kiss. She laughed and wound her arms around my neck.

"I love you," she murmured at the thrumming point of my pulse.

I held her as close as I could. "You are the meaning of it, Little Star."

I jolted when my phone rang from the pocket of my jacket. I didn't let her go as I scooted to the edge of the bed. I banded my arm around her waist to keep her against me as I leaned over so I could dig for it.

She giggled and held on tighter. "You can let me go, you know."

"Nope, I can't. You're stuck with me now."

My smile was too big.

She touched it like she felt the impact of it, too.

I glanced at the screen.

Dean.

My heart climbed into my throat, and anticipation beat a frenzied path through my veins.

Accepting the call, I pressed my phone to my ear. "Dean, what do you have?"

I didn't waste any time with pleasantries.

"It might be nothing, but you said you wanted everything and anything."

I could feel the worry travel through Aster's body. I wound my arm tighter in a silent show of support.

My brave girl who'd only needed someone to remind her of who she was.

Of what she deserved.

"I do. Anything that could possibly be of use."

"Jarek Urso has a pseudo…found the connection a few days ago. Jack Werner. It didn't look like there was much associated with it. A checking account and a couple rental properties."

I didn't realize my teeth were grinding in restraint until Aster started running her fingers down my spine to soothe me.

"And?" I pressed.

"I dug deeper into it and found some flight records from this last summer. At least four trips to Russia. It might be nothing, but it seemed worth mentioning."

Blood thickened and stormed.

"It's definitely worth mentioning. Do you know who he visited while there?"

"That I haven't been able to uncover."

"Keep digging," I told him.

Ending the call, I tossed my phone to the mattress.

I edged back so I could look at Aster, my hands vises that curled around her waist like I could keep her from floating away. "Does your father have business in Russia?"

I only knew what I'd known then—there were no alliances.

Only enemies.

Worry crept across her face. She blinked as she processed. "No. I don't think so."

"Would he send Jarek there for any reason?"

Disconcerted, she swallowed. "I can't believe that he would. I think I would at least know that. This last summer, Jarek was supposed to be traveling to New York. As far as I knew, he was in charge of facilitating a new shipment route."

But her father hadn't exactly been forthright with her over the years, either.

Acting like he was protecting her from his bullshit when she'd merely been a bartering chip.

Hope blazed like a beacon in her eyes. "I need to tell my father."

"I know you're anxious, Aster. I am, too. The thing I want most in this world is to set you free of his power. But we need to wait until we have more. Until we have something solid and substantial to prove Jarek's disloyalty. If we do it too soon, it's only going to give Jarek time to cover his tracks."

Aster deflated, resignation thick. Then she nodded and blew out a strained breath. "I know…I just want this to be over."

"Soon, Aster."

"What happened earlier today when you called? Did you know he was coming for me? I can't believe he went against a direct order from my father."

"I left my office for about an hour. When I got back, it'd been ransacked. Place destroyed. They took my laptop."

That was what unsettled me most.

It'd felt…purposed.

Like they were searching.

The piece of shit would have to search for the rest of his life.

Aster choked. Fear echoed from her depths. From the dark places I wondered if she'd ever fully allow me to go. "He's coming to his end, Logan. He thinks we're playing him a fool, and there is nothing that he cares about more than his pride."

"That's exactly what we're doing, Aster. We're playing him the fool because that is what he is."

And if the fucker came anywhere near her again? He *would* meet his end.

My palm splayed over the side of her head, and my fingers weaved into her hair. "We almost have him, Aster. I can feel it. We just need a little time. And during then, I don't want you out anywhere without me. Do you understand?"

"Logan—"

I cut her off with an anguished kiss.

Praying she would get it. What she meant to me. The terror I possessed at the thought of her being harmed.

Slowing it, I dropped my forehead to hers. "Please, Aster, I couldn't bear it if something happened to you."

Desperation fueled her voice. "I can't remain a prisoner to him any longer, Logan. I won't."

My thumb stroked her chin. "No, Little Star, you are no prisoner. You are free in me."

Chapter Thirty-One

Aster

Recklessly in love…

MY SWEET, WONDERFUL SECRET.
My defender.
My lover.

My North Star.

My beautiful boy who crash-landed in a foreign land where he didn't belong.

Maybe it was a rescue mission. Your descent into enemy lines to rescue a prisoner who was being held against her will.

But was I really an outlander if I had been born within the confines of those walls? If that tainted blood was what supplied my life?

But somewhere along the way, it was you who became the supplier. The lifebeat that pounded within me.

You stood for me. Fought for me. Then you loved me beneath the expanse of hidden stars.

The very next day, I crept into my papa's office, my knees knocking but my chin lifted high. "I won't marry Jarek, Papa, I won't," I'd said.

Papa scoffed, barely glancing my way as he studied the paper in his hand. "Do not start, Aster. You know your purpose. Your role in this family. You will honor it."

"He's a bad man." It came like supplication.

Papa's brow furled. "We are all bad men, mia vita, but Jarek Urso will respect you. Care for you. Protect you and this family. And one day, when your uncle Antonio and I are gone from this world, he will take the place as the head of this family, and you will sit at his side."

I took a frantic step forward. "No, Papa, not all are bad."

The air had shivered as he paused, and he turned to look at me with a face made of stone but with eyes that understood. "Your head has always been full of whimsy, Aster, but Jarek Urso is your fate. I pray you do not act so foolishly that I will have to do something that you and I will both regret."

That regret was already written in the lines of his expression.

Telling.

A warning.

He told no lies.

I ran from him then.

I should have run away, but instead, I ran to you.

I hid with you.

I wrote you a thousand stars and loved you a million times.

In secret.

In the shadows.

In the rain and in the office.

You gave me your mouth in the library, and I gave you mine beneath your desk.

You took me on the counter in the bathroom and against the wall on the side of the house.

Reckless.

Reckless.

We didn't care.

Not when it was the only thing that mattered.

But it was in our sacred spot when I told you.

"I'm pregnant." I was terrified saying it would make it true.

But I'd known it was true. I hadn't bled in three months.

You froze for a moment before you had me pinned against the grass.

You smiled this brilliant smile that shattered the sky and sent the stars soaring higher than where they hung.

Our own constellation.

"Are you sure?" you'd urged.

I gulped and nodded. "I took two tests."

"Aster." It was a rasp of awe, and you pulled me into your arms, so tight I didn't know how either of us could breathe.

"Aren't you angry?"

"How could I be angry?"

Manic laughter had bubbled from my mouth. "Because this is going to cause more trouble than either of us have the ability to deal with, Logan. Because I'm a Costa princess and you're an Iron Owl. Because I'm not even supposed to talk to you. Because I am pledged to another man."

Because my father will kill you.

That was the one I couldn't speak.

"We'll find a way," you'd promised. "We'll find a way. I'm going to get you out of this place, Aster, if it's the last thing I do."

And that was the promise I was terrified of coming true…

Chapter Thirty-Two

Aster

THE NEXT TWO WEEKS PASSED IN A BLUR.

It was easy to do when I'd been living in Logan, and he'd been living in me.

He'd go into the office during the day, and I'd stay in because he was right—it wasn't worth risking it—not until we had proof and we could finally bring this to an end.

Plus, it'd given me time to plot out what I would say to my father. How I would free myself of the chains he'd kept locked around my wrists. I'd written for days, filled journals full of every thought and shaped them into stars.

I'd poured out every dream and every fear. I'd built my courage with each word and my case with each point.

One way or another, I would make my father understand.

He would see me.

See me as a person.

A human being.

As his daughter.

As someone who was going to stand for herself.

In the evening, Logan would come striding through the door.

A vision.

Fierce and perfect and the most gorgeous thing I'd ever seen.

He'd be wearing that smile that promised I was in trouble, then he'd toss off his jacket, and it was on.

The two of us were nothing but desperate hands, pleading bodies, and unrelenting need.

Insatiable.

I loved it. I loved the way he loved me.

As if I was precious.

As if I was a treasure.

But oh god was he ruthless while he was doing it.

The man wasn't shy to take what he wanted.

Rough and hard and demanding.

"Girl, you should see your face right now. Red as a tomato. I know what you're over there dreaming about. Mmhmm."

Gretchen's voice snapped me out of the daydream I'd gotten lost in while I was wrapping Christmas gifts at the island.

Christmas was only four days away. It was the first time since I was a child that I was excited for it. There was a buzz in my blood that whispered of love and grace and faith.

That I was a part of something that mattered.

I sent her a soft scowl. "I have no idea what you're talking about."

Gretchen scuttled into the kitchen. "Oh, I think you do. That man has been eating you alive for weeks. I don't know how you're walking."

Yeah, I really didn't know how I was walking, either.

"He does no such thing."

"Oh, I'm pretty sure he does all the things." She waggled her brows as she filled a watering can at the sink.

"Gretchen." It was an affectionate sigh that squeezed my chest.

God, how much I loved this woman.

She smiled. Pure Cheshire grin. "Just enjoy it, sweetheart. It seems the two of you had a little catching up to do."

I looked out the window where the last of the day sank toward the horizon, winter holding fast to the air.

"I guess we did, didn't we?" I admitted when I looked back at her.

Her expression softened. "It's good you're here, Aster."

A war went down inside me. The part that kept worrying what I was doing was wrong. That it was selfish, staying here, dragging this family into my mess. The danger I was bringing to his door. I'd done it before, and look where that had gotten us.

Was I nothing but a fool for pressing it again? For getting us back into the very position we'd been in then?

"At what point is loving someone selfish? At what point is the cost too great?" I finally asked her.

Gretchen glanced at me in speculation. "For which of you?"

I huffed a perplexed sound, my attention focused on winding ribbon around the package I'd wrapped for Juniper, this little family that wasn't mine yet felt like my own. My voice was a tremor when I admitted, "For Logan because I'm pretty sure I'd sacrifice anything for him."

Gretchen hummed and went to watering the plants in the living room. Her back was to me when she spoke, "Well, from my perspective, that man is about as over-the-top as they come. Filling up the space like a blinding star every time he walks into a room."

I felt that truth to my soul.

"Livin' life to the extreme, but I'm pretty sure it was gonna burn out. You can't keep shining when you only shine to cover the darkness you hold onto."

Emotion climbed to my throat.

Thick and sticky.

She glanced at me. "I've cleaned house for Logan for the last five years. He was always a goof...joking, coming in and making a scene every chance he got, but there was always something beneath the surface. Couldn't put my finger on it. Not until my Jonnie passed about a year ago."

Grief curled through her expression, and an ache lit in my spirit. "I'm so sorry."

"Well, I am, too, but we had quite the life together." She went back to tending to the plants, musing as she did, "I lost him about the same time Logan was moving into this place. He told me he couldn't handle things without me, but I knew him asking me to stay here didn't have a thing to do with him needing the help."

Pausing, she fiddled with a leaf before she continued to speak, "That's a good man, you know, as wild and rough as he can be, bringing me in to live with him because he was worried about me being alone."

She hesitated, the tease normally held in her tone waning to soft affection. "I'd been living here for about two weeks when I heard it one night. Probably should have minded my business, but you know I'm not so good at that, so I let myself into his room when I heard him whimpering in pain and he didn't respond to my knocking."

Soft laughter rolled from her. "The man was fool drunk, tuckered out on a bottle of whiskey, laying on his back on the floor staring up at the ceiling like it was the sky. He told me about a star he'd caught once, one that'd burned him so bad that he'd had to let it go."

Everything squeezed, and my breath locked in my throat when she looked at me. "Every so often after that, I would hear him calling out for that star in his sleep. Aster."

Moisture bleared my sight, joy and sorrow clutching my chest. "He haunted my dreams, too."

She moved across the room so she could reach out and touch my cheek. "It's only a nightmare if it ends bad. You just make sure that doesn't happen."

We both jumped when the door suddenly banged open and a disorder spilled in.

"Pivot!" Jud shouted, the man cracking up as if it were the funniest thing he'd ever said as he and Logan attempted to wrangle an enormous tree through the door.

"Idiot." Logan shook his head, but he was wearing the biggest grin I'd ever seen as he struggled to squeeze the giant fir through.

Joy poured from it.

Real, true joy.

"That's my line, man, my line," Jud grunted. "And you are the one who begged for your big brother to come and do the heavy lifting. You'd better watch yourself or I'll knock you flat. You don't want to go and embarrass yourself in front of your lady now, do you?"

It was all a razzing.

Logan rolled his eyes. "Dude, I just helped you get your tree into your place half an hour ago. Who was begging who?"

I took the chaos in, and the air hitched in my throat when Logan's gaze turned to tangle with mine.

As his smile turned slow.

Sweet.

"Merry Christmas, baby. I got us a tree."

He and Jud propped it up near the fireplace.

I nearly dropped to my knees.

"Of course, this asshole right here had to have the biggest one. Surprised it fits." Jud gestured at Logan, but it was pure affection.

"What do you think?" Logan stretched out his arms.

My heart swelled.

So big.

An outpouring of devotion.

"I think you're the best thing I've ever seen." I couldn't keep it in. This feeling that swept through me like a warm, spring breeze. Something that promised better things were to come.

Jud chuckled a rough sound, and he tossed an aimless punch in Logan's direction as he passed. "Last thing this guy needs is any more ammo for his ego. Head's already bigger than that tree. Puff him up any more, and he's the one who's not gonna fit through the doorway."

Jud was all burly stride and easy smiles as he came our way. He acted like my presence was normal.

Required.

He dipped in and pressed a kiss to Gretchen's cheek before he reached out and wrapped his massive arms around me.

A gush of surprise left me when he hugged me tight.

He lifted me off the floor and whispered in my ear so no one else could hear, "Love him. Love him right. Love him whole. Because he fucking loves you with everything he's got, and he's willing to give it all."

Then Jud set me back on my feet, turned, and walked out.

Chapter Thirty-Three

Logan

IT WAS CRAZY, WHAT LIFE DID. THE WAY YOU COULD BE MOVING along with the day to day, living each one because that's really all you could do. Your lot had already been cast, for good or bad or whatever it was worth. Mistakes had already been made that you had to live with, and you did the best with what you'd been given.

Even when it sucked.

I glanced at Aster where she sat in the passenger seat of my car as I drove in the direction of Eden and Trent's place. I squeezed her hand, and she sent me this adoring smile that sailed through my spirit like eternity.

And I knew, sometimes fate took favor on you, scooped up the dice you'd rolled, and tossed you a pair of snake eyes for the fucking win.

Contentment lapped in the bare space between us, peace and joy wrapping us in a blanket of comfort as we drove into the quaint neighborhood to celebrate Christmas Eve with my family.

Night had fallen, and the houses were decked out in lights,

decorations glowing from porches, families tucked inside the warmth of the walls.

And I wanted to keep it. Wanted it with every part of me. To make it ours.

I pulled to a stop at the curb in front of Eden's house and killed the engine. Silence descended. The only sound was our deep, rasping breaths as our attention hooked on the huge window that fronted the house.

The drapes were open, and my family was inside. Eden laughed at something Jud said to her, and Trent held her from behind, Baby Kate in my sister-in-law's arms. Salem walked through, holding Juni, and the two of them stopped to look at an ornament on the tree.

Gage appeared below them, his caramel hair bouncing when he jumped and pointed.

It was this perfect picture that sent my heart angling in a direction I'd spent the last seven years convincing myself that it couldn't go.

"Do you want that, Aster?" I realized it was close to a plea. "Children? Family? A home?"

I knew my saying it was ripping a wound wide open.

But if I peeled back the exterior?

The walls I'd built—the façade I'd lived in for the last seven years?

That was a wound that hadn't come close to healing.

It was raw.

Throbbing.

A fucking hole that ached with confusion and tumult because I still couldn't understand how Aster had done it.

Her spirit roiled. I felt it flow, whisper and moan on a ripple of grief.

Yearning struck me, so intense that I was inhaling every veiled question that lingered between us.

Aster stared out the window, bobbing in a turmoil that'd caught her unaware.

"I'm sorry, Aster, I didn't mean to put you on the spot, especially tonight. It just—"

"Hurts," she filled in, not looking my way.

"Yeah, it fucking hurts."

The dreams, the plans, the promises we'd made.

But she was the one who'd had to exist on the other side, and I was the one who'd done the very thing she'd begged me not to do.

"It's a pain that won't ever go away, Logan."

Grief rose high, threatening my windpipe, but I forced myself to push for more.

"You said you'd never allow it to happen…that you'd never put a child in the same position as you'd been put in. That you refused to have Jarek's children because—"

She cut me off by whipping her attention my direction. "You asked me if I wanted it, Logan." Her voice had gone haggard. Hopeless and hopeful. Fueled by her own misunderstandings. She touched her chest. "I've always wanted it. I just wanted it with you. I wanted to run away with you. Live with you. For you. For us. A family and a home and our child."

"And I was too late."

Through bleary eyes, she blinked. "Maybe time didn't really exist for us."

"No, baby, no. It did and it does. Time might have been cruel, but we're real, and this *time*? It's ours. Fuck thirty days, I'm taking thirty thousand." Aster smiled a soggy smile. Emotion thick. Her faith finally coming to fruition.

I dove forward, capturing her mouth while this girl captured my soul.

Hell, it'd always been hers. It was time we were finally free to revel in it.

A pounding hammered at my driver's side window.

Aster yelped and jerked away, and I whirled around to find the threat.

Gifts stacked to the sky, Tessa waved back manically with one hand as she tried to balance them.

Shit.

I drew in a fragmented breath and tried to reel in the violence that had been instant.

"Hello, hey, Merry Christmas. Get your asses out of that car because I'm freezing mine off, and you know this tushy is way too cute for that."

I scrubbed a palm over my face.

Fucking Tessa.

I glanced at Aster.

On a giggle, she gave me a small shrug. "You're the one who told me she was only half insane."

A light chuckle got free, and I leaned forward and gave her a peck to the lips. "Come on, it's family time."

Mine.

Hers.

Ours.

This time, I was going to keep it that way.

Chapter Thirty-Four

Aster

FAMILY TIME.

I guess I never understood quite what that meant. Had never experienced it this way.

Family to me had always meant secrets. Loyalty without question. Submission without opposition.

And here we were, a mess of people piled in Trent and Eden's little house. The only one we were missing was Gretchen because she was spending the night at her sister's for the holiday.

We'd eaten and drank and laughed.

Chatted about the mundane that felt like the most important topics in the world because they were the things that mattered to these people.

And the truth of it was that I felt as if I belonged. As if I were a piece of this beauty. A glimmer in the light.

Held in Logan's tender glances and touches, wrapped in his laughter and teases, the easiness he exuded when he was surrounded by the ones who meant most to him.

I was now certain I was included in that.

Logan and I had found our way back to the other.

The Little Star and the North Star had aligned.

And as we gathered around the tree to exchange presents, I already knew I'd been given the greatest gift.

A gift that for so long I'd been too fearful to ask for.

Juni crawled over to me and set a present on my lap. The child beamed at me with her adorable dimples. "There you go, Auntie Aster."

Auntie Aster.

My heart clutched.

"That one is super extra special because I made it alls by myself and because I love you all the way to the stars."

The roots in my spirit dug deeper.

Logan squeezed me from where he and I were snuggled on the floor together, that man wrapped around me from behind with his legs stretched out on either side of me.

Emotion thick in my throat, I glanced back at him.

To the stars, he mouthed.

"Well hurry it ups then," Juni Bee said with all her sweet exasperation.

I choked over the lump. "I'd better then."

"You don't want to get on that one's bad side." Mimi laughed from where she sat on the couch beside Eden's father, Gary.

"That's right, my Motorcycle Dad taught me how to take you down, so you don't want to go messin' with me." Juni issued it with pure pride.

Jud chuckled from where he sat on a small, plush chair in the corner with Salem on his lap. "That's right, Juni Bee. You tell them."

"That I'm the best wrestler ever?" She grinned with excitement.

"Hey, that's my title. Champion!" Gage jumped up and threw his hands into the air.

"You're both the champions," Logan said, his arms curling tighter around me. "You're not gonna find me messing with either of you."

"That's because you're the smart one of the bunch, right, Uncle Logan, right?"

Logan roughed out an affectionate chuckle. "That's right, buddy. Smartest Lawson of the bunch."

Trent scoffed. "You just go on tellin' yourself that, man."

"Says the guy to the one who made him filthy rich."

"Yeah, yeah. Take all the credit, man, I see how it is." Trent fought a grin as he scrubbed a tattooed hand over his face.

"Don't worry, honey, you're smart, too." Eden rubbed Trent's back like she was stroking his ego.

"Well, he married my new mommy, so he's at least gotta be a little bit smart." Gage said it so matter of fact.

Tessa cracked up where she was squeezed next to Mimi. "I'm pretty sure it's Gage here who's the smartest of the bunch. You tell it like it is, little man."

"Well, I have to speak the truth because lying is bad and we gotta follow the rules."

Affection pulsed, so intense, a warm slide of comfort that fluttered through the room.

Juni nudged at the present that was still on my lap. "Well, are you gonna open it? You has to hurry because it's almost time for Santa to come, so we need to wrap this up before he skips right over."

I ran my finger under the wrapping paper, freed the tape, and opened the box. Emotion tugged at the edge of my mouth when I took out the hand-drawn picture.

It simply said *Best Friends* in crude handwriting with a bunch of hearts around it.

Juni climbed up closer, resting her hand on my shoulder so she could peer around at what she'd drawn. "Do you like it? I figures if Uncle Logan isn't your best friend in the whole wide world, you need one, so I think it should be me."

I pulled her to me, held her against my chest.

"I would love that," I told her.

She wiggled all around, hugging me tight before she scooted back and shot an unsympathetic look at Logan. "If you snooze you lose."

I cracked up.

Logan wrapped his arms fully around me, his face pressed into my hair as his chest jostled with his laugh. "Guess the girl really does love to bust my balls."

Salem shook her head, fighting amusement. "As I said before, don't listen to a thing your uncle Logan says, Juni."

"But he's gotta tell the truth, too, Auntie Salem." Gage blinked at her.

Love billowed, rolled and streamed from each person in the room.

And I knew...I knew...this was right where I belonged.

Three hours later, we banged into the apartment.

I didn't know what it was, but something had overcome us tonight.

Joy.

Excitement.

It was like freedom had sat under that tree and, with each gift that had been opened, it had become ours.

Logan's hands were all over me. Sliding around my waist and running over my ass before they were gliding back up my spine and he was taking my hair in a dominating fist.

He jerked me against him, kissing me as if his life depended on it. As if he would find the next beat of his heart within me.

I kissed him back because it was true. He was the blood in my veins. The air in my lungs. The hope in my soul.

He spun me, twisting me out of my jacket and dropping it to the floor as he edged me across the room.

I felt frantic.

Wild.

Giddy.

A giggle got free.

He swallowed it up.

"I love you, Aster Rose." It was a rumble at my mouth.

My fingers dragged through his thick hair, and my kiss was frenzied between each rasping word, "I thought I'd never get to love again. I thought I'd have to hold it in forever. Hide it so deep inside me that one day I would disintegrate."

Cease to exist under the weight.

"But I can't hold it back any longer, Logan. I love you. I love you."

He kept kissing me through the confession, and suddenly, we were beside the giant, twinkling tree.

Logan pulled back to stare down at me. "You are the existence that forever burned within me, Aster. You are the belief that I can live right. Do fucking better. Proof I can have a bigger purpose than this superficial bullshit that I've been chasing after. When I walk into a room? I want to walk in it for you. When I get up in the morning? I want to rise for you. When I live this life? I want to live it for you."

My chest stretched tight, and emotion raced my throat.

My North Star.

I touched his face, and he took my hand and kissed across my knuckles before he stepped back.

It would have been close to a smirk tweaking the edge of his mouth if it weren't for the nerves that carved his features in severity. The way his breaths were harsh clips of oxygen.

Fueled by intensity.

"One more gift tonight, Aster. But you should know it's a gift for me." That time, it was an affected smirk, so sweet my stomach twisted.

He slipped his hand into his pocket and pulled out a small box before he knelt on a knee.

"Logan." A shocked whisper got free, and my attention darted between the urgency in his gaze and what he held in his hand.

"I've had this for seven years, Aster."

Seven years.

Emotion rushed. A tidal wave that came from the depths and rose to the surface. It crashed over me in an inundating swell. Tears blurred my eyes, and my hand covered my mouth.

"Logan," I whispered it again.

Taken.

Overcome.

Unable to stand.

I slipped to my knees in front of him.

He set the ring beside him and took me by both sides of my face. He stared me down, his expression carved in fervency.

"When I came to you that night, Aster, I came with this ring and the promise that I was going to do whatever it took to convince your father you belonged with me. This ring? It was a promise of what I felt for you. I was going to tell him I was going to marry you, and we were going to have a family, and I was going to take you away from that place because you deserved so much better than the life he had planned for you. But I didn't fight for you like I should have."

His hold intensified, his big fingers digging into my hair and his thumbs running the angle of my jaw. We were so close our noses touched, our eyes wide and feeling, sucking every ounce of devotion in.

"I let anger and pride take me over, instead. I let your words impale me rather than recognize the torment that was in your eyes. That's what I chose to see, the hatred and the bitterness, rather than to see you were hurt. That I'd hurt you, too. But that promise I came to make you that night? It still burns bright inside me."

His eyes glassed over as they searched my expression. "Little Star... marry me because I'm tired of looking at the sky without you in it."

I threw myself at him, my arms around his neck. "Yes."

I knew we had to deal with Jarek. Finally put it in the past. But we would, and it would be us. Forever.

"It was always yes."

A groan of relief vibrated through him, and he rose up high on his knees, taking me with him as he hugged me against the raging thunder in his chest.

He was grinning when he eased back and took out the ring.

My hand was shaking like crazy as he slipped it onto my finger. Tears streamed free.

But these tears?

They shouted of forever.

Joy squeezed me tight when I lifted my hand to admire it. It was dainty and delicate, the band rose gold with a floral filigree, the diamond small and perfect and represented everything I'd ever dreamed.

"I'll replace the stone." His jaw flexed.

I choked out a laugh and held my hand protectively against my chest. "Don't you dare, Logan Lawson."

His expression turned tender. As if he saw something in me that he'd once thought missing.

And looking at him?

I saw what I'd once believed of him.

My beautiful, sweet man.

Fierce.

Loyal.

Right and good and kind.

My everything.

My North Star.

Chapter Thirty-Five

Logan

Los Angeles, Nineteen Years Old

L OGAN RUBBED THE STAR-SHAPED NOTE BETWEEN HIS fingers as he slipped out the back door of the office and into the night. The second he stepped outside, his heart rate spiked.

Anticipation.

Need.

A sticky, heavy dread.

Because he could feel it catching up to them.

He felt her presence emanating from behind the outbuilding, her sweet spirit stretching out in a slow build of seduction.

His Little Star that shined so bright.

"Why are you hiding?" he muttered.

Intensity flashed, and she peeked out from around the corner. "Because I have to."

"Are you going to get into trouble?" It was purely a tease.

They were already in so much trouble.

So much trouble.

"No. I'm going to get you into trouble."

He couldn't help but smirk at their little game. "Do I look like the type of guy who really minds?"

Besides, there would be no more hiding soon.

"I'm afraid you will."

"I'll do anything for you."

He moved forward, through the dense foliage to where she waited. Her chest heaved, making the necklace he'd given her twinkle in the bare light. He touched her belly that had barely begun to swell, felt the joy spring up from the places he'd believed he'd never feel.

Aster tipped her face up toward him. A fire burned in her agate eyes. "Then take me away from here. Let's just go. Disappear forever."

He blinked. "We can't just leave, Aster. How am I supposed to take care of you and the baby? What about my family? We have to play this smart."

Moisture filled her fevered gaze. "Family is what we're supposed to be now. And if I stay here any longer…"

She choked on her fear.

He stole forward, wrapped her in his arms, and breathed out a weighted sigh. "You are. And I'll do anything for you. I just…what if we tell your father? Convince him you belong with me? I don't want you to have to hide for the rest of your life. For the rest of our lives. There has to be a better way. I mean, I've been making him a shitton of money, Aster. He respects me. What I do."

Pride carved itself into the middle of him. Logan's cut had gotten bigger and bigger, and Aster's father had told him he'd never met another so promising.

Aster edged back a fraction, and her gorgeous face pinched. "He'll kill you, Logan."

"And what if he doesn't? What if he gives us his blessing?"

"He won't."

"Then I'll ask Trent and Jud for help." He didn't believe it would come to that.

In despair, she blinked. "And how many members of our family have to die for us to be together?" Her hand fisted at the hem of his shirt. "Let's just go."

He rushed to gather her up, pressed his lips to her forehead, and murmured, "Okay."

Okay.

Whatever it took.

He'd already promised her that.

Something rustled in the bushes about twenty feet away, and they jumped apart. Logan peered into the dusky shadows where the leaves waved and lapped.

He couldn't make out anything.

But he felt it.

The grim darkness that flashed over the night.

Swallowing hard, he turned back to Aster, grabbed her by the outside of the arms, and squeezed. "If you really want to go? Then we have to do it soon. We'll leave this week. Be ready."

A fist pounded on his bedroom door, and Logan jerked upright in bed.

"Logan, get up, family meeting in two." Trent's voice radiated through the air, lined in a hard, manic edge.

Logan glanced at the clock. It was just after ten a.m.

Apprehension surged.

What the hell was going on?

Whatever it was, he knew it was big. He could feel it echoing through the house, banging the walls like a warning toll.

Logan scrubbed a hand over his face to break up the sleep, then he tugged on the pair of jeans he'd left on the floor, and he fumbled out.

Late morning light seeped through the drawn curtains, and Trent was pacing the living room.

Jud sat on the very edge of the couch with his hands clasped together, conflict tangled in his being. Logan moved to sit beside him as unease curled through his spirit.

Nathan came out from his room, his eyes wide and trained on Trent, in tune with his twin.

"What's going on?" Concern filled Nathan's question.

Trent roughed an agitated hand over the top of his head, and he inhaled deep before he swung back around. "We've got a problem. Pit's girl is pregnant."

Confusion bound everyone's tongues.

"It's mine," he clarified.

Logan felt like he'd been zapped.

Shocked.

Stunned.

It seemed he wasn't the only one who'd found trouble. The only one with a child on the way.

He knew this was different, though.

Trent wasn't close to being in love. Wasn't close to fighting for a family that'd barely begun.

He'd been sleeping with Juna as a way to get at Pit. Pit was the man Trent had been hunting since the day their mother had been gunned down. The man Trent believed ultimately responsible for her hit.

He'd been doing everything he could to get close enough to take him out since.

It appeared he'd diverged paths.

"She's dead if he finds out," Trent continued. "I'm taking her out of here to keep her safe until the baby is born. I'm gonna raise it myself. We're leaving. This city and this life. We're gonna disappear, start over. It's a bad life, and I won't bring a child into it."

A sound pitched out of Logan without his permission.

Relief.

Stark, gutting relief.

He bent in two, trying to clear his head. To process it.

They'd just been offered an out on a silver platter.

"It's okay, man. It's gonna be okay. Promise." Jud squeezed his knee, thinking Logan was upset while Logan wanted to shout with the out they'd been given.

He could have Aster and his family.

There was a better solution.

Logan barely processed the conversation that ensued. Nathan

asking him if raising a kid was what he really wanted. If he would be happy.

"You make me happy. The three of you, that's it. And…" Trent choked. "And this kid."

This kid.

Logan understood it to his soul.

Trent cleared his throat. "Have a deal to see through tonight. Big one. I don't show, our father will be coming to collect. Don't want to raise any suspicion. Get ready. Pack only what you need. Meet here at four. We roll an hour before sunrise. That is if everyone is with me?"

Logan's head spun as their destinations became clear.

Trent said to only pack what they needed, and the only thing that was going to be was Aster.

Aster.

He wanted to shout it, claim her, but he figured it was going to be a whole lot easier to ask for forgiveness than for permission. Trent was already going to lose his shit when he found Aster with him.

But he also knew his brothers would stand beside him.

Just like they all did with Trent. They moved to him and set their hands on his shoulders. "We're with you."

Five minutes later, Trent and Jud's bikes were roaring down the street.

Nathan looked at Logan, eyed him intently. "What are you going to do, man?"

Logan shrugged like it was clear. "I'm bringing her with us. She and our kid."

Disbelief flushed Nathan's expression then he almost smiled. "Shit. And here I thought you were supposed to be the smart one, and you got yourself into the same kind of mess as Trent?"

Emotion throbbed. "Nah, man, it's not a mess. Not when it's the best thing that ever happened to me."

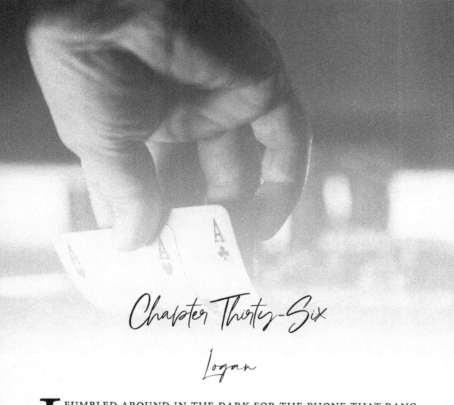

Chapter Thirty-Six

Logan

I FUMBLED AROUND IN THE DARK FOR THE PHONE THAT RANG from my nightstand.

It was late, after one, Aster fast asleep where she'd been curled into my side with the ring I'd kept for years securely fashioned on her finger.

My chest tightened.

Overcome by the sight of her laying there in the swath of muted, milky light that covered the bedroom.

Mine.

In the truest way.

The way she was always supposed to be.

The phone rang again.

Squinting, I sat up on the edge of the bed and picked it up.

Disquiet trembled my nerves, goading deep as I answered the call, my voice quieted when I answered, "Haille?"

"I'm sorry to bother you at such a late hour."

"It's fine."

"I have something that I thought would be of interest to you."

"Yeah?"

"A game...New Year's Day at ten p.m. The stakes will be...worth your time."

I glanced back at Aster who was on her side, facing me, lost to sleep. Even breaths slipped between her barely parted lips, the girl at peace and my only purpose.

The tattoo burned on my side.

Greed.

It took no thought to recognize she was the only treasure I needed.

"I think I'm going to have to pass."

Chapter Thirty-Seven

Aster

"MERRY CHRISTMAS." LOGAN GAZED OVER AT ME where we lie on our sides facing the other. Our hearts were slowed and steadied, and a peace unlike anything I'd ever known had seeped deep into my spirit.

"I never thought I would get the chance to share one with you."

He took my hand and pressed the back of it to his lips. "You get the rest of mine, Aster. The birthdays and the holidays and the celebrations. You get the days that will never make history and the ones that we will remember every detail of for the rest of our lives. You get every day."

"That's good because I'm going to require every single one." My smile was tender, and Logan grinned, emotion cresting his brow.

We relished in it for the longest time before I brought what we kept trying to keep at the back of our minds into the forefront. "What are we going to do, Logan? I have one more week before my father expects me to return to Los Angeles."

He inhaled a shaky breath. "We won't let that happen."

"We need a plan. I'm going to get in touch with my sister and see if she has made any progress, but I'm not sure we can continue to rely on that."

Jarek hadn't shown his face since the altercation in the alley. But I could feel his dark presence looming over the city.

Watching.

Lurking.

Waiting for the perfect opportunity to strike.

"No. We can't." Logan kept kissing over the back of my hand in a soothing manner, even while the ferocity flashed through his face. "I spoke with Jud and Trent last night. Jud has an old connection who's familiar with the Russian families. He's going to make contact with him to see if we can find any ties to Jarek."

Worry and hope flooded my bloodstream. "I don't want to involve your family, Logan."

He wound an arm around my back and pulled me flush, his voice turning to grit. "They're your family now, Aster. Yours. And this family fights for each other."

Emotion surged. Love and adoration and this lingering fear I would never shake. "Is it wrong I find so much joy in that?"

Those green eyes flashed, though this morning, the stony depths were transparent. "This joy is ours, Aster. It's ours."

Then he placed the softest kiss on my lips.

I nearly hit the ceiling when my phone started ringing, and I jerked around to the nightstand to see who was calling.

Panic clawed through my chest. "It's my father."

Logan slipped his palm to my cheek. "Don't be afraid, Aster. You stood up for yourself and came here. Now it's time for you to see it through."

My nerves rattled, and I did my best to swallow it down, nodding at him once before I shifted, removed the phone from the charger, and snuck out into the kitchen area.

My voice was held when I answered, "Merry Christmas, Papa."

"Mia vita, Merry Christmas."

His affection filled my spirit. My love for him real even though he'd caused so much pain and grief.

"It truly is, Papa. It's the first one where I felt whole and right since before I can remember."

Or maybe I never had.

A heavy sigh pilfered through the line. "Please tell me you haven't allowed your whimsical fantasies to delude you, Aster Rose. It's time you come home, where you belong, and leave this foolishness behind."

My mind spun with how to handle this best.

"No. Not yet. I'm so close to finding them, Papa. I've earned his trust." My voice dropped even lower with that. I felt like a fraud saying it, and not because I held any guilt over lying to my father. "I need more time, and you promised me thirty days."

"We miss you here."

My laughter was close to disbelieving. "I'm not sure how you can miss something that doesn't truly exist."

There, I was a shell.

Numb.

A caricature with a false smile.

"You know everything, every choice I've ever made, is because of my love for you."

The sad thing was I thought he might believe it.

"No, Papa. Every choice you ever made was for you because you believed in a lie that was passed down from generation to generation that proclaimed that was the way it was supposed to be. It was wrong. Horrible. A crime. And I will no longer pretend like it's not."

"Aster." His voice was aghast. Low and filled with a warning.

"It's the truth, Papa. And you know it. It's time you came to accept it."

I ended the call before giving him a chance to respond, and the air squeezed from my lungs in spastic quakes.

I was shocked at what I'd said.

Shocked by the truth that I was going to stand behind it.

An overwhelming presence emerged over me from behind. Stark intensity. Mind-bending beauty. Logan wrapped his arms around my waist, and he pressed his nose into my hair until it was sweeping the sensitive spot at the nape of my neck. "Aster. Little Star. My light. My destination. I'm so fucking proud of you."

I pressed my hands over his that were splayed over my stomach. "Together."

"Together," he rumbled back.

And I knew...knew everything would be all right.

Chapter Thirty-Eight

Aster

MY PHONE BUZZED ON THE ISLAND. I ALL BUT SKIPPED over to where I'd left it. I got a full body buzz whenever I thought of Logan, which was basically every second of every day.

So, what if I was happy.

I deserved it.

We deserved it.

Was I terrified? Of course. We had so much to overcome. But we would do it.

Together.

We had to.

There was no other option.

After my conversation with my father two days ago, it'd been cemented. Courage had weaved its way into my fiber, knitting me into a ferocity that I'd never felt before.

The smile I wore completely shifted when I saw it wasn't Logan texting me from the office but rather my sister returning mine from yesterday.

One that'd simply said, *Miss you*, which I'd sent with an undercurrent of a message that she needed to get somewhere private so we could talk.

Taylor: Hi. Are you good?

Me: Yes, are you? Call?

Taylor: Can't. Hidden in a closet at the end of the hall. All stealth like.

Affection sprang into my chest. No doubt, she was thrilled by the scandalous mission.

Taylor: How are you?

I hesitated, warring with what to say, wishing we were normal and we could sit cross-legged on my bed and gossip about boys.

One day.

So I settled on simplicity.

Me: Safe.

Taylor: And well-fucked, I hope?

She had no idea.

Me: Taylor.

I filled as much of a reprimand as I could into her name.

Taylor: Aster.

I could almost see her pouty face as she tossed it right back.

A giggle slipped free, so I gave her a little more.

Me: I'm happy. Really happy.

Her response came in quickly behind.

Taylor: Mmhmm…nothing like some of that good D to make a girl happy.

She capped it with a winky face.

Me: You are ridiculous.

Taylor: Ridiculous and right. Admit it. I can feel your afterglow all the way down in Los Angeles.

Me: Fine.

That was as good as she was going to get.

Taylor: Ahhhhhhhhhhhhhhhhhhhhhhhhhhhh! I knew it!

Light laughter floated out, and I glanced around at the silent apartment. I didn't know why it felt like this conversation had to be covert. I guessed it felt like an extension of what Taylor was going through. The truth that she was taking a risk by trying to help me. I'd put her in a bad spot, but I needed her help.

I hesitated, then let my fingers fly across the screen.

Me: Do you know anything about Papa having connections in Russia?

It took a second for her to respond. My heart thudded in my chest while I waited. Nerves rattling. I could feel it, we were right there.

Taylor: No fucking way. He wouldn't. You know that. His pride is too big for that.

Me: Jarek went at least four times this last summer.

Taylor: SHUT. UP.

Me: That's what we've learned, at least.

Taylor: And you need to know why.

I could see her brain spinning.

Me: Yeah.

Taylor: And you think the why is in that bag.

She didn't even phrase it as a question. Her mind was already adding it up and coming to the quick conclusion.

Me: I have to believe something is in there.

Taylor: Don't worry because I think I figured out how to get inside.

Antsy anticipation slipped beneath my skin.

Me: How?

Taylor: I'm going to seduce the biker.

My heart nearly popped out of my chest when she sent a picture of the scariest guy I'd ever seen. He was outside the house I'd lived at for the last seven years, leaning against the wall with a cigarette dangling from his mouth and his motorcycle boot kicked back on the brick. Dark hair, covered in ink, the patch on his cut claiming *Demon's Day*.

Taylor was right. He looked like kicking kittens was his favorite hobby.

Me: Are you insane? You cannot seduce the biker.

Anxiety clawed through my senses. I couldn't exchange the safety of one of us for the downfall of the other. It was insanity.

A second later, her response buzzed through.

Taylor: Why can't I have sexy times with an uber hot biker if you get to?

Me: Logan is not a biker.

Taylor: Oh, please, that boy may wear a suit, but he has biker blood all the way down in his soul. Piss him off and see what happens.

Okay, fine, she was right, but that didn't change things.

Me: I refuse to put you in danger, Taylor. I only asked for this favor if Dominic could slip in unnoticed, not for you to go on a suicide mission.

Taylor: Death by orgasm. Sign me up.

I tried to hold back a screech of frustration.

Me: Please don't do something stupid.

Taylor: It's not stupid if it's for you.

I could feel the tone of her voice soften.

Taylor: Besides, Dom's out. This mission is on me. And this guy looks like a challenge.

I blew out a sigh, warring, unsure of what to do. She responded before I got the chance to.

Taylor: Trust me, Aster. Please.

The affection that pulled tight across my chest almost felt like pain.

Me: Just be careful. I would never forgive myself if something happened to you.

Taylor: I love you, too.

Me: You know I do.

Me: And delete this thread before Papa sees it, and he locks you away forever.

Taylor: Done, big sister. Don't worry yourself. I have it handled. I'll be in touch soon. Stay safe.

She finished it off with a row of blowing-kiss faces.

While I stood there terrified of what I'd gotten her into.

Chapter Thirty-Nine

Logan

"DO YOU HAVE ANY IDEA WHAT YOU STANDING THERE looking that way does to me?"

I hovered at the doorway of the bathroom and watched Aster get ready in front of the mirror. The girl wore this floor-length white dress that shimmered in the light, a slit riding up to her right thigh, the material slinky and sliding over those lush curves.

Nothing but satin and temptation.

My Little Star that burned so bright it was blinding.

Fire-agate eyes met my gaze in the reflection. I felt her expression all the way to my guts, and my fingers itched with the need to trace the lines of her gorgeous face. She had her hair up in a twist, and a couple pieces hung loose to caress her bare shoulders exposed by the tiny straps of her dress.

She wore the same necklace she'd worn the first night in the basement, the star I'd given her years before, and her engagement ring on her finger that I'd never thought would find its rightful place.

My heart squeezed.

She was a vision.

A gift.

A treasure.

Her gaze slipped over me as I slowly edged forward, and attraction quivered in the space. A deep intensity that whispered and bound and never let go.

"You don't look too terrible yourself."

A rough chuckle fumbled out as I wrapped my hands around her waist and pressed my nose to the flesh behind her ear.

I inhaled.

Hyacinth and magnolias.

"I love it when you look at me like that," I murmured.

A slip of playfulness pulled at the edge of her mouth. "Like what?"

"Like you want me to peel you out of this dress and fuck you until you can't see."

"Well, I was kind of hoping for that later." Her voice was breathy, needy with a shot of a tease.

"It was on the agenda," I rumbled as I kissed a path down the column of her neck.

"It'd better be. You wouldn't want to go and disappoint me on New Year's Eve, would you?"

Savage seductress.

My chuckle grew deep as need burned hot in my stomach. My right hand slipped up the front of her dress, over her stomach and breasts until I was holding her by the front of the neck.

I felt the whimper curl up her throat, and my mouth was back to her ear. "Oh, you won't be disappointed, Little Star. I'm going to ruin you tonight. I promise you."

Desire raced across her flesh.

A growl got free.

"Who do you belong to, Aster?" I held her closer, possession filling my blood.

She met my stare through the mirror. "You, Logan. You."

A hungry groan rolled in my chest. "You have me entranced."

"And you have me ensnared. All of me."

I held her close before I forced myself to step back. "We should go or we're going to be late. We don't want Trent or Jud banging down the door if we are."

There was a big New Year's Eve party at Absolution. I was looking forward to it, if I were being honest, celebrating with my family, with my girl. The other part couldn't wait to get her out of that dress.

"Or worse…Tessa." Playfully, Aster widened her eyes.

I laughed over the amusement. This joy that I could hardly process. "Come on, it couldn't be that bad. She is only *half* insane."

"She might go full straightjacket if we don't show." Affection rippled through her features.

Everything inside me softened. "I love you with them. With my family."

She reached out and squeezed my hand. "Our family."

It was a promise.

Profound and real and everything.

"Our family." I squeezed back.

She tried to hold it back, but I saw the flash of worry streak across her face.

"I know you're worried about what tomorrow will bring, Aster, and we'll face it together. But for now…for tonight…we celebrate us."

Because we'd spent too damn long living without.

"Then tomorrow, we tell *thirty days* it can suck it." A smirk split my mouth.

Aster choked out a soggy laugh. "I like that plan."

I stepped forward and pressed my lips to her forehead. "Me, too, baby. Me, too."

I took her hand and led her out into the main room. Gretchen sat forward from where she was on the couch thumbing through a magazine, and she pressed her hand to her heart.

"Woo wee, you two are gonna cause an accident walking around like that. Holy hell fire and obscenities. Best looking couple that I ever did see, if I don't say so myself. You'd better bring a bat to fight off anyone who gets to looking at your man too hard."

She winked at Aster.

Aster giggled. "Don't worry, G. I'm going to fight for him, just like he'll fight for me."

"Well, if you need backup, you know where to find me. I'm feeling extra frisky tonight. Two of us? They won't even know what hit 'em."

Thirty minutes later we pulled into the Absolution parking lot.

Blue neon lights shined like a beacon through the misty, frozen air. A vibe curled through the night, promising revelry and probably a little debauchery, too.

As usual, the place was packed, but when there would normally be a line winding around the building, tonight it was ticket-only. Trent's general manager, Sage, had organized a kick-ass party. Some super popular band, A Riot of Roses, was playing, and it promised to be a madhouse inside.

I glanced to where Aster sat, and my heart panged in my fucking chest. I couldn't wait to share it with her.

I wound around to the employee lot so we could sneak in the side door, and I was out and opening Aster's door and making her giggle as I rushed to help her up.

"Someone's excited."

Grinning, I tugged her against my chest. "You know I'm always game for a party, baby, and we're just getting started."

"Sounds fun." It was pure innuendo.

Flirty.

Loved that side of my girl, too.

"So much fun," I rumbled, and I dipped down to peck a quick kiss to her lips before I stepped back and took her hand. "Let's get you inside where it's warm."

She was wearing her heavy coat again, but it didn't do a whole lot to cover her legs.

We scrambled over the pitted parking lot and to the side door, both of us cracking up by the time we got there since we'd been slipping and sliding all over the frozen pavement.

Our breath was vapor that misted around us.

Our joy a shout that sang from our souls.

Keeping her close, I reached in and pulled the door open. Milo was standing guard. His smile turned soft when he realized it was us and not some prick trying to sneak in.

"Milo, my man, how have you been?" We gave each other a quick hug with a clap to the shoulder. "Can't complain, now, can I?"

His smile was slow when he turned his attention on Aster. "Good to see you again. I see you're putting up with this guy."

I tugged her back to me then took her by the wrist so I could flash him her ring. "And she's going to be putting up with me for the rest of her life."

His brows went high before he slanted a disbelieving grin at her. "Ah, I see how it is. You went and broke the wild one?"

"Oh, we're just about to get wild," I tossed out.

Aster giggled. "It seems there is no breaking to it, but I'm at least going to keep him reined."

He chuckled. "Good. He needs someone to keep him in line."

"Happy New Year, Milo," Aster said before I dragged her down the hall and out into the mayhem that was Absolution.

People were packed wall to wall, and the band was already on the stage, a disco ball tossing glittering rays over the crowd that throbbed and danced.

I kept my hand snug on Aster's as I shouldered through the crowd toward our reserved booth. We broke through to find Trent and Eden tucked on one side, the girl sitting fully sideways on his lap. Tessa sat next to them. Salem and Jud were on the opposite side, and Jud's arm was draped over Salem's shoulder, and she had her head rested on his chest.

I loved that my brothers had found it. Found what they deserved. What was right.

A flash of grief came faster than I could hold it back. The fact that Nathan had never gotten that chance. He was blameless, no stains, pure, and he was the one who'd gone down for our sins.

A hand slipped up my spine. Warmth and comfort. I let go of a shaky breath and pushed it aside because I'd learned the hard way that dwelling on what couldn't be changed didn't fix anything. It caused more torment. Ate away the good memories and left you consumed by the mistakes.

For so long, my memories of Nathan had been tainted, but I didn't want that any longer.

Tessa popped up the second she noticed us, and she threw her arms in the air. "Finally, you are here!"

"I know you were missing me, but come now, Tessa, at least try to keep your infatuation contained." I let the razzing free. I couldn't help it when it was so easy to mess with the girl.

She gasped then shook her head like she felt sorry for me. "Um, I am infatuated, but that infatuation is with your girlfriend."

Aster giggled.

I grabbed my girl's hand again and waved it like I was showcasing the next prize on a cheesy game show. "That would be fiancée."

That time when Tessa gasped, it was real. "Shut your fucking face. Are you serious?"

Joy burst from Aster. So profound it slammed me like a shock-wave. "It seems he's stuck with me."

Tessa flew forward and grabbed Aster's hand so she could study the ring.

That tiny ring that I'd happily exchange for something bigger and flashier, but Aster had made it clear there wasn't a chance.

Emotion kept rushing from Aster as she was surrounded in attention. Salem and Eden jumped up, too, and the three women smothered my girl in a crush of arms and well-wishes and giggles.

There was no missing the weight of my brothers' stares, though. I hadn't told them yet. I didn't want to get them any more spun up than they already were. The mess that we were in that I still didn't have a fucking clue how to get out of. All that history that we still didn't have an answer for.

Trent slid out, and I took a couple steps his way. He stuck out his hand. I guessed I shouldn't have been surprised when he said, "Congrats, man."

Relief hit me as I shook it, and he used it to pull me in tight, hugging me hard, his words a rumble at my ear, "Congrats. Truly. Want the world for you. You deserve it. And I know you love her, and I want you to know, I stand by you, by her, whatever you need."

Thickness filled my throat, and I nodded as I eased back. "Thanks, brother."

"And you know that goes the same for me," Jud promised as he came in to hug me, too. "Anything. After spending Christmas Eve with you two, it was clear. Whatever shit went down, it didn't have the power to destroy that love you have for each other, and if you have somethin' that powerful, it's your job to fucking hold onto it. Don't let it go. Whatever it takes."

I peeked back at Aster. I felt it way down deep in my soul.

I turned back to my brothers. "I won't."

Tessa whirled around on another gasp, and she slapped her hand over her heart. "I can't believe it...the player tossed in the towel."

She had no idea it was in more ways than one.

Women.

Gambling.

The shady deals.

The greed.

It was done.

Everything except for the overpowering need I had for Aster.

Sauntering that way, I ruffled my fingers through Tessa's red hair, just to fuck with her.

Her mouth dropped open. "How dare you, Logan Lawson? Do you have any idea how long it took me to achieve this perfection?" She shimmied in her electric-blue dress that was so tiny someone was definitely getting a peep show tonight, top or bottom, we couldn't be sure.

"I mean, okay, I'm already perfect, but we went all out tonight. Have you seen us?"

She swished an overzealous hand at Eden and Salem.

Truth was, they were all fucking knockouts, unforgettable in their own ways. But it was Aster who was hiding her laughter off to the side of them who lit me up.

The one who sparked a wildfire in my insides and made me feel like I was being burned alive, and somehow, it still was the best feeling ever.

"Sorry to break it to you, Tessa, but I only have eyes for one girl."

I moved for Aster, relished the way the redness flushed over her chest and up to her cheeks, like maybe she was getting burned alive, too.

"Awww." Tessa looked like she was about to cry.

Salem took her hand. "Come on, let's dance while I can still keep my eyes open."

Eden giggled as she hooked her elbow with Salem's. "Um, no, you're here at least until midnight, lady."

"But my feet are swollen," Salem whined.

"Yeah, and my boobs are leaking. Suck it up."

They started to weave into the crowd. Aster looked back from over her shoulder as they went.

Joy.

It shined all around her.

A halo of light.

My Little Star.

Chapter Forty

Aster

LIGHTS STROBED, AND THE BAND PLAYED, AND THE CROWD rejoiced.

Celebrating.

My celebration was the truth of this man who held me close in the middle of the crush, his forehead dropped to mine and his big hands spread out around my ribs as we swayed. It was close to the way we'd done the night of his birthday.

But then, there'd been so many questions.

It didn't feel that way tonight.

Tonight, it felt as if we'd been lifted.

Elevated.

Exulted above the mess to delight in what we'd been given.

It was half an hour to midnight, and the revelers had turned rowdy. Drinks flowed free as everyone cut loose the weights and worries of the previous year in anticipation of the new.

It sent excitement billowing through the cavernous space.

He edged back to gaze down at my face. "Look at you beneath all those lights, still shining brighter than anyone."

"I think I'm just reflecting off you."

"Hardly."

Our words were barely audible above the din, but we felt them, our spirits swimming together in a sea of exhilaration.

I wanted to stay there forever.

But I was jostled back and out of the dream when the crowd was suddenly torn apart. People scrambled to get out of the way as six big bodies busted through.

Panic.

Fear.

Hate.

They burst in my blood.

No.

Eyes wide with shock, I fumbled back.

No.

My papa was at the helm of the men I knew had come to drag me away. His expression was contorted in disappointment and rueful discontent.

Jarek was at his side, venom in his eyes and vileness in his presence, the man slicked in a sweat that reeked of malevolence. Four men surrounded them, three that I recognized as Jarek's guards and one of my father's.

Violence bristled through the air, and Logan stepped in front of me to create a barricade. Hostility burned from his being.

This man a hedge of protection to shield.

But continuing to hide wasn't going to get us out of this.

The mass continued to throb, oblivious to the ground that had been ripped out from under my feet.

"It's time to leave. Now." Jarek's vicious voice curled over the music.

"That's not going to happen." The words speared from Logan's mouth. I could feel his control fraying in every tremor that rocked through his body.

"I thought by now you would have remembered who you're dealing with," Jarek spat, taking a step forward. He lifted his chin in arrogance, his power gained in the men who surrounded him.

The crowd parted again, a wave that undulated from behind to give way to Jud and Trent, plus Milo and Kult and three other bouncers who came up behind us.

A fortress of strength.

Aggression quivered in the dense atmosphere.

Two groups in opposition.

Trent stepped forward. "I don't appreciate you waltzing into my place of business when you haven't been invited." He cocked his head. "Paying customers only, and all. No offense."

Oh, it was purely offense.

Old hate.

Conflict and contention.

Papa angled his head, his voice controlled. "My daughter is here."

Trent sent a sweeping gaze back my direction before he turned toward my father. "It appears it's where she wants to be."

My father ignored him and looked at me. "You were given thirty days, mia vita. The time has come."

I could see in his eyes he no longer believed I was there to retrieve the stones.

"She's not going anywhere with you. Not any of you." The words were razors that cut from Logan's mouth.

Jarek and his men surged forward.

Logan, Trent, and Jud did the same.

The promise of violence clotted the air.

Stagnant and harsh.

"Then you die tonight." Jarek hissed it.

I could feel the frantic eyes that had gathered. Eden, Salem, and Tessa were suddenly there, terrified, held back by Milo.

They'd meant it when they'd promised to come alongside me.

A feeling washed over me.

Marked.

Potent.

Mandatory.

I was finished being pushed around.

Finished being ordered into submission.

Finished with being told who I was and where I was to be and who I was supposed to love.

Yes, I'd already made the oath to myself, but it felt different staring down the manifestation.

The reality that I either fought for myself or surrendered the way I'd done before.

Do or die.

I pushed between Trent and Jud, coming up to Logan's side. My words were held in a low rasp. "Everyone outside. Now."

Jarek balked as if anything I said was insignificant.

My father put out a hand. A hand that wielded the power. I saw the way it made Jarek flinch with the bite of bitterness.

"Outside. Everyone," Papa commanded.

Logan cast me a searching look. *Is this what you want?*

He'd run with me if I asked him to.

Or fight to the death.

Whatever it took.

I knew he would.

And I loved him even more for it.

I threaded my fingers through his, squeezed tight, and I was the one who led us behind the gambol of my father's men who pushed through the throng until the mess of us were spilling out into the parking lot.

Trent and Jud flanked me and Logan, and Kult and Milo came to stand on either side.

While Jarek glowered and gritted his teeth and silently raged.

The beat of the music pulsed through Absolution's walls while the frozen air wafted in white tufts of vapor from panted mouths.

A stand-off between two warring sides.

I should have known that's what it would come to.

"You wish for a scene?" My father inclined his head.

"No, Papa, I just wish to be heard. To be listened to. To be understood."

"I already granted you thirty days."

"And it's time for you to grant me my life."

His brow curled. "What are you asking?"

"For you to let me go. To give me my freedom. To let me love the man I've loved all along. The one you and Jarek robbed me of."

Logan's hand tightened on mine.

Belief.

Pride.

Support.

I stood firm in it, and I shifted to make sure they could see the ring I proudly wore on my finger.

Rage blistered from Jarek when he saw it. "This is blasphemy. You are *my* wife."

My attention swung to the monster who'd scarred me so deeply. Ugly, gnarled wounds that would forever weep and bleed. "I am not your wife. I am a prisoner you took, one you abused, and I refuse to allow it to continue."

"Bullshit." He surged forward.

In a flash, Jud was in front of him. His hand slammed into his chest. "I'd think twice about that." He leaned in close to his ear, his voice a dark threat. "I'm pretty sure it's you who has forgotten who we are."

My father waved another hand as if Jarek were an unruly child.

"You will stand down, Jarek, as I told you before. We came here for my daughter, not for bloodshed."

Papa's attention swiveled, his eyes narrowed in speculation, focusing in on where Logan and I stood shoulder to shoulder with our hands tightly woven.

"You ask me to leave you with a man who stole from me? A man who touched my daughter when he was forbidden to even speak to her? The man who killed my brother? The same man you promised you would never see again if I spared his life?"

Shock impaled Logan.

An arrow to his heart.

He nearly bowed in two, and his breaths turned ragged, and I could feel the brutal thunder of his heart.

As if a piece of him had simultaneously broken and healed.

Because now he truly knew what it meant when I'd told him there was no other choice to make.

I'd chosen him.

I lifted my chin. "Yes. I'm asking you right now, as my father, to see me as your daughter. As a human being. As a woman who loves and hurts and has needs. I'm asking you to let her finally have the chance to live."

"And if I say no?" That he issued to Logan, a challenge in the rise of his brow.

Logan's hand clamped down so fiercely it was close to painful. "Then we'll have a war I doubt either of us want to fight."

My father chuckled a low, disbelieving sound. "You know, you were the smartest boy to ever pass through my halls, your mind quick and your skill natural, but also the most unwise."

I could almost hear Logan's teeth grind. "If you think my falling in love with your daughter was unwise, then you're the biggest fool of all. Loving her is the only thing I've ever done right."

Emotion welled.

So thick.

So real.

A dubious sound puffed from my father's mouth, and he took a step back, eyed Logan when he said, "I expect you and my daughter in Los Angeles on Friday. We will have a discussion. Without an audience."

He slanted a direct look at Jarek when he stated it.

My own shock had me rocking forward, the ground shaking beneath my feet. *Was he actually hearing me this time?*

It was the same second Jarek snapped. He flew forward in an effort to get around Jud, only it was like slamming into a brick wall.

Jud held him back by the upper arms while Logan positioned himself in front of me. Jarek thrashed and tried to break free, threats ripping from his mouth, "You have just signed your death warrant. I promise you. I will take back Aster and the stones you stole. Where are they?"

Desperation wheezed from his outrage.

My stomach twisted.

The stones had been nothing but a curse.

"Let's go." My father lifted a hand in the air to indicate it was finished.

Jud shoved Jarek back. "I'd suggest you disappear, asshole."

Dizziness spun my head, and I tried to remain upright, unable to believe the possibility.

That my father might actually see.

The group of men moved deeper into the parking lot.

"Papa," I couldn't help but call out.

He barely paused. Barely looked back.

But he did, and I thought what I saw in his expression was mercy.

Thank you, I mouthed.

With a tight nod, he turned and disappeared into the hazy darkness.

In the background I could hear Trent rumble low, "Prick is gonna be back."

"It would seem that way, Sir," Milo offered quietly.

"You good, darlin'?" Jud shifted his attention to me.

I gave him a jerky nod, the welling of shock so thick in my throat I wasn't sure I could speak.

Logan tugged at my hand. "Come with me."

And the truth was, I would follow him anywhere.

Chapter Forty-One

Logan

Los Angeles, Nineteen Years Old

LOGAN TRIED TO CONCEAL HIS HARSH BREATHS AS HE APPROACHED the office where he was rarely summoned. Dread slithered across his flesh, his stomach in knots and his heart beating out of time.

Aster's father had to have found out.

Had to know.

And if that were the case, he doubted much he would make it back out of that room.

Gathering his courage, he knocked on the door.

"Come in."

He inhaled a shaky breath and opened it to the rambling study.

Aster's father sat behind his enormous desk, coolly casual the way he normally was, like there wasn't a thing in the world that could touch him.

An immortal king.

Logan gulped and took a single step forward. "Sir, you wanted to see me?"

"Shut the door and sit." He pointed at a chair across from his desk.

Logan clicked the door shut and tried to keep his knees from knocking as he crossed the room and sat. His muscles ticked as his nerves scattered.

Andres Costa leveled him with his eyes, studying him like he were sifting around in Logan's mind for his secrets.

Finally, he said, "You have been an asset to this family, Mr. Lawson. When your father suggested I bring you in, I was skeptical, but you've proven yourself to be more than worthy."

"Thank you, Sir."

A tiny bit of the tension drained off, but not enough to keep him from itching in the seat. Unsure of where this was going because he definitely felt a *but* coming.

"Inside these walls is much different than when you step outside of them, though." Aster's father swished a hand around the room. "Here, there are fewer mistakes to be made. Fewer temptations to lead you astray. Fewer questions of loyalty."

Logan's chest squeezed.

What was he implying?

Did he know?

He clung to the arms of the chair while sweat gathered at his nape.

Andres Costa eyed him carefully. "And I think it is time we give you the chance to prove that, Mr. Lawson. Your loyalty to me and this family. My brother, Antonio, is to receive a shipment tonight of a treasured family heirloom. I wish you to accompany Jarek to my brother's warehouse to ensure its safe passage here. You will be rewarded handsomely, of course, but more importantly, you'll secure a spot for yourself in this family if you want it."

Pride welled up, a feeling like he'd found his path, what he was purposed to do.

His mind spiraled with a thousand thoughts. Every one of them at odds.

Trent's choice to leave this city. Aster begging him to take her away.

Logan's pulse thundered.

But was that what she really wanted? To be separated from her father forever? From her sister? From all that she knew? And if they left, he could never provide for them the way that he could here.

This was his chance—his chance to earn Aster's father's trust. To earn a place in their family. To show him Aster would be better off with him than with Jarek.

And she deserved the world. Every fucking treasure. A giant house and a big backyard. She didn't deserve to be running and hiding in the shadows for the rest of their lives, terrified of what might be waiting for them around the corner.

He didn't love that he'd be doing it alongside Jarek. That asshole couldn't be trusted. But maybe it was the exact opportunity he needed in order to show Aster's father that Jarek needed to go.

Logan wanted it.

He wanted it.

And this was his one chance.

He had to take it.

"I'd be honored, Sir."

"Good. I have hundreds of men at my disposal, and I chose you to accompany Jarek. This is a mission of the utmost importance. The heirloom is priceless, but more so, it is a personal treasure to me. Its transport is very sensitive, and only the three of you will know its details. Do I have your loyalty and your word, Mr. Lawson?"

"Yes, Mr. Costa. You have both."

Unease trembled in his guts. Trent would be furious, but this was the best way for Aster. For their child. For him.

It would allow them both to maintain connections with their families, but more so, it ensured their safety.

Their comfort.

A good life.

He excused himself and rushed down the hall, newfound purpose pushing his steps forward. He nearly tripped when the hand flew out from a doorway and jerked him to a stop.

"Aster," he breathed, slipping into the room where she was concealed. "What are you doing?"

"Hiding." She let go of a small smile, but it was filled with worry.

He took her precious face in his hands. "And soon we won't have to hide any longer. I just spoke with your father, and he's asked me to retrieve a shipment tonight. He said he chose me over a hundred other men."

Pride brimmed in his spirit, while surprise filled her agate eyes. "What?"

"This is my chance to prove to your father that I'm worthy of you."

"I don't understand. I thought—"

"I was going to find you to let you know my brothers want to skip town. Leave forever. But that means hiding forever. And I don't want that for you, Aster. We'll constantly be looking over our shoulders, running, always worried about being discovered."

"No, Logan."

He pressed on, too excited by the prospect. "Yeah, it sucks this job is with Jarek, but you know what that means…it means your father is placing me on the same level. This is our chance."

Trepidation shimmered across her skin. "No, Logan, I don't like it. I just want to leave. I want to leave this place and never look back."

"But I'll be able to provide for you. For our baby. And you won't have to leave your sister and your father behind. Don't you see? This chance came on the same day as we would have to leave. It's fate. This is an opportunity that isn't going to present itself again."

"No, Logan, I just…" Aster stepped back. Dread radiated from her being. "I don't trust it. I don't."

He rushed back for her, so reckless, the two of them in the house. But it was time. Time.

"You have to trust me."

"Please, Logan, if you love me, let's just go with your brothers tonight. I don't want any part of this world. I don't care about the money, the only thing I care about is our family. Please."

Logan stepped back. "I gave your father my word. I have to, Aster."

"Logan," she begged.

He gripped her by both sides of the face. "You have to trust me."

"And what if it goes bad? What if something happens to you?"

"I will come back to you. No matter what."

"Promise me." It wheezed from her lips.

He dipped down and uttered the words he'd promised her time and again.

"Even if I can't see you, I'll know you're there, and I'll find my way to you."

"And there is no place my heart won't find you. My North Star." Sadness filled her voice when she whispered it, and she touched his chest.

"Don't worry. I'll be back…tonight. Meet me at our spot at one."

"Okay."

∂◦

Logan wavered outside Nathan's doorway where his brother had a suitcase open on the bed packing his clothes.

Logan struggled to breathe, his spirit in an upheaval. He'd been so certain of his decision when he'd sat in Andres Costa's chair, but actually saying it out loud—doing it—made him feel like he was taking an axe and splitting himself in two.

His heart on a chopping block.

Nathan felt his presence, and he slowed to look back at him in question as he tucked another stack of shirts into his suitcase. "What's going on, man?"

Clearly, it was radiating off Logan.

The dissention of what had to be done.

He stepped forward, unease firing from him like bullets through the room. He roughed a hand through his black hair. "I'm not leaving with you guys tonight."

Nathan stilled, a rush of hurt and disbelief radiating from his pores. "What?" he finally managed.

Logan felt like he had a ball of shredded glass in his throat. "I'm staying here, with Aster. I have an opportunity to do this right. Gain the respect of her father. I have to take it."

"Logan…" He paused, gathering what to say. "Those people, they can't be trusted. If you're getting in any deeper than you already are, that has to tell you it's a bad idea."

His head shook as his spirit warred. "I'm not doing anything illegal. Picking up an important shipment and delivering it to Andres Costa. It's a test of trust. That's it."

Nathan scoffed. "If you think whatever you plan to do isn't illegal, then you really are a fool."

Logan shuffled on his feet. "You know how much I love you and this family, Nathan. God…we've been through so much shit together. The three of you basically raised me, and you raised me with the knowledge that family is everything. That we stand by each other no matter what. And Aster has to be that now. I have to make her a priority. Do what's best for her. Live right by her. Protect her and provide for her."

"And how are you going to provide for her? By letting your hands get dirty with her daddy's blood money?"

A frown curled Logan's brow. "Like what I've been doing hasn't already muddied my hands."

"But you know it's different, and if you stay here, if you get further involved, become a *part* of them, it's gonna get ugly, man. You have to know that."

Let's just go.

Her words spun through his mind, his conscience at odds.

Run or stay.

But running didn't feel right.

"She's worth any sacrifice, and by doing it this way, I'm opening up a route to both our families. She and I will be free to see the people who mean most to us. I don't want to spend the rest of our lives with the fear of being discovered. Hiding."

It's what they'd had to do since the day they'd met.

Pain lanced through Nathan's features. "And I'm afraid you're going to find more trouble than you bargained for."

Trouble.

She was always worth the risk.

"I have to see this through. And once we have Aster's father's blessing, we'll come to you guys. Raise our kid with Trent's. I just need to make this right."

Nathan moved across the room. Apprehension oozed from his being, and his dark eyes dimmed as he touched his chest. "I have a bad feeling, Logan. A fucking bad feeling about all of this. Trent and you and all this bullshit that has taken root in our lives."

"Maybe this is the one thing that will set all of us free. But I have to take this chance. For her. I love her. Love her. And I can't ask her to live her life in fear because of her love for me."

Nathan wrapped his arms around Logan. Hugged him tight. Logan hugged him back just as fierce. "I get it. I get it. Just please be careful. I couldn't stand it if something happened to you. To any of you."

"I'll be careful. I promise."

"So fucking proud of you. I hope you know that, Logan. Probably don't say it enough, but you've got it right, man. Your heart. Don't ever fucking let anything taint it."

❧

Logan's heart pounded a riot as they pulled into the dusky alley behind the warehouse. Rain poured from the sky in heavy sheets, the sky cast in severe streaks of light as the storm ravaged the city.

They were on the shadiest side of town, the streets lined with decrepit buildings that housed vile acts and sinister intentions.

Jarek cast him a malicious glance before he killed the engine and the lights went dim.

Nausea gathered in Logan's stomach, this feeling that everything was off. Darkness reigned, only the barest streams of dingy light arching through the bleary expanse from a spotlight hung on the side of the building.

Jarek cranked open his door. "Let's go."

Logan's phone rang, and he rushed to shut it off.

That unsettled feeling only intensified when he saw it was Nathan. The second he rejected the call it started ringing again. Agitation crawled through his being, a feeling coming on strong that Aster and Nathan had been right.

He never should have come here.

Because evilness clouded the air.

Dense and dark and unrelenting.

"Are you already going to puss out? I can't say I'm shocked," Jarek sneered. "You shouldn't be here. You don't belong."

Guilt clawing at his chest, he silenced his phone and tucked it into his pocket. "I'm coming," he grunted.

With a harsh shake of his head, Jarek climbed out of the car and strode through the torrent that poured from the sky. Logan rushed to follow, his shoes splashing through the dirty puddles that had gathered.

Jarek came to what appeared a small metal garage door, and he pushed a button at the side as he peered into a camera.

It buzzed and began to roll up.

Inside stood a man who appeared close to the same age as Aster's father, his hair the same color, his eyes the same shade.

They were less trusting, though, darting around as he held a box to his chest. "My brother should have come himself rather than to trust two boys who know not what they possess."

"I am perfectly aware of the importance of this delivery, Antonio," Jarek shot back. "You act as if he shouldn't trust me when soon I will be married to Aster. I am every bit as much a part of this family as you."

Antonio scoffed. "You have a long way to go before you take the seat at the head of this family."

Bile climbed Logan's throat. Once Aster's father and Antonio both passed, Jarek would be next in line.

Darkness swirled behind them as the rain pelted the ground. Dread filled him full. Logan suddenly realized he wasn't sure if this was a test that could be passed.

Antonio stepped forward into the murky light. He tossed a glare at Jarek as he went to pass the box to him. "Be careful, mutt."

Jarek's nostrils flared.

Anxiety raced through Logan's veins, and he swore he could feel it, the bolt of depravity that struck with a flash of lightning.

A figure emerged from behind, dressed in black and covered in shadow. A mask concealed his face.

Jarek whirled around, and Antonio's eyes went wide as the man lifted an arm, cocking a gun as he edged forward.

"Give it to me," the man snarled.

Antonio tightened his hold on the box. "That would be a very unwise mistake on your part."

"Do you think I give a fuck what you say?"

A shot was fired.

Antonio howled when he was struck in the leg, and he dropped to the ground as the box crashed against the pavement.

The lid busted open, and two necklaces flew out, clattering and rolling across the ground, their giant stones glinting in the bare light.

The man went for them, leaning down to grab one, and Logan took the opportunity to dive onto his back.

He hit him with a thud. They fell to the unforgiving ground, and the attacker scrambled around in the dirty puddle, trying to turn so he could angle his gun.

"Let it go!" Logan shouted as he struggled to pin him, to hold him down. "Jarek, help, get the gun from him!"

Antonio crawled to them, struggling to get the necklace from the man's hold.

"Jarek!" Logan shouted again.

Another shot rang out.

Logan froze as Antonio slumped to the ground. Blood pooled around him.

Shock pierced through him.

Oh god. No. Oh god.

His heart clanged in his chest as Logan fought for the man's wrist that wielded the weapon. He finally curled both hands around it, bending his hand back enough that it forced him to drop the gun.

It skidded across the ground.

Logan grunted when an elbow cut him hard in the side.

The blow loosened his hold, but he managed to knee the guy in the ribs, sending him back down.

On his hands and knees, Logan scrambled for the gun that lay three feet away.

The masked man was on his feet by the time Logan got to it. Logan flew around, lying on his back, and he pointed it in the man's direction.

The man hesitated, his attention whipping between Logan and Jarek before he ran, the single necklace dangling from his hand as he disappeared into the alleyway.

Breaths heaved from Logan's lungs and the world spun.

Horror had him in a fist.

His eyes met Jarek's. Jarek who stalled for one second before he darted for the second necklace.

Logan was faster, on his feet and snatching it up before Jarek could get there. In a flash, he had the gun pointed at Jarek. Rain pelted his face, and he tried to blink, to make sense, to process. "Stop, right there."

Jarek skidded to a stop, hatred on his face. "You did this," he spat in the direction of Aster's uncle who lie face down in a puddle, the water that streamed from him blood red.

"You did this. And Aster's father will know."

Logan realized he'd taken his attention off Jarek for too long when he turned back and he also had a gun pointed at Logan.

Logan's hand shook. "That's not true."

"It is. You killed him." Jarek cocked his gun, but it was Logan who pulled the trigger.

It rang out, at one with the crack of lightning that cut through the night.

Clutching his side, Jarek dropped to his knees.

And Logan?

He ran.

Rain soaked his face as Logan panted for a breath where he had his back pressed to a wall of a building at least a mile from where he'd run. He gasped for oxygen, to see, to keep the ground from slipping out from under his feet.

But it spun and spun and the sickness reigned.

He bent over and vomited on the ground. It splashed on the pavement, mixed with the rain, and Logan thought he would faint.

His hand was curled around the necklace, his other around the gun.

What had he done?

What had he done?

Disoriented, he raked his arm over his face to clear some of the derangement that muddled his mind. He struggled to get it together.

To breathe.

With a shaky hand, he leaned down and set the gun on the ground before he dug his phone out of his pocket.

He had six missed calls from Nathan and a couple messages.

Dread sank all the way to the bone.

He squeezed his eyes shut to try to clear his vision, and he could barely fill his hemorrhaging lungs when he tapped into his messages.

He put it to his ear and forced himself to listen. That dread turned to alarm when Nathan's panicked voice came through. "Logan, answer your fucking phone. I need you. Juna showed here."

The words were haggard, coming between juts of his breaths.

"That job Trent is supposed to do tonight is a fucking trap. Juna and Dad set him up. He's going to kill Trent, Logan…fuck…"

There was fumbling on the other end of the line.

"Juna said she couldn't go through with it, so she came here to stop him, but he hasn't been here since this morning and now he's not answering his phone. We have to stop him. Warn him."

Terror caught Logan by the throat. Frantic, he tossed the gun into the dumpster, then he stumbled out from his hiding place, mumbling, "No, oh god, no."

He pushed out onto the street as the next message came through.

"Fuck, Logan. Answer." Nathan choked a pained sound. "I'm going by myself. God, I hope you're okay. I'm freaking the fuck out. I love you. I love you."

The line went dead.

Frantic, Logan dialed Nathan. He was going to promise him he was coming, all while the reality of what he'd done chased him through the rain-drenched night.

His call went to Nathan's voicemail.

"Shit," he whimpered, trying to focus as he dialed Trent, and he shouted into the messages when he didn't answer, "It's a trap. Fuck, Trent."

He realized he'd cried it.

Begged it.

He stumbled, dialed Jud.

Nothing.

Nothing.

He ordered a car that was two minutes away then stuffed the necklace into his pocket. His limbs were shaking out of control when he slipped into the backseat of the car as a rash of chills washed over him.

He looked down through the dim light to the blood that he didn't realize covered his jeans and his hands.

Just like Nathan had promised it would.

"You okay, bro?" the driver asked.

Logan choked around the knot in his throat. "Just hurry."

Twenty minutes later, the car was at the curb in front of their house, and Logan stumbled out.

Disoriented.

In shock.

He heard the roar of motorcycles screaming up the street. He almost breathed out in relief until he saw it was only two lights.

His eyes narrowed as he tried to make out who it was.

Trent and Jud.

They flew into the drive as the wind howled and the rain battered.

They squealed to a stop, their engines killed, their eyes wild.

Trent fumbled off, soaked in blood.

Jud fell right to his knees.

"Nathan," Logan begged. "Where is Nathan?"

"He's gone. He's fucking gone." Trent wailed it.

It was half cry, half fury.

Logan bent in two.

"No."

No.

Nathan had needed him, and he'd ignored his call.

No.

Agony froze his blood. Burned in his mind.

He swayed side-to-side, and he blinked and struggled to focus.

The only thing he knew was he had to get to Aster and explain before Jarek got there.

His head split with a rush of pain.

Unless Jarek was dead.

He pressed his hands to the sides of his head like he could stop the butchering inside.

"Get in the truck," Trent shouted, racing for the house.

Jud was moaning.

Just fucking moaning where he'd dropped to his knees.

"I have to get to Aster," Logan mumbled.

"What?" Trent shot out in a slash of anger and confusion.

"Aster."

"Are you fuckin' crazy? Aster Costa? I just fucking put our father in the ground after he had Nathan mowed down. We're leaving. Right now."

Trent grabbed Logan by the shirt and hauled him up.

It was when he noticed the blood that saturated Logan's clothes. "What the fuck did you do, Logan? What did you do?" It was horror. His own guilt.

Like he could be the fault of this.

"Nathan," Logan cried.

Trent tossed him into the back of the truck. "Don't move your ass out of that spot."

Logan leaned out the door and vomited again. Two minutes later, doors were slamming and Trent was tossing a bunch of bags into the back.

Jud slid into the front passenger seat, and Trent put it in reverse and gunned it out of the driveway, clipping his bike as he went, metal screeching as it was dragged two feet.

Then he shifted into gear and floored it.

"I have to get to Aster." It was a moan.

Trent whipped his attention over his shoulder to Logan. "You will never step foot in Los Angeles again, Logan. Do you understand?"

"I have to—"

"We're all dead if you do. Promise me. Fucking promise me."

Logan couldn't form the words on his tongue. Couldn't tell a lie that great. Because he had to get to her. To his girl and his baby.

Little Star.

He curled in on himself as they traveled through the night.

It passed one a.m.

She'd be waiting for him.

Terrified.

He called from somewhere near Sacramento when Trent stopped for gas, hidden away in the bathroom so his brothers wouldn't know.

There was no answer.

His spirit screamed.

He tried again the next day and the next.

He called and called for what felt like forever.

He begged the heavens for guidance.

For his Little Star to know he would come for her.

"Even if I can't see you, I'll know you're there, and I'll find my way to you."

It took him two months to slip away from Trent's paranoid eye. He sneaked away with the stone necklace and the ring he'd purchased the week before.

He would go to her father. He would present the one stone he possessed to Andres Costa that he'd been charged to protect and explain to him what had happened that horrible night.

His guts clenched because he still didn't know Jarek's fate. If he were alive or if that bullet had put him in the ground.

It didn't matter, he would beg for a chance.

For a chance to love and protect Aster, swear he would never make that kind of mistake again.

He would give her a good life. A better life. Away from the evil that lurked in that place, just like she'd first begged him to do.

When he got there, it didn't take long until she wandered out to their secret spot.

Only tears covered her face, and her stomach was flat.

He fumbled out from his hiding place.

Shock filled her face before it twisted with horror.

Or maybe it was the horror that consumed him. The way his knees wobbled in a slash of pain, and the words pitched from his mouth on a plea. "The baby."

"I got rid of it," she hissed in disgust and anger, though the words hitched in her throat midway, and she held her middle, too.

Grief whorled through the air as he struggled to process what she'd said.

The hate that had come with it.

He stumbled to the side.

He was going to pass out.

He couldn't stand.

He gripped both sides of his head. "What are you saying, Aster? What the fuck are you saying? Tell me you didn't. Oh, fuck, please."

Sickness flooded his bloodstream.

Their dreams flickered through his mind in black and white.

As if it'd all been imagined.

Unreal.

It was then he noticed the ring that glinted on her finger.

"What the fuck is that?" Pain wheezed out with it, fury following close behind.

"I'm Jarek Urso's wife. What did you think, you could crawl back here, and I'd just be waiting for you? How could you come here? After what you did? You stole from my father. You killed my uncle."

Logan's head shook. "No."

Her face pinched in a disjointed revulsion. "You chose to leave, Logan. You chose this."

Logan stumbled forward. "No, Aster. No. I told you I'd come back to you. That even if I couldn't see you, I would find my way back to you. You promised."

Her eyes slammed closed when he grabbed her by the upper arms. Shivers rushed over her flesh, and she tore herself from his grasp. "Don't touch me. I belong to Jarek now."

"Aster." Her name scraped from his soul. "No, fuck, please."

He couldn't fathom it.

What she was saying.

What she had done.

She hugged her arms over her chest. "It was just a stupid fantasy, Logan. I belong here. With Jarek. I'm a Costa princess, and thanks to you, my uncle is dead, and it's time I took my rightful spot."

She believed that? How could she fucking believe a word Jarek would feed her?

"Aster, no, listen to me."

She recoiled when he grappled to take hold of her again, and her voice twisted with spite. "Don't touch me! Don't. Fucking. Touch. Me. You were never good enough for me, and we both know it."

Agony spiraled with the anger. "Are you fucking kidding me? I would have died for you."

"That's good because you're dead to me." She took a step away. "I hate you, Logan Lawson, and I don't want to ever see you again."

"Aster."

"Go! Do you hear me? I hate you. I hate what you did. I hate who you are. Just…go."

She turned and rushed back into the foliage.

Numbness seeped into his bloodstream as he watched her go.

Dimness clawed.

He'd lost it all for her.

His brother.

Now his child.

Every hope now slayed.

He vomited the sickness onto the ground.

And as he reached into his pocket and curled his hand around the stone, he let bitterness take over every spot where Aster Rose had existed.

He let hatred reign, and he promised himself he would never be in the same position again. He wouldn't stop until he held the power. Until who he was counted. Until he had everything.

Then…then he would make Jarek Urso pay for what he had stolen.

Resolved, Logan turned and slipped into the darkened night as that single, little star burned out.

Chapter Forty-Two

Aster

WITH MY HAND SOLIDLY HELD IN HIS, LOGAN DARTED back through Absolution's main doors, dragging me through the raving crowd that had only gotten rowdier as it approached midnight.

He ducked down the hall where we'd entered, then he was hauling me into a private room and locking the door behind us. He moved across the room and fumbled around at the wall and pushed open a hidden door.

What the hell?

Confusion whirled through my being while my heart soared.

I still couldn't believe what had just happened with my father.

I didn't think I'd ever felt more exhilarated.

More hopeful.

More alive.

Logan slammed it shut and locked the hidden door, too.

It closed us off to the smoky, opaque shadows that swam through the secret room. My attention raced to take it in. It held a game table and a couch and a small bar at the back. The décor oozed of 1920's decadence.

Logan strode out in front of me, as if he couldn't sit still. He roughed an agitated hand through his black hair as he paced.

His spirit was held in a lethal storm.

"What is this place?" I wheezed, chaos whipping through my being.

My breath hitched when he finally whirled around, the sight of his face clipping off my question.

The man was so obscenely gorgeous in the tailored suit he wore.

So magnetic my heart jolted toward him.

Those eyes flashed as they raved over my body.

Copper and green.

Stony.

Malachite.

Yet, still the farthest from opaque.

They were feral.

Angered and awed and everything in between.

"You did it for me." Agony hurtled out with the hardened words.

"You did it for me." Reverent torment. It underscored his disbelief and this vibrant anger that pounded through the room. "You promised your father you would never see me again if he spared my life? That's why you married Jarek?"

My soul shook, and I pressed my hands to my chest. "I had no other choice."

I knew until right then he never had really understood what I'd meant.

Every muscle in his body rippled with severity, edged in strength and rage.

"No, Aster, you could have chosen *you*."

"And exist in a world where I knew you didn't? Know that your love for me had been your end? Never, Logan. Never." The confession wept through the room.

"What did he do to you?" Rage sprang from his spirit and burned from his tongue.

My eyes squeezed closed. "I don't want him here right now, Logan. I don't want him anywhere near us."

Because for the first time...for the first time...Logan and I had a future. A chance. A possibility. The hope of life and a...family.

My heart pounded, and my eyes fluttered open when he murmured my name.

"Aster."

It was acclaim.

Energy crackled, and he slowly moved my way.

"It was to protect me." Coarse adoration filled the sharp edge of his voice. "That night, everything you said was to protect me."

I could barely nod around the sorrow in my throat. "It killed me, Logan, standing in our special spot and telling you the greatest lie. It destroyed me all over again to cause you that pain. But it was so much better than the alternative."

Emotion bottled in my throat. The truth and the secrets and the pain.

Reaching out, he tipped up my chin. Logan's jaw was set, and his heat flamed in the space between us. "For years, I hated you, thinking you'd taken the easy way out. That you'd married a man with a name and power. That you realized I wasn't worth the trouble."

"I was the one who brought you trouble." Soggy affection blew out with the wheeze.

He inhaled a shaky sound, then he leaned in and pressed his mouth to the spot where my shoulder met my neck.

"Little Star," he whispered at the sensitive flesh. "I should have known. I should have known. But somewhere deep inside, my soul knew."

Logan's gaze deepened, locked on mine. "I should have fought for you."

"And what would have happened then? It would have brought more tragedy."

"You were worth the fight, Aster. Whatever it would have cost."

"I didn't believe it then," I admitted.

"Tell me you do now. Tell me you understand the treasure that you are," he demanded. His fingers gripped me by the chin, harsh and tender. "Tell me you understand you are worth the fight."

"I know it now, Logan. I see it in your eyes."

He edged back and slowly turned me around until I was facing an ornate, full-length mirror.

I met his reflection, the stony ferocity that rippled through his gorgeous features. "Beauty. My heart. My poetry," he murmured as his fingertips fluttered down the slope of my neck.

"You are every word I've ever written."

I could almost see the scattering of stars strewn around us. As if each call of my heart had been hung in the sky.

Logan whispered, "Wait right there. Do not move, Little Star."

Through the obscured light, I watched Logan's silhouette move across the room. In the far corner, he pulled back a drape that revealed a massive safe, and he entered a code and pressed his finger to it.

Nerves skidded through my body. This sense that we'd tripped into a new place. That we both finally understood.

Anticipation filled the room.

His and mine.

Mine and his.

It coalesced.

Convulsed and intensified and came alive when he rummaged around for something protected within.

Significance filled the atmosphere.

Thickened and deepened.

The moment hinged on expectancy.

He kept his hand hidden when he slowly edged toward me. He stopped six inches away, his panted breaths lifting chills on the flesh of my back as he gazed at me through the faded mirror.

"You asked me what this room is, Aster. This is the room where I buried all my secrets. Where I attempted to leave my pain and my spite and pretend like every part of me hadn't remained in Los Angeles with you." His breath whispered over my bare skin, illicit chills that crawled like possession.

"I gave myself over to the greed, thinking I could find contentment in excess and wealth. Find purpose in the commitment I'd made to one day make Jarek pay for what he'd stolen from me. But there was no satisfaction in any of it because the truth was all that greed came down to one thing—my love for you."

He pulled what he had hidden from behind his back and draped a necklace around my neck.

A massive stone dangled between my breasts.

A gasp raked free of my lungs.

Shock.

Confusion.

Hurt and hope and abiding love.

The ground trembled beneath my feet.

"One half of the twin stones," I whispered. "How? You said you sold them."

My fingers trembled as I touched it, and Logan leaned closer, his voice a rasp of admission. "It's the only piece I ever had, Aster. I know Jarek told your father that I was responsible, but we were attacked that night, and that man killed your uncle. Jarek stood like a pussy on the sidelines while I tried to stop it from happening. The man ran with the other stone, and before Jarek could get to the second, I took it. I shot him because he was going to shoot me. I told you I always believed that night was a setup. I still do. The night I came back for you, I was going to go to your father and return the stone and tell him everything."

My mind spun with the details.

With the truth that Logan had never done any of the things he'd been accused of.

That it was Jarek.

Jarek.

Deep down, I'd always known it, but I guessed it'd been easier to live through the loss and loneliness placing more of the blame on Logan.

"Why didn't you tell me? You said you sold them, but you had one the whole time? Why do you still have it?"

It was an appeal. Both for then and now.

These stones that had ruined everything.

382 | A.L. JACKSON

Greed.

It was what I'd believed him to be all along, and even then, I'd forgiven him.

Logan's dark brow twisted. "I was going to, Aster. When you broke my heart, I had every intention of leaving there, selling it, becoming more powerful than your father and Jarek combined. I was going to ruin them. But I couldn't. I couldn't do it. Not when I knew it was responsible for taking you from me."

"You didn't tell me? This whole time, you had it, and you didn't tell me?" I wondered how the accusation held no anger.

Logan fiddled with the chain, severity coating his voice. "I didn't trust you, Aster, that first night. You were still just the Costa princess to me." His mouth pressed behind my ear. "My tormenter. My greatest regret. The one I hated myself for still loving."

"And then?"

"And then I was terrified you were still going to leave me. That you were going to disappear. I needed an advantage. An asset to wield if I needed to. Even before you understood it, I promised myself I was never going to let you go."

"And now?"

His hand slipped from my shoulder and down my arm, and he threaded our fingers together. "And now...we do this together, the way we always should have."

"And you don't know where the other half is?" I clarified.

His head shook. "The last time I saw it, the man who killed your uncle ran with it."

Pain lacerated my soul. "Jarek did it."

He'd set up the whole thing.

Disgust blew through the agony. The pain Logan and I had been through.

It was over the twin stones.

I knew it to my soul.

"I've always believed so."

"I hate him so much."

It should be impossible to hate someone so much.

"He's at his end."

Moisture blurred my sight, and that old pain welled fast. I was impaled by the onslaught of the mistakes and manipulations we'd been victims of.

Our child.

Our child.

"Why didn't you come to me that night?"

"Our whole world exploded that night, Aster. I'd just shot Jarek Urso, I didn't know if he was dead or alive, and I only had half of what I'd been sent to retrieve for your father. Your uncle was dead and Jarek had blamed me for it. I was a kid, Aster, a kid who had gotten himself in far too deep. I was fucking terrified and had no idea what to do."

His thick throat tremored when he swallowed, grief the strike of a match in his green eyes. "I made it home only to find out Nathan had been killed. The rest of us were in danger. Trent forced me to leave with them that night, insisted that I never step foot in Los Angeles again. He'd said I'd be signing our death certificates if I did. Even with all of that, I called and called you, Aster, I fucking tried, but you never answered, and I came back the first moment I could sneak away."

My soul shivered, and tears streaked down my cheeks. "You didn't forget me."

A possessive growl rumbled from Logan's chest. "Forget you, Aster Rose? You inhabited every recess of my mind. Every crevice of my heart. And you lived in every drop of blood that beat through my veins. Just like I know now I beat through yours."

He pressed his face to my neck. "I hate what you had to do. Hate that you sacrificed. But I get it because I'd die every single day for you."

"Logan."

"Little Star."

"My destination."

Intensity blistered from his being, and Logan stepped back a fraction to twine a loose lock of hair around his hand. "And here we are," he rumbled.

"And I'm never looking back."

"Never."

"Love me, Logan, and don't you dare stop."

A rough chuckle vibrated his chest. "Stop? Oh, Little Star, I already promised you I was going to ruin you tonight."

His lips fell to my shoulder and ran up the side of my neck.

Fire flamed.

I exhaled a shaky breath as he kissed a path down the length of my exposed spine until he was kneeling behind me.

He bunched the silky material of my dress around my waist.

Cool air caressed my bottom, at odds with the heat that throbbed between my thighs.

I sucked for air.

Lust hissed from his mouth. "Fucking gorgeous. Your ass, Aster. Perfection."

He splayed a palm over my cheek, then he angled down to kiss along the strip of the lace between my crease.

I jolted forward, nearly buckling in two, and I grabbed onto the sides of the mirror for support.

Logan grunted when I did.

"Good girl," he murmured.

He spread my cheeks then pulled the fabric aside so he could let his tongue take its place.

He licked me from my clit to ass.

Desire bloomed, tendrils that spread to embed in every cell.

"Logan."

His tongue rimmed my asshole as he drove two fingers deep inside me.

Pinpricks of pleasure lit.

I pressed back, needing more.

"More."

"You're about to have all of me."

Intensity bounded through the room, and I swore, I felt the walls enclose to box us in.

A dark sanctuary where it was only me and Logan.

As if we were back beneath those hidden stars.

This love that had been twisted and disfigured but had never broken.

It unfurled then.

Complete and whole.

Logan rose to standing, and he undid his pants. Stony eyes searched my face through the reflection as he pushed his fingers between my thighs and rubbed my center. "Say it."

I gasped and whined and angled forward in a plea for more.

"I'm yours."

The second I said it, he grabbed me by the waist and drove into me in one possessive thrust.

So deep it drove a deep sob from my mouth.

"Do you feel that, Little Star?" he grunted.

Logan pulled nearly all the way out before he drove back again.

My thighs shook.

I felt him like an avalanche.

A rolling of bliss.

An undulation of possession.

"Mine," he grated.

It was grit.

Gravel.

A claim.

The truth that I had always been.

"Tell me," I demanded back.

Our gazes tangled in the reflection.

He banded one arm across my stomach, and the other splayed wide while it slowly traveled up my abdomen and chest until he was holding me by the front of the throat.

His hand curled there, pulling me up and forcing me to lean my weight against him, and his mouth came to my ear. "I'm yours, Aster. Fucking yours, and I'm always going to be, and I won't stop until that truth is your peace."

He bent his knees and thrust into me again.

A cry jolted from my lungs.

"That's right, Little Star. Feel what I do to this sweet body."

"I feel everything."

Logan growled and took me harder. "I love you, Aster Rose."

He stepped back, and he pressed his hand to the back of my neck so he could bend me over.

My hands shot back out to hold onto the mirror as he began to pound into me from behind.

He was so big as he filled me again and again.

Overpowering.

Overwhelming.

"Your pussy is perfect, Aster. The way you fit me. Nothing has ever felt better."

Pleasure gathered like the same storm that had brewed in his eyes.

Whimpers ripped from my throat with each relentless drive of his body.

"It's mine, Little Star. All of you."

He reached around and pressed his thumb into my mouth, making me suck, before he withdrew it and began to swirl it around my puckered hole.

Sensation raced.

Beautiful and dark.

"Feel me, Little Star."

He worked it inside, deeper and deeper with each stroke of his hips.

He met the deep, maddening rhythm of his hard fucks.

"Logan," I whimpered, not sure if it was too much or not close to enough.

I pushed back and drew away and got lost in the brightening glow of coming bliss.

"Touch yourself," he commanded.

My fingers fumbled to my clit, unable to keep my knees from bending forward as I held onto the mirror with my other hand to keep myself upright.

Whimpers and cries of desperation flooded from my mouth, his name a prayer I would never cease saying.

He took me harder then.

Impossible.

Too much.

Too right.

His cock and his thumb ruthlessly, perfectly in sync.

My fingers frantically tried to keep up.

Stroking and stroking as pleasure swarmed.

It was a sea of sensation, rising from the deepest abyss. Growing stronger. A current that surged and swept.

He took me ruthlessly.

Merciless in this offering.

Vicious in this atonement.

I could feel nothing else but the man who consumed me.

Body and soul.

Mine.

He'd meant it.

And in it, I found the most beautiful bliss.

"Look at me, Aster," he grunted through his raving strokes.

My eyes met the severity in his.

"Do you have any idea what you do to me? Your tight cunt and this gorgeous ass and your unforgettable face. I won't ever let you go. Not this time. Not ever again."

"I love you, Logan." It came out with the air that wheezed from my lungs.

"Everything," he muttered in return.

Our hearts raced, and our spirits shook, and our bodies begged.

Merged and twined and became one.

That dark sea swirled and thrashed.

Sensation erupted from the depths. From the places I didn't know.

It eclipsed reason and sight.

He drove and possessed.

I split apart.

Soared.

Ripples of pleasure raced to touch every cell, to infiltrate every fiber.

"Oh god," I cried, my knees going weak as pleasure took me whole.

Logan tightened his arm that was banded around my waist because I could no longer stand.

He continued to drive into me as my walls throbbed and pulsed around him.

"Aster...fuck...yes."

He took his pleasure, and he gave me mine.

Wave after wave.

Unending.

Infinite.

Logan grunted low as he buried himself completely.

His body quivered and poured.

Bliss cracked through the room.

A blackout.

Dark, dark ecstasy.

Spent, I dropped to my knees when he loosened his hold, but Logan only scooped me into his arms.

His heart raced at a jagged beat, and his breaths pitched from his lungs.

"Logan."

I bit my lip at the way he was looking at me. The man so gorgeous my stomach quaked all over again.

"What are you doing?" I whispered.

My heart twisted when he smirked. "I thought you'd get it by now that I take good care of what's mine. Get used to it, baby, because I'm going to be doing it for the rest of my days."

Shouts seeped through the walls. The countdown had begun.

"Ten, nine, eight..."

Logan held me tighter as his spirit danced with mine.

"Five, four, three, two..."

Logan mouthed the last, *One*.

"Happy New Year, Little Star."

I pressed my face into the warmth of his neck. "It's not just happy, Logan. It's every wish I've ever made."

Chapter Forty-Three

Logan

MORNING LIGHT SLOWLY BROUGHT ME TO consciousness. I was face down on my stomach, one cheek buried in a plush pillow and the blankets pushed around my waist. Glittering rays streamed through the window and illuminated the room in dancing golds and sparkling gems.

Or maybe I just felt like a motherfucking king.

I flopped onto my back and listened to the sounds echoing through the walls. A smile stretched wide as I heard the clattering of pans and the subdued pat of her bare feet.

The girl was a song that whispered in my ear and lured me to standing.

I shuffled into the bathroom, took a piss, and brushed my teeth before I tugged on a pair of sweatpants.

The whole time, I could feel her moving through the apartment.

This girl my destiny.

I sensed her like a tie in my being that could never be undone.

Quietly, I edged out of the bedroom. I stopped outside the door to take in the sight.

Aster was there, in the kitchen. She was barefoot and wearing the same button up I'd worn last night. She had the sleeves rolled up, the fabric swallowing her frame in the most exquisite of ways, hitting her right above those lush, gorgeous thighs.

Dark brown hair was piled in a wild knot, and there was a fresh dusting of flour on her cheek.

So fucking pretty.

So fucking right.

I could see the etching of a smile tug at the corner of her mouth while she whipped something in a bowl. "Are you just going to stand there and stare all day?"

Her voice was light, full of wonder and a tease.

My chest panged, and I leaned a shoulder against the wall and stuffed my hands into the pockets of my sweats. "Seems like a pretty good way to spend New Year's Day to me."

"Why only look when you can touch?" She tossed it out with a slight shrug, pure seduction and ease.

A rough chuckle scraped up my throat, and I strode that way, every step tightening the muscles in my abdomen, my mouth watering for a taste.

I wound myself around her from behind, loving the way she felt, the way she sank back and let go of a satisfied breath.

"Happy New Years, baby," I murmured as we began to slowly sway.

"I can't believe I'm here with you, celebrating the New Year."

I glanced at her ring that glinted in the rays of morning light. My chest expanded in a possessive beat. I pushed my nose into the hair behind her ear.

Hyacinth and magnolia leaves.

"A hundred more new years where this came from."

Soft affection rolled from her mouth. "A hundred, huh?"

"A thousand." A smile fumbled on my lips.

She giggled and sank deeper into my hold. "I'll take as many as I'm given, just as long as I get to spend them with you."

"Every day." My hands splayed over her stomach.

"You'd better be careful, I might get used to this," she whispered like this entire thing was a dream.

I kissed a path down the side of her neck.

Another giggle. "You're distracting me."

"That's the plan."

"Can't you see I'm busy?" It was coy and sweet.

I lapped it up, wrapped myself tighter, and peered down from over her shoulder. "What are you making?"

"Cookies."

I grunted. "You're the one who'd better be careful, or else I'm going to be the one getting used to this."

"What, me barefoot and pregnant in the kitchen?"

My breath caught in my throat. I forced it down. "Don't tease me, Aster."

And not about the kitchen thing. Fuck that misogynistic shit. The men who'd held her down. I was going to hold her up.

She stilled, her breaths going shallow as she set aside the bowl and whisk. She placed her hands over mine and pressed me closer to her, and her voice thinned out. "I'm not teasing, Logan. I think I might be pregnant."

Everything stalled.

Time.

The staccato of my heart.

Before it all raced to catch up.

I rushed to spin her around, and I tipped up her chin so I could take in her sweet, gorgeous face that was held in worry and fear and something bigger than life.

Energy bound the air in a dense knot.

"What are you saying?" My hands trembled as I slipped my palms to either side of her neck. "What are you saying, baby?"

Her eyes were wild and intense. "I think I might be pregnant, Logan. I should have had my period last week, and I thought I was just off with the stress and the worry. I've been nauseous, but again, I thought it was just from everything that is happening. But this morning, I vomited, and in that moment, I think I just knew. My shot was due right before I came here, and I missed it, but I thought it would be fine—"

"It's more than fine." I cut her off, my voice squeezing on the words. "More than fine. As far as I'm concerned, it'd be a fucking miracle."

She inhaled a shattered breath.

"I'm scared, Logan. I'm scared that I'm making the same mistakes all over again. That it's too close and feels too familiar. But if it's true? I will do everything to protect this child. Everything, Logan." A fiery oath lit in those agate eyes. The girl a warrior. One who would stand and fight.

"There is nothing I want more than to have a family with you."

"Are you sure?" She blinked up at me.

"I promise you, Aster Rose. I promise."

I lifted her hand and kissed her ring, and I leaned in to murmur in her ear, "And I'm going to make sure that becomes Aster Rose Lawson soon. Very soon."

Aster laughed. She laughed this disbelieving, joyous sound that rang in the air and reverberated from the walls.

A thrill.

Euphoric.

"I can't believe it," I murmured.

It felt like I was suffering from a bolt of shock.

The best kind.

"I can't believe it!" That time, I shouted it, and I picked her up and spun her around.

She squealed and laughed and clung to my shoulders as she flung her head back and let the peals of delight paint the walls of the apartment a new color.

Vibrant.

Beauty.

Light.

"We don't even know for sure." She giggled it.

I held her up high, and she looked down at me, smiled that smile that slayed.

Cut me wide open.

This girl my destiny.

"But you know," I hedged.

Her expression softened, so tender that she melted through the middle of me. "Yes, Logan, I know."

I took her mouth.

My kiss was fevered and hers was overjoyed.

Panted laughs and giggled whispers. "I love you, Logan. I love you."

"I love you, baby, so much."

I kept spinning her around while I kissed her, this girl the wildest, best ride I'd ever taken.

I set her down on the edge of the table.

She yelped then grinned while I palmed her on the outside of the thighs. "Look at you...a perfect present wrapped in my shirt."

Another giggle, and redness was lighting on her cheeks.

"Are you going to unwrap me?" The tease slipped from her tongue.

"Oh, Little Star, you bet I am."

I reached for the material and tore it open. Buttons pinged as they scattered across the floor.

Aster squealed then gave me the fakest pout. "Hey, I liked this shirt."

"I like your tits better."

Small and round and already pebbled up so tight as her chest heaved toward me, peeking through the shirt where it was split open.

The only thing she had on under it was a patch of black lace held together by three bands on each side.

Need fisted my guts.

"Is that so?" A seductive smile pulled over her mouth. Joy rushed beneath it.

"Oh, it's so, Aster. You are a fucking dream, spread out on my table."

My cock was stone. It pressed against the fabric of my sweats, and the muscles in my stomach flexed in anticipation of the best kind of relief.

Aster sank her teeth into her bottom lip as those eyes raked over me. "And you steal my breath, Logan. Look at you...my North Star."

A growl rumbled in my chest, and I leaned over her so I could devour that mouth.

She bucked up, her lace-covered pussy rubbing against my abdomen.

I devoured her, and she laughed some more, close to delirious.

I understood the condition. The way my head was spinning and the only thing that mattered was getting inside this girl.

Wholly.

Fully.

Footsteps skidded to a stop just inside the living room.

I jerked back, still gripping deep into Aster's thighs.

"Oh my," Gretchen wheezed as she slapped a hand over her heart.

"You should probably head on out, G, because I am most definitely about to take it out."

Aster covered her face with her arm, trying to hide her laugh of embarrassment.

Gretchen waved a hand in the air and started in the direction of the door, calling, "Don't mind me. I'm half blind, anyway. Didn't see a thing. Half deaf, too, so don't worry yourselves a bit. I'll clean up the mess later."

When the front door banged shut behind Gretchen, I let out the chuckle I was holding.

Aster dragged her arm free. Her face was beet red.

"Logan," she chastised. "You are horrible."

"And you are mine." I cracked a smirk. "Now where were we?"

"I think you were admiring my tits."

I ran a knuckle over a peaked, hard nipple. "Oh, that's right. I was admiring these tits."

I palmed them both before I kissed down her stomach and edged back so I could drag her underwear down her legs. I dropped them to the floor, then I angled down while peering up at her when I murmured, "And now I'm getting ready to *admire* this perfect pussy."

She bucked up. Completely bare. Drenched and swollen and throbbing.

Straightening, I freed my cock, lined myself up, and plunged into the hilt.

Aster bowed.

Body and soul.

"That's right, Little Star. You and me."

You and me and this little family.

It was all I was ever going to need.

I took her slow this morning.

My hips rocking in deep and measured strokes.

Early morning light poured in the window to shine over her entrancing body.

I touched her.

Loved her.

My girl came three times.

I came hard in her pussy in deep rutting thrusts.

Pure motherfucking ecstasy.

I heaved for a breath as I fell over her, my ear pressed to the hammer that raged in her chest. She searched for air, and she languidly ran her fingers through my hair as awestruck laughter rolled from her mouth.

"That was amazing."

I lifted my head. "You're amazing."

We just stayed there for a minute, staring at the other, unable to believe we'd made it to this place.

"Why don't I go grab a test and you finish the mess on the counter that Gretchen is going to have to clean?"

Aster giggled. "I don't think that was the mess she was referring to. She's never going to eat on this table again."

I nuzzled my face in her neck. "I plan to eat on this table many, many times."

She smacked at me playfully.

I helped her to standing, then I kissed her nose. "I'll be right back."

"I'll be waiting."

∽∾

I jogged to the small drugstore down the street where I bought ten tests.

I couldn't help it.

I was excited.

Because Aster and me?

We were never looking back.

I paid, then rushed back up the sidewalk to my building. I entered through the main lobby and went directly to the elevator, my knee bouncing in anticipation as I rode it upstairs.

I all but ran to the door.

Only when I got to it, I skidded to a stop.

My heart hurtled into my throat that was covered in bile.

The hinges were busted.

Dread spiraled through my being, and I ran into the apartment, ready for any fight that awaited.

Only I froze when I was impaled by the energy that filled the space.

Dark and grim.

The paper bag slipped from my hand and all the tests spilled onto the floor.

Because I knew in an instant, my girl was gone.

Chapter Forty-Four

Aster

I WAS GRINNING WHEN I WENT TO THE CLOSET AND PULLED another of Logan's shirts from a hanger. I put it on and buttoned it, then I padded back out into the kitchen to finish mixing the batter for the cookies.

There was no wiping the smile from my face. The joy that had seated itself deep.

It was amazing what could change in thirty days.

Thirty days.

It was funny that I'd intended them to free myself of Jarek's chains. Even that should have been impossible.

Still, I'd known I had to fight to find my freedom.

To find *myself*.

And I did.

I did.

But I'd also found so much more.

I'd found joy and hope and love. I found the family I'd been missing. I found the belief in a man that I'd lost long ago.

We'd thought our dreams crushed.

But in those thirty days?

We'd found revival.

A resurrection.

Redemption.

A small giggle floated out when there was a tapping at the door. I grabbed a hand towel and wiped my hands and started across the room on my bare feet, a smile tugging at my mouth when I called, "What did you forget? I hope it was another kiss."

I let the playfulness roll out with it.

This joy that possessed.

Logan had only been gone for little more than a few minutes, and I was already missing him.

There was no response.

Frowning, I pressed my ear to the wood to listen. "Logan?"

A shot of unease rippled through.

Dread slipped like ice down my spine.

Cold as it spread.

Because in that second, I knew it. I knew it just as sure as I knew the child that grew in my belly.

And I'd never let it happen.

Not this time.

I turned on my heel to run for my phone. That was right when two huge bangs crashed against the door. Wood splintered and metal twisted.

Alarm pounded through my bloodstream.

No.

On the third hit, it busted wide open.

A scream ripped up my throat, and I kept running as I looked back to find a man in the doorway who held a metal battering ram.

Jarek stepped around him and came through the doorway.

Evil curled through the air.

My knees nearly buckled, but I forced myself to hold down the fear.

I just had to make it to the bedroom where I'd left my phone and everything would be okay.

My bare feet slapped on the dark floor, but it was the sound of the heavy footsteps that grew closer and closer that sent terror ripping through my veins.

With each thudded step, his vile presence swarmed the room.

I pushed myself harder, flying into the bedroom and going for the nightstand.

I heaved a breath when I grabbed my phone, but Jarek was on me before I could even bring the screen to life. His hand flew out in the same motion, smacking me across the face. The force toppled me onto the bed. "You stupid bitch."

Horror tore from my throat and banged against the thick walls.

No.

No.

I couldn't let this happen.

He grabbed a handful of the shirt at the neck and jerked me up to standing. "Where is it, Aster, where is the stone?"

My head violently shook, and I clawed at his hand. "I don't know."

"You're a fucking liar." Hatred burned in his expression. "You think you're going to ruin everything, don't you? Stop me? I will have what I want. He will not make a fool of me again."

Jarek jerked me forward and began to drag me back through the apartment.

I tore at his arm, fighting his hold, screaming, "No, someone help! Please, someone help me."

He pulled my back to his chest and cupped his palm over my mouth. "Keep screaming and you die. At this point, I'm beginning to believe you've worn out your use."

Still, I kicked and flailed as Jarek half carried, half dragged me into a stairwell meant for the maintenance team.

They quickly rushed down the stairs, the two men's feet pounding on the concrete steps.

The whole time, I fought. Desperation thick, I scratched and clawed at Jarek's hand while trying to sink my teeth into his palm.

It wasn't enough.

It wasn't enough.

They banged through a door that led into the back of the building where there was an employee parking lot for the stores and restaurant that housed the main floor.

I kicked and flailed my bare legs into the frigid, ice-cold air. "No!" It slurred against his palm.

Right outside, a man waited at the back door of a limousine. He opened it, and Jarek tossed me inside.

I shouted with everything I had as I slid into the leather seat on one side.

"Help! Please." Frantically, I smacked my palms against the glass.

Jarek climbed in. "Shut your fucking mouth."

Two doors slammed shut and the car jolted forward, the tires squealing as we peeled from the lot.

I banged both palms against the glass as if I could break free.

The low, sinister laughter that curled through the limousine made my head whip around to find another man I hadn't realized was there.

Haille Manchief sat across from me with a smug smile on his pompous face. His head was cocked to the side, studying me as if I were the most interesting element in this twisted-up game. "Ah, there you are. I thought you were going to prove interesting."

He took his attention from me and set it on Jarek who raged beside me.

"He'll come. Just wait. It is done."

Chapter Forty-Five

Logan

AGONIZED VIOLENCE BURNED A HOLE THROUGH THE MIDDLE of me. I stormed back into the kitchen. Unable to sit. Unable to think. Prisoner to the torment that clawed through my insides.

I nearly choked on the sight of the half-made cookies where Aster had left them. Seized by the rage, I grabbed the metal mixing bowl and threw it across the room. It smashed against the wall and clattered to the floor.

"Logan, man." Jud's voice was low and sympathetic where it fell over me from behind, and I pressed my hands to the counter and dropped my head between my shoulders in an effort to get it under control.

My brother set his hand on my shoulder and squeezed it tight. "We're going to get her back, man, promise you."

My heart ping-ponged against my ribs.

My vision red.

The fury blinding.

"I can't—" The words cracked in my throat as another wave of desperation slammed me.

It didn't matter that I'd already known she was gone, that I'd known it the second I stepped into the frayed, oppressive air her spirit had left behind, I'd searched every inch of the building.

It had taken my brothers less than fifteen minutes to come storming through my busted apartment door after I'd called, sure that monster had taken her.

Where, was the problem.

We'd already gone to the hotel where he'd been staying. It'd only taken a stack of cash to get it out of the receptionist that he'd checked out three days ago.

Torment howled through my body, and I pulled myself from where I was sagged against the counter and raged back across the floor, both hands dragging through my hair like it could tame what ate me alive.

Aggression.

Violence that streaked.

I needed to keep them. Rein them until they could be unleashed.

"Logan," Trent said, approaching me like he was approaching a rabid animal.

It wasn't far off.

"I have to get to her." It was a rasp.

Hatred.

Fear.

Agony.

A dangerous cocktail that was going to blow.

"Knew that prick wasn't goin' to stand down. Was clear as day last night. He's out for something."

"For my girl. I shouldn't have left. God. I shouldn't have left."

I dropped to my knees on the rug, gutting weakness taking me over.

I shouldn't have left.

I clutched the hollow ache that moaned in my chest. "If something happens to her..."

To them.

Nausea spun.

"We'll find her," Trent promised as he came to crouch in front of me. I'd rambled everything I could give them when they'd first shown, confessing everything I'd held onto for years.

"Do you have details? Any clue? Could he be headed back to Los Angeles?"

I shifted onto my butt, leaning against the couch and blinking through the turbulence that narrowed my sight.

"Possibly. If he was going to use her against her father?" My head shook as I searched for an answer. "I don't fucking know."

The only thing I knew was I was going to destroy him.

And if he hurt her?

My ribs flared as I drew in a ragged breath.

I flew to my feet when there was suddenly a commotion at the door that gaped open.

Trent did, too, and Jud raced over to take up my side.

Only it was a young woman who stepped through. "Hello?"

A tatted-up biker followed her in, all kinds of protective and wearing a cut with a patch that said *Demon's Day*.

Trent fucking hissed, and both he and Jud stepped forward, a sharp edge riding their demeanors as they stared down a man that rode for what had been our club's mortal enemy.

Trent and Jud spread out, filling the space with their distrust and animosity.

In a stupor, I tried to make sense of the woman standing there.

"Taylor? Is that you?"

I didn't know if it was relief or panic that struck me at the sight of her.

I hadn't seen Aster's sister since she was twelve. A child. She was now a woman. Her hair and eyes were close to the same color as Aster's, although she was a couple inches taller and curvier.

Her expression dampened when she looked around.

As awareness gave way to the air of desperation, of horror, of malicious intent.

"I'm too late," she whimpered. She looked like she might collapse when she slowly drifted into the vacant space.

I moved for her. The biker came forward, too, stepping in front of her.

Trent and Jud flanked me.

"Watch it, Demon," Trent warned low.

"I'm just here to protect the girl. Your boy needs to calm the fuck down before he gets any closer to her. Looks like he's about to snap," the Demon spat.

Taylor shoved around him, putting out her hand. "This is no time for a pissing contest. What happened to my sister?" She begged that.

"He has her." Strained terror heaved out with the words.

He had her, and I had no fucking clue where he intended to take her or how I was going to get her back.

A sob ripped from Taylor's throat. "No. He can't. I…"

She spun around like it would stop this fucking endless cycle of torment.

I'd promised Aster I'd protect her. Promised her that bastard would never touch her again.

And he *had* her.

Lightheadedness pummeled me, suffocating, everything so tight that I thought my lungs would implode.

This crushing, devastating weight.

"I got it." Taylor hugged a satchel to her chest. "I got it for her and she's not here and he has her. Oh god, he has her."

Her knees went weak, and she nearly toppled over, but the Demon caught her around the waist. "We'll get your sister."

"What's in the bag?" I demanded.

"She needed proof." It was a wisp of pain.

"What is in the bag?" I stumbled forward, about to lose it.

To snap, just not on Taylor like the Demon had implied.

I was about to fly out that door and go on a rampage.

Hunt until I found him.

Until I could wrap my hands around his neck and choke the life from him.

Taylor passed it to me while the biker continued to keep her supported. "There are documents in the case condemning Jarek's disloyalty to our father, just like Aster thought. But I found something else, Logan, I think I found what she really needed."

Urgency spun around me as I dug into it.

I didn't know if it was relief or disgust.

A part of me had always assumed.

Had always known.

Hell, I wasn't even surprised.

But there it was, the second twin stone.

My chest clutched tight, and my stomach twisted.

Sniffling, Taylor looked at me, and her expression deepened in emphasis. "It's worth only a fraction without its partner."

"It's what he wanted all along. The second stone."

"Do you have it?" she asked through her tears, her voice cautious.

The confession climbed my throat, the truth that he had likely been plotting how to get it back from me for all this time.

Our family's whereabouts had been unknown for years, until a year ago when Gage's mother had exposed us.

Clearly, that was when Jarek had found our location, too.

I sank onto the couch because I couldn't keep standing.

"I have it," I forced out.

Taylor seemed to have to compel the words out. "The documents in there...what Aster had sent me after? They're in code, but we believe them to be records of his connections in Russia."

She glanced back at the biker before she returned her attention to me. "It appears there was some sort of arrangement. If Jarek could acquire both stones, then he was assured his new position as head of LA. There is a plot to take my father out, but he had to procure the missing piece before he could do it."

My chest burned, and she pulled something else out of her bag and slowly edged forward.

Confusion pulled across my brow as she handed me a keepsake box.

"This was in Aster's old room back at our father's house. Hidden, but I always knew where she kept it. I brought it thinking she would want it and would probably never go back."

My spirit thrashed as I set it on my lap, as I carefully opened it to find it filled with folded star notes.

Little Star.

My spirit thrashed, silently reiterating the promise again and again.

"Even if I can't see you, I'll know you're there, and I'll find my way to you."

I would. I would find my way to her. No matter what it took.

She moved and knelt in front of me, and she reached in and produced one that was awkwardly shaped, too thick to really fold with the number of pages it held.

"I'm not sure what she's told you, but I think you need to read this one. So you fully understand. It's important."

Emotion filled my eyes.

Fuck.

I couldn't handle any of this shit.

My mind spun with every scenario.

Aster hurt.

Scared.

The baby...

My breaths clotted off as my throat thickened in a vise of agony.

"She loves you," Taylor urged.

"I love her. More than life. And I promise you I will get her back." Razors filled the last words.

"I know you will."

It was then my phone buzzed with a text. I scrambled to grab it, praying for a miracle.

That this whole thing was a misunderstanding.

That she was safe.

I frowned when I saw it was a text from Haille.

> Haille: It's rude to turn down a thoughtful invitation, no? My house at 10 or I'll have to find a more interesting way to entertain myself. She is an intriguing artifact.

A cold sweat broke out on the nape of my neck.

Haille: I think you are well aware of what tonight's ante is. I hope you don't disappoint me.

A tacky awareness slipped over my skin.

Prickles of disgust and disbelief.

Greed.

It had driven me for years.

I'd believed I'd had something to prove.

Had hungered for the power.

For the gain to rise superior over my enemies.

So I'd sat at that man's table and made friends with the beast.

I'd filled my cup with treasure until it'd overflowed with wealth.

But in the end, there was only one thing I wanted.

Chapter Forty-Six

Aster

When the light goes dim…

MY LOVER.
My life.
My North Star.
What did you do? What did you do?
Grief blew through me like a parched, stricken desert.
Dry and brittle.
No stars or light or reason.
A total eclipse.
I'd only wanted to go. To leave. To escape.
Money didn't matter. My comfort was in you.
So I'd trusted you to whisk us away. To come to your senses. For you
to turn your back on the greed that had tainted my family.
Our time had come and gone.
One a.m. then two.

Dread had filled me to overflowing and threatened to wash me away in the undertow.

I'd heard the frantic footsteps that pounded the compound, the shouts and the anger and the disbelief.

With my heart barely beating, I'd sneaked back inside and slipped down the hall where I'd pressed my back to the wall outside of Papa's office, listening to the chaos that ensued inside.

It was filled with men, but it was Jarek who'd ranted in stark pain. "That asshole," he'd hissed, holding himself way up high on his side. "He killed Antonio in cold blood, Andres. He tried to kill me. He took the stones. He took them," he gritted in abhorrence.

Devastation curled.

Wound and whispered and made me sink farther against the wall to keep myself from slipping to the floor.

My uncle? My uncle was dead?

How could I believe it?

That you would do it?

In shock, I'd peered into the room as if it might paint a different picture.

But it was blotted in red.

Disfigured and mangled and wrong.

The light on Papa's desk shined through the darkness and illuminated the blood that dripped onto the floor.

Jarek's shirt was soaked in it.

To me, it'd looked like death.

If only I could have hoped to be so lucky.

That there would have been a measure of grace in this torment.

You'd betrayed my father.

You'd betrayed me.

Because you didn't come.

And it had come to this.

I'd heard my papa's voice, his fist that'd slammed against the desk, the horrible words that crashed out, "He will die for this. His whole family. See to it."

So I'd run.

Run down the corridor with frantic gasps raking from my lungs.

I'd known I had to get to you. Find you. Understand why.

Why?

Why?

Why?

I'd run back to our secret spot, praying you would be waiting. That you would explain it all.

Again, you weren't there.

I waited and paced some more.

You still didn't come.

But Jarek did, his dark shadow covering me when he appeared from behind.

Scorn lined his face. "He's dead, Aster. He's fucking dead and you're mine."

Fear had slithered like the coil of snakes down my spine, pooled in my stomach as he took a step toward me, like the rage that held him had eradicated the wound that oozed from his side.

Instinctively, I'd set my hands over my stomach.

Over our child.

As if I could protect him.

Jarek's eyes had gone there, and I'd lost air when I'd seen the flash of contempt light in his eyes the moment he knew.

I'd turned to run.

To flee.

I screamed when he grabbed me by the hair, when he yanked me back, when his fist found my face.

He dragged me deeper into the hidden places in the garden.

I'd kicked and pled, but there was no mercy from a merciless man.

"He will die for taking what is mine. Both the stones and this body."

Agony overwhelmed as he struck me.

Each blow had come harder than the last, powerful enough to shatter bone, to shatter courage, to shatter sanity.

His fists and his boots and the grip of his gun.

So much pain.

But still, I'd fought. With every part of me, I'd fought.

I'd rolled to my side, rocking, curling into a ball to keep him protected.

Jarek had ripped my head up by my hair, and the vile voice whispered like it could be a balm in my ear. "Don't cry, Aster. This is what was meant to be. You'll see. You'll see."

He'd hauled me to the side gate while I'd prayed for you. I'd even prayed for my father.

The guard had let him pass. I'd pled for help, but the man, he didn't listen, he didn't care, the same as Jarek.

Monsters who looked at me like a possession.

Treasure or waste.

Whatever their pleasure.

Jarek pushed me into the front seat of his car.

I'd screamed for Papa. Prayed for him to come and save me. Or maybe he would stand aside and allow Jarek to ruin me.

Maybe I really was nothing to any of them.

Jarek had groaned as he'd gotten into the driver's seat, his hand pressing on the wound before he'd hit me with his gun again.

"This is your fault, you cunt."

I was so disoriented when he'd begun to drive. Blood ran in heavy streams down my face. My skin was busted open, throbbing and swollen.

Consciousness had come in and out of focus.

I was almost relieved when I realized we were at the Costa physician. He was the one who repaired gunshots and stab wounds and the evidence of beatings when my father's men couldn't be seen at the hospital.

He would help me.

He would help me.

But Jarek tossed me into the room, grated, "Get rid of it."

It'd taken one look at the coldness on the physician's face to understand what Jarek had meant.

I'd lost all sanity.

All sense of prudence gone.

I had raged, flying across the room to the locked door.

"No!" I'd screamed as I'd pounded my palm on the unforgiving metal. "Please, someone help!"

I jerked from a hand that grabbed me by the upper arm, and I ran through the room, tossing trays and supplies onto the floor.

They'd crashed.

The clanking metal piercing and loud.

The panic so fierce.

I had to get away.

I had to.

A needle was stabbed into my arm.

I fought for coherency.

I'd fought, Logan, I'd fought.

But I should have known it from a young age.

I was a possession. Property. Inanimate.

I never had a chance.

I'd awoken the next day with my father sitting beside me where I lie on an unfamiliar bed, my sight partially obstructed by a swollen eye. It took half a second for me to come to awareness. To the gutting, horrified recognition.

Still, my hands flew to my stomach.

To the emptiness that would forever ache within me.

A wail climbed from the depths. So deep and severe I'd thought it would rend me in two.

"Foolish child," my father had said. But it was soft, his fingers brushing through my hair.

Everything hurt. My broken face and my beaten body and my shattered soul.

Another sob ripped up my throat and banged from the walls.

A grief so deep I'd thought I'd perish right then.

"I warned you not to do something so foolish. Something that would force me to do something I would regret."

My father had the audacity to let tenderness fill his voice.

"Is Logan dead?" The question cracked, so thin and brittle. I didn't know if I would survive the answer.

"It seems he and his entire family have fled. But we will find them."

It was the smallest fraction of relief.

A shooting star that passed in a blink through the sky.

"You cannot hurt him, Papa," I'd begged.

"He betrayed me, mia vita. He took my brother." His own sorrow wound with his words. "Betrayed me. Stole from me. Touched you."

"I love him, Papa."

Even after what you'd done. Even after what you'd cost.

Everything, everything.

I still loved you.

"You must not." It was a demand. "You must fulfill your duty. To me. To Jarek."

Jarek.

Sickness clawed through my consciousness.

I began to weep. Guttural cries that came and came.

"Please, Papa."

Pain.

Intense.

Unending.

"He will be held accountable for his actions."

Yet my father sat there and looked at me with the evidence of what my tormentor had done. This was the man he'd intended to be my husband, and he sat there and looked at me as if it were my fault?

At the realization, my broken spirit split apart.

"I will die if you have him killed."

"Blasphemy."

I didn't know if in that moment it was true. It must have been because I was sure my father saw the truth of it in my eyes.

Frantically, I grappled to take hold of his hand. "I need one thing from you, Papa, please, grant me one thing. I need him to live."

"Aster Rose," he'd warned, torment in his voice.

My hand had grasped at his. "I'll do anything, Papa. Just promise me you'll spare him. Promise me, and I'll do what you demand."

He'd wavered, but in it was a glimmer of the humanity I prayed he possessed. His lips had thinned then he'd said, "Okay, mia vita. I will spare him and his family, as long as he never shows his face here again."

◦◦

Two months later, you came. You stood in our spot after what you'd caused.

I was so angry.

So angry.

Depression had come, dark, eternal rage its partner.

So lost. So sad. So empty.

"The baby." It was the first thing you'd said.

The impact of it nearly knocked me to my knees.

Tears fell and fell, but I held on to the anger.

"I got rid of it." I'd tried to spit it like venomous truth, but halfway up, the lie had stuck in my throat.

You'd swayed to the side.

Gutted.

I knew it.

I saw it in your face.

And I hated you even more that you'd made me put you through this.

If you'd only listened.

If you'd taken us far from here.

We could have hidden away together.

That's where I'd always wanted to be—hidden away with you.

I knew the second you saw the gaudy, disgusting ring on my finger.

A shackle that maimed.

"What the fuck is that?" Your voice was so hard. Shocked and outraged.

I was outraged, too.

"I'm Jarek Urso's wife. What did you think, you could crawl back here, and I'd just be waiting for you? How could you come here? After what you did? You stole from my father. You killed my uncle."

How could you?

How could you?

God, you were still so beautiful out there beneath the hidden stars, even with your face contorted with disgust.

I'd wanted to go to you.

Fall on you.

Beg you to take me away from this horrible place.

I had to guard myself from your words. From the desperate pleas that fell from your mouth.

I couldn't listen.

I couldn't hear.

Because I'd bartered my life for yours, and I hated you for that, too, and it was now my responsibility to see to it that you never returned again. Just your standing there could have been a death sentence.

So I'd forced out the bitterness that was bottled inside me, tried to claim the lies as truth. "Don't touch me! Don't. Fucking. Touch. Me. You were never good enough for me, and we both know it."

"Are you fucking kidding me? I would have died for you."

Your words broke through, and my soul screamed that I *was dying* for you.

"That's good because you're dead to me." *I'd forced myself to take a step away.* "I hate you, Logan Lawson, and I don't want to ever see you again."

Then I'd turned and run.

And that was the night my North Star went dim.

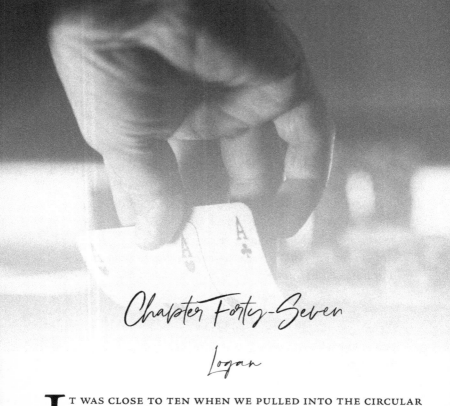

Chapter Forty-Seven

Logan

IT WAS CLOSE TO TEN WHEN WE PULLED INTO THE CIRCULAR
drive of the mansion hidden deep in the forest outside Redemption
Hills. Night stretched long and dense across the heavens.

A shroud of debauchery.

An oozing of sin.

My knee bounced uncontrollably as I tried to breathe around the
ten-thousand-pound weight that sat squarely on my chest.

I fought with the urge to jump from the passenger seat to go
storming the castle like some kind of twisted knight.

My soul reeled from the star Taylor had asked me to read.

It consumed me in a fist of grief and a thirst for vengeance, tortured by what Aster had been through.

Her sacrifice.

Her loss.

Her pain.

While hatred burned so hot toward Jarek I thought when I saw
him he might burst into flames.

Disintegrate into ash.

Like he felt me getting ready to splinter apart, Trent muttered, "Play it cool, man," as he pulled his Porsche to a stop in the drive.

Jud was in the backseat.

Tension coiled in the air, bands that stretched taut between us and made every single one of us feel like we were going to snap.

I knew it.

I could feel it radiating off my brothers.

The truth that we were waltzing into the lion's den.

"Are you two sure you want to go in there?" One last chance for them to back out because I wasn't coming out of that house without my girl.

Whatever it cost.

"Like we'd let you go in there alone and miss out on all the action? I don't think so, brother," Jud cracked.

"Yeah, not gonna happen," Trent added. "Besides, it looks like you're going to need more than two hands for this little endeavor. And that's what this family does…we lend a helping hand when it's required."

He smirked at that because we all knew this was a whole lot more than a *helping hand*.

Things were bound to get wild in there.

Would likely end bloody.

It would be dangerous and unpredictable.

I took a steadying breath, opened the door, and pushed to standing, hand gripping tight on the case that held the stone.

Ferocity simmered in my blood, close to boiling.

My nostrils flared.

I could feel it.

I could feel her spirit crying out from within the walls.

My chest tightened with the promise. "*Even if I can't see you, I'll know you're there, and I'll find my way to you.*"

"Easy," Jud said as he came up to my side. "Know you want to run in there with guns blazing, but we have to play this smart."

"Good thing smart is what he does." Trent almost grinned.

My hand squeezed on the handle of the case that held the box. It was fucking ironic how the whole goal for that bastard was getting the second stone back from me, and he didn't have a goddamn clue that I now possessed both. The other stone that Taylor had raided from his house was safe with her and the Demon where they waited for us back at my place.

Steeling myself, I started in the direction of the mansion, and Trent and Jud followed suit.

The three of us walked toward the imposing stairs, our footsteps crunching below us while the atmosphere throbbed and quivered with depravity.

I could feel it seeping out from below the door in a sinister cloud and slithering across the ground.

I wondered why I'd never felt it so distinctly before.

Or maybe the ugly truth of it had been that I'd ignored it. More than likely, I just hadn't cared.

Greed.

Now it felt like a sickness I was going to expel.

One side of the double doors opened when we got to the top step.

Jud and Trent were ready to go if it was a straight-up trap.

Oz was there, his gaze wary and hard as he widened the door.

"Mr. Lawson."

"Oz. It's a pleasure to see you again. I brought friends." I grinned like it was just another game, and I was inviting a couple unwitting fools to the table while my heart beat so hard I thought it would bust through my ribs.

I pretended like I didn't want to punch the prick in the face for having any part in this.

"I'm afraid they will have to wait outside," Oz said.

Trent scoffed. "And I'm *afraid* that's not gonna happen."

The scar on Oz's face slashed down as he frowned. "I was told there might be trouble."

"Yeah, and that trouble will come if anyone laid a finger on the girl inside."

He actually had the nerve to cringe. "She is whole, Sir."

"That's good because every last one of you will die if she's not."

Jud growled a low sound at my side as I issued it. I didn't know if it was to warn me to cool it or because he was underscoring the promise.

Oz let his gaze wander over the three of us before he seemed to settle on something, then he turned to me and asked, "Did you bring your ante, Sir?"

He eyed me, something deeper and more pressing than I'd seen in his expression before.

"I did."

Anxiety pulsed.

The oxygen outlined in razors.

Each breath strained and painful.

A short fuse burning quick.

One wrong move and things would blow.

"I'll need to search you," Oz said, and he began to pat me down. I knew he would. Which meant this whole thing was going to be tricky.

Trent and Jud assured me they'd had to get creative many times.

For years, this would have been a routine night for them.

I hated dragging them back into it, but there wasn't anything else we could do.

No way to get Aster back if we didn't take a risk and pray this time the dice landed in our favor.

When we were clean, Oz led us down the same corridor I'd traveled before, but tonight it felt like those odds were stacked against us.

Dead men walking.

Oz opened the double doors and began to lead us down the spiral staircase.

My chest tightened.

In dread.

In determination.

In the truth that I would do anything to set her free. This time I would see it through.

Jud and Trent followed behind, every muscle in their bodies coiled in severity.

Ready to strike.

I lost my fucking breath when we wound down and the scene in the basement came into view.

Haille was there, rocked back in his chair like the sadistic monster I should have truly recognized him to be.

Because Aster—Aster was on her knees at the side of his chair, a gag in her mouth, her hands bound behind her, a chain around her neck.

He held the opposite end.

Rage howled and screamed, sharp talons that tore up my insides, desperate for a way out.

To get to her.

To wrap her up and hide her away like I should have done years ago.

I wanted to tell her I knew what she had been through. That I hated myself for leaving her and would never do it again.

I bit down on my tongue to keep the words from spilling out.

Still, a small sound of pain escaped her gag when she saw my descent, and Haille's grin only widened when he saw my brothers in tow.

"Ah, so this is a family event. I can't say I am surprised. I suppose just this one time I will allow it."

Sick motherfucker.

I saw it in his eyes. He'd take pleasure in bleeding all three of us out, just for the fun of it.

Violence howled beneath the surface of my skin when my gaze moved to find Jarek sitting at the same spot as last time. He slowly shifted to watch as we came, his spine going straight, fear and hate in his eyes.

Rage thrashed where I kept it caged.

That's right, motherfucker, be afraid.

I rounded the table to my spot, as cool as could be while my insides shook like an earthquake.

Oz didn't retreat upstairs like he normally did. He stood behind Haille, a sentry standing guard.

Fuck. This was bad.

My odds dwindling with each second that passed.

Trent and Jud felt it, too. Their nerves scattered and zapped.

I sat and tossed Haille a smug grin. "You wanted a game...you have a game."

You vile, deviant piece of shit.

Haille's brow lifted. "And I am to assume you brought your ante? Tonight's stakes are...high. A single hand, all in."

He chuckled like it was all in a night's fun.

He wanted a show.

A play.

But I also knew he wouldn't let me walk out of here with either Aster or the stone.

If he and Jarek had been hunting it for the last seven years, they wouldn't willingly let it go now. I'd gladly trade it for her. In a heartbeat. Without question.

But I felt their intentions seething through the basement.

Perversion.

Wickedness.

Still, I went along with it like I could trust him. "I win, I walk with both the girl and the stone, and this time, I think it'd be fair if you forwent your cut."

It toppled out like sarcasm.

His expression was wry. "That seems fair. A game is a game, after all."

Yeah, and neither of us played by the rules.

The whole time, Jarek fermented in his depravity where he sat across from me.

I set the case onto the table and lifted my chin in challenge.

He angled over to grab the chain from Haille and dragged Aster forward on her knees, the girl sliding across the floor like she was a piece of meat to be traded.

A whimper of terror skidded from her throat.

Fury stabbed through me like a hot blade. I nearly lost it right then and dove over the table to take the motherfucker out.

Trent grunted from behind me. *Stay cool. Stay cool.*

I didn't know how I was going to manage it when it felt like I was being burned alive.

Sweat slicked my skin and the knots in my guts tightened.

I opened the box and pulled out the stone.

Jarek salivated.

"Beautiful," Haille murmured. "It seems we have a game."

The dealer stepped forward and dealt the dirty hand.

One.

Two.

Three.

Four.

Five.

Back and forth to Jarek and me.

Jarek glared.

I sent him a cocky smirk while I wanted to rip him in two, my knee bouncing with the unspent violence that wanted to break free.

He laid two cards facedown.

I did three.

I manipulated.

Worked my magic, if that's what you wanted to call it, because my wins were nothing more than sleight of hand.

In a normal situation, I would have been gloating as I laid down another straight flush.

But Jarek and Oz had already pulled their guns, just like I'd expected them to, while Haille sat there smug, enjoying the show.

I jumped up before either could anticipate it and tossed the table onto its side.

Aster screeched, and she scooted back on her ass, using her heels to push herself away while Jarek shot to his feet.

Cards flew, but I knew the biggest distraction would be the stone that went sailing.

It spun and spiraled, almost in slow motion as it arced in the air.

Haille and Jarek's eyes were wide as they watched it, their hunger for its beauty enough to enrapture them as they watched it soar.

It was our only chance.

Jud was already on his way, stealth as he moved around the table to get to Aster before anyone would notice. His job was to get her and get the hell out.

Trent and I would take care of the rest.

"Get it," Haille shouted at Oz.

Trent moved along close to the wall in an effort to sneak up on Oz. The man was our biggest threat.

Trained to kill.

The same as my oldest brother.

My heart stampeded as I went to jump over the table to get to Jarek who'd let his arm drop to his side, his gun dangling limply at his thigh, too fucking caught up on watching the stone clatter to the floor to notice what was coming for him.

Out of the corner of my eye, I saw Oz step forward, and dread thrashed through my system.

Fear for Trent.

But I had to focus.

Focus on getting the gun from Jarek.

Only Oz swung around to the side, and he didn't have his gun pointed at me or Trent.

Rather, it was pointed at Haille.

In confusion, I stumbled a step, and his frosty eyes met mine in clear implication as he dug into the inside of his jacket with his free hand.

When he pulled it out, he tossed a handgun in my direction.

"It seems you forgot something, Sir."

Shock slammed me as I caught it. I stared at it for a beat, my whole being contorted in a giant *what the fuck?*

Everything flash-fired from there. The motion set from slow to triple speed.

Haille went for the gun at his side that he'd thought himself too untouchable to require, blustering, "What do you think you're doing? Get the stone, you fucking idiot."

"I am no longer indebted to you, you sick bastard," Oz gritted.

Oz pulled the trigger. The gunshot rang out through the room.

Disorienting.

High-pitched confusion that banged against the walls.

Haille slumped over in his chair, blood pouring onto his shirt from the hole in his chest.

Holy fuck.

Aster screamed.

I whirled toward Jarek.

Jud started to move faster, and Jarek felt him coming, and he swung the barrel at him. He fired off two erratic shots.

Jud had already anticipated it and ducked and rolled behind a piece of furniture at the wall.

Adrenaline pumped.

Sweat across my skin.

Desperation in my bones.

Jarek turned, yanked the chain, and dragged Aster back across the floor.

She screamed and shouted against the gag, and he jerked her up to hold her back to his chest.

The pussy was using her like a shield. "One step closer and she dies."

A whine came from her soul.

Fire-agate eyes flaming with intent.

Together.

Together.

We were no longer doing it separate. We weren't sacrificing *us* for the other.

Trent and Oz enclosed, but it was Aster who shifted in a blur of fury. She wrenched out of his hold, whirled around, and threw a knee to his groin before he could make sense of it.

Jarek howled, then he had her by the hair as I was jumping over the table. Aster kicked him again, the girl going rabid, fighting with everything she had with her hands still bound behind her back.

Trent went for him on the side.

Jarek felt it, fired another wayward shot.

Desperation flooded him.

He shot again, this time toward Oz, desperate to keep us back.

Another bullet pinged through the air.

A muffled scream tore from Aster, and she lifted her leg and kicked him with the bottom of her foot low in the gut.

He stumbled back a foot.

And my girl—she gave us our chance.

I pulled the trigger.

His eyes went wide with shock as he blew backward three steps.

Violence roiled through my being.

I'd hit him up high, close to where I'd struck him seven years ago.

"I'll kill you," he grunted, but it was the monster who was dropping to his knees.

He let the chain go to cover the wound with his hand.

Defiance filled his expression.

Hate and animosity.

"I will kill you and this bitch and your whole fucking family."

Straightening, I took a step toward him.

My brothers came up to my sides, and Oz gathered beside Trent.

Fear blistered from Jarek's flesh.

"You won't get away with this," he ground out, his words fractured. "You are all dead. I will see to it."

My teeth ground as I angled forward, ignoring his threat.

Hatred boiled from my tongue. "That shot was for Aster. For hurting her. For the pain you caused her. For treating her as anything less than the miracle she is."

Agony and contempt rasped from his breaths, and he tried to rebound, struggling to lift the gun that dangled at his side in his other hand.

I stood higher, and that time, I aimed the barrel between his eyes. Eyes that widened in terror.

"And this? This is for our kid."

I fired.

Aster screamed into her gag.

She screamed and screamed as she backpedaled with her feet to get away from his body that toppled to the floor.

A gush of air wheezed from my lungs, a moment of shock, of relief, of sickness, of every mistake and sin that had ever been committed.

The gun slipped from my hold, and I rushed for Aster. I dropped to my knees in front of her and ripped the gag from her mouth.

I took her face in my hands, my attention racing over every inch of her, searching for any injuries. "Are you okay? Baby, are you okay?"

My thumbs frantically brushed over the tears that soaked her cheeks. The right one was swollen and bruised, and there was a cut on her lip.

Fury flamed again.

"Little Star," I begged.

She gasped a cry, and I freed her hands, and she threw her arms around my neck. "I'm fine. We're fine."

I slumped to the ground on my ass, and I pulled her onto my lap and curled mine around her.

I held her tight as our jagged breaths heaved and jutted and our haggard hearts screamed.

I breathed out because I was never going to let her go. "It's over, Aster, it's over."

"Logan," she sobbed and buried her face in my neck. "Logan."

"It's okay. It's over. It's over."

I ran my fingers through the tangled locks of her dark brown hair.

Hyacinth and magnolia leaves.

My breath.

My blood.

My life.

My Little Star.

"Well, shit," Jud said, scrubbing a giant palm over his face as he looked around the scene.

Trent jutted his chin at Oz. "We need to dispose of these bodies. You have bags?"

Oz nodded. "Three of them. They were intended for you. They knew you would come."

Oz shifted his attention to me where I held a trembling Aster on my lap, my lungs squeezing the oxygen up my constricted throat.

Questions rushed from me without sound.

He'd turned on Haille.

Had stood for us.

"Why?"

He swallowed hard. "You were not to walk out of here, and the girl was to be slain in front of her father. I would not let that happen."

Aster choked over the fear that still rambled through her being. Trembles rocked her head to toe, the girl in shock.

If it was possible, I gathered her closer.

"Thank you," I told him, barely able to get the words to cooperate.

"I have done awful things in his name, and I could no longer be a prisoner to his bidding. I needed out as badly as you, and for a long time, I've been looking for a way. But when I learned of what they intended? I knew there was a purpose that I was still here. That it was my duty to stop this from happening. My conscience cannot bear more innocent blood."

"We're going to have questions," Trent muttered.

Oz almost smiled. "And I have answers."

Chapter Forty-Eight

Aster

I GRIPPED LOGAN'S HAND WHERE WE STOOD IN THE HALLWAY outside my father's office door.

Logan sent me a gentle smile, and my heart fluttered in my chest.

"Are you ready for this?" he asked.

"Yes."

I was.

I was so ready.

Ready to stand for myself.

Ready to stand for Logan.

Ready to stand for our family.

Still, my insides shivered as I glanced around.

Memories of this place echoed down the corridor.

The hope we'd had and the sorrow that we'd found.

For so long, we'd secreted ourselves away, hidden, our love nothing but a prayer and a whispered chance.

And today, that prayer would become our reality.

Even though my father expected us, Logan reached out and knocked on the wood.

"Come in," was a muffled reverberation from the other side.

Logan opened the door, and together, we walked through, our hands held tight.

A promise to the other.

We were never letting go.

My father sat behind his desk, his expression cautious and somehow contrite.

My heart panged at the sight. Bitterness and hurt and the love I'd always held for a man who'd caused so many wrongs.

"Papa," I couldn't help but whisper, the long-used affection a rock in my throat.

"Please, come in and sit." He gestured to the two leather chairs that sat across from his desk.

Tentatively, Logan and I moved that way and settled into the chairs, though our hands never loosened their bond.

"Mr. Costa." Logan's voice was hard.

"Logan." My father sighed a disbelieving sound. "Much has happened since the last time we met."

It seemed impossible that had only been four days ago when it almost felt like a lifetime removed.

It'd been a blur of torment. A day of terror.

But Logan—Logan had found his way back to me.

Just like for the rest of my life, I would always find my way back to him.

I would fight.

I would love.

I would cherish, and I would work for our joy and our peace.

But our days would no longer be counted as sacrifice.

It was an oath he and I had both made.

"You could say that." Logan's voice was strained.

I understood the animosity he felt sitting across from my father.

My father's expression dimmed. "Jarek and that man Haille intended to overthrow me."

Logan cleared his throat, glancing at me with all that adoration before he returned his attention to my father.

I'd asked him to provide the details so I could prepare myself for the rest.

"Yes," he said, completely blunt. "Oz, Haille's first guard, turned. He chose to protect your daughter over his loyalty to Mr. Manchief. He gave us everything he knows, plus there are plenty of condemning documents that were found at Jarek's home here in LA."

My papa lifted his chin. "And?"

Logan angled his head, ferocity coming off him. "They wanted the stones, Mr. Costa. They have always wanted the stones."

My father hissed. He still didn't even know of their fate. Had no idea both of them were currently sitting in the box that rested at mine and Logan's feet.

All thanks to my sister who had seduced a biker.

"That night seven years ago, it was a setup," Logan continued. "Haille and Jarek had made an alliance. Haille knew of Jarek's standing in the family, and apparently Haille had made the greedy asshole an offer he couldn't resist. Jarek was charged with securing both stones, and once he presented them to Haille, he was promised all of Los Angeles. Haille's men were also promised to Jarek, that they would come here and end the Costa reign. Jarek wanted power and he wanted Aster, and he didn't want to wait for it. Besides, he believed Haille more powerful than you."

It was a straight shot to my father because it was true.

Haille would have destroyed him and this entire family.

But it'd all been put on hold when Logan had disappeared.

"That night, one of Jarek's men came to make it look like a regular heist, but you had sent me, and things didn't go exactly as planned. I tried to stop the thief, but the man ended up shooting Antonio. The assailant managed to get away with one stone. My gut told me it was all a setup, so when Jarek went for the second stone, I grabbed it. He was going to shoot me, so I shot him first."

"And you ran," my father surmised, horror in the wobble of his voice.

"I ran. I never should have. I should have come back that night and fought for Aster."

Logan turned those eyes on me.

A thousand shades of green.

"I was a fool," he murmured my direction as he traced his thumb over the back of my hand. "But I will never make that mistake again."

My chest pulsed with adoration.

I love you, I mouthed.

Logan heaved out a breath when he turned back to my father. "They have been hunting for it for years. Once they discovered my location a year ago, Haille set a plan of his own because he no longer trusted Jarek to do it. He rented a house nearby and came to me to manage his less than legitimate finances."

"He wanted on the inside." Papa blew air through his nose.

"Yes. And when he still didn't discover the necklace's whereabouts, he brought in Jarek. Jarek never disguised his hate for me, and Haille was correct to assume that hate went both ways. He figured eventually Jarek's presence would draw the stone out. Haille had believed I would eventually confide in him that I had possession of the stone. He believed that would be the easiest course. It didn't go that way, so they came for Aster."

"And we all nearly died because of it," I heaved, sitting forward. "Because of all of this, Papa. Because of the greed and the thirst for power. Because of the sins and the crimes. I was to be killed as a punishment to Jarek for messing up the first time, as a lesson, right here in your office, before they killed you. This...this is the life you chose. This is the life you forced onto your daughters. And it's a life I will no longer live."

His face paled. "I am sorry, mia vita, you don't know to the depths."

Tears blurred and tripped from my eyelids, faster than I could stop them. "You sat there by my bedside, knowing what he had done. That he'd beaten me. That he robbed my baby from my body. You condoned it, traded it for Logan's life."

"Aster," he begged.

Agony spun, a swell of lightheadedness rushing through my brain, but I pressed on and pushed to my feet.

Logan squeezed my hand in a show of support before he released it. I spread both palms over my still-flat stomach.

Love abounded.

This rising hope.

This blazing joy.

"And now…now I have a chance at finding what you and Jarek stole, and I'm taking that chance. I'm taking it, and there is nothing you will do or say to stop me."

Desperation curled from his throat. "I have wronged you, mia vita. I stood behind years of tradition, turned a blind eye as if it were just the way. I allowed abhorrent things to happen to my own daughter. Will you ever forgive me?"

"I will always love you, Papa, but I don't know if I will ever forgive you for what you caused."

"I could never forgive myself."

I leaned forward and planted my hands on his desk. "Then you remember that, Papa, you remember that when it comes to Taylor. Because I promise you, with my last breath, that I will never allow you to do to her what you did to me."

He gulped, turned away when he forced out, "On my shame, I swear to you, it ends here."

Relief blew from me in a breath.

I almost slumped over, my entire being rocking forward with the rush of adrenaline and the surge of perseverance.

I would stand.

I would stand.

Then Logan was there, at my side, his arm sliding around my waist.

He leaned down, pulled the box from the case, and set the box on the desk. "I came here seven years ago with the one stone I had. I was going to offer it to you, promise my allegiance, and beg for the chance to give your daughter a good life. Now, I'm telling you. Take the stones, and I'm taking Aster, and we are never looking back."

Confusion bound my father, and with a shaky hand, he reached out and slid the box the rest of the way across the desk. Carefully, he undid the latches.

He gasped at the twin stones set inside, his attention jerking up. "You're just…giving it back? After all these years?"

Logan's arm tightened around my waist. "The stones have always been yours, and Aster has always been mine. I no longer have any use for what does not bring us joy."

Stunned, my father rocked back.

I swallowed around the rock lodged in my throat, and I shifted to take Logan's hand in a show of solidarity, then I lifted my chin and said, "Goodbye, Papa."

Because I was turning my back on this ugly world, and I would never see him again.

"Goodbye, mia vita."

Together, Logan and I walked across the floor. The second we stepped out into the hall, Logan spun me around and gripped me by both sides of the face.

My beautiful man.

My dark defender.

My North Star.

He smiled down at me, pride and love gushing from his soul, and with the pads of his thumbs, he brushed away the tears I didn't even realize were still falling.

"Run away with me, Little Star?"

"Running away with you is all I've ever wanted to do."

His forehead dropped to mine. "Never look back."

I curled both my hands around his wrists, my eyes dropping closed when I promised, "Never look back."

Epilogue

Logan

"WHERE ARE YOU?" I CALLED.

Giggles floated through the cool, evening air as footsteps rushed over the earth.

I followed them slowly, tiptoeing along, holding back the laughter that wanted to billow out as I hunted my sweet little thing.

"Why are you hiding from me?" I sang, popping my head around the trunk of a tree.

Megan squealed like mad from behind the bush where she squatted.

"I got to hides, but you found me, you sneaker!"

A chuckle rumbled up my throat, the child so goddamn adorable I hardly knew what to do with myself.

Discovered, she jumped up and came rushing out of her hiding place, the same place she hid every single time, mind you, lifting her little arms to me as she ran my way.

My chest pressed full.

Overflowed.

I swept her up and pressed my nose into the soft curls of her dark brown hair.

Hyacinth and magnolia leaves.

Just like her mother who gazed over at us.

My heart squeezed and devotion pumped through my bloodstream.

I held our daughter tight as I stared at my wife.

My world.

My gravity.

My soul's destination.

"Come here," I rumbled to Aster.

A soft smile filled her face as she edged over the grass on her bare feet, the woman looking at me with those eyes that slayed me through.

With joy and peace.

Her love so fierce for the little girl I held in my arms.

Our hope complete.

"What, you want to find me, too?" she teased.

Happiness bounded around us.

This place that'd become our home.

I tucked Aster to my chest, our daughter squeezed between us in this never-ending embrace.

I leaned down and pressed my lips to Aster's forehead. "Oh, Little Star, no matter where you go, I will always find you."

For an expanded bonus epilogue, head to my website, aljacksonauthor.com

About the Author

A.L. Jackson is the *New York Times* & *USA Today* Bestselling author of contemporary romance. She writes emotional, sexy, heart-filled stories about boys who usually like to be a little bit bad.

Her bestselling series include THE REGRET SERIES, CLOSER TO YOU, BLEEDING STARS, FIGHT FOR ME, CONFESSIONS OF THE HEART, and FALLING STARS.

If she's not writing, you can find her hanging out by the pool with her family, sipping cocktails with her friends, or of course with her nose buried in a book.

Be sure not to miss new releases and sales from A.L. Jackson - Sign up to receive her newsletter http://smarturl.it/NewsFromALJackson or text "aljackson" to 33222 to receive short but sweet updates on all the important news.

Connect with A.L. Jackson online:

FB Page https://geni.us/ALJacksonFB
A.L. Jackson Bookclub https://geni.us/ALJacksonBookClub
Angels https://geni.us/AmysAngels
Amazon https://geni.us/ALJacksonAmzn
Book Bub https://geni.us/ALJacksonBookbub

Text "aljackson" to 33222 to receive short but sweet
updates on all the important news.